ADAM J. SCHOLTE

THE LEGION HAS COME

THE RAMULAS CHRONICLES

The Ramulas Chronicles Book 3: The Legion Has Come

Paperback edition ISBN: 978-1-7638864-4-5
eBook edition ISBN: 978-1-7638864-5-2

Published by Adam J Scholte
www.adamjscholte.com

This second edition: April 2025
First edition: November 2023

A catalogue record for this book is available from the National Library of Australia

Editor: Jason Martin
Design and Typeset: Kristine Joy Magno
Printed in Australia.

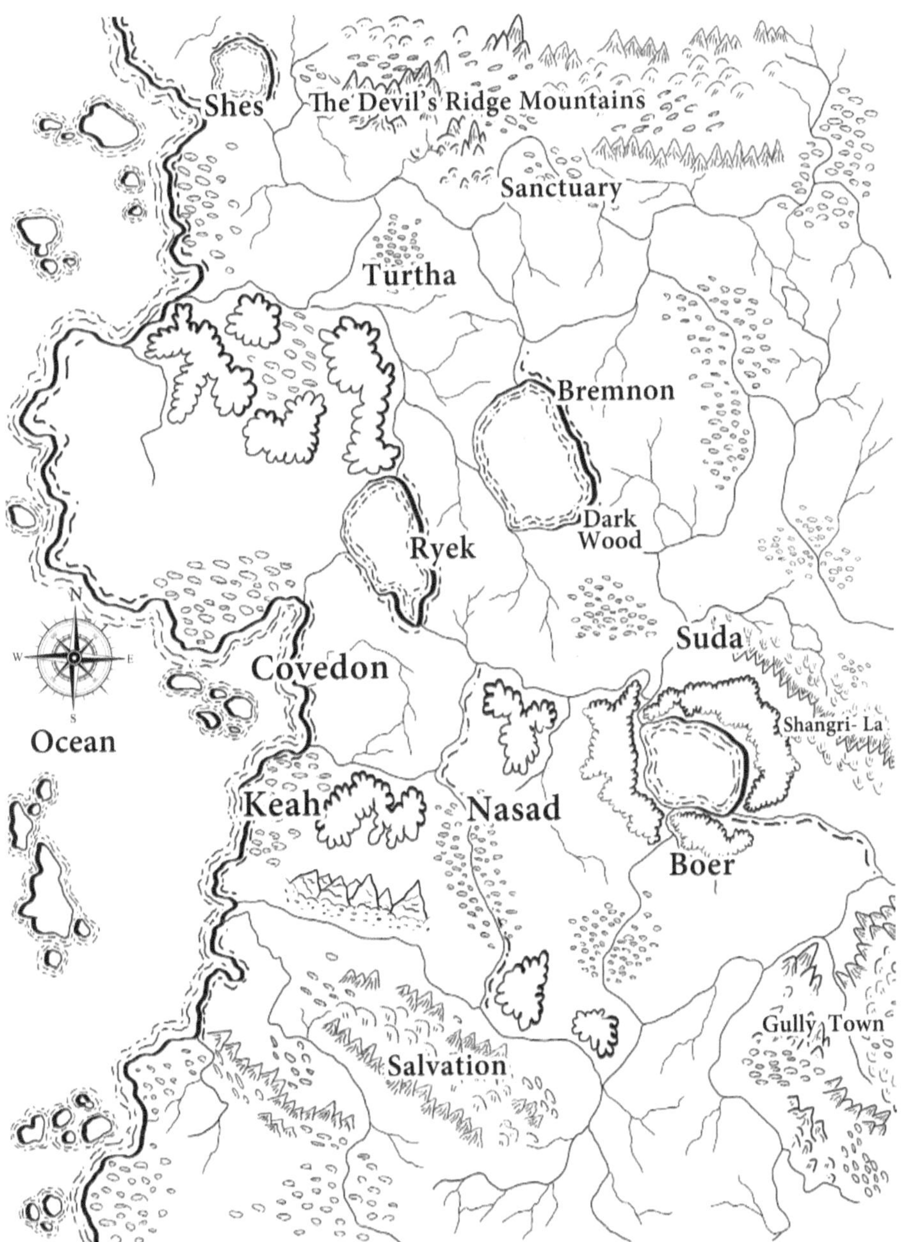

Shes
The Devil's Ridge Mountains
Sanctuary
Turtha
Bremnon
Ryek
Dark Wood
Suda
Covedon
Shangri- La
Ocean
Keah
Nasad
Boer
Salvation
Gully Town
N
W
E
S

Character list

Aleesha—King Zachary's daughter

Alpha—One of the Warlords chasing Oriel.

Benji—Former thief, friend of Pip and now member of the fallen angels, an elite army with Sanctuary.

Beta—One of the Warlords chasing Oriel.

Captain Aldrich—Member of King Braydon's army.

Declyn—Magician to King Braydon.

Druids—A faction of the feared druids have come to aid Sanctuary.

Eady—Leader of the Dryads.

Edwin—A Dwarf helping dig the tunnel to Oriel.

Emily—An ancient spirit trapped in Sanctuary for hundreds of years.

Fenris—A young Hell hound.

Grace—Daughter of Ramulas, affected by his magic and that of the Dryads.

Iguchi—A warrior from across the sea, trainer of the fallen angels.

Jacqueline—Wife of Ramulas.

Jenna—Sister to Pip.

Kate—Eldest daughter of Ramulas, who has unique fighting skills.

K'ayden—Head of the Khilli people.

Lodi—A giant living near Sanctuary.

Logan—Spy for king Zachary

Lucas—Head of King Zachary's royal guard.

Makayla—Jenna's daughter.

Master of shadows—Head of the thief's guild in Keah.

Michael—Member of the fallen angels.

Miles—former thief and member of the fallen angels, and close friend of Benji.

Nathaniel—Brother of Michael who is trapped near Oriel in the mountain.

Old John—Member of the shadows, thief's guild of Keah.

Omega—One of the Warlords chasing Oriel.

Oriel—A being of pure magic hiding from the Warlords who wish to kill her for her powers.

Owain—Blind archer from Shangri-la.

Pip—Former member of the shadows, and now fighting partner of Ramulas.

Private Anderson—Member of King Zachary's army.

Ramulas—Twin to Remus, leader of Sanctuary and protecter of his people.

Reckoning—A captain of the legion.

Redemption—A caption of the legion.

Retribution—A captain of the legion.

Remus—Twin of Ramulas, head Warlord chasing Oriel.

Royce—Earth elemental

Rygar—Dwarf and adoptive father to Lodi.

Rufus—Ramulas' warhorse.

Shayn—Earth elemental

Shigar—Magician to King Zachary.

Tao—Son of Jenna..

Tilly—Sprite living in Sanctuary's Forest.

Valkyrie—Mother Hell hound.

Zachary—Ruler of the Kingdom.

Contents

1

Nathaniel screamed in pure rage.

His gauntlet and sword had floated out of the cave searching for a new owner, then a part of him died when the spirit within the sword found someone worthy to wield it. When Nathaniel first held the sword, the spirit of the blade attempted to possess and take control of him; after a quick battle, he defeated the spirit. But if a mortal held the sword, then the spirit could easily control them.

Since Oriel had come to the mountain, Nathaniel's magical power had slowly begun to return; his strength and eyesight increased, and his wings easily lifted him from the ground. He had come so close to retrieving his weapons after several hundred years.

He thought back to the events that led him to being locked away in this mountain.

He paced in front of the doorway, clearly agitated. He was an angel, but for him, being an angel was not enough—he craved the same power as the gods themselves, and the spirit within the sword felt his frustrations.

'You deserve more power than the gods have given you,' Heaven's Reign said, hoping to force him into action. 'Bring me forth and I will freeze all in our way.'

Nathaniel nodded. 'I want what is rightfully mine.'

Two other angels noticed his distress and came over to him, hoping to calm him down before he made a decision that he would regret.

'My dear friend,' one of them said, smiling calmly, 'why do you put yourself through such torment?'

He turned to Michael. 'How long have we been mere tools for the gods, doing as they bid without question? For eons, we have worked watching over the humans, who pray to the gods for mercy. We are given nothing for this.'

Michael's smile grew as he held up his hands in a mock defeated gesture. 'We are angels and should be grateful for our existence.'

Nathaniel shook his head and thrust his finger at Michael. 'I deserve to be as powerful as the gods themselves.'

The other angel, Gabriel, stepped toward Nathaniel. 'You must rid yourself of this anger before it is too late.'

A gong sounded; its tone seemed to come from everywhere and nowhere. A door opened before them, and the angels saw a kaleidoscope of swirling colours.

'Any who wish to enter the hall of the gods must first wield the hammer of the gods,' a deep voice said. 'This will allow them to have the power of the gods.'

A silver-scaled gauntlet floated in front of Nathaniel, and it was a thing of beauty for him.

'I wish the right to have this,' he shouted through the doorway.

'To be worthy of the gauntlet, you must first kill your brother angels.'

Heaven's Reign released thoughts of pure joy as Nathaniel pulled it out of its scabbard. A thick wall of mist flowed from the blue crystal blade once it was free. Michael and Gabriel stepped away from Nathaniel, who dashed at Michael with a thrust. Michael's mouth opened in shock as the blade entered his chest. With a thought, Heaven's Reign unleashed its power, freezing Michael from the inside.

Gabriel took a few steps back, pulling out his own sword. The intricate arcane symbols glowed with magic. With a slight flick of his wrist, Nathaniel pulled out his sword from Michael and shot a blast of ice at Gabriel, who was transformed into an ice statue.

Two quick steps brought Nathaniel close enough to strike at Gabriel, breaking the statue and sending its fragments along the hallway.

The gong sounded once more, and the gauntlet floated towards him. Stepping forward, Nathaniel held up his hand, allowing the gauntlet to slide on. He smiled in satisfaction as the power flowed through him.

Nathaniel eagerly stepped into the doorway, and as soon as he entered, his whole body was assaulted with pain. As the pain increased, he felt the weapons pulled from his hands, and he lost his sight.

Something had gone terribly wrong.

Then it dawned on Nathaniel. He had been sent to the plain of eternal darkness. He knew there was no escape for him here.

All this time, his anger and frustration had festered and grown. With Oriel close by, he would soon have enough power to break free and regain his weapons.

Everyone would feel the wrath of a fallen angel once he was free.

****

'How long have the First Legion been in the mountains?' Ramulas asked.

'A couple of days, but Remus has kept his presence hidden from me until now. He wants me to fear that he has arrived.'

Ramulas shook his head. 'But why wait until now to show you that he is here?'

Oriel sighed. 'He wants me to know fear, but in doing this, he has allowed me to see how much of the Legion he has brought with him. Something went wrong as they crossed over—just over seven thousand arrived here, and a few red wizards and warlords. The portal has closed, and he has no way of returning home.'

Ramulas smiled. 'That is good; seven thousand is better than ten, and not as many magic-users. Do you know when he will leave so we can prepare?'

Oriel shook her head sadly. 'If Remus comes with what he has, the people of Sanctuary will not survive. They are still recovering from the battle with the kingdom army, and Legion soldiers are far better than they are.'

Ramulas knew this was true. As he thought of the people putting on brave faces while they fought their own inner battles, he held out his hands. 'What are we to do?'

'Wait; there is more,' Oriel said, holding up her hand. 'There is both good and bad news.'

'Tell me the good news,' Ramulas blurted.

'Winter is fast approaching, and Remus will not march until the snows' end.'

Ramulas nodded as a smile played on his face. For as long as he could remember, winter around Bremnon was harsh and in the mountains even more so. It would be almost impossible for the Legion to survive the thick snows. 'We have time to prepare.'

'The bad news is that Remus is forming an alliance with the Symiaks on the mountain for when he marches for me.'

'How many?'

'A few thousand.'

Ramulas thought back to when he and Pip encountered them in their barren wastelands in the mountains, where the taste of dust hung in the air. A mixture of luck and magic saved them. He shuddered to think of what would happen if the Symiaks marched alongside the Legion. Just talking about the creatures brought fear into the ordinary person. How would the people of Sanctuary react if they came to their home?

He pushed the thoughts away. There were too many other things that needed to be discussed.

'Something happened to the green dragons when they were feeding. K'ayden and I were stopped as a dragon wanted to eat an injured soldier I was carrying. Then Emily came and the creature was truly scared of her. I have never seen such a thing. How can she have this power?'

Oriel nodded. 'When you first came to this castle, I told you that there was much for you to learn. I said that Emily was a very powerful spirit who had not crossed over to the other side. Everyone in Sanctuary was killed in a war and she chose to stay.'

Ramulas nodded.

'The magic of Sanctuary has shown me what really happened. An evil force came here in search of something that would give them power. The people of Sanctuary were warriors and unafraid. Even though the enemy greatly outnumbered them, it did not matter. Wave after wave of attacks were pushed away from the wall for a week until most of the dead came from the invading force.

'The warriors of Sanctuary thought the battle won when the evil force retreated into the forest leaving only a small chest behind. The victors took this into their home as their prize. Try and try as they may, no-one could open the chest, but later that night, when most were sleeping, the chest opened quietly.

'Spirits of the slain enemy came forth. This was the reason they threw themselves into battle so willingly: they knew that they could not die. Some spirits opened the gate while the rest attacked the people. Weapons were useless, as they passed through the ghostly forms.

'Then the evil force flooded in from the forest and slaughtered everyone within the walls. They were unable to locate what they were looking for, so they drifted away, leaving Emily's spirit behind. The echoes of each of the people reside within her. Emily relives the battle every day and the ancient magic of Sanctuary makes her very powerful.

'But for the dragon to fear her, Emily must be almost as powerful as you.'

Oriel shook her head. 'Emily is more powerful than I am.'

'What? That cannot be possible,' Ramulas said as he thought of the small girl he and Pip met in the forest when they discovered Sanctuary. He could not understand how an innocent child could be so powerful.

'Everything is possible. I was created a few years ago, and Emily has had hundreds of years to hone her magic, but because she possesses the mind of a small girl Emily doesn't realise her potential; this is the same with Grace.'

'What about Grace?'

'Within ten years, she will have more magical ability than you. That is why she will need guidance.'

2

Remus and the Legion soon came to accept life in the mountains—the hard, unforgiving ground and winds that would appear out of nowhere, kicking up swirling dust storms that peppered the skin and left fine grit in their mouths.

Over the past few days, Remus had sent out spies amongst the Symiaks. He had learnt that the city of Keah was where the king resided, and their army was large enough to keep these creatures at bay. As soon as any Symiaks were seen at the base of the mountains, alarms would sound, and the king's army would chase them back up the mountain.

From what Remus could see, there was a lot of distrust amongst the Symiak tribes, and they had never fought for a common goal. The only thing stopping the tribes from fighting was their greed. Tensions still simmered under the surface, but the presence of the Legion was enough to dissuade them from fighting.

A seventh tribe had joined them from across the mountains, and Remus called a meeting with the chieftains. As they entered the large tent of animal pelts, Remus looked to the west. He ignored the freezing winds pulling at his robes and focused on a shaft of thin red light marking Oriel's position.

'After all this time, Oriel, we will soon be reunited.'

Redemption appeared at his side. 'My warlord, they await you inside.'

Remus nodded and entered the tent. All eyes focused on him as he stood in the doorway slowly scanning from left to right, holding the gaze of each chieftain before moving onto the next. He took slow, deliberate steps to a stool that, as he sat, forced the seated Symiaks to look up at him. He needed to show dominance for his plan to work.

'The person I look for—the one with your shiny gifts—hides in the mountains west of here,' Remus said slowly.

This brought looks of confusion from the Symiaks.

'Him comes from west mountain,' Grunch said, pointing to another Symiak.

"No, no,' Remus said, shaking his head. 'Past Keah and many towns, walking for many days.'

The chieftains snarled and began to hoot and stomp their feet. Remus felt his hold over them slipping away.

'Little ones in mountains, we will smash them,' Grunch said, rubbing his hands together thinking of the dwarves, who were their most hated enemy.

This brought another round of stomping and hooting. Remus let it die down before he spoke.

'I need to see the king of Keah.'

'Why you see king?' Grunch said as he stood clenching his fists. Generations of hatred of the humans came forth, with memories of the everlasting war between the races.

Remus looked to the three captains of the First Legion and slightly shook his head. A fight with these creatures would be won but at the cost of the men he needed. He needed to win these creatures over.

'You have told me that when the humans see you, they always attack you,' he explained calmly.

The chieftains nodded.

'After I get the person with shiny gifts, I will give you the city of Keah.'

'How get Keah?' Grunch asked eagerly.

'I will need to speak to the king of Keah,' he said slowly, as if talking to a child. 'I have a plan to take the king's army away.'

The Symiaks began stomping and hooting until Grunch held up his hand. 'When you see king?'

'Soon; very soon. I need to work out what to say to the king.'

The Symiaks hooted and stomped in joy. For generations they had fought the humans, and now they would he given the city of Keah.

***

Zachary woke after a fitful sleep. Nightmares of the black dragon had woken him several times. Sounds of the soldiers walking past, fires crackling, and smells of food brought him out of his tent. Two members of the royal guard stood to attention as their king walked into the makeshift camp in the pre-dawn light.

Men huddled in groups around fires, breathing plumes of mist into the morning air. Every now and then, a soldier would glance fearfully at the forest two hundred yards away and the sky. Zachary investigated the trees; he was certain that something dark and foreboding waited just beyond the shadows. He understood the uneasiness within the camp.

'How long until we march for home?' he asked as Lucas walked over to him.

'Within the hour.'

'How many men survived?'

Lucas sighed. 'Almost three hundred were left on the field, two hundred were injured in our haste to flee the dragons, and half of the supply wagons were left as well.'

Zachary cursed softly. At this time the day before, he had led his army toward Sanctuary confident of victory. A day later, his forces had been decimated and he was thankful to be alive. Too many unexplained events had happened the previous day—the Khilli running to join Sanctuary and the Lord of Sanctuary rising from the dead before calling the dragons.

Thoughts of Shangri-la returned to him. Zachary could not allow another group of people to be independent from the crown, but the dragons protected Shangri-la, and now they appeared here—what could this mean?

Lucas had decided for a small group to ride ahead to Turtha and make ready for when they arrived later that day. The sun had just begun to rise when Zachary accepted a warm bowl of porridge from a sergeant. It had no taste, but he enjoyed the warmth.

Orders were called out around the camp and Zachary watched as men scrambled, pulling down tents, packing wagons, and gathering horses. The men's demeanour was subdued, and a few tried to lift morale as they worked, but they all wanted to be as far away from there as possible.

Zachary looked towards Turtha across the plains, thankful that the rolling hills would replace the forests.

***

Ramulas and Pip stood on the wall looking down at the clearing, which still had arrows, shields, swords, and a dozen wagons near the tree line.

'We need to clean this mess. Everything comes inside,' Ramulas said.

'The wagons?' Pip asked.

'Everything.'

She smiled up at him. 'The wagons might have some nice things.'

'I know.'

'I keep what I find,' she called as she raced for the stairs.

'Ask the people to help you,' he called out as Rygar came up to him.

He watched as she quickly spoke to a few groups before running out into the clearing, stopping at the wagons, unsure which one to search first.

'Hurry, Pip. People are coming!' Ramulas laughed as he called down to her.

She dashed to the closest wagon as people started coming out into the clearing. She called out instructions for all the weapons and shields to be picked up before they came to the wagons.

'She's a crafty one,' Ramulas said.

'Aye, that she is,' the dwarf agreed. 'The kingdom shields should be o' top o' the wall.'

Ramulas looked at him puzzled.

'Hang them to show the Legion that you have already defeated an opponent.'

'Are you sure?'

Rygar looked up at Ramulas and winked at him.

***

Over the next hour, everything was taken into Sanctuary. Ramulas and Rygar came down into the courtyard.

'Everything will be shared amongst the people,' Ramulas said as the Fallen Angels stepped forward handing out items.

Ramulas walked into the castle with Pip and Iguchi appeared by his side. 'This is very wise, Lord of Sanctuary. You keep nothing for yourself and give to the people. This will make them even more loyal to you.'

Ramulas shrugged. 'I gave it away because I needed nothing.'

'Even so,' Iguchi said, shaking his forefinger, 'other rulers would have kept most of the bounty.'

Ramulas thought of King Zachary as they walked into the castle. They came into the throne room to find Oriel, Shigar, K'ayden, Owain, and the druids.

'Welcome, everyone,' Oriel said. 'As I have told Ramulas, the Legion has arrived and is in the Symiak mountains.'

A few gasped before multiple questions were fired at Oriel.

She held up her hand for silence. 'All I know is that the portal they used to travel here has collapsed and they have no way home. The Legion has been left with no other choice: they must come here and the warlords kill me for my powers.

'This is their only way home. Once Remus has my powers, the First Legion will march from town to town, killing and enslaving. Then Remus will bring the other Legions into this world.'

Ramulas thought of the most direct route for an army of that size to get there from the Symiak mountains. They would come down from the rocky terrain and move across open plains, passing forests and lakes before entering the forests of Sanctuary. Ramulas knew that this would take some time.

'We need to stop them,' Shigar said.

Remus will bring the Legion here just after winter. Not all the Legion came through. He will only bring seven thousand with him.'

'Oh, is that all?' Pip said sarcastically.

Oriel shook her head. 'No. He is also talking with the Symiaks in the mountains, and a few thousand might be marching with him.'

Pip's mouth fell open as the rest of the group shared concerned expressions. The Symiaks were feared across the kingdom, especially by those from Keah.

'I have spoken to Oriel,' Ramulas said, 'and we need to look at where we went wrong in the last battle. Too many mistakes were made, and we can't afford these this time.'

'As the Lord of Sanctuary, you should not ride into battle,' Shigar said.

Owain, Rygar, and Iguchi nodded.

'All generals and leaders are found at the rear of their forces during battle,' Iguchi stated.

Ramulas held out his hands. 'I thought that I was to lead my people into battle. Why have I spent all this time training?'

'Training provides you with your magical abilities. You will be able to use this in battle. When Remus comes, he will seek you out. He does not take defeat lightly. Last time, you caught him unaware—this time, he will want to make an example of you.'

He looked down, slowly shaking his head. 'I don't know how to use my power. I don't remember what I can do.'

'We can help,' Shigar said as he stepped forward with the druids.

One of the druids held up his scaly hand. 'We would be better fighting the enemy from outside the castle. We have honed our craft in the Darkwood; we will attack them in the forest.'

'And I have a trick or two for when the Legion arrives,' Shigar said with a smile.

'Lord of Sanctuary,' Iguchi said, 'a small group of men can do greater damage. The king's army came into the forest unchallenged; this time, I will take my Angels out to harass the Legion as they come.'

'Where will you meet them?' Ramulas asked.

'Days away from our forest.'

'I can give you more men with your soldiers,' Ramulas said.

Iguchi quickly shook his head. 'My Angels are all that I need.'

'Ye done wrong when the king's army came into the clearing,' Rygar said. 'Ye let them line up in fancy rows; when the Legion comes, don't give 'em time to think.'

Iguchi nodded. 'This is right. We must allow the enemy no rest as they travel here.'

"Ramulas, you will need to talk to the dryads,' Oriel said. 'They will be able to use their unusual talents to slow the Legion as they come through the forest.'

'I will see them now.'

'I'm coming too,' Pip said.

Ramulas quickly turned to Oriel. 'I almost forgot—we used the black dragon's scale; now we will need any miracle we can find.' He sighed, thinking that was going to be a blow to the Legion, but now Sanctuary was still recovering from their battle with the king.

'We can use Heaven's Reign,' Michael said, walking into the room.

'How can the sword help?' Ramulas asked.

Michael shrugged. 'For now, I cannot tell, but when my brother possessed it, he could cause a lot of damage.'

For too long there had been too many unanswered questions regarding Michael, the weapons from the tunnel, and his brother.

'How do we know Heaven's Reign won't hurt the people of Sanctuary?'

'I have felt the spirit within the sword,' Oriel said, 'and it waits for the real enemy to come before it fights.'

'I got Heaven's Reign in the training grounds; I'll be seein' what this fancy sword can do,' Rygar said.

'What about you, Michael?' Ramulas asked. 'Who is your brother to have such power, and what about yourself?'

All eyes turned on Michael as he took a deep breath and let out a slow sigh. 'My brother was banished from home a long time ago; I have come to bring him back.'

'Where is your home?' Ramulas asked.

Michael's shadow moved along the floor behind him, then it grew as it moved up the wall, and then a collective gasp could be heard as the shadow grew wings.

***

Lodi and Heaven's Reign stood in the middle of the training grounds. It was the only place in Sanctuary that was bare of any stonework or paving. People watched from the border, leaning on the railing. The giant had been a curiosity for them since his arrival in Sanctuary; now they whispered about Heaven's Reign since Jason had transformed after touching the magical sword.

'Your sword is pretty, Rain; can I touch it?' Lodi asked hopefully.

'I am Heaven's Reign. Why do insist on calling me Rain?

'Sorry, Rain,' Lodi mumbled. 'I just wanted to see what your sword can do.'

Heaven's Reign snarled, pulling the sword from its scabbard. 'You bumbling oaf. I will be glad to show you.'

A wall of mist fell from the blue crystal blade as the people spoke in hushed tones and Lodi's eyes widened.

Heaven's Reign thrust the sword at the giant. A stream of ice shot from the blade toward Lodi, who recoiled in shock.

A foot away from Lodi, the ice exploded with the sound of shattering glass. The fragments of ice hung in the air for a moment before transforming into hundreds of butterflies made of ice.

Lodi's jaw dropped as the butterflies danced around him. He reached out to touch them as Grace ran squealing into the training ground with Fenris close behind. She waved her hand through the air and the butterflies followed her commands.

Kate followed with Valkyrie, holding her hands out with an expression of wonderment and laughing each time a butterfly touched her fingers.

Lodi had recovered from the initial shock and hopped around trying to catch them. Each time he touched one, it burst with a faint chime. Then the people watching from the fence started coming toward the magical creatures. After a few moments, all the butterflies had vanished. The looks of joy turned to disappointment.

Grace glanced at the mist falling from the crystal blade, and her face screwed up as she wiggled her fingers. A second later, Heaven's Reign's eyes widened.

A stream of ice shot from the sword ten feet into the air, where it exploded into hundreds of ice butterflies. The people in the training grounds became excited as they reached for the sky.

'Grace, you stop that this instant,' her mother called as she walked towards them.

Grace dropped her hands, and the butterflies fell to the ground with a tinkling sound. She knew that she was in trouble. Jacqueline smiled to the crowd sheepishly as she ushered her girls to the castle. Both girls hung their heads as they followed.

'What were you thinking, Grace?' Jacqueline asked as the entered the castle.

Grace mumbled while still looking at the ground.

Her mother squatted down and lifted her daughter's chin to look into her eyes. 'What were you doing out there?'

She shrugged. 'I just wanted to play with the butterflies.'

'Your magic could have hurt someone,' Jacqueline said, shaking her finger. 'That's why Oriel and Shigar teach you. Your father will not be happy when he hears about this. Outside of the castle, no-one knows you have magical abilities, and Kate, you should know better.'

'What did I do?' Kate asked, holding out her hands.

'You are the eldest and should lead by example.'

Kate glared at Grace as they were led deeper into the castle.

3

Oriel and Iguchi were the only ones who were not surprised at Michael's shadow on the wall.

'The Fallen Angels,' Iguchi said, waving to Michael as if that explained everything.

'What?' Ramulas replied.

'Watch the way a person moves when they think no-one watches, and you will see their true intentions,' the little man said.

Michael's shadow had returned to normal, and everyone looked at him in awe. They had an angel to help them fight the Legion.

'Are you a real angel?' Pip asked, walking over to him.

Michael nodded as he smiled.

'You can help us,' she said excitedly. 'You can kill the whole First Legion.'

The angel slowly shook his head. 'In order to come here, I had to lose most of my powers, and I am forbidden to kill. I am here for my brother when he is released.'

This brought questions from everyone and Ramulas held up his hand for silence and turned to Michael. 'The most important question is, can you help us when the Legion comes here?'

He nodded. 'My presence with the Fallen Angels will bring them luck during the battle. They will be able to move in ways never seen before.'

'This is good,' Iguchi proclaimed. 'He will bring what the enemy does not expect. Long ago in my land, a castle was under siege. The lord knew the enemy numbers to be too great for a victory. He called down, asking for the townspeople to be spared and he would surrender, as he cared greatly for them. And, in an act of good faith, he would remove his soldiers from the wall as he gathered his people.

'Soldiers reappeared on the wall as the gates opened and the towns people slowly made their way out, their heads bowed, carrying their possessions and shuffling their feet. As agreed, the enemy force parted, letting the commoners through. But once the townspeople were in the middle of the enemy, they dropped their bundles and drew hidden weapons.

'The soldiers had changed clothes with the common people and walked out to an unsuspecting force. On this day a larger force was defeated.'

Iguchi had just finished when Jacqueline gave a polite cough at the door.

Ramulas saw Grace smiling proudly next to her mother. 'What happened?'

'Grace used her magical powers in the training grounds.'

She quickly outlined what she had seen with her daughters. Once Jacqueline had finished, she asked Ramulas to talk to Grace.

He nodded. He would talk to Grace while he and Pip visited the dryads.

***

They walked through the forest with the hell hound close by Grace. The air was damp, and the smell of decaying leaves was thick in the air. Most of the trees had lost their leaves, but they were still alive with the sounds of birds and wildlife.

'Tell me, little one,' Ramulas said with amusement in his tone, 'why did you use your magic in front of people today?'

'I wanted to see the butterflies.'

Ramulas shook his head. 'You let other people know you can use magic. You mustn't do that until you are much older.'

Grace sighed as she dropped her head. 'I'm sorry, Da.'

'From now on, only use your magic in the castle.'

She looked up at Ramulas with glowing green eyes and gasped in surprise. 'Da, the dryads are in the trees.'

Three males stepped out of the trees a moment before Tilly buzzed into view.

One of them smiled. 'Welcome into our home. We wondered how long after the battle you would come to us.'

'I have come to ask a favour,' Ramulas said.

The dryads waved as they turned away. 'Come to the sacred clearing where the others wait for you. Tilly will show you the way.'

Ramulas nodded as the dryads melted into the trees. The sprite moved away from them, and Grace reached up for the creature, but Tilly beat her wings, flying just out of reach. Grace became frustrated and clapped.

Tilly sneezed and dropped just low enough for Grace to grab her by the foot. The sprite squeaked and pulled out its short sword.

'Grace!' Ramulas shouted.

Startled, she released the sprite, who flew to the treetops.

Ramulas sighed. 'I just told you not to use magic outside of the castle.'

Grace's expression caused Pip to laugh and Ramulas looked to the sky for divine intervention. Since finding out that his daughters had acquired magical abilities, he could see the different ways they handled this. Kate was extremely uncomfortable when her ability showed itself, and Grace wanted to explore everything about hers.

***

They arrived in the sacred grove to find all the dryads waiting for them. Grace ran off to play with the children as Eady walked up to them. Ramulas noticed that this part of the forest seemed warmer as dappled sunlight filtered through the foliage and the mystic pool shined with a life of its own. 'Welcome. We heard of the battle, and we mourn those who passed.'

The mention of the fallen felt like a knife twisting in Ramulas' stomach, but he quickly pushed the feeling aside.

He sighed. 'There will be an even bigger battle after the winter. An army from another world will march on Sanctuary. If we cannot stop them, they will destroy everything, including your home.'

'What will you have us do?' Eady asked.

'During the last battle, I asked the dryads to stay hidden, but now I fear that I will need your assistance. Will the dryads fight alongside us?'

Eady cocked her head to the side. 'Will this army harm women and children?'

Ramulas nodded. 'I have seen them do terrible things, and they will show no mercy when they arrive.'

Eady spread her hands. 'We are a peaceful race. We will only fight if we agree that there is no other way. Come tell us of this army that comes.'

Ramulas and Pip spoke to the dryads of what they knew about the Legion though Oriel's visions. When they had finished, the dryads agreed to help with the Legion. Ramulas just hoped that he had enough help by winter's end, and wondered what the Legion was doing to prepare.

***

Three more Symiak tribes arrived in the camp, which made their total three thousand. A meeting was held with promises of shiny gifts for all who helped with retrieving Oriel.

Remus saw tensions boiling just below the surface and understood why these tribes had never come together—there was animosity and distrust between different groups. He had learned that the tribes had been fighting for generations and, therefore, they could never take the city of Keah.

Remus had organised three fights to distract the tribes. He needed them only to focus on Oriel. The bouts were between his captains and three of the best Symiaks.

The Legion soldiers and Symiaks formed a circle around a fighting pit that had been dug three feet into the rocky ground using magic. The red wizards and warlords had cast friendship spells over the creatures, allowing the Legion to mingle with them around the pit.

Remus wanted this to be a show of unity between Symiak and soldier. He was putting all his eggs in one basket with this ploy.

One wrong move could spell disaster.

He saw the three Symiaks who were to fight his captains and was fully confident that his captains would prevail; however, to win the creatures over, each bout needed to appear as if the Symiaks were close to winning before they lost.

***

Man and creature had now lined the cliffs and rocks surrounding the pit, anywhere they could find a vantage point. The first Symiak walked out to the cheers of soldiers and Symiak. He was Aggar of the Stone tribe; his skin was dull grey and covered in arcane symbols. Long, dark hair flowed down his back, and he held two swords made of stone.

Redemption walked into the ring swinging his twin spiked batons and smiled at the cheering crowd. He moved with the grace of a seasoned fighter.

Aggar rushed forward, hoping to catch him off guard. He didn't understand that the three captains could never be surprised. As the stone blades came down towards Redemption's exposed side, he waited until the last moment before stepping to the side and rapidly hitting the blades with his batons.

Aggar screamed in rage and swung a sword at the captain's head. Redemption parried the strike, which sent the baton spinning into the crowd. Men and Symiaks cheered as Redemption ducked and weaved out of harm's way, occasionally blocking with his remaining baton.

Each swing of the swords seemed closer and closer, and then Redemption lost his footing on some rocks that had fallen into the pit and fell back. Aggar rushed in with a wild swing. Redemption recovered and hit his baton on the inside of the creature's wrists several times, causing the creature to drop its weapons. The captain jumped up to kick Aggar in the face, stunning the creature. Then Redemption swung his baton in an upward arc, hitting Aggar between the legs.

Its eyes rolled back as Aggar fell to the ground.

Both soldiers and Symiaks cheered at the victory, and the pit was cleared for the next bout.

***

Slesht of the river tribe stepped into the pit. He was older, with a shaved head. He was very tall but thin, wearing a vest embroidered with the skeletons of fish and birds. His choice of weapon gave the creatures reason to cheer—hanging from a thick chain was a thick spiked ball. It glowed red from within and thin trails of grey smoke flowed from it.

Reckoning stepped into the pit, wearing only a pair of loose dark leggings and holding up his gauntlets with curved claws attached to them. Each gauntlet had three claws three feet long and sharp enough to puncture armour. He saw these as an extension of himself.

The two opponents slowly circled around the pit, Slesht flicking his spiked ball and filling the pit with smoke, which snaked into the air.

Reckoning smiled, knowing the creature would attempt to use the smoke as cover, but he had the other captains communicating with him. He took advantage and rushed the Symiak. Slesht hesitated and was slashed by one of the claws. He saw a line of blood across his chest.

The Symiak's weapon glowed as he swung it in a tight vicious circle at Reckoning's head. The captain ducked while using his claw to deflect the move. The swings continued as the ball's glow intensified. Reckoning always stayed just out of reach.

Frustrated, Slesht dashed forward, swinging the ball, which wrapped the chain around one of Reckoning's claws. The captain smiled, as this is what he wanted. Men and creatures cheered as the chain was pulled with Reckoning tumbling forward through the dust and loose stones.

Then he recovered and ran at the stunned Symiak. Before the creature could react, Reckoning jumped over its left shoulder and pulled the chain with him. The creature was off-balance when Reckoning looped the chain around its neck and began to choke him.

The crowd of onlookers fell into a frenzy as the Symiak fought against the chain. In a few moments, Slesht ceased his struggle and collapsed. Reckoning un-looped the chain and raised his hand in victory.

Remus watched closely as both soldier and Symiak cheered for the victor.

A hush came over the crowd after the pit was cleared. The Symiaks had lost the last two bouts. Grunch walked in with the expectations of all the tribes to win this one. Retribution followed, wearing loose pants and sweeping his twin swords through the air in intricate patterns as he circled the Symiak.

Grunch roared and held up his hand. A giant spiked club was thrown in from the crowd, and he caught it with ease. He snorted and slowly walked towards the third captain; an expression of murder intensified with each step.

Retribution launched his attack as soon as Grunch came close. The blades of his swords hummed through the air as they became almost invisible. Grunch roared in fury and slammed his club to the ground, narrowly missing the captain, who rolled out of the way.

Small, precise cuts could be seen on the Symiak's forearms.

Time and time again, Grunch swung wildly at Retribution, only to miss by the narrowest of margins. Each time, the captain would dance in and out, spinning his twin swords.

Within a minute, Grunch's arms were covered in blood. It was as if both arms had been dipped into a barrel filled with blood. Scores of well-placed cuts had been delivered to the Symiak's arms during the exchange. The more blood Grunch saw, the madder he became.

Then he took a wild swing, and his blood-covered hands lost their grip on his weapon. As the spiked club flew over the stunned crowd, Retribution jumped up, slamming both hilts of his swords into Grunch's temples.

The Symiak swayed for a moment before falling like a giant tree. Remus smiled as both man and creature cheered. He needed unity to march for Oriel and those who protected her.

***

Ramulas walked up to Owain on the wall and could have sworn that the blind bowman was looking over the forest. 'Owain, I have a question for you.'

He nodded. 'Welcome, Ramulas.'

'The Legion will come at the end of winter, and we need all of the help we can get. Is there a way for you to contact the black dragon and bring it back?'

Owain shook his head. 'I have no hold over the black dragon. It hates the greens and would be far from this place.'

Ramulas' eyes widened. 'What about the green dragons? Would they come to help us?'

A sad smile crossed Owain's face. 'I have left Shangri-la and the greens would no longer take heed of my words. They will only listen to those of my old home.'

This comment felt like a blow to the stomach for Ramulas. He gave a nod of thanks and walked away, devastated that his hopes were shattered so quickly. How were they going to stop the Legion without the dragons? Then he saw Shigar.

'My friend,' the magician said, 'you seemed troubled. What is wrong?'

He quickly explained his conversation with Owain, and how dragons could help with the coming battle.

Shigar smiled. 'Come with me, my friend. I have been working on a few things that will lift your spirits.'

Ramulas followed Shigar to his chambers with bookshelves lining every wall, holding books of various sizes, scrolls, and potions. Piles of books, scrolls, and potions also littered the tables and floor. The musty smell of cloves hung in the air as he walked in.

He showed Ramulas to a clean section. 'Wait here for a moment, my friend.'

Shigar searched through his books and scrolls with growing excitement, and then with a maniacal grin, he started to chant.

Crackling energies filled the chamber and scrolls and paper rustled in an unseen breeze; a small, dark cloud appeared before Shigar, making his hair stand on end.

Ramulas gasped as his body was covered in goosebumps.

Shigar's chanting became louder and more frantic as the cloud rose above him and grew. He pulled something from his robes and threw it into the dark cloud with a shout.

The head of a black dragon materialised from the cloud, its eyes focused on Ramulas as its mouth opened and it shot towards him. He jumped back as his weapons appeared in his hands, and a warm sensation flowed through him as purple flames danced on his shoulders.

And then, with a pop, the dragon vanished.

Shigar laughed softly as Ramulas glanced at him in confusion. 'It looked real, did it not, my friend? But it was just an illusion. I will create an even bigger one for when they come to our home.'

Ramulas laughed. 'This explains why I have not seen you much. I just hope your magic is enough for the warlords.'

***

Remus sat in the large tent with the chieftains. The three captains, the red wizards, and the warlords stood behind him. He looked at Grunch, whose arms had been healed and left scars of the battle. He wore them proudly.

'I have called you here to talk about Keah,' he said calmly. 'I will soon take my men into Keah and ask the king to bring his army with us to get the person.'

An eruption of protests filled the tent.

Remus waved his hand, casting a spell of calming, and spoke when everyone had quietened down. 'Let me explain. I have promised you the city of Keah after we have found the person I am looking for.'

Grunch stood and shook his head. 'We not go with Keah. You take men, then we come into city.'

This was met with grunts of approval from the other Symiaks.

'The army will not leave the city after seeing so many of you in the mountains,' Remus explained.

'Then why go with Keah men?' Grunch asked.

Remus smiled. 'We go with Keah soldiers and let them fight for us. Then, when they are weak, you attack from behind, kill them, and Keah is yours.'

The Symiaks stood, hooting and stomping. Then, after a moment, Grunch raised his hand for silence and looked at Remus. 'When you go Keah?'

'Soon,' Remus said. 'Very soon.'

4

Amessenger was intercepted by the king's royal guard two miles out of the town of Covedon where the road headed towards the ocean. After a few quick words, he was rushed to Zachary.

'My king,' he said, 'two messages have come out of Keah.'

Zachary took the two silver tubes and read their contents. A confused expression crossed Zachary's face as he re-read them, and then he handed them to Lucas. 'Read them.'

Lucas smiled grimly. 'I have already been told, my king. The Symiaks are gathering in the mountains in numbers never seen before.'

'And the city is without its army,' Zachary added. 'We cannot tarry. We must push the men as hard as we can. If the creatures come down from the mountain, we could lose the city.'

They arrived at Covedon a short while later. The tangy taste of salt in the air, mixed with the sounds of the sea birds, reminded the army of the docks in Keah, but this town was smaller than the docks of Keah, and all the people survived one way or another by living off the ocean.

The people of Covedon seemed subdued with the army outside its gates and the small force of royal guards that entered the town. The fat mayor and sheriff greeted them in the centre of town.

'My king, I trust your journey was pleasant,' the mayor said while playing with the material of his shirt.

A bolt of anger shot through Zachary as he looked at the poor excuse of a man in front of him. He glanced at the sheriff. 'Lock this dog meat away and send him on the next wagon to Gullytown.'

Both the mayor and the sheriff stood in shock for a moment before the sheriff called a pair of soldiers to drag the mayor away. Zachary then promoted the sheriff to the position of mayor.

'How many boats do you have in your harbour?' Zachary asked the new mayor.

'One ship leaving for Shes in the hour and five fishing boats.'

'I will need the ship and boats,' Zachary said calmly. 'I need as many of my men to go to Keah as soon as possible.'

Thoughts raced through the mayor's head. The ship would need to be stopped and the fishermen spoken to. There would be protests of bloody murder, but these protests would very soon go quiet.

With an awkward bow, he ran off to the docks.

Zachary arrived soon with the royal guard to find the mayor in a shouting match with the ship's captain and fishermen. The sounds of the waves crashing on nearby rocks, the cry of the gulls, and the creaking of rocking boats would have seemed almost tranquil to Zachary if this was not so urgent.

'I don't care if the king himself comes down here,' the captain shouted, 'the ship is not going to Keah.'

Zachary cleared his throat a few times as he walked closer to the captain, who turned and paled at the sight of the king. The other dock workers and fishermen backed away in stunned silence. For a few moments, the only sounds were of the waves and gulls.

Zachary wore an evil smile. 'I believe you have something to tell me.'

The man's eyes widened as he shook his head, unable to speak.

'I suspect that you were going to tell me that you were going to unload your ship and take as many of my men as you can to Keah. Is that correct?'

The ship's captain regained enough composure to give a slight nod.

The mayor quickly ran to the fishing boats and, with the king's presence, there were no more arguments. Zachary looked at Lucas. 'Fetch me Logan,' he said in a bored tone.

Logan, the captain of the royal lancers, came down to the docks, his long blond hair flowing in the breeze. It stood out in contrast to his dirty uniform, which showed signs of battle. Logan's hair always appeared as if it had just been washed, and he seemed out of place surrounded by soldiers covered in grime from the battle.

Zachary waved him closer. 'I need you to go back to Sanctuary and follow up with our plan. Take a horse, but only as far as Turtha. Eat well; you will be leaving at first light.'

Logan stood. 'My uniform?'

Zachary waved. 'Leave it on. It will help with your story. If you fail me, I will send you to Gullytown.'

Logan gave one of his cocky smiles. 'If I fail, the people of Sanctuary will kill me.'

He raced off as the soldiers began boarding the ship and fishing boats. Within the next hour, seven hundred soldiers set sail for home.

***

Ramulas stood on the balcony in the early morning light. He was able to see most of the town. Against the rear wall, the statues of the fallen seemed to sparkle in the sunlight, and the magical flame still danced above the altar.

This would be the first day of training. The people of Sanctuary, dressed in armour, filed past the fallen, pausing for a moment before continuing. Ramulas was amazed by the reverence they showed the fallen.

'What is she doing?' Pip asked by his side.

'Who?'

She pointed to Emily, who was behind the fallen and walked to the magical flame. She cupped her hands behind it until a soft light filled her hands, then she walked away holding the light close to her chest. She stopped behind one of the fallen and pushed the light into the statue, causing a faint shimmer to spread across its body.

Emily returned to the flame and repeated the process until she had touched all the fallen. After Emily touched the last one, Ramulas blinked, and Emily was gone.

'What!' Ramulas gasped. 'Where did she go?'

Pip's emerald eyes glowed as she scanned the fallen and people filling past, and then she turned to him with an expression of disbelief. 'One moment she was here, and the next she was gone. I can see through walls, but I can't find her.'

'Training has started again. Come with me and watch Rygar put the people through their paces,' Ramulas said.

Ramulas' mind wandered as they walked thinking of how much his life had changed in such a short time. If they were able to defeat the Legion, he would be free to go back and rebuild his farm, but would he really want something like that?

'That's not a good sign,' Pip said.

Ramulas looked up to see himself at the fence of the training grounds next to Pip. Two large groups faced off. Rygar shouted a command and the left group charged twenty feet to attack the other group. After a brief scuffle, the dwarf whistled, and the roles were reversed. This continued until the people struggled to hold their weapons.

As the two groups walked away, Ramulas saw the expressions of determination on their faces, and then he noticed Heaven's Reign leaning against the opposite fence of the training grounds. Ramulas had heard that the people had followed Lodi's example and now called him Rain. At first, Heaven's Reign had been furious, but then he accepted the new name.

Rain had repeatedly asked to train with the others, but Rygar was unsure of what the crystal blade would do.

For now, Rain would wait. For now.

***

Pip stood on the wall watching Owain train the archers in the clearing. She had been switching her attention from the archers to the wildlife and the dryads in the forest.

Then something caught her attention a mile away in the trees.

She saw a man stumble through the forest toward Sanctuary. He would stop every few feet to lean on one of the trees. Looking past the man, Pip saw the Fallen Angels following him, which brought a smile to her face.

As he came close, she could see that he wore a filthy kingdom uniform, and he was covered in bruises and abrasions.

She called down to Owain, 'Someone's coming through the forest!'

He smiled up at her. 'I know. I heard them coming a while ago.'

Pip silently cursed herself for not realising how good Owain's hearing was. As the soldier came into the clearing, she raced off to find Ramulas.

Logan collapsed as he entered the clearing, and the Angels surrounded his prone figure.

'This man is very lazy,' Iguchi said. 'He did not have far to go. Bring him to the Lord of Sanctuary, where we will learn of his fate.'

Miles and Benji picked up the limp body and brought him inside, where the people gathered in wonder at this new development. Iguchi led the Angels to the throne room, where Ramulas, Pip, and Oriel waited.

Ramulas pointed to a table. 'Place him there. Pip, find Shigar and bring him here.'

She raced out of the room as Logan was laid on the table and Ramulas came over to inspect him. Thoughts raced through his head as to what implications this could bring to Sanctuary. It had been almost a week after the battle with the kingdom army, and now one of the soldiers lay injured before him.

'Were there any more in the forest?' he asked Iguchi.

'The Lord of Sanctuary need not worry; when we saw this one, we searched the forest, and there were no others.'

Oriel came to stand by Ramulas, holding her hands over Logan, and he was soon covered in a fine purple mist. Her arms dropped and she looked at Ramulas with concern.

'He has been beaten and travelled for days on foot without food or water, and I looked into his soul—the king has sent him back to spy on us.

Miles stepped forward, drawing his sword.

'No,' Iguchi said, raising his hand. 'It is good to have a spy with us.'

Ramulas appeared confused. 'It is?'

Iguchi nodded. 'It is better to know that we have a spy and feed him false information than to have a spy without knowing. A good spy can destroy his enemies; a bad spy destroys his master.'

At that moment, Pip returned with Shigar and came over to the table.

The magician gasped. 'This is Logan, the captain of the royal lancers. What is he doing here?'

Ramulas told Shigar and Pip what they had just learned about Logan.

Shigar shook his head. 'He was always a shifty character. What do we do now?'

Ramulas smiled. 'We go along with whatever story he tells us and see what we might learn from him.'

'Other than Rygar, only the people in this room are to know the truth about Logan; if too many people know, he will find out,' Ramulas said.

Everyone nodded.

'Oriel, heal him.'

Oriel held out her hands once more and red mist drifted down to cover Logan. This time, he softly moaned as his wounds healed. After a minute, he opened his eyes.

'Shigar!' he said in astonishment. 'Where am I?'

The magician smiled. 'You are in the castle of Sanctuary.'

'And we are curious as to how you are here,' Ramulas said.

Logan slowly looked around at the people surrounding him. 'I was with the king's army when we marched on Sanctuary, thinking I was on the right side, then something changed my mind.'

'What was that something?' Ramulas asked.

'Dragons,' Logan said with awe. 'When I saw the dragons in the sky, I knew that I wanted to change sides. Once the king's army ran into the forest, I could not shake the dragons from my mind. After a few days, I had spoken to some trusted friends about leaving the king's army—I wanted then to come with me.

'But word got back to the king. I was charged with treason and sentenced to death. I killed the soldier guarding me and fled here.'

'You expect us to welcome you after twenty-eight of my people were killed?' Ramulas said in a low tone.

'I killed no-one and didn't even fight.'

Ramulas thought for a moment. 'You may stay a few days until we know what to do with you.' He turned to Iguchi. 'Have your Angels show him a room in the west wing.'

The small man nodded and motioned for Michael and Benji to take him. Once he had gone, Ramulas breathed a sigh of relief.

'My friend, you were a little harsh on Logan,' Shigar said.

Ramulas smiled. 'If I had not acted in this way, he might have been suspicious, and the west wing has a lot of empty rooms. I want him to think he has freedom. Now all we need to do is wait for Logan to make his first move.'

5

After days of meetings, the Symiaks finally agreed to Remus' plan of going to Keah. The sun had begun to drop, covering the mountains in a light mist that formed into small pockets at the edge of the camp, and in a few hours, it would be dark. Howling, freezing winds tore across the mountains. Remus hoped it would not be so harsh in Keah.

He told the Symiaks that he would leave in the morning with the Legion. After the snows, he would return to take them to shiny gifts.

Grunch promised many more Symiaks would come by then. Remus smiled, knowing that he would throw the stupid Symiaks and Keah's army at whoever was helping Oriel. The red wizards, warlords, and soldiers began preparations for leaving in the morning.

As the freezing winds tugged at his robes, Remus knew that he needed to gain the trust of Keah's king as soon as possible. They needed to find a common ground, otherwise, life could be difficult for both sides.

***

Zachary led his army through the gates of Keah just before sunset. He was happy to see the seven hundred sent by sea standing on the wall. Entering the gate, the anger of losing the battle came forth within him. He had lost the Khilli and was betrayed by Shigar.

Zachary dismissed his soldiers, ordering them to rest, while his royal guard followed him into the castle. A sergeant waited outside Zachary's chamber and saluted his king.

Barely able to contain his rage, Zachary said, 'Tell me what happened with the Khilli.'

The sergeant told of the small force invading the castle wearing face paint, with two hell hounds, a dwarf, a female with purple hair, and a man wearing purple and green armour whose weapons were covered in magical flames.

The group was led to the Khilli families by four Khilli warriors with them. The soldiers attempted to stop them several times but were overrun. The other group fought in a way they had never seen before.

He then showed Zachary to Shigar's chambers, where the group had last been seen. Lucas opened the door and Zachary peered inside. The king felt a knife twist inside his stomach as he walked into the magician's chambers. It was almost bare—most of the books, scrolls, and potions had been taken.

'Was Shigar seen with this group?' Zachary asked the sergeant.

When the sergeant shook his head, Zachary turned to Lucas. 'Search this place for any clues, then burn everything. I want to know how they escaped.'

After a quick search, Lucas ordered for the room to be destroyed. Zachary walked away to the sound of shelves being broken, but it did not give him the satisfaction he thought it would.

The group the sergeant described seemed familiar to the one in Sanctuary, but it could not be the same group. How could they travel from one place to another so quickly? Shigar was somehow involved. Zachary wanted to know how the magician helped.

'My king, we have found something,' Lucas called, coming out of the chambers.

Zachary followed the captain into the chamber to a rear room where they found a hidden doorway with a stairway leading down into the darkness. One of the bookshelves had been moved to show this door.

The king smiled. 'Fetch the torches. We will see where this takes us.'

***

Four soldiers held a torch and led their way into the darkness with the sergeant. The royal guard and Zachary were close behind. Then the sergeant stopped at the start of the hallway and looked back at Zachary.

'My king, this does not feel right.'

'If you do not continue, I will send you to Gullytown,' Zachary promised.

The royal guards pushed him forward before he could answer. He stumbled a few feet before the hairs on the back of his neck stood on end.

The sound of soft moaning and whispers came from the darkness.

The sergeant looked around frantically. 'What's that?'

Two spectral figures floated toward the torches and grabbed the sergeant with skeletal hands. He screamed in terror as they dragged him into the darkness.

'It's a trap!' one of the soldiers shouted just before he, too, was pulled into the darkness, and his torch fell to the floor.

The royal guard formed a cordon around their king and raced upstairs. Once they were in the small room, Lucas pushed the bookcase in front of the opening.

'What was that?' Zachary gasped as he fell to the ground.

When no-one answered, he gestured for Lucas to pick him up and for them to go out into the hall.

'I want this door to be kept closed and never opened again,' Zachary said as he tried to understand what had happened.

Zachary and the royal guard waited near the door for a few minutes to see if the ghostly figures would come out. When none appeared, Zachary headed for his chambers.

***

Joshua paced in his kitchen, trying his best to ignore his wife. His best friend was one of the fallen, and he had fallen into a deep depression. Try as he might, Joshua could not let go of the pain of missing his friend. He had missed the last three days of training. He had spent every waking hour either at the statues of the fallen or sitting in his kitchen staring into space.

'Why don't you even look at me?' He heard his wife's voice through the haze. 'Everyone else has moved on; I'm alive, and if you're not careful, you will lose me as well.'

'*Come to me,*' a voice whispered, barely touching his consciousness.

Joshua's head snapped toward the sound, and he quickly made his way toward it. For the first time since the battle, Joshua's eyes were full of energy.

'Oh, you have finally come to your senses,' his wife said, coming to embrace him.

'*Come to me,*' the voice repeated with urgency.

Joshua brushed his wife aside and walked out into the street. It was an hour past dawn and a light drizzle had settled over Sanctuary. Small groups of people dressed in armour made their way to the training grounds. No-one took notice of Joshua, who was of average height with brown eyes and short dark hair. The only thing different about him was that he was stocky and broad across the shoulders.

The voice continued to call him as he walked to the tunnel, ignoring everything around him. He did not even hear his wife yelling as she followed.

Six people stood at the tunnel entrance, each taking turns to grab the gauntlet that hung in the air. The men laughed each time it danced away.

Joshua pushed his way through the group and looked at the gauntlet. He knew this was calling him.

'Hey there,' one of the men protested.

Joshua stepped forward and held his left hand up, and the gauntlet floated down to cover his hand and forearm.

***

Michael's eyes widened as he felt the energy of the gauntlet. It had found an owner. The Fallen Angels were in the training grounds with Rygar.

He quickly told Iguchi what had happened before running off with the Angels close behind.

***

Joshua gasped in pain as the gauntlet shrank and moulded to his arm and hand. He fell to his knees, desperately trying to pull it off.

'Help me take it off,' he moaned.

Several people rushed in to help without success, and then the gauntlet began to glow a soft white light, which soon intensified into a blinding white light. Everyone shielded their eyes.

When the light faded, everyone looked in shock at Joshua.

Joshua stood radiating power. His short dark hair had now been replaced with long, curly blond locks that fell to his shoulders, and his brown eyes were now bright blue. The most noticeable thing about him was that he was snarling like a wild animal, his blue eyes full of hate and his teeth bared at any who came near.

He opened and closed his left hand a few times. 'Leave me now,' he growled.

One of the people stepped forward in concern. 'What has happened?'

Joshua hit the man with a backhand, sending him flying ten feet through the air, and then he rushed the group, scattering them like leaves in a storm.

People gathered to see others moaning on the ground, and everyone watched Joshua with a mix of fear and uncertainty.

'Look 'ere, what yer doin'?' Edwin asked Joshua as he came out of the tunnel.

Joshua leapt fifteen feet to land in front of the dwarf with a growl, only to be hit in the side of the head with the dwarf's shovel. The handle snapped and the head fell to the ground.

'Oops,' the dwarf said as Joshua picked him up by the vest and threw him back into the tunnel.

'Stay back,' Michael called as the Angels surrounded Joshua, followed by Rygar and Lodi.

Joshua crouched in the centre of Angels and growled.

'Oh no,' Michael whispered when he saw that the person wearing the gauntlet had his brother's eyes and hair.

Joshua crouched in the middle of the circle the Angels had made around him.

'He must be stopped,' Michael said. 'Beware the strength of the gauntlet.'

'Alive!' Iguchi called.

Miles and Benji glanced at each other before rushing Joshua from opposite sides. Joshua moved faster than anyone thought possible. Benji was sent flying through the air, only to be caught by Lodi, and Miles was sent sliding across the wet ground. Four more Angels ran in, only to be knocked aside with ease.

Then Lodi pushed passed the Angels. Joshua smiled at the challenge of fighting a giant. As Lodi reached down for him, Joshua launched himself at the giant, delivering a brutal left hook. The power of the punch caught Lodi off guard, his arms waving as he stepped back.

Joshua ran forward and received Lodi's boot in his face. He fell onto his back and the Angels pounced on top of him. Edwin came running out of the tunnel with Royce and Shayn close behind, each carrying an armful of rocks.

'Hold his legs!' Edwin called.

The Angels held down his legs as Royce and Shayn moulded the stone around Joshua's legs and feet. When they had finished, Iguchi motioned for the Angels back.

By this time, a large crowd had gathered to witness the chaos caused by the gauntlet.

Joshua stood, his eyes burning with fury at being held by the stone around his feet.

Iguchi walked forward. 'This one is very angry, and he finds his strength through his anger.'

Joshua screamed in rage as he bent down and began beating at the stone moulded around his feet. Chips of stone flew in all directions, causing people to shield their eyes.

Michael shook his head. 'This is a very bad sign.'

Rygar nodded as one of his feet came free and Lodi stepped forward, but Iguchi rushed in front of the giant and stabbed two ridged fingers into the enraged man's neck. Joshua gasped once before collapsing to the ground.

***

Remus watched the Legion as they lined up in columns alongside the supply wagons. The sun began to rise over the mountains, throwing distorted shadows along the ground.

The Symiak tribes gathered one hundred yards away. They had come to watch the spectacle of the Legion leaving for Keah.

'I will return at the end of the snows,' Remus said to Grunch.

The creature grunted. 'Grunch will wait with many hundreds of Symiaks. You will take us to gifts?'

Remus smiled without emotion. 'I promise you will get what you deserve.'

The Symiaks hooted and stomped their feet, sending clouds of dust into the air as the Legion made their way down the mountain.

***

It took hours to navigate pathways down the mountains before reaching the road to Keah, and before too long, they were within site of the city walls. Travellers coming and going from Keah had seen this army and raced back to the protection of the city.

Remus signalled for a halt as he cast a spell allowing him to see the city walls as if he were only one hundred yards away. Soldiers looked down at the panicked people as they pointed towards the Legion. In turn, the soldiers waved and shouted to those in the city. Remus looked to the west at the bay filled with all manner of ships and boats.

A short while later, the gates opened, and the army of Keah raced out to meet them. Clouds of dust rose behind the army, and Remus noticed several red banners with a black eagle in the centre.

'They come,' Remus said calmly. 'Remain at attention.' The sound of rolling thunder increased as the kingdom army closed in. Remus called for the warlords, red wizards, and his three captains to come to him.

They rode two hundred yards and waited for the army of Keah to meet them.

Lucas held up his hand, stopping his forces one hundred yards away. A force of riders holding long silver lances, followed by a score of royal guards, fanned out onto the grass on either side of the road. Lucas walked his horse up to the warlords as Remus removed his hood.

Lucas' eyes widened as he saw the escaped prisoner leading an army and wearing a red breastplate covered in magical symbols. 'What trick is this?'

Remus held out his hands, clearly confused. 'What do you mean?'

Lucas knew something was out of place. This man looked exactly like the escaped prisoner, but there was something very different about him. He whispered to a royal guard who turned and raced back to the city.

'Do I need to concern myself with this?' Remus asked nodding to the vanishing rider.

Lucas shook his head, 'You look like someone we know, but I can see you hold yourself differently.'

Remus held his chin in a cupped hand, looking off into the distance thinking of the man he fought in the mountains. 'What can you tell me of him?'

Lucas shook his head. 'Someone will be very interested in seeing you. Please wait until he arrives.'

Remus gave a slight nod to cover his irritation. He was not used to being told what to do but knew that he needed to be on good terms with the people of Keah.

Lucas observed Remus and his army with fascination. The uniform was different and nothing like those in Sanctuary, and the most noticeable thing was the lack of the symbol on the side of his face.

A short while later, Zachary rode into view, flanked by three scores of knights riding warhorses. Zachary pulled up next to Lucas as the royal guard formed a tight circle around him.

The king's eyes widened in shock, which quickly turned to anger. 'Where are your dragons, Lord of Sanctuary?' He sneered.

Lucas leaned in to whisper in Zachary's ear. After a few seconds, he gasped and looked closely at Remus' face. 'Who are you?'

'I am Remus, warlord of Lodec. We have come to you to ask for your assistance.'

Zachary shook his head in confusion. 'Where is this Lodec? I have never heard of it.'

Remus motioned toward the city. 'It would be preferable if we could discuss this in a more comfortable setting. I know what I have to say will benefit both of us.'

Zachary motioned for Lucas to come with him to the side of the road, where they spoke for a few moments before he returned. 'I will allow a small group to come into the city to talk, but your army must remain outside the walls.'

Remus glanced up at the sky and saw it was close to midday then turned to Redemption. 'Stay with the Legion until we return.'

Redemption rode through an opening made by the royal guard and used hand signals to have the Legion sat up a temporary camp. The knights on warhorses surrounded Remus and the king as they made their way to the city.

***

Remus smiled as he was led through the city. People lined the streets watching them in awe. Little did they know, the fox had been brought into the chicken pen. Within minutes, they were shown into Zachary's chambers.

Zachary sat on his throne observing the newcomers. 'Strange things have happened over the past few weeks. Please excuse my ill behaviour toward you; a person appearing very similar to you has caused much grief throughout the kingdom,' Zachary said to Remus.

Remus frowned. 'What has this person done?'

'I will tell you soon, but first please tell me what has brought you and your army into my kingdom.'

Remus waved his arm behind him. 'We have come from a place far from here in search of someone who possesses something of ours.'

The statement confused Zachary, as he had been told the Legion came from the direction of Salvation. He would have known of an army like the Legion in those parts, and there was nothing but barren land beyond Salvation.

'Did you come by ship and then travel across land in order to come here?' he asked.

Remus took a deep breath, knowing this would be the telling moment. 'We come from another world.'

Zachary's mouth fell open as he searched his chambers for an explanation. The royal guards were visibly shocked.

Remus smiled inwardly, knowing he had the upper hand. 'Our world is ruled by magic, and the person we seek has taken this from us and fled to this world. She is to the north of here at the base of a mountain range, and she is surely being protected by people.'

Zachary's first thought was of Sanctuary. 'When did this person escape?'

'A few weeks ago, but our concept of time differs from yours.'

Zachary was silent as he thought of when Shigar told him that a powerful artifact had come into the kingdom. Soon after that, they had caught the Lord of Sanctuary, only to have him escape with the crystal, and then thousands of people across the kingdom joined the traitor Shigar in Sanctuary.

'I think the person you are looking for is in a place called Sanctuary.'

'Remus' eyes widened. 'How can you be sure?'

Zachary quickly told the story from when Shigar felt the artifact to the battle at Sanctuary.

'And you just returned last night?' Remus asked.

Zachary nodded while Remus silently berated himself for spending too much time in the mountains. If they had come a few days earlier, the Legion would have walked into an unguarded city. He pushed these thoughts away. He would use the king's army to retrieve Oriel.

'Our world will die if we do not bring this person back. You have been to Sanctuary; I would ask that you show us the way. After we have her, we will leave gifts for you.'

Zachary leaned forward on his throne. 'What gifts?'

Remus pulled a pouch from his robes, pouring the contents onto the patterned rug. Gems, crystals, and diamonds silently bounced, catching the light as they danced.

'The person who has these is named Oriel; she will have enough to fill this room,' Remus said with a wave of his hand. 'When we retrieve Oriel, you will get gifts.'

Zachary was speechless. He wanted revenge against the Lord of Sanctuary, and his prayers were answered in the form of the Legion. He would be rich beyond his wildest dreams. He wanted to return to Sanctuary.

Then it hit him.

'We cannot go to Sanctuary until after winter; it snows heavily along the mountains.'

Remus saw the greed and cunning in the king's eyes. 'If you march with the Legion after winter, we will take Oriel and leave the rest for you. Together, we can defeat the people of Sanctuary. The one thing I ask is accommodation for my men over winter.'

'How many men do you have?'

'Seven thousand.'

Zachary balked at such a large number. That was almost a quarter of the population of the city. 'It would be difficult to house that many in my city. Give me a moment with my council.'

Remus nodded as Zachary walked away with the royal guard. He waited patiently until the king returned.

'I can only house five thousand here, and a thousand each in the towns of Covedon and Turtha, which are a few days' travel to the north.'

With great reluctance, Remus agreed. He did not want his forces divided; however, the king's army would be used to soften Sanctuary's defences when they marched for Oriel. 'Allow me to prepare my men.'

6

Lodi carried the still-unconsciousness Joshua into the throne room. The rocks had been removed from his feet. He was dropped in front of Ramulas.

'What happened here?' Ramulas asked.

'The gauntlet has found a new owner,' Michael said, walking into the room. 'It has sent this man insane; he was attacking people near the tunnel.'

'How bad was it?' he asked, walking forward with Oriel.

Iguchi led the Angels into the room as Michael said, 'He hurt several people before attacking the Angels and gave Lodi a good hit before Iguchi stopped him.'

Ramulas turned to see the swelling under Lodi's eye, and he gasped. 'He did that to you?'

Lodi did not reply, instead choosing to glare at Joshua.

Oriel walked over to the unconscious man and held her hands above him until he was covered in a faint white light.

She frowned and shook her head slightly. 'The gauntlet is driving him mad; it feeds off his anger. He has skin almost as hard as stone, and he is almost as strong as Lodi.'

'We could use him when the Legion comes.'

Half the room jumped when Pip spoke, as she walked into the room silently.

'Until that time, I will place a tranquillity spell upon him,' Oriel said, waving her hands as purple mist covered Joshua. 'His strength and anger have now been halved; the people of Sanctuary are now safe.'

She clicked her fingers, and the light around Joshua faded. He moaned softly and opened his eyes to see the gauntlet on his arm. 'Please take this off me,' he pleaded to Oriel.

She shook her head. 'It has formed a bond with you. If I remove it, you will die a painful death.'

He glanced around the room in defeat. 'Am I cursed to wear this until I die?'

Oriel shook her head. 'When the true owner of the gauntlet returns, he will take it from you. He is close to me in the mountain, and I feel his anger. When he is free, he will come for his weapons. But for now, do not worry; I have placed a calming spell on you.'

Rygar stepped forward and slapped Joshua on the back. 'Don't ye be worryin'. I'll take ye back to the tunnel and explain what happened.'

As they left, Ramulas asked Oriel, 'With a stone-like skin and being almost as strong as Lodi, is he going to be like this all of the time?'

'No, only when he is angered.'

'This is good,' Iguchi said. 'I know a weapon for one such as he.'

***

Logan had recovered quickly and was walking around by the next day. His first destination was the throne room, where he was met by Ramulas at the door.

He gave a friendly smile. 'I know that I have only been here one night, but I wish to prove my worth. I want to help in some way.'

'I will talk to the others on the council to see where you might fit in, but first, remove the kingdom unform and replace it with ours.'

Emily appeared behind Logan holding a dull grey tunic and a pair of leggings.

'Emily will follow you to your room and escort you around the castle. Rumours of you have surfaced so, please, for your safety, stay here for a few days.'

Ramulas smiled as he shut the door in Logan's face. Logan fought to control his anger as he walked away. He was left with a child. He would not allow this humiliation to interfere with his mission.

***

Logan came out of his room and found Emily waiting for him. 'Leave me be, child,' he said as he brushed past her.

He stopped in shock when she grabbed his tunic. He snarled and raised his fist to strike her.

Shigar's laughter stopped him. 'You may not like children, but this one is to be left alone if you value your safety."

He nodded at Emily. 'Does she belong to the Lord of Sanctuary?'

'Emily is the child of Sanctuary.'

He glanced down at Emily and jumped back when he saw dark energy flowing from her eyes.

Shigar smiled. 'You will find that Sanctuary is very different from the city of Keah,' the magician said before walking away.

Logan saw Emily walk around a corner and raced after her. He needed to know everything about Sanctuary. He rounded the corner to find no trace of the girl, which meant he was free to search the castle.

He spent an hour walking the halls and searching rooms. He marked all that was locked and would return later. The castle was different from Keah. The design of the stone and marble was unlike anything he had seen before.

He could not risk being caught at this early stage. He needed to build trust. Then he walked out of a room to find Emily waiting for him.

'Why were you in there?' she asked.

Logan ignored the question. 'Where did you go before?'

'I do not like you, and I want you to leave the castle.'

'I go where I please, and no child tells me what to do.'

Emily smiled and pointed behind him. Logan turned to see nothing was there. When he looked back, Emily had vanished again.

***

Emily stepped out of a secret passage after he had left, watching Logan walk away.

'What are you looking at, little one?' Pip asked.

'I do not like him; he is bad on the inside.'

'Do not worry. I will keep an eye on him.' Pip winked at her before running down the hallway after Logan. Shortly, she caught up with him and stayed out of sight. Logan glanced around before quickly entering a room. Pip counted to ten before making her way to a wall opposite the room.

Logan walked out to find a smiling Pip casually leaning against the wall.

'I know who you are, thief,' he said, walking towards her. 'I almost had you a few times in Keah.'

She shrugged. 'Almost is not good enough.'

'How does someone like you end up in a place like this?'

'Oh, I don't know; kill a few kingdom soldiers,' she replied innocently.

Logan stepped forward as anger flared in his eyes and reached for a sword that he no longer wore.

Pip smiled as she opened her robes showing her throwing knives. 'You can borrow one of these if you like.'

'Are you threatening me?'

'No, just warning you not to call me "thief" again.'

'The Lord of Sanctuary will hear of this,' Logan said as he stormed off.

'Tell him I said hello.'

***

Ramulas found Pip on the wall looking out over the forest. The cold air from the mountains whipped her hair and clothes. 'Oriel told me you would be here.'

'I'm waiting for the leaves to die,' she said softly.

'What?'

Pip pointed to the trees filled with multi-coloured leaves. 'I see the last of the energy drain from the leaf before it dies. The trees are pulling their energy into their roots for winter.'

He smiled. 'Logan came to see me. He told me that you threatened him. What happened?'

'He called me a thief from Keah, and I asked him to stop.'

'We know that he is a spy for the king. Try not to upset him too much.'

She winked at him. 'I'll try.'

Ramulas was about to answer when Pip grabbed his arm and pointed to the edge of the clearing. 'Something is under the ground.'

They both saw something push its way through the grass. A small hut with a domed roof stood near the trees as if it had always been there.

'What is that?' Ramulas asked.

Pip shrugged. 'We need to tell Oriel.'

***

They entered the throne room to find an excited Shigar talking to Oriel, his arms moving as if they had a mind of their own.

An image of the hut appeared in from of them. 'Sanctuary's ancient magic has brought us something to help with the Legion.'

'I felt the energy when it came,' Shigar said, dancing on his toes.

'What is it?'

'It is part of a trap for those who wish the people of Sanctuary harm.'

Pip screwed her face. 'What can one small hut do?'

'Inside the hut is a lever, and when it is pulled, a passage will appear. Any who enter the passage will die.'

'I want to see how it works,' Pip said, racing for the door.

Ramulas and Shigar followed her out into the clearing, where she eagerly waited for then next to the hut. It was discoloured by lichen and emitted a deep earthen smell. Ramulas smiled and gestured for her to pull the lever.

She ran inside and pulled the lever. At first, nothing happened, but then a rumbling sound came from near the gate. They felt the vibrations beneath their feet before a passageway rose from the ground. The trio walked over for a closer inspection.

It ran from the wall with a slight decline of fifty yards into the clearing. It was a few feet higher than Ramulas, made from granite, and wide enough for five men to walk abreast.

'Once inside, the enemy will have shelter from our archers; this will have them running into the trap,' Ramulas said.

He and Shigar walked away from the tunnel when Pip grabbed both by the arms and turned them around. 'There is a hole at the base of the tunnel.'

They both looked but could see nothing.

She shook her head in frustration as Shigar cast a spell and the hole was visible just beneath the surface. 'This gives me an idea of a good trick for when the Legion comes.'

***

Ramulas walked out into the clearing with Logan, who hid his nerves well. He had not been told why he needed to come out there and was worried that he had been discovered looking around.

Ramulas brought him to the small hut. 'Do you know what this is?'

Logan shook his head. 'Is it some kind of shelter?'

'No. If the people of Sanctuary are forced out of their homes, this will be our way in.' He walked in and pulled the lever.

Logan gasped as he ran outside as he heard the rumble, and his mouth hung open looking at the tunnel. He knew that scores of men with battering rams could enter the passage.

Then his eyes widened as an idea came to him. 'What's to stop the enemy from using it?'

Ramulas nodded to the hut. 'Pull the lever.'

Logan rushed in and began pulling without success, his temper almost boiling over as Ramulas laughed. 'Try twisting the handle slightly before you pull.'

Logan did as instructed and was rewarded with a rumbling sound. He raced out to see the passage disappear. He hid his smile, as he knew how happy the king would be with this information.

'The Legion will not know how to pull the lever,' Ramulas said.

'Who is the Legion?' Logan asked.

'An army coming here from another world to kill and destroy everything.'

For the first time since arriving in Sanctuary, Logan felt that he had bitten off more than he could chew.

***

Rain walked through the training grounds watching Rygar work the people through fighting drills and approached a pair. 'May I join you?'

Both nodded and faced him with their swords ready. Rain drew his blue crystal sword from its scabbard and a curtain of mist fell from the weapon. The duo circled Rain, searching for an opening. Rain playfully tapped the sword to his right before the man rushed at him with a flurry of strikes.

Rain tilted his sword and a blast of ice shot out covering the man's chest. He fell to the ground screaming in pain and holding his body. The other man backed away as Rygar ran over and the man on the ground began turning blue.

'I'll be needin' blankets and warm water quickly,' he said as he slapped away the ice.

As people came with blankets and water, the dwarf turned to Rain. 'Ye best keep that sword away from 'ere until ye can control it.'

Rain walked away smiling as the man was brought to Oriel.

***

Nathaniel sat in his dark world and brooded. Both of his weapons had found other owners. With them gone, it felt as if a part of him was missing, even though he had not held them for hundreds of years.

He could feel Oriel close to him and her magical power growing stronger with each day. The stronger she became, the more he was able to do.

Now he had the ability to take on astral form. He moved through the rear sections of the tunnel. The first thing he thought strange was the two earth elementals working on the walls alongside humans. As he walked, he listened to the conversations about the importance of freeing Oriel soon—this meant that Nathaniel would also be free.

He felt the faint echoes of his weapons outside where he could not go and was almost driven mad by this. One of his first things to do when he was free was to destroy those who held his weapons.

$$7$$

Ramulas and Pip stood in front of four Legion soldiers. The room smelled of stale sweat and blood. She was still shocked when he came within fifteen feet of them and they transformed from straw dummies into beings of flesh and blood.

They glared at the duo with open hatred and were unable to move until Ramulas gave the command.

'We should fight all four of them,' Pip said eagerly.

Ramulas shook his head. 'We have not fought them since the battle; we start with two.'

Pip snorted. 'I can handle two by myself.'

He smiled, activating two soldiers. They exploded into action, drawing their red-bladed swords and charging. Ramulas turned away, spinning his weapon, knocking a thrust away with his axe. Twisting slightly, he swung his war hammer, hitting the soldier in this breastplate and sending him back two steps. Ramulas spun the other way, leading with his battle axe, cutting through the armoured mid-section and spilling loops of entrails to the floor with wet slaps. The soldier's eyes widened as two throwing knives appeared in his neck.

Ramulas turned to Pip with an open mouth, seeing her opponent was down. She smiled and shrugged. 'I told you that I could beat two of them.'

'What! Mine was almost dead.'

She winked. 'Almost, but I finished him.'

He was speechless at her attitude. He saw that the soldiers' wounds were healing, and he knew that they would be ready to fight again soon. Pip had retrieved her knives and swaggered back.

'Are you ready?'

She nodded as Ramulas activated them again and quickly stepped away. One of the soldiers rushed Pip with a combination of strikes, allowing the other to come at her from behind. Ramulas held himself back as Pip ducked and weaved her opponent's strikes looking for an opening.

Then she found one.

She dropped to one knee, slicing the inner thigh of the soldier, and heard movement behind her. She rolled to the side and saw the sword of the second soldier hit the floor where she had just been. Two knives spun towards the soldier, which he knocked aside with his shield.

Pip smiled as she leaned forward and thrust a knife into his groin. The soldier screamed as he pitched to the floor. She stood and gave Ramulas a mock bow.

'Next time you may not be so lucky,' Ramulas said sternly.

'You would never let any harm come to me.'

Ramulas shook his head. 'Be careful what you wish for.'

***

Logan closed the door silently as he entered the room. A quick glance told him that it was a child's playroom, and he searched the chests and drawers looking for anything of importance. When he found none, he decided to check other rooms.

He opened the door to find Grace reaching up for the handle. Her eyes widened and screamed as energy exploded within her. An invisible force picked Logan up and threw him ten feet back into the room. Fenris growled and charged down the hallway to come skidding to a halt in front of Grace.

The hell hound bared its teeth and growled, slowly inching toward Logan. Logan scuttled back as fast as he could.

'No! Please, it was a mistake!' he said, gasping for breath.

Grace patted her thigh. 'Fenris, here.'

The hell hound stopped and walked back to Grace. Logan got to his feet and held his side watching Grace and Fenris. He wondered where the hell hound had come from to hit him so hard.

'I am lost and came into this room by mistake; now, please move your dog, and I will leave.'

Grace pulled Fenris aside so Logan could pass. 'I am sorry that I hurt you, but you scared me.'

Logan shook his head. 'You should have more control over your dog.'

***

Logan walked the streets of Sanctuary until he came to the training grounds. Watching the groups train, what bothered him was the people around him talking about the Legion coming to take Oriel. Who were they?

He continued walking and found himself in front of the statues of the fallen. Stepping closer, he saw that one of the statues shimmered and he jumped back in shock. For a split second, he could have sworn the statue was alive.

Pip watched the spy from a nearby rooftop. She had followed him from the training grounds. She smiled every time he would backtrack or loop around to see if anyone followed, but he never thought to look up.

He walked along the base of the cliff and stopped suddenly, studying an oddly coloured rock. He pushed on it, and a door opened in front of him. He stepped back and glanced around to see if anyone else had seen it. No-one was around. He turned to see the door closing. Logan quickly made his way to the castle.

Pip was torn between following him or waiting for him to return because if she, as a thief, found a secret passage or door, she would need to look inside. Through her new-found vision, Pip studied the door and was surprised that she had not seen it before.

She was rewarded when Logan came back a short while later with a sack over his shoulder. He opened the door and stepped into the darkness.

Pip settled in and waited for him to return.

***

Logan stepped into a circular room and saw a lever in front of him. As he stepped forward, the door closed, and he was plunged into darkness. He knelt and took a torch and flint out of his sack and, in a few moments, the torch was lit.

Logan looked around the circular room of plain smooth rock and found it only had the lever and the one door he had walked through; the air was stale and reminded him of a room that needed airing out.

He walked over to the lever and pulled it until he heard a click. The room started to turn; the door moved from behind him to directly in front, showing the entrance to another room.

Logan quickly walked in to find it was the same as the first. He quickly pulled the lever and this room also began to turn. This was repeated fifteen more times until Logan found himself out in the clearing two hundred yards from the edge of the wall in the forest. He searched the side of the cliff and found the same-coloured rock that would open the door.

He smiled to himself at this amazing discovery and made his way back to Sanctuary through the rooms. He walked out full of confidence at what he had found—a back door into Sanctuary.

***

Miles let out a sigh of relief as Logan walked back through the hidden doorway. One more step and he would have bumped into the Fallen Angel.

'It's a good thing we saw the door opening,' Benji said. 'He walked out into the middle of us and didn't know we were here.'

The forest around the two came alive as the rest of the Angels stepped forward. To a normal person, the Fallen Angels were virtually invisible, even when they were close enough to reach out and touch you.

Iguchi nodded. 'This is good. Michael, you must run to tell the Lord of Sanctuary what we have seen.'

***

The door closed behind Logan and made his way back through the rooms to Sanctuary. In the third room, the air around him grew cold rapidly and plumes of fog came out with each breath. The hairs on the back of his neck stood on end as he heard faint whispering.

'Hello; is someone there?' he asked, turning around and drawing his sword.

There was no answer, but Logan felt as if someone was watching him. He quickened his pace to Sanctuary.

***

Pip smiled as the door opened and Logan stepped out to join with the people of nearby streets. She ran across the rooftops, knowing that she had enough information to tell Ramulas.

Entering the throne room, Pip found Michael talking to Ramulas and Oriel. 'He walked out amongst us and did not know we were there. He came out of the mountain and looked around before going back in.'

Ramulas nodded. 'And you said that he needed to use a rock on the cliff to open the door.'

Pip walked up to Michael's side. 'There is another entrance near the waterfall with a secret door. I watched him go in and waited for him to return. I have never seen them before with my vision, but now that he has used it, the door and rock glow for me.'

'He will relay this information to the king, for use if they choose to attack again,' Ramulas said.

Oriel stepped forward. 'I only became aware of the doors yesterday as Sanctuary's ancient magic continues to open up to me, but I do not know much about them. More will be revealed to me soon.'

'What is inside there?' Pip asked.

'There are several rooms and an evil spirit as old as Emily inside there.'

Ramulas grew concerned. 'Is there any chance of the spirit coming out to attack the people of Sanctuary?'

Oriel shook her head. 'No, it is trapped within the mountain. It waits for the living to enter to consume their souls.'

'But Logan went through,' Pip said.

'Logan went in by himself. The spirit is smart and knows that others will soon follow.'

Oriel walked over to a long table and waved her hand. The others followed to find a small model replica of Sanctuary, the forest, and mountains.

Two red dots indicated the entrances of both doors.

Ramulas pointed to the dot inside of Sanctuary. 'If we are busy at the wall, Logan could lead them in behind us and do a lot of damage. This would be very tempting to use. How many people could get past the spirit?'

'Only a small group will be allowed to enter, then they will be trapped inside with the spirit and it will feast on their souls.' She turned to Ramulas, her expression serious. 'I have news of Remus.'

'What news? Has he begun to march?'

She smiled sadly. 'He has brought the First Legion into the city of Keah, where he was welcomed by the king.'

'What does this mean?'

She shrugged. 'For now, I do not know, but the Legion now live in the city.'

'This cannot be a good sign,' Ramulas said.

Oriel had already said that Remus had arranged with the Symiaks. If the kingdom army joined them as well, Sanctuary would fall. But it was not possible for Symiaks and humans to unite—they had been at war for generations. What could Remus be planning?

***

Remus was not happy with dividing his forces, but he would use this to his advantage. He would send two of his captains with a thousand men each to Turtha and Covedon.

He spoke to Zachary about the important role that his Legion would have in the distant towns, explaining that the people of Sanctuary may want to retaliate through the winter.

'I have mayors in those towns. They rule under me, and they will have control of your soldiers when they are there,' Zachary said.

Remus smiled while slowly nodding his head. 'I do not wish to take control from you with a strange army new to your lands; however, our world has known war for generations. By the time your mayors see trouble and inform my captains, it may be too late.'

Zachary's eyes widened. 'What do you suggest I do?'

'Before I tell you, I would like to hear more details about the battle at Sanctuary so that we may be better prepared.'

With the help of Lucas, Zachary told of the first attack as they moved through the forest up until they were chased away by the green dragons.

Remus frowned as he thought of when Oriel changed into a dragon before she escaped. Dragons and giants could pose a problem, but the combined magic of the warlords and red wizards would rectify that.

Remus sighed as he formulated his lie. 'We have dragons and giants in our world. What would your mayors do if Sanctuary marched on the towns with dragons and giants?'

Zachary's jaw dropped, knowing they would run as fast as they could.

'If you give control of the towns to my captains just over the winter, we will ensure that Sanctuary will not attack and then march on to this city.'

Zachary's eyes widened, and he glanced around desperate for an answer, then he excused himself to talk with his royal guard.

A short while later, he returned with Lucas by his side. 'Messages will be sent to the towns telling them of your coming and to accommodate your men. Letters of authority will be given to your captains only during the winter, with the mayors to have a say in any decisions made.'

'Deal,' Remus said.

***

Reckoning and Retribution walked through Keah with their soldiers, with the rest of the Legion lining the streets. After they left, the remaining Legion were shown their accommodation in empty warehouses and abandoned buildings. The warlords and red wizards would be staying in the castle.

Remus smiled to himself at the thought of what they were going to do to the people of this land after they retrieved Oriel.

8

Logan watched as the first snowflakes fell in Sanctuary. The children ran out into the street, laughing as they held out their hands to catch the snow. They became more excited as the snow piled up on their hands. The laughter and squeals of joy became louder and infectious. This brought the adults out into the streets, and magical energy flowed through the people as the adults held out their hands as well.

Logan felt a smile grow on his face as his hands reached out for the snowflakes. With a jolt of realisation, Logan pulled them back and fought against the magical euphoria sweeping the streets. He stepped back from the balcony into the castle and walked to his room.

Once inside, he thought, *What kind of magic was strong enough to affect everyone in Sanctuary? It must be Oriel; the way people talk about her is with awe.*

By this stage, he was used to seeing the Khilli people walking freely through the town. The people of Sanctuary had embraced them into their lives.

Logan crouched down at the end of his bed to open his chest and pull out a pile of papers. He sorted through the notes and maps he had made since his arrival in Sanctuary. He quickly added what he had seen before leaving the room again.

As the door closed, Pip stepped out from behind a large tapestry and went to Logan's chest.

***

The snow fell in the forest around the Fallen Angels. They stood motionless, each carrying a sack full of rocks and soil, which were heavy and uncomfortable on their backs. Iguchi told them the route they needed to run; they awaited his signal.

'It is cold,' Iguchi said, watching plumes of steam come out as the Angels breathed. 'You must run to keep warm.'

As one, they ran through the trees in pairs before disappearing. An hour later, they returned at a slower pace, and a few fought for breath. Iguchi waited for them to gather before he spoke.

'You are very noisy; I thought a herd of elephants were stomping through the forest.'

This brought a few weary smiles from the Angels. 'You must run again, this time with less stomping.'

The smiles vanished as the Angels ran once more.

Even though they were tired, the Angels finished the course quicker, and some were close to collapsing.

'Quickly,' Iguchi said. 'The enemy is coming. Divide into two groups and make shelter.'

Without thought, the Angels dropped their sacks, broke off into groups, and used the sacks to make a low wall around the group. Branches and stone were used to build the wall higher. The Angels soon finished and stood within the three-foot-high walls.

'These are good shelters, but they lack doors. They will be made again over there,' he said, pointing to a grove of trees.

Without complaint, the Angels dismantled their shelters and brought them to the appointed place. Iguchi watched them with a sense of pride. He had pushed them past their physical and mental limits, and now he needed them to be able to function when pain filled their minds.

He waved them to him once they were finished. 'If you wish to attack an enemy, you need to know how they will react to this attack, and who they will call on for help. Remove these people first and you will cause chaos. Thrive in chaos and you will win the battle before it begins.'

'If the enemy attacks us, you will fight, but if the enemy feels as you do now, they will avoid fighting. We must make sure that the Legion is very tired by the time they reach Sanctuary.'

The Angels had started to relax when Iguchi pointed to Benji. 'Do you feel like walking to that rock near the tree?'

Benji shook his head seeing the rock one hundred feet away.

'Good. Miles will carry you to the rock and you will carry him back. The rest will find a partner and do the same.'

The Angels suppressed groans, picked up their partners, and walked to the rock.

***

Rygar paced up and down in front of the group of soldiers. 'Keep yer arms straight.'

They raised their arms higher; they had been holding their swords out in front of them for half a minute, and they had begun to tire. The strain on the faces came through as they struggled to hold the weight. The dwarf silently counted to thirty before allowing the swords to drop.

After training drills, they held the swords in their left and right hands to strengthen their arms. They would do this until they could not hold any more. He dismissed this group and called another forward. As they came, he saw Lodi holding his huge club out in front of him. He had been following the drills using his club as a sword.

Then something caught his eye, and he walked over to the giant.

***

Rain stood in front of a thick wooden pole, holding his sword. A thick wall of mist cascaded from the blade, blanketing the ground at his feet. He lunged at the pole and struck at the pole several times before twisting to avoid any counter attacks. Every time he hit the pole, small puffs of fog filled the air.

When the pole was almost covered in fog, Rain tilted his sword and a blast of ice shot into the fog. The fog cleared, showing the ice-covered pole.

'Now that's a good trick ye just done,' Rygar said, walking up to him.

Rain turned, lowering his sword. 'The spirit within the sword speaks to me, showing me what I can do. I practise here away from the people.'

Rygar placed his hands on his hips. 'Well then, have ye learned any more tricks?'

Rain smiled as a sparkle of amusement lit up his blue eyes. He lifted the tip of the sword until the blade was horizontal at waist level. A thick wall of mist dropped from the blade, and then the mist thickened to form an ice wall half an inch thick.

Rygar's eyes widened as he came over to tap on the ice with his knuckles. 'Could ye make this any thicker?'

'I could try later.' Rain shrugged.

'Well, ye just keep tryin',' the dwarf said, walking back to the training Angels.

Joshua stepped out of the stables as he left. 'They accept you more,' he said to Rain. 'They push me to the side in fear that I might hurt someone.'

Rain smiled. 'They will find a place for you soon. They will need us when the Legion comes. We will be welcomed then.'

A bolt of anger shot through Joshua as an expression of pure rage flashed across his eyes, and then as quickly as it surfaced, he pushed it away.

'The people treat me with fear. Even my own wife fears me. Don't they understand that I cannot control this gauntlet?'

Rain shrugged. 'People fear what they do not understand. All the people know is that the gauntlet is making you mad.'

Joshua fought back the rage as Rain spoke. He wanted the gauntlet gone, but its power was so intoxicating. A part of him wished Oriel had not placed the tranquillity spell on him.

Joshua wanted his full potential unleashed.

***

The Fallen Angels had built several small platforms that were fixed to the top of upright logs of varying heights. The lowest platform was two feet high and the highest was fifteen feet from the ground.

Iguchi stood in front and gestured to the platforms behind him. 'You must be like the wind and light on your feet, like so.'

With a quick hop, Iguchi jumped onto the small platform and seemed to float through it as he jumped from platform to platform. When Iguchi was finished, he indicated to the Angels to follow his lead. With their training, the Angels did not find the task too difficult.

Benji was one of the last to complete this and smiled. 'That was easy. I could do this with my eyes closed.'

Iguchi nodded. 'Agreed. You will all do this with your eyes closed; Benji first.'

Benji's mouth fell open as the Angels moaned. He sighed, stepping up to the first platform and closing his eyes. He made it to the third platform before falling off.

'Start again,' Iguchi called.

***

The Fallen Angels made their way back to Sanctuary at a slow, painful pace. Each of them was sore and tired. They had spent almost twenty-four hours training without sleep and little food. Their only thought was placing one foot in front of the other.

They entered the clearing to find all of the archers on the wall waiting for them.

'To return home and rest, you must pass the archers,' Iguchi said.

The small man waved his hands, and the archers readied their bows. All the arrows had lead ball tips for bruising, not killing. Iguchi led the Angels to the gate as the arrows rained down around them. Despite their tired bodies and minds, the Angels were able to dodge while holding their shields above them. They only rested once through the gate.

Then pails of water dropped on them from the wall and the Angels spun in shock at the unexpected attack.

'Oh, no,' Iguchi called out in his sing-song voice. 'My Angels have been burned alive with hot oil.'

The Angels looked at him in disbelief.

He shook a finger at them. 'Even when the battle seems finished or won, you must always look for dangers. Eat and rest. Tomorrow is a big day.'

***

Iguchi walked with Ramulas into the training grounds, where Lodi and Rygar waited for them. The giant held a length of chain in his hand. Attached to the chain was a solid metal ball one foot in diameter.

'O Lord of Sanctuary,' Iguchi said, 'with the help of Oriel and the short one, we have made a new weapon.'

Ramulas nodded. 'That looks impressive and heavy, but Lodi already has his club.'

'It's not fer me boy. We made this fer Joshua. Lodi will show ye how it works.'

The giant walked over to two wooden targets and stopped ten feet away. He lifted the ball above his head and began to swing it in tight circles. When he gained enough momentum, he sent the ball into the first target, smashing it to pieces. Lodi repeated the process and the other target exploded in a shower of splinters.

Ramulas' jaw dropped at the damage caused, picking up a piece near his feet. 'This was an inch thick.'

He gestured for Lodi to drop the chain near his feet, and Ramulas picked up the thick chain and struggled to lift the ball two feet from the ground.

'How do expect Joshua to carry that, or even throw it?'

Iguchi nodded. 'He will need to train, and when the Legion comes, Oriel will lift the tranquillity spell.' The small man pointed behind Ramulas. 'Our friend has come now.'

They turned to see Joshua and Rain come into the training grounds, and Ramulas waved them over.

'Joshua, we have made something for you to use against the Legion. Tell us what you think.'

Joshua picked up the ball with ease but struggled to hold it over his head.

Rain leaned into his friend and whispered, 'You must learn to control your anger to give you strength.' An expression of determination and anger crossed Joshua's face. With a soft grunt, he lifted the ball and swung it three times above his head before letting it fall to the ground.

'They have taken my strength,' Joshua said as his shoulders slumped.

'But there is more inside of you, my friend. All you need to do is look.'

A moment later, Joshua's lips curled back to reveal his teeth and he emitted a low growl. He picked up the ball, swung it, and sent it at the remains of the first target fifteen feet away. With a jerk, he pulled the ball back and struck out at the second target.

Rain gave a nod. 'That was much better.'

Ramulas was speechless after witnessing what Joshua had done. He would hate to be around when the tranquillity spell was lifted.

***

Grace sat cross-legged in the throne room surrounded by twelve druids; they each had their hoods pulled back revealing bald, green scaly heads. Their taloned hands rested in their laps as they watched the magical prodigy.

Grace was barely able to contain her excitement as she waited to see what they would teach her.

'Tell me, child, how did you make ice butterflies come out of Rain's sword?' the leader hissed.

Grace clapped her hands. 'I like butterflies.'

'Do you know how they came out of the ice?' he asked as his hands opened like flowers greeting the morning sun.

She shook her head. 'I thought about them, and they came.'

He reached into his robes and pulled out an acorn and held it out in the palm of his hand. 'Druids have much in common with the dryads.

The trees and nature play a big part in our lives. The dryads move through trees, and we worship the spirits within the trees.'

Grace gasped at this news. 'Do spirits come out of the trees?'

He shook his head. 'No, they live in the ground but talk to us through the trees.'

'What do they say?'

'They teach us the cycle of life and the balance of nature which must not be broken. For each death must be balanced with a life. Many old and sick give their lives so that the young may survive. Under the forest floor during the winter snows are layers of rotten leaves, which give food for the acorn to grow into a mighty oak tree.'

He tossed the acorn to Grace, who caught it in mid-air and gazed upon it in awe.

'You now have the essence of a tree in your hands. A tree waiting to be brought to life. It takes years for the acorn to become a fully grown tree. We can make it grow faster by using our magic. We want to take you to a place in the forest where we can teach you how to use magic on this acorn.'

Grace looked up at the druid and then back at the acorn in her hand. Static energy filled the room as she began to murmur, and her eyes glowed a fierce emerald.

The druids glanced at each other as the acorn floated out of her hand. It stopped just above her head and popped open. Before their eyes, roots and branches grew from the acorn. The druids quickly stood and stepped away from the rapidly growing tree.

'Child, you must cease this at once,' the head druid ordered.

Grace sat on the floor in a trance-like state with her eyes closed, slowly waving her hands through the air. The energy in the room increased as the tree grew to ten feet and the roots touched the slate floor, turning the tree into a thing of living stone.

'Grace!' Oriel shouted while clapping her hands.

A shockwave of energy rolled across the room, cancelling Grace's spell. Grace collapsed in front of the now twelve-foot stone oak tree.

Oriel was shocked at her level of magical ability. The stone oak tree became the newest addition to the throne room.

The druids parted as Oriel came over to Grace. She held out her hand as a light mist covered the small girl. 'You silly girl.'

To grow the tree, Grace had given up her life force. Another thirty seconds and she would have died. Grace would need to rest for the next few days to recover.

***

Pip watched the interaction of Grace and the druids from behind a tapestry. She knew the druids were going to teach her magic and Pip wanted to watch. With her new eyesight, Pip saw Grace's true form of a juvenile purple dragon. It was as tall as Grace with small wings and a stubby tail.

She also saw the druids' true form—they were dark, shadowy figures with deformed bodies. Their spines were twisted, so they shuffled bent over as they walked.

The acorn floated out of Grace's hand and the purple dragon seemed to grow as the tree took on life. A constant stream of flame from the dragon fed the tree growth. When Oriel called out for Grace to stop, the purple dragon curled up into a ball and slept.

'Pip, I need you to find Ramulas and bring him here,' Oriel said, looking directly at Pip.

She jumped in shock, thinking that no-one knew she was there. She gave a quick nod before going back into the series of secret tunnels.

9

Pip returned with an anxious Ramulas; she had only told him that something had happened to Grace practising magic with the druids. Ramulas stopped with his mouth hanging open as he entered the throne room.

He gazed in wonder at the stone oak tree in the middle of the room, and then he saw his daughter lying at the base of that tree with Oriel beside her.

He rushed to them, knelt beside Grace, and looked at Oriel. 'What happened?'

She explained how the druids were teaching her life magic and what she had done with the acorn through using her life magic and the effects it had on her.

Ramulas felt a mix of anger and frustration build within him hearing how close she had come to dying. 'You were to watch her as she used her magic. Her mother will not be happy when she hears this.'

'Grace's magic has grown faster than I thought possible. Now this has happened, I think she needs time away from magic.'

Ramulas nodded. 'She needs to do things that others her age do. I will tell her that there is no more training until after winter.'

The druids came up to them. 'We are sorry, Lord of Sanctuary. We have never seen a tree grow this fast before with magic.'

'You can grow trees with magic?'

'Yes, but it takes a year to grow a tree of this size.'

'How long did Grace take to grow this one?'
'Two minutes.'

***

Logan checked to make sure the hallway was clear before taking his lock picks out. He knelt down and made quick work of the lock, smiling as he heard it click open. He pushed on the door and froze when he heard rapid footsteps from within the room.

The door was pushed closed in front of his face, and he heard the door lock once more. He was confused, and then stunned, as he saw someone peering at him through the keyhole at him. Anger quickly surfaced when heard a woman's laughter from behind the door.

Logan demanded, 'Who are you? Open the door and show yourself.'

'This door was locked for a reason; you don't need to be in here.'

Logan's eyes widened. 'Thief, I will tell the Lord of Sanctuary about this.'

'Fine, and I will tell of you picking locks.'

A cold shock washed over Logan as he stood and scanned the hall. If she told, he would have some explaining to do. He needed to make sure Pip did not talk. He looked through the keyhole to find she was no longer there. He picked the lock again and entered.

Logan saw that he entered a small bedroom as he closed the door. It only had a bed and chest. He dropped to his knees to find under the bed empty, and the chest was as well. Then he looked out of the open window three storeys above the streets and saw no sign of her. He shook his head as he left the room.

If Logan had bothered to look behind the large tapestry on the wall, he might have seen the outline of a hidden door.

Pip made her way through the network of hidden tunnels, smiling to herself at how quickly she angered Logan. She would pay his room a little visit.

Over the past few days, she had been entering his room when he was out, copying his maps and notes. She was close to showing Ramulas.

The maps of Sanctuary and the castle were very detailed. He had even gone to the trouble of marking down distances between places and the training drills of the people.

This could only mean that the king wanted to return to Sanctuary.

***

The Khilli warriors walked into the training grounds and the people of Sanctuary gathered around the boundary. Word had spread quickly of them coming to train.

It would be the first time that the people had seen them train. The Khilli had been spoken about in whispers for generations. It was said that a lone warrior could beat up to four kingdom soldiers in combat.

The Khilli stretched and rubbed their muscles. They paired off and began a slow dance moving slowly back and forth, always keeping within arm's reach of each other. Slowly elbows and knees were brought into the dance.

Then without warning, they exploded into a flurry of movement, just missing each other with strikes from knees, elbows, hands and feet. K'ayden walked up and down in front of them, calling out in their language. When the elders were killed, he was elected as their chief.

The morning was cool, and the clouds above told of a storm later that day, but the warriors only wore loincloths. They trained for hours, steam rising from their bodies as they went through their fighting routines.

K'ayden's chest filled with pride watching his people. They had been freed from the kingdom and would soon be returning to their homeland. They would fight the Legion with everything they had, and that still would not repay Ramulas for freeing his people.

***

Ramulas and Jacqueline sat by Grace's bed for a day and a night until she woke. Both had not slept or wanted to leave their daughter's side.

Ramulas looked at his youngest daughter, thinking how different she was from Kate, who was uncomfortable with her abilities.

Grace moaned softly and Fenris wagged his tail at the end of the bed. Jacqueline pounced on her daughter, engulfing her in a hug. 'Thank the gods you have woken.'

Ramulas sat back, allowing his wife time with Grace, and then he explained to his daughter that she would no longer be using magic until winter's end. She seemed to collapse within herself.

***

Grace and Kate walked into the throne room with their mother. The three of them gasped when they saw the stone tree.

'Look, Da; I made a tree,' she said to Ramulas, who stood near a window.

'That you did, little one.'

They all looked at the tree in awe. Even though it was made of stone, its leaves and branches moved as if a wind came through the window.

'Look, Da. The castle is moving,' Grace shouted, pointing to the balcony.

He turned in time to see the balcony sliding out one foot away from the room.

'Wait here,' he said, walking to the balcony.

Ramulas looked around the outer wall of the castle. Small ledges were coming out of the wall at different heights. He came back into the throne room to find a smiling Oriel waiting for him.

'Welcome, Ramulas,' Oriel said as power radiated from her.

'What has happened to you?' he asked.

'My power is returning; I will be able to leave the mountain soon.'

Ramulas heard his daughters' laughter and turned to see them running around the stone tree. He remembered what Grace had said about the castle moving.

'I saw the outside of the castle moving.'

Oriel looked at Jacqueline. 'I need to show Ramulas something. Do you mind if I take him for a moment?'

Jacqueline nodded while Oriel walked out into the hallway. Ramulas was frozen in shock; he had never seen her leave that room before.

'As I told you, my power is returning. I can do more things now.' She gestured for him to follow her. They went to a balcony on the seventh floor and showed him the wall.

Several balconies had formed on each level. Each had a parapet. 'If the Legion makes it into Sanctuary after the maze, they will suffer heavy losses from the archers on these ledges. The growth comes from the materials dug from the tunnel.'

'How far do they need to dig to free you?'

She smiled. 'They are very close.'

'I will gather more workers to free you sooner.'

A sad smile crossed her face. 'Edwin and the elementals are doing all they can. More people will get in their way.'

'But I need to try to do something.'

'Do not worry about things you cannot change.'

He sighed, wanting to say something reassuring but, lost for words, he smiled at her before walking away to find an answer.

****

He walked into the tunnel, passing workers pushing carts full of rock and earth. It had been a while since he was here last. Every twenty yards, a torch had been placed on the wall, throwing dancing shadows along the tunnel.

Then he passed the side tunnel where the magical sword and gauntlet were found. He paused to look when a cold wind buffeted him from nowhere. He shielded his eyes while steadying his feet then, almost as soon as it began, the wind stopped.

He warily looked around before making his way deeper into the tunnel. A moment later, the cold wind hit him from behind. He pulled out his weapons and turned as warmth flooded through him. Wind in a tunnel this deep was very unnatural, and he felt it was a form of magic. Purple flames danced along his weapons, and once again, the wind stopped.

He walked away thinking about these events and soon came across Edwin and the elementals at the end of the tunnel.

The dwarf smiled. 'Welcome, me lord; what brings ye 'ere?'

'Just wanting to see your progress.'

Edwin smiled proudly. 'Over three hunerd yards we have come. And these two say that the mountain is talkin' to 'em.'

Ramulas looked at the elementals and Royce smiled. 'When we have freed Oriel, we have been given a choice of joining the mountain.'

'What does that mean?'

'We can become one with the mountain. This is where we truly belong.'

'If that is what you want, I will be happy for you both.'

They smiled, and Ramulas made his way back to the castle.

***

Nathaniel felt a strong magical presence enter the tunnel. He had felt this a few times before. He investigated through his astral form and found Ramulas in the tunnel.

Rage flooded through the angel as he flew at Ramulas and went straight through him. He saw a reaction from the Lord of Sanctuary and the glow of the magical weapons on his back. Nathaniel though of these weapons as Ramulas walked away.

If he could not have his own magical weapons, he would take Ramulas'. He flew at Ramulas once more. When he was ten feet away, the Lord of Sanctuary turned and pulled out his weapons and was covered in purple flame. Nathaniel could feel the power and knew that he was not yet ready.

When he was finally free, Nathaniel would find this man to see which one was the strongest.

***

Ramulas walked the streets and saw a commotion near the courtyard. A crowd had gathered and were talking excitedly. As he came closer, Pip pushed her way through the crowd.

'Tilly has come searching for you.'

A moment later, the sprite flew over to him. 'You are wanted in the sacred grove.' She flew out of the gate, and they followed her. They walked into the sacred place of the dryads and were shocked at the lack of snow. They had walked through inches of snow in the forest. Even the branches of the surrounding trees were weighed down by snow, but there was none here.

Ramulas and Pip were greeted by all the dryads as Eady stepped forward with a smile. 'We have discussed ways of helping when the Legion comes.'

She held out a small bundle of leaves wrapped in a ball which seemed to be humming softly.

'What is that?' Ramulas asked.

'It is something that will keep the enemy busy,' Eady said as she turned the ball in her hand to show wasps trying to crawl out of the hole.

'When this hits something, the leaves will open, and the wasps will attack everything nearby. You will need to run quickly when you see these thrown.'

As they walked back to Sanctuary, Ramulas was happy with the dryads' surprise. He had seen people's reaction to a single wasp; imagine if it was a whole swarm of them?

Iguchi and the Fallen Angels were coming out of Sanctuary as they came in. 'Hello to you, Lord of Sanctuary, and to you, thrower of knives.'

'Are you taking your Angels out to train again?

'Yes. It will be many days and weeks of training,' he said, turning to his Angels. 'Why do you stand there when I talk of training? Run along the mountains.'

Ramulas and Pip watched them run into the forest.

'Given enough time, I will turn them into steel, but first, they will need to go through three stages.'

'What are these stages?' Ramulas asked.

Iguchi smiled. 'First, I will make them think they are going to die; second, they will know death is very close; and last, they will accept that death is a way of life.'

Ramulas' mouth dropped. 'Isn't that pushing them too far?'

Iguchi shook his head. 'No, for once you accept your own death, you realise that anything is possible. When the Legion comes, my Angels will need to do the impossible.'

Ramulas sighed. 'I know they are coming; I just wish there was another way.'

'A hard road travelled will always make the better person,' Iguchi said before running after his Angels.

Iguchi caught up with his Angels near the base of the mountain. An inch of snow covered the ground and several large rocks.

'Look at all this snow. There is too much, and I want this area cleaned, but you will only use the blade of your swords. If you cut too deep, you will damage your weapon—not deep enough and you will leave snow. You must practise your striking techniques.'

Without a word, the Angels began cutting into the snow. Benji found the proper technique, using his sword like a shovel. The others followed his lead. After a short while, the snow had been removed from the area.

Iguchi clapped his hands and the Angels stood to attention. 'The time of snow and frost is a good season to train a person. It is much harder to hide your tracks with frost-covered grass. I will go into the forest. You will follow after thirty seconds. If you do not find me, training will be hard.'

The time had passed, and the Angels went to where Iguchi disappeared to find he left no tracks. Benji stepped into the snow and removed his foot. They all saw the imprint left by him. The Angels would need to rely on other methods to find their master.

After searching the surrounding forest, they returned to the clearing to find Iguchi waiting for them. 'Have you no eyes to follow my tracks? Have you no ears to hear me stomping through the trees?'

The Angels knew that Iguchi could move as silently as a mouse without leaving a trace. He gestured to ten logs cut by the Angels the previous week. They were twelve feet long, thick, and heavy. 'Five Angels for each log. Pick them up now and hold them above your heads.'

The Angels broke into groups and held each log over their heads. Iguchi nodded his approval as he walked in front of them, and then he mimicked holding a log against his chest before squatting down. He raised his hands above his head before standing then lowered his hands to his chest and squatted once more.

'This is one movement; you will show me.'

As one, the Angels repeated Iguchi's movement.

'Again,' he called.

This exercise was for building teamwork. If one person did not put everything into this, then the others would suffer. The Angels did this fifty times before their bodies showed signs of stress. Arms and legs shook as the logs tilted one way or the other.

'Stop. We will now run,' Iguchi called.

Benji sighed with relief, pushing his log away. The rest of his group did the same.

Iguchi shook his head. 'Pick up the log. You will be running with it.' Benji almost collapsed. 'Benji, pick up the log now.'

He turned to Iguchi. 'How are we supposed to run carrying that?'

'Very carefully. If you drop the log, you start again.'

The Angels picked up their logs and followed Iguchi as he ran through the forest. They returned after a two-mile circuit and Iguchi gestured for them to drop the logs. Most of the Angels collapsed to the ground fighting for breath.

As the Angels lay gasping for breath like a fish out of water, Iguchi was secretly very proud of them. They were supposed to fail this task. They had become stronger than he could have hoped, but he needed them to be mentally strong when the Legion came.

It was easy to be strong when you were winning, but it was another thing to be strong when your friends were dying around you. Iguchi knew this battle would bring a lot of deaths.

The midday sun fought to break through the thick clouds as Pip followed Logan through Sanctuary. She smiled to herself, jumping from roof to roof. He always looked around him but never up. He backtracked multiple times, constantly searching for signs that he was being followed. Pip saw a score of children led by Grace as they walked past Logan.

Pip's eyes flared when she saw that Grace's aura had become very strong. She was in a dilemma—should she follow the children or Logan? Pip made up her mind in an instant and chose the children. There were a handful of people in front of the statues of the fallen when Grace arrived. She walked up to the statue and the far end and placed her hand on its shield.

'This is Matthew—he used to train with Rygar and Lodi. He was very brave. He died fighting the king.'

Grace said, 'Come and say hello to him.'

What Pip saw almost caused her to fall from the roof. Every time a child touched the shield, a faint purple light would shine in the statue's chest. The glow faded after the last child removed their hand. This was repeated with the remaining statues.

Once the children had left, Pip thought of the last time she had seen something strange with the statues—she had seen Emily put the flame of the altar into the chests of the statues. With what she had seen with the children, Pip was unsure what this meant.

10

Remus stood in his chambers within the castle of Keah. The warlords and red wizards sat in a circle chanting as mist rose from the floor. The three captains had always been able to communicate with each other; however, over vast distances, it was harder. This would only be a short communication.

Redemption had received word that the other captains had arrived in their towns, and they awaited council with Remus. The wall behind the chanting group transformed into a wall of glass, with faint images of the two captains side by side.

'I trust you are both alone,' Remus said.

They nodded in unison and Remus turned to Reckoning. 'Tell me of your reception in the town of Turtha.'

He smiled. 'We were welcomed at the gate. The mayor received word of our coming and met us at the gate. He read the documents signed by the king. He didn't seem pleased, but he agreed to the terms.'

Remus nodded. 'That is all that matters. I only care that they are compliant.'

Remus addressed Retribution. 'What of your town?'

'This mayor is new and willing to do anything that will please his king. He will follow the documents and does not want to be sent to a place called Gullytown.'

Remus snorted. 'The documents written by Zachary are vague at best. I want to take advantage of this. Join the guards at the gates and on the wall. Within two weeks, I want complete control of the towns. The king sends messages by pigeon—I want every one coming or going read by you.'

Both captains nodded, and Remus continued. 'The king may think that separating our forces weakens us. He will be proven wrong. Train the Legion hard during winter. Make any problems disappear.'

The two captains smiled without emotion before their images vanished.

Remus thought of this strange city and its customs. He did not think he could get used to the colder climate of this world. In his world, winter was cold, but it never snowed. Keah could fit into a small section of any one of the cities back home. The people and soldiers moved without urgency or purpose. They would easily be slaughtered by his Legion; who would be strong enough to stop them?

***

The Fallen Angels came out of the forest into the clearing just after dawn. They walked slowly, with every fibre burning, and all they wanted to do was sleep.

'Do you wish to tarry, or do you wish to gain some well-deserved sleep?' Iguchi said.

Miles and Benji looked up at the wall to see it was empty. They nodded to each other and walked through, followed by the others.

Buckets of cold water were dropped onto the Angels once they were inside the passage.

'Oh, woe is me! I have lost my Angels, for they were careless and burned alive with hot oil!' Iguchi wailed.

Benji held out his hands. 'There were no archers on the wall. We thought it was safe to enter.'

Iguchi shook his finger at the Angels. 'You must never think that you are safe. Always look for the assassin behind every tree. Only then will you be safe.'

The Angels walked into Sanctuary hanging their heads in shame.

***

Logan stood in the courtyard as the Angels came into Sanctuary. He had seen them leave the previous morning and was curious to know what they did. He walked up to Iguchi. 'I would like to know what you do with the Angels in the forest.'

Iguchi shook a finger at him. 'What we do is secret.'

'I want to come the next time you take them out.'

'I only train Angels, and you are no Angel.'

Logan fought the frustration. 'I only want to come once.'

Iguchi nodded. 'Wait here until you are called,' Iguchi said before running up the stairs to the top of the wall.

A moment later, he waved at Logan from the wall for him to come out into the clearing. When he was just past the gate, Iguchi called out, 'Now look to the trees.'

He stood with his back to the gate, searching the trees, and a bucket of water was dumped on his head. He looked up in shock to see Pip smiling down at him. She blew him a kiss before disappearing.

He shook with rage, feeling humiliated. 'What is the meaning of this?'

'You asked for the secrets of Angel training; thus, I have shown you.'

Logan spun on his heels and stormed back into Sanctuary, where he found Pip talking to Emily. 'You dare throw water on me.'

'Me?' Pip said innocently. 'I was only doing what I was told. I would never take the pleasure of upsetting you.'

'You will pay for this,' Logan said, stepping forward and raising his hand. Emily's eyes grew dark as dark energies crackled around her. Steam rose from Logan's clothes as the air around him heated up. He quickly stepped back, lowering his hand, and saw that people were watching them.

'I don't like you,' Emily said.

Pip noticed Logan's eyes darting around. 'You don't want to cause a scene in front of everyone, do you?'

He shot her an evil look before walking into the castle.

Logan changed clothes in the privacy of his room and thought about his time in Sanctuary. He had documented the training of the soldiers, archers, and cavalry; he had drawn maps of every part of the town and forest.

He had written down details about the people digging into the tunnel to free Oriel. Every time, he was refused entry and told that his place was outside. He was confident he had enough information for the king to defeat Sanctuary. Then he remembered the dragons—he had not seen or heard of them since he had arrived. He decided to talk with Ramulas.

He entered the throne room to find Shigar talking with Oriel. 'I am looking for the Lord of Sanctuary,' he said.

Shigar shook his head. 'He is not here. Perhaps we could assist you.'

'I have come to ask about the dragons. I saw them at the battle, but none since coming here.'

Oriel smiled. 'They have flown over the mountains to the north and will return when we are in need.'

'Oh. I was hoping to see them.'

She shook her head. 'They will only come in time of need.'

Logan smiled awkwardly, left the throne room, and headed back to his room to write that the dragons still protected Sanctuary.

As Logan wrote, he pondered about Sanctuary as a town that people had come to a few months earlier, and yet it felt like the people had lived here for years. Logan had spent his whole life in Keah and could not understand the way the people worshipped the Lord of Sanctuary.

In all his travels, Logan had seen places of worship in every town and city of different gods and deities, but here in Sanctuary, everyone came to the fallen to pray at the altar. This was a very strange place indeed.

***

The druids gathered in a small snow-covered clearing to see how their improved magic would perform. The head druid held his wand up to his face and gently blew on its tip. Three green bubbles the size of apples came out. He waved his hand, sending the bubbles toward snow-covered trees.

The first bubble hit a tree and exploded, sending sticky green fluid in all directions. This knocked snow from the tree's branches and caused the other bubbles to explode as well. The fluid quickly hardened to become a strong, sticky web covering many trees.

One of the druids walked up to the web, placed a stick on it, and tried to pull it off unsuccessfully with the help of a few others.

'It is strong enough,' the head druid said. 'Now we must control the flight of the bubbles.'

The druids spent the rest of the day moving their bubbles through the trees. They started off with one, guiding it around the trees, then moved on to multiple bubbles. They began by following the bubbles and, by the end, they were able to move them from a distance. This would give them the opportunity to attack without being seen.

Ramulas and Pip were brought to watch. The head druid indicated for Pip to step forward and produced three apple-sized bubbles. 'Do not let them touch you.'

Pip nodded as he waved his hand, causing the bubbles to float towards her. The former thief stepped back and hid behind a tree, quickly cursing as they followed. She yelped and rolled through ankle-deep snow into the clearing.

The other druids joined in moving their bubbles through the clearing; they surrounded Pip and slowly closed in. She had heard of the bubbles and did not want them touching her. Pip ran at a group of bubbles with the snow crunching beneath her feet and rolled underneath them.

She found her escape blocked by green webs between the trees. She turned to see the bubbles close. She threw two of her knives, which burst the bubbles and blocked her retreat. More knives flew at as many bubbles as she could see, but her luck ran out when one touched her from behind and burst.

She screamed when covered in the sticky fluid, and it tightened as she moved. One of the druids touched the web and it dissolved into dust, freeing her. As Pip gathered her knives, Ramulas spoke to the head druid.

'How many bubbles can you send out at once?'

He held out a hand. 'Only a few at a time. Any more and we would lose control over them. When they burst, we can send more.'

'They seem stronger than the last time I saw them.'

'They are much stronger; they will hold a person for up to half an hour.'

Pip smiled. 'The Legion soldiers will look like flies in a web.'

***

Logan watched Ramulas and Pip talking excitedly as they came back into Sanctuary with the druids. Curiosity burned within and he needed to know what had happened in the forest. He quickly followed them into the castle.

Ramulas and Pip entered the throne room to find Rygar talking with Oriel. Ramulas explained what they had seen with the druids and wanted to know how to use them in the upcoming battle. He asked Oriel to bring up the map of Sanctuary.

She waved her hand and the town of Sanctuary appeared on the long table; they walked over to inspect the translucent model.

***

Logan heard people talking as he walked into the throne room and saw Ramulas, Pip, Rygar, and Oriel in front of the long table making battle plans, then he jumped seeing the stone oak tree in the middle of the room.

'What is that?' he asked, pointing to the tree.

Ramulas waved at it absently. 'Oh, it's just a tree. It appeared there one day.'

Logan tore his eyes away from the tree and came over to the table, seeing it bare.

Oriel's voice echoed in the minds of Ramulas, Pip, and the dwarf. 'Do not worry, only we can see the model. He only sees the empty table.'

Rygar smiled, drawing his finger along an imaginary line, 'We should spread them out here.'

Ramulas shook his head and pointed to another part of the table. 'No, that leaves us open here. We should split the forces and have half here.'

'What are you doing?' Logan asked.

Ramulas smiled. 'We are working out the best defence for Sanctuary. You have experience in fighting—where would you have the men?'

Logan scratched his head, looking from the table to the people in the room. 'Um, there is no map here.'

Pip winked at him. 'Why don't you use the map that you have of Sanctuary?'

Logan's heart beat faster in his chest as his mouth went dry. 'I don't have a map of Sanctuary. Why would I have one?'

Rygar winked at Logan, stepping towards him. 'I know ye have a map of Sanctuary; we all know ye do.'

Logan almost fainted as the three closed in on him. He had never felt this trapped before and was looking for a way to escape when Rygar tapped the side of his head.

'Thee map inside yer head. That's the one we been usin'.'

Logan sighed with relief. 'Um, where is the castle?'

'Where do you think it is?' Ramulas asked.

Logan placed his finger on the table, which placed him in the image of the mountains.

Rygar placed his finger a foot away. As Logan looked down, the dwarf winked at Ramulas. 'How did you get there, when my castle is here?'

'No, the castle is here,' Ramulas said, pointing to the opposite side of the table.

Logan's jaw dropped. They were making plans without the use of a map and not having a clue what the other was doing. This was going to be easier than he thought.

The dwarf turned to Logan. 'The enemy will attack through the forest. There is no other way into Sanctuary. Do you know of any other way in here?'

The spy shook his head.

'Well, it looks like we will be ready for the Legion,' Ramulas said.

Logan gave a weak smile before excusing himself. He ran back to his room and went through his papers. The only thing that would stop the king was the dragons.

***

Oriel nodded. 'He has moved away now.'

Pip held her stomach as she laughed. 'Did you see his face when we asked if he had a map? I don't know if he was going to cry or run from the room.'

The rest joined in the laughter.

Ramulas said, 'He must think us mad.'

Rygar nodded. 'Let him tell that to yer king.'

11

Remus walked through the snow-covered streets of Keah to one of the warehouses near the docks, where some of the Legion were housed. A cold wind blew in from the harbour. He saw that he was not the only one pulling his robes tight to fight the chill. It was mid-morning, and the streets were filled with people dashing from store to store through the light snow.

Remus entered the warehouse, removed his robes, and shook off the excess snow. He stamped his feet, bringing feeling back to them. As one of the soldiers took his robes, Remus wondered how difficult it would be to try to take Oriel in these conditions.

He was handed a cup of what these people called coffee. It was hot and bitter but warmed you during the cold. Redemption walked over, his twin batons swinging on his hips. The Legion stopped their training and lined up in columns.

'How are the men's spirits?' Remus asked.

Redemption tilted his head. 'Considering we are in a strange land where we are treated as outsiders, they fare well. They look forward to winter's end, when we can have fun with the people of this kingdom.'

Redemption's formality was lacking, but allowances were given. They were far from home, surrounded by people who openly showed dislike for them. Reports have been coming in of hostility toward his men in certain parts of the city.

Tensions were building on both sides. He needed to ensure the Legion maintained their self-control until they marched on Sanctuary, otherwise, they would war with the king and waste precious fodder to throw at the dragons. The last thing he needed was to come this far and fail.

He nodded to Redemption. 'Train them harder with shorter rest periods. I only want them thinking about Oriel. I will talk to king Zachary about his own people.'

Redemption nodded and walked back to the Legion making hand signals, and they continued their drills. Remus walked back out into the cold to the castle. He would ask king Zachary more about Sanctuary, promising him more crystals and gems.

Remus smiled to himself, thinking of the king. Zachary was like the donkey trying so hard to get the carrot hanging in front of him that he could not see the stick about to hit him from behind.

***

Remus walked into Zachary's chambers to find his warlords and a red wizard talking with the king. The red wizard sighed with relief when he saw Remus, and the royal guards stepped away from their king.

Zachary smiled. 'Ah, Remus, it is good that you are here. There have been some negative reports of your soldiers in my city. A few are unsettling.'

'Tell me what they are,' Remus said, knowing the answer.

'Several different groups of people across the city have made complaints about your soldiers by the docks. I have given my word as king that I will resolve this issue.'

Remus nodded, holding back his rage. 'People of this city are going into the areas where my Legion trains and is housed. You told me there would be no problem. I was led to believe we would be left alone.'

Zachary smiled condescendingly at Remus. 'I have allowed your men to stay in my city and towns and offered hospitality as my guests. I only ask that you control your men. '

The red wizard saw the change in Remus' expression and back-pedalled. He wanted to be far away when Remus lost his temper.

Remus bit down on his tongue, not trusting himself to speak. After a moment, he calmed himself. 'We have paid more than you asked. I could gather my men if they are causing too much trouble and move back into the mountains with the Symiaks—they would be happy to help us with Oriel. But that would mean your towns will be unguarded if Sanctuary retaliated.'

Zachary's reaction was more than he could have hoped for. Remus had no intention of leaving Keah until winter's end, but the king need not know that.

Zachary leaned forward with his eyes wide. 'Please stay. I will talk to my people to be more understanding of the soldiers.'

'And I will speak with my soldiers to show courtesy to the people in your fine city. My men will walk through your city in small groups, I think this is for the best.'

Zachary looked like a trapped animal. 'But the reports.'

Remus shrugged. 'It will be easy to return to the mountains.'

'I will talk to my people.'

Remus gave a slight bow. 'King Zachary, we must take our leave. There is much work for us to do.'

Without waiting for a response, Remus led his group out of the chambers. Small victories like this sent messages of who was really in control.

***

Remus entered his chambers and turned to his warlords when the door closed. 'Who does he think he is? If we were home, he would die painfully.'

'What would you have us do?' Omega asked.

Remus smiled without emotion. 'For now, nothing. We need fodder to throw at those guarding Oriel. I need to talk to Reckoning and Redemption. There has been a change in plans.'

Omega tilted his head. 'What change?'

'After we kill Oriel, I was going to open the portal to bring the other Legions through, but not now. We will come back to this fine city of

Keah and raze this place to the ground. The soldiers may do what they want with the people, but Zachary is mine. I have things to show him.'

Omega smiled. 'But what of his army?'

'Between the people of Sanctuary and the Symiaks, none will make it home.'

Laughter filled the chambers as each thought of what they would do when returning to Keah, and then Remus signalled for the communication of the two captains. In a few moments, they stood together on the wall.

'Are there any issues in your towns?' Remus asked.

Both shook their heads.

'Keep the men training until the end of winter. We will be taking the city of Keah after Oriel.'

'We have intercepted a message from the king,' Reckoning said. 'It was to revoke our power in this town. We are to be guests and nothing more, and our power is stripped. The massage was to be sent to Covedon.'

'Who else has seen this message?' Remus asked.

'The pigeon master, but now his wife and children stay with the Legion. He will not talk.'

Remus nodded. 'Send him the message that the Legion has stepped down. I will talk to the soldiers in Keah about our plans for Keah. You both will do the same—give the men something to look forward to.'

Remus sent his rage in waves in the direction of Sanctuary. He wanted Oriel to feel fear before he saw her next.

***

Oriel felt Remus' anger like a hot tidal wave washing over her. Something had happened in Keah since he arrived. He was angered and trained the Legion harder.

This confused her. The feeling was so brief she was unable to hold onto it for long. Oriel wanted to find out what had happened. Taking her astral form, she flew across the lands until she came to the walls of Keah.

She almost ran into the faint shimmering blue wall in the snow. Remus had placed wards around the city to warn of intruders. She returned to Sanctuary, thinking of some way to find out what was going on in Keah. Oriel sent out a psychic call for Ramulas to meet her in Shigar's chambers.

***

Ramulas and Pip walked into Shigar's chambers and greeted Oriel and the magician.

Oriel smiled sadly. 'Something has happened in Keah to anger Remus. I cannot enter the city—he has placed wards to warn him. We need to know the goings on behind the walls.'

Ramulas looked at Shigar. 'Are you still able to use your magical doorway to get into your old chambers?'

'Yes, but I will be recognised by the soldiers almost immediately.'

'I'll go,' Pip said. They looked at her in surprise. 'I can blend in as soon as I am in the castle, I will contact the thieves' guild and they will tell me everything.'

'Are you sure?' Ramulas asked.

She smiled up at him. 'Look after my family while I am gone.'

***

Pip said her farewells and wore a thick grey clock over her black one as she stood before the magical door.

'Welcome, Pip. This will bring you into my old chambers in the castle of Keah. You will need to close the door once you are through. When you do this, it will only leave a faint outline on the wall, to come back you must knock on the wall as if it's a door. I will hear you and open it from here. Be sure to knock in the right place or I may not hear you.'

Pip nodded and stepped through to Keah.

Her jaw dropped as she entered Shigar's old chambers. Tables and shelves had been smashed to pieces; broken furniture lay strewn across the room. She gently closed the door, and it disappeared, leaving an outline.

She moved around the shards of wood to the door and her emerald eyes glowed as Pip saw no-one was outside. She walked through the hallways with confidence, as if she were meant to be there. She waited near the kitchen door until a young girl came out. Pip grabbed her and the girl's eyes widened.

'Sarah, I have returned and need to see the master. Can I leave with the workers?'

Sarah nodded and placed her hand on Pip's face. 'Your eyes are green; how did that happen?'

'Magic. Now, I will wait here until you finish.'

***

Sarah came out and led Pip with the other workers. The guards at the gate did not give them a second glance. Once on the streets, Pip grabbed Sarah, 'I have moved away from the city; is the master still in the same place?'

Sarah nodded.

'Watch for me; I will return soon,' Pip said before melting into the crowds.

Pip knew it would be dark in a few hours and she needed to send word of her return. She had been gone a while and was not sure of the reception she would receive.

Pip made her way to the docks and caught her first glimpse of the First Legion. Four soldiers dressed in red and black walked through the streets as if they were one. Pip followed them for a while and entered an inn where she was known.

She was met with a familiar sight. A girl Pip's age sat with a fat merchant old enough to be her father. He had a ring on each finger; each glittered with a different stone or gem. The girl leaned in to whisper something in his ear and led him into a darkened back room.

The score of patrons did not look up as two heavy-set men rushed into the room. Angry shouts were heard before the sound of flesh hitting flesh and the merchant begging for his life. A moment later, the merchant ran out of the inn, his face swollen and his rings missing.

The two men walked out of the room and were shocked to see Pip.

'I need to see the master,' she said.

They opened another door and motioned for her to enter. She had been gone a long time without word—others had died for less.

'We have had no word from you since the day you broke into the castle with the prisoner. Where have you been?' one of them asked.

'A place called Sanctuary.'

The men's eyes widened. 'Then the rumours are true. The king's army lost a battle in the mountains.'

Pip nodded; she knew this would be dangerous for her to come back.

'Go to Amra's inn. You will be called when the master is ready.'

Pip wanted to ask about the First Legion, but she was unsure what her status in the shadows was. She would find out when the master came. Pip just hoped he could forgive her.

***

Pip walked into Amra's inn and winked at the two half-giants who watched the door. The eight-foot twins grunted in response. They were broad across the shoulders, their fists as large as melons, wearing loose leggings and vests.

She ordered an ale from Amra and then took it to a dark corner of the inn and waited. She let her thoughts wander on how she felt about coming back to Keah. Pip had only been gone a few months, and yet it seemed like a lifetime ago. After living in Sanctuary, she knew that she had finally found a home for herself and her family.

Besides the way people acted with the Legion, nothing else had changed. This was a city where Pip loved every aspect of its underworld. She sighed, thinking that now she felt unclean in a place that was a way of life.

Being in Sanctuary had shown Pip what life really was.

Pip watched as people came and left. None of them were looking for her. Then four Legion soldiers walked in. They stopped by the half-giants, who slowly backed away from them. The four slowly scanned the inn before walking to a table by the fireplace.

Amra quickly sent a serving girl to them. He wanted no trouble from the Legion. He heard rumours. The serving girl had left their table as eight rowdy teamsters came in noisily talking amongst each other. They walked up to the bar and were served drinks. They watched the Legion soldiers.

One of them stepped forward and spoke to the Legion soldiers. 'Hey there; you're sitting at our table.'

The soldiers glanced at the men briefly before turning away.

'You better move yourself away real quick,' another teamster said.

Amra leaned over the bar. 'I will have no trouble in my place. If you're looking for trouble …' He finished by glancing at the half-giants.

The teamsters were in shock. 'Are you taking their side?' one of them asked.

Amra shook his head. 'I take no sides and want no trouble.'

Amra left and they spoke softly amongst themselves. One of them walked to the soldiers holding two ales. As he neared them, he pretended to trip, emptying one of the ales on the soldiers.

He winked at his companions. 'I am sorry, sirs, I seem to have tripped.

The men at the bar laughed and slapped the bar while Amra paled. The Legion soldier who had been covered slowly stood as he looked down at his wet uniform and gave the teamster an expression so dark that everyone dared not breathe.

'I accept your apology,' he said before sitting down.

The teamster could not believe his luck. Winking at his friends, he poured the second ale over the soldier's head.

With an explosion of movement, the soldier stood, and the blade of his sword rested on the neck of the teamster, whose eyes were wide with terror. The two half-giants walked to the table as the other soldiers stood.

'Hold!' Amra called to the giant-kin, who stepped back. 'I want no trouble.'

The soldiers glanced at Amra with eyes devoid of emotion, then the soldier with the sword placed it on the table, unbuckled his breastplate and put it near his sword, 'I have dishonoured the Legion and must be shown the way,' he said as he kneeled.

The teamster's bravado had gone, and he quickly returned to his companions while the other soldiers surrounded their Legion friend.

'Are you ready?' one of them asked.

He nodded. 'Let it begin.'

The three soldiers stepped in and began to punch and kick the kneeling soldier. Not once did he raise a hand to defend himself. After ten seconds, he collapsed while the beating continued for a short while.

Suddenly, the soldiers stood back and helped the soldier to his feet. As he stood Pip could see cuts and abrasions covering his face. He stood smiling, with blood coming from his mouth and nose. One by one, the other soldiers hugged him, and then he walked over to the bar placing two silver coins on the bar. 'We are sorry for any trouble here.'

After they left, Amra stood in shock. They walked past the half-giants as if they did not exist. One of the teamsters caught his attention. 'You're to blame for this—out with the lot of you.'

'But they pulled a sword; you saw it,' one of them said.

Amra shook his head. 'I saw you lot cause trouble and they walked away without a fight. They saw what I saw,' he said, pointing to the half-giants, who moved towards the teamsters.

'We're leaving. We want no more trouble,' one of them replied.

Barely controlling his anger, Amra said, 'You've caused enough trouble. Leave and do not return.' He turned to the half-giants. 'Escort them out, and do not be gentle.'

They smiled as they closed in on the teamsters.

The sounds of furniture breaking, combined with the screams of mercy filled the room. Pip watched with amusement as they tried unsuccessfully to fight back. They were all thrown out into the snow.

Once the broken furniture had been cleaned up and stacked by the fireplace, the front door opened, and ten heavily armed men walked in. Pip gasped as a broad-shouldered man walked in behind them. He scanned the room, seeing the blood stains and broken furniture, before laying his eyes on Pip.

There was something familiar about this man, something Pip could not put her finger on. Her instincts screamed that this man was somehow extremely dangerous. He reminded her very much of the master of shadows. Then it hit her like a bucket of iced water.

This was the master of shadows—he was tall, broad across the shoulders, and walked with the utmost confidence, but the master she knew was black-skinned and bald. The man at the door was tanned with wild spiked blond hair.

'Master, is that really you?' Pip asked.

He chuckled softly. 'Yes, my favourite thief. I am the master of shadows. Since the Legion has arrived, there have been some people of influence disappearing, and I needed a little disguise.'

The half-giants took a step away from the master as he walked to Amra at the bar. 'Tell me what happened here. I do hope Pip was not involved.'

Amra quickly told of what occurred with the Legion and teamsters. When he had finished, the master spoke.

'I have need of your establishment. Leave now and return in two hours' time.'

Amra walked swiftly to the door, taking the giants with him. The master glided over to Pip while the men went to the bar.

'Pray tell, child, where have you been? I have heard news that you were in Sanctuary.'

Pip nodded.

'Tell me of your time there.'

Pip spoke in detail of travelling with Ramulas and meeting Oriel in Sanctuary, the people who came and trained, defeating the king's army, and that Oriel had said that the Legion was in Keah. She told him she had been sent to gather information.

'When you left, we received word that your sister had left Bremnon. You left the thieves' guild without permission—do you know what that punishment is?'

Pip glanced back at the men near the bar. They all had their weapons drawn. She knew each of them, and could best four or five, but not all ten.

Tension filled the air.

Pip had broken the rules and needed to be punished. 'The punishment is death,' she whispered.

With speed that belied his size, the master swung a hatchet at Pip's head. She was too slow to react.

The last thing she felt was the cold steel hitting her.

***

Remus stood at the end of the largest warehouse, which held all five thousand Legion soldiers. The red wizards had cast spells to keep this meeting private.

'The king has spoken to me about the problems his people were having with us being here. After speaking with him our plans have changed. Once we have Oriel, we will return to Keah and the city will be razed to the ground. Do what you want with the people and watch my wrath for King Zachary. But for now, do not allow them to provoke you. We will have our fun once we return.'

Remus smiled, knowing there would be no more problems.

Remus walked into Zachary's chambers with Beta, Alpha, and Omega. The king waved away his council.

'I have spoken to my men and there will be no more trouble as they walk through this grand city.'

'Through Keah?' Zachary stammered. 'I thought they would stay near the docks?'

Remus smiled. 'The people already know of the Legion in this city. I have spoken to my men; have you spoken to your people?'

Remus almost laughed seeing the expression on Zachary's face as the king processed what he needed to do.

12

Iguchi stood with his Fallen Angels in the clearing that was covered in a thin crust of snow. Across from them was Owain and the archers. Each had a quiver of fowling arrows. Ten feet behind the Angels were five targets. Iguchi called Miles, Benji, and Michael to stand in front of three targets. Plumes of steam came from everyone as they breathed.

Owain called for three archers to come forward, and the others stepped back. Fifty yards separated the Angels and archers. Miles, Benji, and Michael needed to get close enough to the archers to touch their bows. The archers would be shooting the targets behind the Angels as they came. The trio slapped their arms as they jogged on the spot making patches in the snow beneath them. They could not allow the cold to slow them.

The Angels walked forward as the first arrows flew. They had to walk in a straight line and were only allowed to parry or dodge the arrows. For the first twenty yards, they easily avoided the arrows, then Benji was struck, and he fell to one knee. Miles was hit in the shoulder, and then ten yards later, Michael was stuck as well.

The archers lowered their bows as Iguchi stormed over to his Angels. 'My three Angels are dead,' he cried to the clouds above. 'I taught them well, but they did not listen.'

He motioned for them to stand and come closer. 'Have I not told you to watch the archer load his bow and steady his aim? Your movements are to be made before he shoots, and yet all three hesitated and now are dead. My wisdom has been thrown to the wind.'

Benji spoke. 'The snow slows our progress; we will try again.'

Iguchi slowly shook his head. 'You three have brought great shame to me. Remove yourselves from my presence.'

They walked to where he indicated with heads hung low. Iguchi called for five more Angels to repeat what they had done. These wanted to do better.

Again, the Angels were struck halfway, scolded by Iguchi, and told to join the first three. This was repeated until all the Angels stood to one side.

'Oh, woe is me,' Iguchi said, pacing in front of them waving to the path made in the snow. 'The wisdom I have taught you has been thrown away, like gems into the mud. I give you a simple task and you all failed me. Owain, I want three archers to shoot the middle target.'

Owain organised his archers while Iguchi walked over to the target. Once there, he nodded, and the arrows flew at him. For the first twenty yards, Iguchi seemed to move in slow motion as he plucked the arrows out of the air. He dodged and twisted at impossible angles to avoid the others. In the last ten yards, he rolled forward and stood before the archers. In his hands were their bows.

Iguchi turned to his Angels. 'Look at me; I am old and frail, and yet I touched their bows where you could not.'

'You are as frail as an old bull,' Benji said before Miles could stop him.

Iguchi's eyes locked onto Benji as the Angel attempted to disappear. 'Come to me. I have a lesson for you.'

Benji slapped his head as the other Angels shook their heads. When he stood before him, Iguchi said, 'I will show you Jitsu. Now, strike me with your sword.'

Benji hesitated for a moment until Iguchi motioned for him to strike. He drew his sword and slashed at the small man's neck. Iguchi stepped inside the strike, grabbed Benji's forearm, and twisted. Benji dropped the sword and was sent cartwheeling through the air. Iguchi spoke when he landed.

'I come from farming people who were always attacked by bandits with swords. Farmers were forbidden to have weapons, so we discovered Jitsu.'

Benji stood slowly and Iguchi motioned for Miles and Michael to stand next to their friend and to remove their swords, then he waved for the three to attack him.

Michael rushed Iguchi ten feet away, only to grab air and fall to the ground. Benji ran at Iguchi, followed by Miles. Benji reached Iguchi and found himself spun around and pushed into Miles. They were both stunned as Iguchi ran up and sent each flying in different directions.

He bowed, saying, 'I will teach you the basics of Jitsu: how to use your opponent's energy against them.'

The Angels were paired off and went through motions, each taking turns to throw the other around. They tried with everything they had after failing the previous test.

***

Nathaniel felt a subtle change in the magical energies. In an instant, he knew what that meant. He was no longer restricted to the rear of the tunnel. He sent his astral form to the tunnel entrance.

He flew through people pushing carts of dirt and rock, and he increased his speed when he saw the light. He was forced to a stop by a faint blue barrier at the entrance, so he watched people walking by.

After a while, he was almost driven crazy by the energy of Heaven's Reign coming toward him, and this feeling increased as the sword came closer. A soldier walked by with his sword swinging on his hip. Nathaniel screamed in rage as he beat on the barrier calling for his weapon.

The soldier stopped, placing his hand on the hilt of the sword. He investigated the tunnel and smiled. Nathaniel saw the man's blue crystal eyes and knew that the spirit within the sword had bonded with this man.

The soldier caressed the sword while giving a knowing look into the tunnel before walking away. Nathaniel beat at the barrier with renewed fury until the soldier was out of sight. He knew that, with his sword, he would be able to break free of this prison. He went back to the rear of the tunnel where the earth elementals were working.

Oriel's magic had become stronger, and he knew she would soon be free. His freedom was connected to hers. Once free, he would reclaim his weapons, and then every living thing in this town would feel his wrath.

***

A group of fifty soldiers stood in formation as Rygar paced in front of them. 'When the battle begins, ye will be fightin' more 'an one person. Every enemy ye kill, two or more will replace 'em. Ye need to train fer this.'

He waved his hand behind him, showing four other groups the same as theirs. The defending group braced themselves as the first group came forward.

Rygar called out, 'Aim fer their bodies. If yer hit, walk away from the rest.'

The two groups met with the sounds of wooden swords hitting shields and grunts. Rygar had told the attacking groups to strike without thought of defence, whereas the defending group was told to be patient and wait for openings to attack. This battle lasted four minutes and the first group of attackers were defeated.

'Next,' Rygar called.

The defenders had now found a rhythm of falling back and striking out at the attackers. They moved as one, slowly breaking down the attackers, but they still lost numbers.

Each group of attackers was confident, with the defending group growing smaller and smaller. By the time the fourth group had finished, there were only five defenders left. Rygar held up his hand and called everyone to him.

'Yer enemy will grow in confidence seeing a smaller group. Give 'em a good surprise and attack 'em when they don't expect it.'

***

Ramulas walked through the halls of the castle. He felt sick in his stomach worrying about Pip. She had left the previous morning, and it was a few hours after midday. This feeling had been growing since the night before.

He entered the throne room to find Oriel looking out of the window. 'I think something has happened to Pip.'

Oriel turned to face him. 'Why would you say that?'

He shrugged. 'I have had a bad feeling about her. Have you heard anything?'

She shook her head. 'Remus has wards to block my magic. Talk to Shigar, but remember, Pip can handle herself better than most. You should not worry.'

They went to the magician's chambers and Ramulas explained his ill feelings.

'I have been waiting by this door for her to return. The way is blocked, and I will open it once she knocks. All I can do is wait.'

'So even if she needed our help, we could not give it.'

Shigar smiled sadly. 'That is correct.'

***

Joshua was covered in sweat despite the light snow falling around him. He suffered cramps in his stomach and his whole body ached from practising with the ball and chain.

He wanted to be able to use it without the help of the gauntlet.

'You need not push yourself so hard,' Rain said, walking up to him.

Joshua growled. 'You know nothing of what I am doing.'

Rain smiled, shaking a finger. 'Oh, that is where you are wrong, my friend. We both have something very much in common.'

He pulled out his crystal sword, and Joshua watched as a thick wall of mist fell from it. 'We both possess items that have changed us and given us power beyond comprehension, yet the people of Sanctuary fear us. They are controlled by fear of the unknown, and what we might do to them. When the Legion comes, we will be expected to fight for those who loathe us.'

Rain saw that Joshua's blue eyes danced with amusement. 'You are making no sense.'

Rain held his sword up to his face. 'The spirit within this sword talks to me, showing me what true power is. Our weapons were wielded by the same master. We are meant to train together. What does your gauntlet say to you?'

Joshua growled, backing away. 'You have gone mad. Leave me now.'

Rain laughed. 'I am not mad, only a person who has been shown the truth. I am the only one who truly understands you; the only one who does not fear you.'

'What do you know?'

'We are asked to train on our own, so we don't harm the people here, and yet, when the Legion comes, we are expected to fight alongside these very people.'

Joshua looked at his gauntlet with pain in his eyes. 'We have both harmed people here. My wife fears me every time I come home. This is driving me mad. I do not want to be seen as a monster.'

'I have come here to show you the truth of who we are,' Rain said.

'What are you talking about?'

'I have learned to control my gift so I will not harm anyone, yet I am kept away. I want you to know what it is to be free.'

Joshua nodded.

'I will not lie to you, being free is painful.'

Joshua braced himself as Rain pointed the crystal blade at him. A stream of ice shot out at him, which he blocked with the gauntlet. The ice seemed to blast right through him. The sound of breaking glass echoed around them as the tranquillity spell was broken. A mix of power and rage flowed from Joshua as the ice poured from the sword.

The ice stopped and Joshua felt the minute sensation of pain. He growled, flicking the iron ball with ease.

'Good. You are almost there. Push through the pain and you will be free.'

Joshua growled, feeling every muscle in his body tighten and constrict. Even breathing was extremely painful. He growled again and pushed through the wall of pain. Just when he thought he would pass out, the pain subsided.

Rain laughed and erected an ice wall four feet high in front of Joshua, who swung his iron ball through it, then Rain produced another and another, always keeping one step ahead of Joshua.

'Kill you,' Joshua growled.

Rain nodded. 'Oh, you will kill, but it won't be me. When the time comes, you will kill more than you could hope for.'

This enraged Joshua even more.

'Yes, my friend; be free.' Rain laughed.

13

The druid held the arrow in his hand near his wand and blew gently, sending small bubbles onto the tip of the arrow. He lifted it up so that the bubbles shone in the light and handed it to Ramulas.

'You must be careful putting this onto the bow. It will explode on contact,' he hissed.

Ramulas nodded. 'I will keep that in mind.'

He nocked the bow and aimed at the target thirty yards away on one of the lower floors. He shot the target and green goo covered everything within a three-foot radius. He let out a low whistle as they walked over to the target.

'This is a lot faster than the bubbles; we should have all our arrows covered in this,' Ramulas said.

The druid shook his head and gathered five other arrows that were covered in bubbles. He placed them into a quiver and shook it gently. They exploded, almost instantly covering him. He tapped the goo with his wand, and it turned to dust. 'This is the danger of using too many.'

***

Joshua stood in the mist, unable to see anything.

'Now is the time for you to learn control,' Rain said from behind.

He spun around swinging his ball.

'Do not allow the gauntlet to control you. You must look deeper within yourself to be free.'

Rain stepped forward and placed the crystal blade on the side of Joshua's head. Pain flowed through every fibre of his being as he fought to remain standing before he fell to his knees.

'No, you must stand and fight.'

Joshua grunted and forced his way up. 'Too much pain.'

'Then I will remove your gauntlet—take your ball and chain from you.' Joshua roared and walked through the pain as the mist flowed into him, and then the pain vanished. 'Now do you understand what it is like to be free?'

'Power,' Joshua growled.

Joshua stood, feeling the raw primal power flowing through him just below the surface, waiting to be called. Knowing he could control this was intoxicating.

'Now we are able to work together to bring out the best in each other,' Rain said with a smile.

'Would ye look at all this ice,' Rygar said, walking over. 'Ye have come up with more tricks with yer fancy sword.'

Rain gave a slight bow. 'Yes, I have.'

He formed an ice wall ten feet away and Joshua exploded into motion, throwing his ball through the ice. Rygar was shocked by the power coming from Joshua, and then he saw the expression of pure rage on his face.

'I am free,' Joshua growled.

The dwarf stepped back. 'What has happened here?

'I took the spell from him. Now he is free to control the gauntlet.'

Rygar looked around for the Angels, or anyone to help, but he was alone with two powerful, unstable beings.

***

Jenna gently knocked on the throne room door. Ramulas and Oriel waved her in.

'I am sorry to trouble you,' she said softly. 'I have been worried about Pip.'

Ramulas forced a smile. 'I am sure that she is fine. She will blend in, and the Legion will not notice her.'

'I am not worried about the Legion. It is the thieves' guild and the master of shadows—Pip made a lot of money for them, and he would not be happy that she had left. Others have been killed for that.'

'Do not worry. Pip has sent a message,' Oriel lied. 'She will return in a few days.'

Jenna blushed and looked at the floor, missing Ramulas' jaw dropping at the lie.

'Oh. I feel foolish for asking now.'

'Do not feel foolish. We are your family, and you should feel free to talk when you need,' Ramulas said.

Jenna smiled and left thinking how wonderful this place was and that this was the happiest she had been since her parents were taken to Gullytown. Pip had always spoken of finding a better place for them to live, but not in her wildest dreams could Jenna imagine living in a place like this surrounded by so many loving people.

Ramulas turned to Oriel. 'You lied to her.'

'The truth would have caused her much pain and worry. After the death of their parents, Pip is her only family.'

'I hope my feeling about Pip is wrong.'

***

Pip woke to a world of pain.

Opening her eyes brought stabbing pain through her head. A soft moan escaped her before closing her eyes. A warm damp cloth was gently placed over her face, and she heard a voice that sent shivers through her body.

'You need to rest,' the master said. 'You have lost a lot of blood. It will take a while to recover.'

The last thing she remembered was the hatchet coming towards her, but she should be dead. Pip wondered where she was and why the master was with her.

'Why am I alive?'

He sighed. 'An example needed to be made of you. What was I to do when my best thief walked away without punishment? The shadows would fall apart. They would turn on me."

Pip understood. If he had shown weakness, the stronger shadows would have attacked him like a pack of wolves. 'What happens now?'

'Most of the shadows think you dead. Only a few know you live and why I allow you to live.'

'Why?'

'I have a very bad feeling about this Legion. Beneath their false smiles there lies something very evil. They plan to march to Sanctuary at winter's end with the king's army. I do not think it will bode well if they return victorious. I fear then the Legion will show their true colours.'

'What do you want from me?'

'You came here to find out about this Legion?'

Pip nodded weakly.

The master told Pip everything the shadows had observed and heard about the Legion. He followed with two things that truly shocked Pip. The shadows would assist the Lord of Sanctuary, and Pip was to take Amra and his half-giants back with her to Sanctuary.

'Amra is in fear of the Legion and has asked for my help.'

'How much did he pay?' Pip asked.

'Amra has left all he owns to the shadows.'

Pip smiled. Even in dark times, the shadows always found a way to profit.

'But wait,' Pip said. 'The magical doorway to Sanctuary is in the castle. How do I get to it with the two half-giants?'

'You are Pip, the greatest thief in the kingdom's history—you will find a way.'

Pip sighed; how did she always get herself into situations like this?

***

Pip sat up in a small room while the morning sun came through the window. Her pain was numbed as she chewed on the highly addictive stardust leaf. This would dull the pain for a short while, and addicts would do anything to retain this feeling. Pip's willpower was stronger than this.

Pip hated the use of drugs, but this was the only way for her function to do what was needed. Her mind worked overtime trying to figure out how to get two half-giants into the castle. Then the answer came to her. She almost laughed at how obvious it was.

Pip waited opposite the servants' gate at the castle and thought of Amra and the two half-giants that stood behind her. There was no use in trying to hide them—they were too large. Instead, they each held a large empty crate on their shoulders. She would walk them into the castle in plain view.

***

Sarah walked towards the gate as Pip stepped out of the shadows. The young girl's eyes widened. 'The master of shadows killed you; all the shadows talk of it.'

Pip shook her head. 'I was punished but not killed. I need you to help me get those two into the castle,' she said, pointing to the giant-kin across the road.

The small girl looked in disbelief at the half-giants, both holding crates and trying to appear as if they belonged, but people on the street and small patrols of Legion soldiers paid them no heed. Pip whispered her plan to Sarah, who thought it was madness but always trusted Pip and her actions. She agreed to help.

Pip dashed across the road and returned with the giants. The small group was twenty yards away from the gate when the guards noticed them. Four of them blocked the gate with drawn swords.

'What are you doing here?' one of them asked.

Pip stepped forward with an annoyed expression, pointing at the giants behind her with her thumb. 'This just came from the docks. It's for the lunch banquet. We need to take it to the kitchen.'

'By order of the king, only workers are allowed passed the gate. There was no mention of giants.'

Pip rolled her eyes while sighing. 'The king himself told us to bring these in. There's a special guest in the castle he's trying to impress.'

The soldier felt unsure as to what to do. He looked to his companions for support and received non-committal shrugs. He turned to Pip. 'We were not told of this.'

'Well, we are an hour late already, and I would be happy for you to question the king to see if he did order these. I will be very happy to inform him that you doubted his word,' she said, folding her arms and smiling.

His eyes widened at the thought of angering King Zachary, and Pip added, 'Or you can let us take these to the kitchen, and we'll be on our way.'

While the soldier considered this, Pip walked to the gate with the group following her. The other soldiers parted allowing them through.

'Wait! I will come with you,' the soldier said.

Pip forced a smile. 'Fine. Keep up, then.'

Her mind raced as they walked into the castle. It was hard enough with the half-giants, but what would they do with the soldier in tow? The halls were filled with servants and the kitchen door was fifty yards away.

Pip turned to the soldier at the door. 'Wait here. We will return soon.'

She knew they could disappear if they entered the kitchen alone.

He shook his head. 'I need to come with you.'

'Damn,' she swore.

Pip forced a smile. The others were on the verge of panic as she led them into the kitchen. Amra and Sarah shot concerned looks her way. Entering the kitchen, the sounds of banging and shouting filled the air, mixed with the smell of freshly baked bread. Despite the predicament, Pip's mouth began to water.

Turning to the soldier, Pip asked, 'Do you want to see the kitchen?'

When he nodded, Pip turned to one of the half-giants. 'Show him the kitchen, then.'

He did not catch her meaning until she winked. A smile grew on the giant's face as he picked up the stunned soldier and threw him across the kitchen. He flew twenty feet before crashing into a pile of pots and plates. Then came the shouts of alarm.

Amra looked at Pip. 'What do we do now?'

'We wait to see if he brings us food,' she answered sarcastically. 'We run. Follow me.'

People screamed and jumped out of the way when they saw two half-giants running through the halls. This was the last thing Pip wanted and knew that word would spread quickly. They needed to get to the magician's old chambers.

***

They raced up the two flights of stairs two Shigar's chambers, and there was no-one in sight. The effects of the stardust leaf were wearing off—Pip's body ached, and her mind was slowing.

Pip looked around, hearing pursuit as the soldiers came up the stairs. She shook her head to clear her thoughts. They only needed to run a few hundred yards and then they were safe. 'Let's go; this way.'

She led them down the hall, giving a quick prayer to whatever gods were listening. She wanted to reach Shigar's chambers unnoticed. The gods didn't hear her. Twenty yards from the door, six soldiers came out into the hall.

Both groups froze.

'Run!' Pip shouted.

The giant-kin roared as they ran, picking up Sarah and Amra. After the initial shock, the guards called for them to halt. It was a race to see who would reach the door first.

Pip opened the door, and the half-giants pushed her through. She shut the door in time to hear the soldiers pounding on the other side. The handle moved and the door was pushed open an inch. Pip screamed and was pulled away by one of the giants who blocked the door with his body.

Pip ran to the outline of the door. She beat her fists on the door, screaming 'Open up!' They all looked at her in confusion. 'It's a magical door; you need to knock on it to open it.'

Then the effect of the stardust leaf wore off. Pip slumped to the floor with her back against the wall. Shigar had promised to open the door when she knocked.

Something heavy began to hit the outside of the door, and she saw the wood splinter. The soldiers would be in the room soon. Pip had led them into a trap.

'I'm so sorry; I tried,' Pip said before falling into unconsciousness.

14

'Now, me lad,' Rygar said. 'I don't think it was wise for ye to take away the spell.'

'I was chained like a dog,' Joshua growled. 'Only to be released when the enemy came, then to be locked away again.'

The dwarf shook his head. 'Now, me lad, we were only doin' what we thought was best fer ye.' Joshua slowly walked to Rygar, swinging his ball with ease. 'No-one will chain ye again. Just stay out of trouble.'

Rygar quickly went to the throne room to find Oriel and Ramulas talking. 'Rain took yer spell away from Joshua.'

They were both stunned at this statement.

'I felt a slight shift in the magical energies before, but I thought nothing of it,' Oriel said, closing her eyes. 'I can feel Joshua now. He will not harm anyone in the state he is in. Rain and Joshua want to be accepted by those in Sanctuary. We need a way for them to train with the others.'

'But they have both hurt people,' Ramulas replied.

'They want a chance to feel like they belong here with the people. Give them this one chance. They are willing to die for the people. Let them be accepted.'

Ramulas nodded.

***

There had still been no word of Pip, and Ramulas had begun to worry even more. He walked into Shigar's chambers to ask for news.

'Well met, my friend,' Shigar said as he entered.

'Any word of Pip?'

The magician shook his head and pointed to the magical door. 'I have waited by the door for days and nothing.'

'I am very worried; she has been gone too long, and I think something has happened to her.'

Shigar saw the worry on his friend's face. 'Come with me. I will take you to a place I go when I feel troubled.'

He led Ramulas to a heavy wooden door and showed Ramulas out onto a balcony with a view of the snow-covered Devil's Ridge Mountains. 'This, my friend, will take away your worries.'

As Shigar shut the door, a faint knocking could be heard from within his chambers.

'Is this not a beautiful sight?'

Ramulas nodded.

'The sight of the mountains and sky takes all my troubles away. The night-time is even better.'

They both stood on the balcony lost in their own thoughts. Then they heard the sound of someone pounding on wood. The two looked at each other for a second before realisation set in.

'It's Pip!' Shigar called, running into his chambers.

As they raced inside, the pounding was almost deafening, and Shigar wondered what Pip was hitting the wall with. He reached the door and pushed it open.

He jumped back when two half-giants charged through the door, one of them holding Pip's limp form.

Ramulas pulled out his weapons and was instantly covered in magical purple flames. A man ran through the door holding the hand of a young girl. 'Shut the door—soldiers are coming!'

Ramulas saw a score of soldiers running to the open door. He screamed, raising his war hammer and releasing a stream of energy through the portal. The front line of soldiers was picked up and thrown back into the others. Shigar quickly shut the door and rubbed off the outline of chalk.

Ramulas fought off the wave of fatigue that washed over him as he turned to the half-giants. 'What happened to Pip?'

'She was punished by the master. She agreed to help us leave Keah.'

'Why would you want to escape Keah?'

'We have had trouble with the Legion army that now lives in our city.'

'Why would Pip want to help you?'

'Because we are her friends,' Sarah answered.

Ramulas looked at Pip. 'She is hurt. We need to take her to Oriel.'

Ramulas followed the half-giants as they entered the throne room. He was not happy they were in Sanctuary, but his priority was Pip. She was still in the arms of the giant-kin, and after Ramulas' display of magic, they wanted no quarrel with him.

Amra introduced them all on the way, but Ramulas would not trust any of them until Pip was awake.

Oriel gasped in shock seeing the young thief. 'Quickly, lay her on the table.'

She waved the half-giant away and started to chant. The former thief was covered in a faint purple light. 'What happened to her? Her skull is fractured, and she is close to death.'

Amra stepped forward. 'She was punished by the master of shadows for leaving the shadows.'

Oriel shook her head and waved at the group. 'Leave me; there is much to do.'

Ramulas led the others to the other side of the room. 'What happened in Keah, and why was she gone for so long?'

Amra told of Pip returning after leaving without permission, the trouble he had with the Legion, the rumour of Pip's death, and then how she came into his inn with a plan to take them to Sanctuary, bringing them to the castle.

'But wait,' Shigar said, holding up his hand. 'We heard a loud pounding on the door. Pip sounded too weak for that much noise.'

Amra nodded to one of the giant-kin. 'He pounded on the door when Pip fell.'

Ramulas smiled. 'So, that's why we could hear you. By the looks of things, you were in trouble.'

Sarah said, 'The soldiers just broke down the door.' Then she smiled, running to Pip who had just sat up.

'We made it,' Pip whispered as Sarah wrapped her arms around her neck.

Pip winced as she hugged the girl and gently pushed her away. 'Amra, the half-giants and Sarah are friends. I have been told of the Legion and we need to be prepared.'

Oriel smiled. 'For now, you need rest.' She waved her hands and Pip was covered again with a purple aura and was soon asleep.

***

Remus walked through the castle followed by Omega and Beta. He was attempting to control his rage, which threatened to explode at any moment. A few moments earlier, one of the red wizards had come to him with news that a small group including half-giants were running through the castle and trapped in a room.

Once the soldiers broke into the room the group had escaped via a magical doorway. The Lord of Sanctuary had appeared, casting a spell that threw them across the room, and the door disappeared.

He also found out that this magical doorway was used to help free the Khilli people. Zachary should have told him about this room.

Remus pushed past the soldiers guarding the magician's old chambers and saw Lucas talking with Zachary near a far wall as a dozen soldiers searched through the broken furniture.

'Show me where this magical portal was,' Remus said.

Zachary and Lucas turned, and the king said, 'I was told it was somewhere here on this wall.'

'Why was I not told about this?' Remus said in a taut voice. 'We could have laid a trap for them and entered Sanctuary.'

Zachary shrugged. 'We did not think that they would use this door again.'

Remus turned to his warlords. 'Search the room.'

They chanted while waving their hands in tight circles. A faint red mist filled the room. The outline of a broken doorway appeared behind Lucas and Zachary. Remus, Omega, and Beta quickly went to the wall. The broken outline began to sparkle as the magic entered it.

Remus lightly brushed it as he gave Zachary an emotionless stare. 'I heard the Lord of Sanctuary used his magic here.'

Zachary nodded.

'Which means that this door leads to Sanctuary.'

Zachary nodded. 'We know.'

'This door has been sealed from the other side. There is no way for us to get through.' Remus said as if talking to a child. 'If we had been told of this before, we could have placed a ward on this room, which would have kept the door open and told us when they were here. Now we will lose many at Sanctuary.'

'What do you mean, "lose many"? How?' Zachary asked.

Remus sighed. 'We go to war after winter. In all wars, men die. Now, is there anything else you would like to tell me?' Zachary shook his head too fast for Remus' liking. 'Are you sure there is nothing?'

Zachary and Lucas shared a knowing look.

***

Logan walked back into Sanctuary. He had been enjoying his freedom ever since Pip had left for a few days. He was planning to leave soon and wanted to remove one of their assets.

He was unable to get close enough to Ramulas, Rygar, or Iguchi, and Pip was out of the question. Over the last few days, he had been talking to Lodi, slowly gaining the giant's trust. So far, he had gathered enough poisonous roots and berries to kill a horse.

Before Logan left, he would feed Lodi his last meal.

***

Pip sat alert in the throne room at the head of the table. Ramulas, Owain, Rygar, Iguchi, K'ayden, and the druids waited for her to talk.

She took a deep breath and began. 'The Legion arrived just before winter and made an alliance with the king. Both armies will march at winter's end. Two thousand of the Legion have been sent to Turtha and Covedon.'

'Why do they have soldiers in those towns?' Ramulas asked.

'There were too many to be housed in Keah, and Zachary is afraid of you retaliating.'

'Zachary must be desperate to allow the Legion inside Keah's walls,' Shigar said. 'He would not have been happy losing the battle. He would see the Legion as a gift from the gods.'

Pip shook her head. 'There has been a lot of tension between the Legion and Keah's people since they arrived.' She quickly outlined what had happened at Amra's inn, saying there were several other instances like this.

Oriel said, 'Remus would have the Legion on a very tight leash and looking at the long-term goals. If he was not after me, the Legion would have killed everyone and burned the city by now.'

Ramulas nodded. 'We know they will come at the end of winter; we just have to keep an eye on Turtha and Covedon.'

'I will tell you as soon as they walk out of the city,' Oriel said.

'It will take a long while fer an army that size to reach Turtha and Covedon, and then to 'ere.'

'My Angels will welcome the Legion as the make their journey here. I, too, wish to know when they leave.'

The war council spoke of their plans, each taking a turn stating what their role would be in the upcoming battle and how they could assist after playing their part. The discussion lasted for hours and finally, everyone was happy.

Ramulas stood. 'We have come further than I could have dreamed, but we have a lot of work and very little time. Let's get to work.'

As everyone left, he motioned for Pip to stay. 'What are we going to do with your new friends?'

'They are my friends. Sarah will stay with me, and there is room for the others.'

Oriel spoke. 'I have looked into their souls, and they will do what they can to help.'

Ramulas sighed. 'Show them to their new home.'

***

Pip took Amra and the two half-giants into the training grounds to watch the drills. They gasped as Lodi walked across the street. The giant froze seeing the two giant-kin.

The three stood silent for a moment before running at each other. Lodi tripped as the first half-giant dived at his ankles. As soon as Lodi hit the ground, the other kicked him in the face. A crowd of people gathered to watch the fight with concern.

Lodi recovered quickly, jumping to his feet. He picked up one of the half-giants and slammed him to the ground with an earth-shaking thud. The other jumped on Lodi's back and punched him in the head repeatedly.

Rygar pushed his way through the crowd, pulling out his axe. He watched the fight for a moment before speaking. 'Bah, they're just playin''

He put his axe away and walked over to Lodi, who had both half-giants on his back. 'If I find ye have broken anything, ye'll have hell to pay.'

Lodi pointed to the two on his back. 'But I wasn't do anything bad.'

'One thing,' Rygar said before walking away.

The dwarf smiled as he walked away with the fight resuming. After all this time, his son had someone to play with him.

***

Iguchi walked into the throne room to find Ramulas studying battle plans. 'Hello to you, Lord of Sanctuary.'

Ramulas looked up in surprise. 'I thought you had taken your Angels out.'

'They have left. I will join them soon. The battle plans are good, and we must not stray from them. We must force the enemy's hand and keep them off-balance. We need to take away their control and not allow them to rest. This will help us win.'

Ramulas sighed. 'This is going to be hard.'

Iguchi shook a finger at him. 'You must not think of the whole battle. This will be won through many smaller battles. We will make their journey here very difficult. My Angels are blocking all the small paths of the forest, leaving them only the road to come here. This is one of the places my Angels will attack. By the time the Legion arrives, they will be tired, and we will attack again.'

Ramulas saw a hint of amusement in the small man's eyes. 'What have you got planned?'

'To cause the enemy much grief and sorrow.'

Ramulas was intrigued. 'Tell me more.'

Iguchi held up a finger. 'Have you ever walked over an ant's nest? You will see the neat lines of the ants coming and going into the nest. But when you stomp on the nest, the lines are soon forgotten, and the ants look for the intruders. Once the ants calm down, they return to their neat lines. This is my plan for the Legion.'

'Will this be enough?'

Iguchi shook his head. 'By itself, no, but if this is used along with other battle plans, not allowing them to rest—only then will the enemy make mistakes.'

Ramulas nodded his approval.

'One more thing, Lord of Sanctuary. I will need ten of the archers to learn how to shoot arrows while riding horses.'

'Why would you need that? They are training every day.'

'I need them for the battle. An hour a day is not too much to ask if we are to win this battle.'

***

Ramulas stood with Owain in the clearing watching ten archers on horseback. It was easy to see that they were not natural horse riders, but they were the best of the archers.

Whenever a horse felt the rider was unsure it would play up and do its best to remove the rider, but Ramulas communicated with the animals, calming them. Iguchi had instructed Owain to have the riders pass the targets and shoot.

The first few tries shocked everyone as most of the arrows had missed completely from twenty yards away. They were not accustomed to shooting while moving.

Iguchi motioned them to stand aside while he climbed onto a horse. He had a bow and five arrows. He raced out to fifty yards away, where he moved the horse back and forth. Iguchi nocked an arrow and fired, and everyone gasped in shock when he hit the centre of the target. Then the other four arrows found their mark in the other targets.

Iguchi rode the hose back to the archers and jumped off, landing like a cat. 'With practice, you, too, can do the same.'

***

An explosion followed by screams stopped Ramulas in his tracks. He ran from the courtyard to the source of the sound. Then he heard another explosion from the training grounds. He moved through the streets and pushed through the crowd and saw Lodi throw a crude-looking spear. It arced in the air to land in between two crates. The spear exploded, sending splinters of wood flying across the training ground.

'What is this?' Ramulas asked.

Lodi's eyes widened as his jaw dropped. 'I didn't do it. They was already broken,' he said, dropping a spear in his hand.

'Do ye like me new spears?' the dwarf asked, walking over to Ramulas.

'What are they?'

'Pieces of broken steel held together with fire-oil. I make the spears and let 'em dry for a day and they're ready.'

'What is fire-oil?'

Rygar smiled, tapping his nose. 'That's a secret o' me clan. It's safe unless ye give it a hard knock, then *boom*.'

The dwarf fetched a hammer and put a drop of fire-oil onto a flat rock. He hit the rock, which split with a resounding *bang*. 'Now, if the Legion comes with their shields held high, these spears will blow 'em away.'

'How many have you got?'

'I have made meself twenty so far.'

Ramulas glanced around. 'Keep your work away from prying eyes.'

Rygar looked up to see Logan watching from the crowd. 'Don't ye worry, me lord. They'll be safe.'

***

The archers had been riding for weeks and were able to hit a target from twenty yards away at a trot.

Iguchi had shown them how to control the horses using their knees. Owain constantly clicked his tongue to see how they were fairing; they were more relaxed riding, which helped with their aim. Plumes of steam came from the horses' nostrils as they paced up and down the snow-covered ground.

Owain tilted his head as he felt the slight change in the weather. The end of winter would be here soon, and the archers would not be ready by then. Then needed more time to train; they had an important part to play in the battle.

15

Emily walked up to Ramulas in the courtyard. 'Oriel wants to see you.' As they walked, Ramulas looked at Emily who, according to Oriel, was a very powerful spirit. 'Where have you been? We have not seen you in a while.'

'I play in the forest with the dryads.'

'There are children here for you to play with.'

'Too many people here,' she said in a soft voice. 'There has not been this many since …'

Emily's thought drifted back five hundred years, the time before the demons killed everyone she knew. Emily was a normal girl with loving parents and other children to play with, but now she was unsure why she remained here all this time, surrounded by people she did not know, which brought back the pain of everything she had lost so long ago.

'Damn,' Ramulas swore at forgetting what she had been through as he looked up at the castle. He looked back down, and Emily had gone.

He walked into the throne room to find Oriel waiting for him. 'Welcome, Ramulas. I have been looking into the souls of Joshua and Rain. They both have control of their magical weapons. They can safely train with the people. This will help unify everyone at this important time.'

'What about their weapons?'

'The weapons are still connected to their former master, who is trapped with me in the mountain. I feel him becoming stronger as he feeds off my magic. He yearns for their return.'

'What can we do about him?'

'For now, nothing, but bring Joshua and Rain out to train with the others.'

***

Rygar and Ramulas stood in front of fifty soldiers. Joshua and Rain were twenty yards away. The dwarf motioned for ten of the group to move towards the pair.

'The snows will be finished soon enough, then the Legion will be here, and I plan to give a hidin'. That's why ye will be fightin' these two.'

The dwarf walked over to Joshua and Rain. 'Ye play gentle with them.'

They nodded and walked towards the group. Joshua and Rain separated, casually walking on opposite sides of the group. The soldiers waited with swords and shields ready. Joshua growled while slowly swinging his ball. He feigned a strike before moving away. Rain flicked the tip of his sword at the ground, shooting a blast of ice beneath the soldiers' feet.

Joshua dropped his weapon and charged the group, knocking down four before they could find their footing. A couple of swords bounced off his hardened skin and, being as strong as a giant, Joshua shrugged them off.

Rain attacked from the other side, parrying a few swords away before using his crystal blade. Short, controlled bursts of ice were aimed at swords and shields, giving them additional weight, and making them harder to hold up, and then Rain filled the area with a thick mist.

One by one, the group was pulled into the mist, followed by the sounds of a brief struggle before Joshua grabbed another. Then the fight was over. The mist dissipated, showing Joshua standing with ten moaning soldiers at his feet.

'What in the nine hells do ye call that?' Rygar said, waving his arms about. 'All o' ye have been training hard, and only to be beaten by these two.'

The dwarf watched as the group pulled themselves up and walked to the side, brushing the ice and snow from their uniforms. They were sore and in disbelief at how quickly they were bested.

Joshua and Rain patiently waited for the next group. Ten more broke away and stepped forward, looking far from happy. This fight ended faster than the one before. They lay on the ground in shock as Rygar came storming over.

'What were ye thinkin'? Ye had no fight in yer eyes. Ye gave up before the fight even started just because ye seen what happened to the last ones. This doesn't mean you give up. That's when ye rush in. I gave ye trainin', now use it!'

The dwarf sent the groups away feeling frustrated. *This is no good,* he thought, *they've been trainin' fer months and they fell apart in a real fight.* He knew they would stand no chance against the Legion when they came. He needed them to find a purpose and desire to fight, wanting to run to the enemy no matter the odds.

'That did not go well,' Logan said, walking up to the dwarf.

Rygar shook his head. 'It was not pretty.'

'Will they be ready when the Legion comes?'

Rygar shook his head. 'They're far from ready, and we run out of time.'

'Is there something I can do to help?' Logan asked.

Rygar waved at him. 'Leave me be.'

Logan fought hard to keep the concerned expression on his face as he walked to the castle. He needed to document this—under real pressure, the people of Sanctuary would fall apart. If not for the dragons, King Zachary would have won the last battle.

***

Rygar walked up to Joshua and Rain in the middle of the training ground. Both were ready for more action. 'Yerselves lookin' fer another fight?'

They nodded, and the dwarf called for Lodi, who came out followed by the two half-giants. Since the arrival of the half-giants, the giant-kin

131

had been inseparable. A small group stood by the fence waiting for the fight.

Rygar looked up at Lodi. 'These two are looking for a fight. Have some fun, but no broken bones.'

Rain slowly pulled out his crystal blade and sent puffs of mist into the air while Joshua swung his ball with ease. Lodi roared as he picked up both half-giants by their vests and threw them at the pair.

One was hit with a blast of ice just before he knocked Rain to the ground, the crystal sword falling. The other was hit in the side by Joshua's ball and became entangled in the chain, which was what Lodi was hoping for.

Lodi jumped over the half-giants and delivered a punishing right cross to Joshua, sending him back. He swung at Lodi, narrowly missing the giant. Lodi answered with a few punches to Joshua's midsection. The half-giants were now up and ready to join the fight.

However, so was Rain, who had regained his sword. He shot a blast of ice at Lodi, who howled as he was thrown from Joshua. Rygar watched the two groups fight as the crowd of onlookers grew. No-one could find the advantage. He wanted the people of Sanctuary to fight like these two groups in front of him.

Then the answer came to him. It was so obvious and so simple. He walked up to the fighting groups and separated them. He saw that they were bruised but still ready to fight. He sent them away with a plan to use them tomorrow.

***

Ramulas steadied himself, holding both hands before him as Shigar shot another blast of energy at him. A small ball of white light formed in between Ramulas' hands and shot out to meet the energy blast. A shower of multi-coloured sparks filled the space between them. Ramulas ran through the sparks, pulling out his battle axe and swinging at the magician.

Ramulas had no fear of harming the magician, who was covered in a magical shield. Just before his axe reached Shigar, Ramulas saw green bubbles floating down.

'Damn,' he swore as they touched the blade of his weapon.

In an instant, he was covered in a constricting green goo. Ramulas fell deep within himself, feeling explosions of warmth in the pit of his stomach. The goo began to freeze, then he moved quickly, and it shattered, freeing him.

He looked up in time to see Shigar's wand tap him on the nose. 'You are now dead, my friend.' Ramulas' mind raced, thinking of a way out of this situation. 'Do not worry, my friend. Your magic is good, but you need to get better. Soon it will be easier, but now we must rest.'

Ramulas fought the dizziness that threatened to overwhelm him. 'I want to be better.'

Shigar smiled, 'The first thing I learned about magic is to know your limitations, or you will become exhausted like you are now. This could mean danger for you, just like with young Grace.'

Ramulas nodded, which sent throbbing through his head. They had been using magic for twenty minutes and the tiredness had set in. He said farewell to Shigar and went to his quarters knowing he would sleep as soon as he lay down.

***

Rygar stood in front of the same group as yesterday. They all held wooden swords and shields and were in the centre of the training grounds. Joshua and Rain stood twenty yards from them, and behind them were the giant-kin standing in front of a large black curtain.

Rygar motioned for ten soldiers to come forward. 'Now, yer fight yesterday with these two showed ye ain't got yer fightin' spirit. When the Legion comes, they will show ye no mercy. If they had the chance, they would kill yer loved ones.'

The dwarf waved at Lodi, who pulled away the curtain. It fell and the ten soldiers' mouths fell open. They saw their wives and children locked in a cage, calling to be released.

'What is this?' one of the soldiers called, stepping forward.

'Ye best be ready. Lodi has a ring o' keys, and when I wave me arm, he will try an' find the one that fits the lock. When he does, the half-giants will have their way with yer women.'

This statement brought louder cries from the cage as the half-giants came closer. The soldiers protested and one grabbed the dwarf by his tunic. 'Release them now, or I will tell the Lord of Sanctuary.'

The dwarf smiled. 'Ye have to pass Joshua and Rain.'

He waved his hand and Lodi ran to the lock fumbling with the keys, trying the first one in the lock. The women and children screamed in terror.

The man released Rygar and joined the others charging at Joshua and Rain. The dwarf watched with a grim smile as the desperate group ran. Joshua broke a wooden shield with a swing from the iron ball, knocking the man down.

But two others took his place and swung wildly with their swords.

Rain tilted his sword and shot a blast of ice at the group's feet. They fell but quickly scrambled to their feet again, the screams giving them strength. The first to rise received a blast of ice on his shield. He yelled in rage, throwing the shield away, and towards Rain swinging.

He was hit with two blasts of ice but was too enraged to notice and kept moving forward. Then four members of the group were past Rain and Joshua. They waved their swords, running at the giant-kin.

Rygar saw that they had fought with a determination not seen before against almost impossible odds. They threw themselves at the enemy without worrying about themselves.

He waved to Lodi. 'Step away, me boy.'

The giant dropped the ring of keys and Joshua and Rain stopped fighting. The door to the cage flew open. Women and children ran crying into the men's arms.

Rygar motioned for the other forty to join this group. 'The cage was never locked; it was always open.'

Rygar smiled at the expressions of the men at being deceived. Behind them, other groups watched on. They came in to hear what the dwarf was saying.

'What ye just seen was a nasty trick. The soldiers thought their families were in danger, but they were in on the trick, knowin' they would not be hurt.' He paused to see the looks of shock in the crowd. 'I seen yesterday that the fightin' spirit had left ye. Ye need to train every day like your family's lives depend on it, because yer families will suffer if the Legion gets inside Sanctuary.'

He saw the expressions of everyone change to a fierce determination. 'Stop standin' there. We got trainin' to do.'

***

Ramulas sat on the floor with his legs crossed opposite Shigar. A multi-coloured cube the size of an orange spun in between them.

'When the cube turns red, you must defend yourself; when it is blue, you must attack.'

Ramulas nodded and the cube spun faster, turning blue and red in rapid succession. Ramulas lifted his hands, covered in purple flames. He proceeded to defend and attack the cube every time it stopped. He blocked out everything that wasn't the cube.

Then he saw a few green bubbles floating down. He continued to battle the cube while watching them come down. When they were five feet from him, he moved them with a thought.

Then the cube shot Ramulas in the chest, making him wince.

'I told you to concentrate on the cube,' Shigar said.

'But the bubbles were floating down. I did not want to be covered in web. There was no other way.'

'You waited until they were too close. If a threat can be seen, deal with it straight away.'

More bubbles drifted down from the ceiling and Ramulas moved them. 'Is that better?'

He smiled as they moved just behind the magician.

The cube began its spinning once more. Ramulas knew that he needed to stop this and brought the bubbles onto Shigar's back, where they exploded, covering the magician.

'That was not nice. Now I know where Grace gets her sense of humour from.'

Ramulas sat on the floor of Shigar's chambers fighting three cubes at once while bubbles floated down. Two druids stood to the side and threw a handful of stones, which transformed into wasps that flew around the room.

One by one, Ramulas moved the bubbles into the path of the flying wasps. After the wasps were dealt with, Ramulas waved his hands, and three green bubbles surrounded the cubes. The shafts of light bounced around inside the bubble until all the cubes had destroyed themselves.

'You have come a long way in a short time, my friend.'

'I feel different with my magic somehow.'

After giving thanks to Shigar, he made his way to his family. After a week of training with the magician, Ramulas could feel his magic flow through him.

***

Iguchi stood with Owain in the clearing, watching the archers race by the targets and hitting close to the target from fifty yards away.

'They have improved. Today would be a good day to show them the platforms my Angels have made,' Iguchi said.

Half an hour later, Iguchi stood on the centre platform in the forest, which overlooked the road to Sanctuary. The three platforms were virtually invisible hidden in the trees. It would be a good place for an ambush. The trees in the forest were covered in snow, and the occasional branch would break from the weight. The air was fresh, and the sunlight seemed the sparkle of the surface of the snow-covered ground.

The archers arrived. 'We are here, 'Owain stated.

Iguchi nodded. 'I have heard you stomping around for ten minutes. Have you seen my Angels?'

The archers shook their heads, and then the Fallen Angels stepped out of the surrounding trees, causing the archers to jump.

'My Angels stood in plain sight along the path you took, and they followed you here. The enemy will come along this road very soon and we must be ready.'

He motioned for everyone to come onto the platform with him. 'Three archers will be on each platform, and one will watch the horses. You will see cloth-covered boxes on the road below. Separate onto the three platforms and show me how you can hit them twice and run to your horses. My Angels will harass you as you ride. You must shoot them while riding.'

The archers nodded as they shot at the covered boxes on the road and raced toward Sanctuary along the forest path. Each rider held a loaded bow ready. A few moments later, a couple of Angels stepped out from the trees. The archers shot at them, hitting the Angel's shields and pushing them back.

They nocked another arrow as they rode. By the time they had reached home, the archers had passed six sets of Angels.

'You have done well,' Iguchi said, stepping out from the trees.

'How did you get here?' one of the archers asked.

'I ran through the trees watching you.'

'We did not see you.'

The small man smiled holding up a slender finger. 'I did not want to be seen.'

The archers looked at the ground and were shocked to see that Iguchi had not left any footprints in the snow. It was as if he had floated above the surface.

16

Logan had spent the past week taking his horse into the forest for hours at a time. He was happy to have the freedom to do this without prying eyes. The first few days were to see if anyone was following him.

When Logan was satisfied that no-one was watching, he brought his maps and documents to a large oak tree and buried them in an oil-covered pouch. He was happy to be leaving. The longer he stayed, the more he was beginning to fall under the spell of everyone else in Sanctuary and have thoughts about switching sides like Shigar.

'Today will be my last,' he said, walking to his horse.

As he left, a dryad stepped out from a nearby tree and watched him ride away. A low buzzing could be heard through the trees, and Tilly appeared near the dryad. 'Do I keep following him?'

The dryad looked down where the pouch was buried. 'No. We tell the Lord of Sanctuary.'

Tilly flew to land on the dryad's shoulder, and they entered the tree. A moment later, they came out of the tree and the sprite flew through the gates, into the courtyard and then the castle, flying through the hallways. She came across Grace and some children.

Fenris barked at the sprite while Grace jumped up to try to catch her. 'I want to play with you.'

Tilly shook her head. 'After I see your father.'

Grace pouted. 'On the third floor.'

Tilly flew up the stairs, searching for Ramulas. After startling a soldier, she was shown to the throne room where Oriel and Ramulas turned to her in shock.

'What are you doing here?' Ramulas asked.

Tilly quickly explained the events surrounding Logan in the forest. Ramulas and Oriel looked at each other in concern.

'So, the time has come,' Ramulas said. 'Iguchi wants us to allow him to leave. Pip has told us everything he has written. His main plan will be to use the secret tunnel. Let him leave thinking he has outsmarted us. There is no harm he can do before leaving.'

Logan watched Rygar train the soldiers for a few minutes, then walked away confident the dwarf would be busy for a while. He adjusted the sack on his shoulder, making his way to the warehouse that Lodi and the dwarf called home.

He walked in to find the giant waiting for him. 'What is in the sack? What do you have for me?'

'Shhhh,' Logan said, looking around in mock terror.

Lodi looked around terrified. 'What happened?'

Logan emptied the sack on the floor in front of the giant. Cakes, breads, and pastries tumbled out. 'I told you that I would bring you nice things.'

Lodi did not answer as he shovelled the food into his mouth. Logan smiled, knowing that each piece of food was laced with poison. In less than a minute, the food was gone.

Logan took the sack and shook his finger at Lodi. 'You are in trouble now.'

The giant's mouth hung open. 'I didn't do nothing.'

'I said that I was to bring you one thing, and you ate the whole lot. What am I to tell Rygar? He will be mad with you.'

Lodi snarled at Logan. 'You not to tell Rygar nothing.'

Logan stepped back, holding up his hands. 'I will not tell if you don't.'

He smiled as the giant nodded.

***

Rygar returned to the warehouse after training to find Lodi curled up on the floor, his snoring sounding like distant thunder. He had never known Lodi to sleep during the day. He tried several times to wake him without success. He would talk to him later.

***

An hour after midnight, Logan led his horse behind the warehouse. He removed a water skin from his pouch and poured lamp oil over the wall, looked around, and then took two candles out and placed them halfway into the wall.

Turning away, he lit a tinder and carefully brought the flame up to light the candles, knowing that it would light the oil in ten minutes. He moved to the front door of the building, placing wedges into the frame, blocking any exit. With the giant dead, Rygar would not be able to escape.

He climbed onto his horse, took one last look around, and rode out the front gate.

***

Pip's emerald eyes glowed as she watched him ride out into the forest. She had been keeping a close eye on him for the past week. She listened to Ramulas when he told her to let him think he would get away with this.

She glanced back at Sanctuary and saw something out of place. Something was burning behind the warehouse. Pip went to investigate.

She stood behind the building fighting for breath. She saw the candles and oil covering the wall. The flame was almost ready to touch the oil and burn everything. She pulled out the candles and saw an eye peering at her from the hole.

'What ye doin' there, girl?' Rygar asked as she jumped back.

'Logan has gone and left us a present,' she said holding up the candle.

'Can ye help open the door? I can't do it, and Lodi won't wake up.'

Pip opened the door. She and Rygar ran around the back, wiping all the oil away with rags and blankets and throwing them all into a pile of wood.

Rygar tossed the candle onto the pile, and it took off straight away. 'Logan will be wantin' a fire; I'm thinkin' to give him one. Follow me lead.'

Rygar screamed 'Fire!' and Pip joined in. In a few seconds, scores of people rushed out into the night. Pip filled them in on their plan. People ran off to return with anything that would burn and tossed it on the growing pile screaming as well.

Ramulas came running around the corner with Iguchi and the Fallen Angels. Rygar walked over to fill them in then signalled to the people that no more fuel was to be put on the fire. By this time, the whole township had gathered.

Ramulas stepped forward, magically amplifying his voice. 'A spy for the king has left. He thinks that he has caused us harm, but instead, he has shown his hand, and we will be ready when they return.'

The crowd cheered.

***

Logan sat on his mount a mile down the road and watched the smoke as it blocked the full moon in the clear sky, then he smiled hearing the shouts of alarm.

The smoke grew thicker and the cries louder. By now, the warehouse would be fully alight, and the dwarf and giant would be dead. He turned his horse and raced for home. King Zachary would be in for a surprise when he returned.

Logan rubbed his hands together in an attempt to bring feeling back to his fingers, and the rich earthy smell clung to him after digging through the frozen ground for his possessions, but it was worth it to help the king attack Sanctuary again.

Logan did not see Tilly and the dryads watching him from the trees.

***

Logan rode through the night and half of the morning before reaching Turtha and was annoyed when the guards stopped him one hundred yards from the gate. A score of archers had their bows trained on him. After a few moments, he was escorted into town. This was not the Turtha he knew. All the towns would accept a royal lancer without question.

He was shocked when his sword was taken and his hands bound in front of him by soldiers in red and black. No-one would listen to him as he was taken to the quarters of the mayor, who Logan recognised as the former sheriff.

The mayor looked up from his papers to deliver a cold stare as four of the strange soldiers walked into the room. 'Give me one reason why you should not be put to death.'

This simple statement struck Logan like a slap to the face. A cold chill swept through his body. 'Do you not recognise me?'

The mayor sneered. 'I do not know Sanctuary scum.'

Logan looked down and cursed himself a fool. He had ridden into town wearing Sanctuary's uniform. Everything could fall apart if he did not choose his words carefully.

'How has your leg healed since coming off your horse? After the battle of Sanctuary, you limped into the king's camp. It was morning and you brought word of the Khilli escaping Keah.'

The mayor's eyes widened as Logan spoke. How could he know these things? He turned to the soldiers. 'He is with us—one of the king's soldiers. Then he turned to Logan. 'These men are from the Legion. They will be marching with us to Sanctuary.'

Logan smiled. 'I am Logan James, Captain of the Royal Lancers. King Zachary sent me back to spy on Sanctuary to gather information. Check the pouch tied to the horse.'

Two Legion soldiers walked past Logan, one holding his pouch. It was placed in front of him. After looking at the contents, the mayor had him untied.

'Rest and have food brought to you and a fresh horse. You will leave after midday. Remus will need to hear this,' one of the Legion soldiers said as the mayor nodded.

Logan was dumbfounded. The Legion soldier was giving him orders and the mayor did not say a word.

'Send a pigeon,' Logan said.

The soldier shook his head. 'We need you to get to Keah as fast as possible. You will rest, and then we will give you a fresh horse.'

'I have information the king will need to see.'

The Legion soldier shook his head. 'Remus will want to talk with you. Rest for now.' With a slight nod, Logan was escorted out of the room.

Logan wondered how much had changed since his time in Sanctuary.

***

It was past midday and Rygar was worried. Lodi was still sleeping and turning pale. He quickly went to see Oriel.

'What troubles your dear dwarf?'

'It's me boy. He's been asleep since yesterday and lookin' sick. Could ye come look at him?'

She shook her head. 'I am unable to come out of the castle. I have called the druids. They will assist you.'

A moment later, four druids walked into the throne room. Rygar told them about his adopted son, and they left with him.

They examined the giant for a few minutes before talking amongst themselves, and then the lead druid turned to Rygar. 'The giant has been poisoned. We will make a potion to draw it from him.'

Rygar was shocked. 'How could he be poisoned? Who would have done this?'

Then it hit him like a kick to the stomach. Logan was the only suspect. He would make him pay if he ever saw him again.

The druids left the warehouse and returned with Ramulas and the potion. They fed the foul-smelling liquid into Lodi, and a short time later the giant winced before emptying the contents of his stomach on the floor.

They spoke to Lodi and found out that Logan had tricked him and given him cakes.

'Ye sneaky dog,' the dwarf said. 'He also tried to burn us in here.'

Ramulas looked out the door. 'I wonder what trouble he is causing now?'

***

Logan made it to the town of Covedon just after dusk. He was shocked to see the king's soldiers on the wall with men in red and black armour. He stopped at the gate asking for the captain. One of the soldiers in red and black came forward.

'Come with me. I will show you to the captain of this town.'

Logan did not move as he fought the uneasy feeling inside. 'Why should I go with you and not the kingdom soldiers?'

The soldier smiled. 'Because the Legion controls this town.'

Logan saw the kingdom soldiers give slight nods as he was led into town. He wondered how something like this could have happened. He saw more Legion soldiers walking the streets as if they owned them.

He had been here many times before and every time the people here were friendly, giving a slight nod or a wave to each other, but now people rushed around with their heads low. It seemed that even the cries of the gulls were trying to tell him something.

They stopped outside a large inn and Logan was shown inside. The common room was filled with Legion soldiers talking to one another, and then the room fell silent when the door closed. The silence was deafening, and Logan had never felt so small in his life.

The soldier motioned for Logan to follow him into a rear room. The two guards at the door moved away as he came in. Logan saw a man in a red hooded cloak sitting at the table and the four soldiers in the room became alert.

'Why is he here?' Retribution asked.

The soldier gestured to Logan. 'He came from the north.'

Redemption stood and walked to Logan, gazing with emotionless eyes. 'Why are you here?'

'I am on my way to Keah; I have news for the king.'

'Your king gave us control of this town; you will give the message to me.'

Logan's head swam as he attempted to understand what was happening. He held out the pouch containing the documents. 'Do you know of the battle with Sanctuary?'

'Yes, your king told us of this. We will march with him at winter's end.'

'I have spent the winter in Sanctuary as a spy for the king. In my pouch, you will find information to help with the next battle.'

Retribution took the pouch and searched through the contents, then slowly looked up at Logan. 'You have been there all winter?'

Logan nodded.

'Have you seen Oriel?'

'Of course. Everyone there has seen her.'

He motioned for the soldiers to close in around Logan, and once again he felt helpless. 'You will come with me.'

They marched through the common room and into the street. As they walked, Logan was stunned when he realised the only people out were the Legion soldiers.

They arrived at a large warehouse by the docks. He was led into a small room with a crystal ball sitting on the table. Redemption lay his hands on it for a few seconds, and it began to glow.

The glow faded and a face took shape in the crystal ball. Logan jumped back. Staring back at him was the Lord of Sanctuary wearing a red robe and a red breastplate covered in magical symbols.

17

'Who is this?' the image in the crystal ball asked.

Retribution smiled. 'He is a spy for the king. He has spent the winter in Sanctuary, seen Oriel, and has maps and notes for the king, Lord Remus.'

Remus' eyes narrowed. 'Bring him to me in the morning and I will ask him of Oriel. I must thank the king for telling me of this spy—what is his name?'

Retribution nudged the spy.

'My name is Logan.'

He received a sharp, painful slap to the back of his head. Logan turned to see Retribution glaring at him. 'You will show respect and end with "Lord Remus".'

'I am Logan, Lord Remus,' he said, feeling like a chastised child.

'Bring him tomorrow morning,' Remus said before the image faded.

'You will rest tonight,' Retribution said. 'Tomorrow, you will tell Lord Remus about Sanctuary.'

'What of the king? I was to tell him.'

Retribution shrugged. 'Things change.'

He was led back through the streets until they returned to the inn full of Legion soldiers and shown upstairs to a room.

'Food and drink will be brought up to you along with our uniform. You will wear it. You will stay in this room.'

'Am I a prisoner?' Logan asked, taking off his sword.

'No, but you are of importance to us. Keep your weapon. We do not fear you.'

Logan tossed his sword on the bed and walked over to the window. Looking at the boats in the ocean, and smelling the tang of salt in the air, he wondered how much had changed while he was away.

***

Remus walked into Zachary's chambers with Omega and Beta. They walked past the guards at the door.

Zachary looked up from a meeting with councillors and forced a smile. 'To what do I owe this pleasure?'

Remus did not speak until he was ten feet away from the throne, and then he locked eyes with the king. 'We are waiting.'

Zachary looked around confused. 'What are you waiting for?'

Remus smiled and spread out his hands as if to reveal a surprise. 'Logan, the spy you sent to Sanctuary.'

Zachary's mouth dropped and he almost fell off the throne, then he regained his composure. 'I was waiting for Logan to return before telling you about him. If he returned. Sanctuary is a dangerous place.'

Remus sighed. 'Logan is in Covedon and will come here tomorrow. When he does, I will show you courtesy of being there when he is questioned.'

Zachary stood with rage coursing through him. He had never been spoken to like that. Lucas and the four royal guards slowly circled the warlords. 'You dare talk to me this way in my city?'

Remus ignored the royal guards. 'Do you wish the march on Sanctuary to be successful this time?'

'What has Sanctuary got to do with the way you spoke to me?'

'Everything, my dear king. You failed to tell me about the secret door in the magician's room, and now Logan. If you spoke with him in private, you would only allow me certain knowledge.'

He paused and waited for Zachary to deny this. When he was silent, Remus continued, 'Withholding information from me is a tactical mistake. It could mean taking Sanctuary in a day or waiting outside the wall for weeks, with the loss of so many men. When Logan arrives, we will speak to him together.'

Zachary felt like a child caught stealing. 'I agree about Logan. I should have told you. I will send for you when he arrives.'

'Thank you, King Zachary,' Remus said with a low bow. 'We will take our leave.'

Zachary looked at the door in shock as the warlords walked out, wondering how he had lost the balance of power.

***

Logan was brought to the same warehouse and was shocked to see one hundred Legion soldiers in formation, eyes void of any emotion.

Retribution had his back to Logan as he spoke. 'I trust you rested well.'

'I did. I was told that I would not need a horse for Keah. How do I get there?'

Retribution laughed softly as he turned with amusement in his eyes. 'A way will be made for you, but now you wait. It won't be long.'

'What won't be long?'

Retribution gave a knowing smile and remained silent, and then a low humming filled the air around them. The hairs on Logan's arms stood on end. A door of light opened ten feet in front of Logan, who stepped back. Retribution grabbed his shoulder and pushed him into the light.

***

Logan tripped and fell through the door of light, his eyes blinded by the brightness. He was caught by two pairs of hands; he blinked a few times until his sight returned.

The first thing he saw was Remus standing before him. 'You are Logan.'

Logan nodded as Remus smiled. It was cold and devoid of emotion. When Ramulas smiled, it was full of warmth. He walked over and laid his arm across Logan's shoulders as if they were friends.

'Walk with me, Logan. We have much to discuss.

They walked by the lines of Legion soldiers all still as statues. There were at least a thousand, he thought. Then they came out of the warehouse and two soldiers stepped out to walk on either side of him. Other soldiers joined the small group, lining up in front and behind him.

'Walk as one with the group, Logan, or you will suffer quite a painful death. Do not talk or move out of turn.'

Logan shivered at Remus' tone. The threat of death was said so casually. He knew that his life meant nothing to this man.

Then he almost tripped and missed a step. He saw that they were at the docks of Keah, but how was that possible? He was in Covedon one moment and now he was here. As they walked, he saw several groups of kingdom soldiers walk within feet of him. Not one recognised him, and he was not surprised when they walked unchallenged into the castle.

He had been gone too long. Too much had changed. Keah did not feel like home anymore to Logan.

***

Logan's mouth dropped when they walked into the king's chambers as if they owned the room. The royal guard stood to attention while Zachary sat forward on his throne. 'Welcome, Remus. I have had no word of Logan. Why are your soldiers here?'

Remus smiled and nodded while motioning his soldiers to form a line to his right. 'I understand your discomfort, but they are here to bring Logan to you.'

Zachary gave a dismissive wave. 'They can wait in the hall.'

Remus' smile grew. 'Logan is already here, in this very room.'

Zachary's eyes darted around the room looking for Logan while the royal guard stepped forward to search as well. 'Where is he?' the king asked.

'Logan, step forward and remove your armour,' Remus said.

Logan came away from the soldiers as he removed the breastplate. He saw no recognition. As the breastplate fell to the floor, Logan's blond locks flowed over his shoulders.

Zachary gasped when he realised Logan stood before him. 'How did he get here, and why does Logan wear your uniform?'

Remus bowed slightly. 'We have our ways. The most important thing is that Logan is here. He was brought to you as soon as he arrived. I have not spoken to him of Sanctuary.'

Zachary looked at Logan, who nodded. 'I will gather my council, and we will learn how to win this time.'

***

When everyone had arrived, Remus handed Logan his pouch of documents, which were emptied onto a large round table. He quickly unfolded the map of Sanctuary, and everyone huddled in for a better view. It was very detailed, showing the castle and other buildings in the town.

'Where have you seen Oriel?' Remus asked.

Logan unfolded a few other maps and pointed out the throne room. 'She appears in this room, but it is just an image. Oriel is deep within the mountain. The people are trying to free her.'

'Tell me, have you seen the treasures with Oriel?'

Logan shook his head. 'I was not allowed in the tunnel.'

Remus smiled. 'Do not worry, King Zachary, you will get everything you deserve when we find Oriel.'

'What of the giant and dragons?' Zachary asked.

'The dragons are across the Devil's Ridge Mountains and will come when they hear battle. The giant is now dead, along with his adoptive dwarf father who helps train the people.'

Everyone looked at Logan in shock as he explained the relationship between the giant and dwarf, and how important they were in training.

Remus stopped him several times, asking about the training drills, and Logan finished by saying how they both died. He stopped allowing what he said to sink in.

'But there is more,' he said. 'Shigar lives in the castle along with twelve druids.'

Those from the kingdom gasped. Remus and his party looked at them in confusion. 'Who are these druids?'

Zachary shook his head. 'They are evil. They live in the Darkwood. They come and take people every now and then. They cannot be stopped.'

Remus raised an eyebrow. 'Why hasn't your army gone into this Darkwood and dealt with these druids?'

Zachary shook his head as his eyes widened. 'The Darkwood is full of monsters.'

He quickly explained the story of the druids and how all the monsters from across the land were betrayed and now take people.

Remus glanced at Logan. 'Do the people of Sanctuary know druids live there?'

He nodded. 'The druids walk through the streets and play with the children.'

'Play with the children?' Zachary asked in disbelief.

'They create bubbles for the children to chase.'

'Show me the tunnel where they dig for Oriel,' Remus said.

Logan pointed to a section of the map.

'What is here?' Remus asked, pointing to the maze.

'It is a maze. You hear stones moving. I think people are working in there, but I have not been in there.'

'What else can you tell us?' Remus asked.

'A magical sword and gauntlet floated from the tunnel and are now possessed by two people in Sanctuary. The sword shoots ice, and the wearer of the gauntlet is as strong as a giant. I have also found a back way into Sanctuary through a set of rooms which can only allow a small group at one time.' Logan pointed to where the entrance was.

Then Logan looked up and smiled. 'The Lord of Sanctuary showed me a way to attack the gate without arrow fire from above.' He explained the small hut and lever which produced a tunnel to allow them to ram the gate without being attacked themselves.

Remus spoke. 'Tell us of this Lord of Sanctuary.'

'Well, he looks a lot like you.'

'So I have been told.'

'The people of Sanctuary worship him as their saviour and would lay their lives down for him. He wears magical armour which moves like a second skin. His weapons are covered in purple flame when he trains.

There are rumours that he was a farmer before going on a quest to be captured by the king. He escaped and fought half of the king's army before coming to Sanctuary. He has a wife and two daughters, who are followed by pet hell hounds.'

'Hell hounds?' Zachary asked in shock.

Logan nodded. 'They follow his daughters everywhere and protect them.'

'Does he care for the people of Sanctuary?' Remus asked. When Logan nodded, he said, 'That is a weakness we will use against him.'

Logan went through his paperwork, describing everyone's role within the town, from the archers to the people digging the tunnel. He was stopped every now and then, and by the time he was finished, Logan was so tired he could hardly think straight.

'We have enough information for now,' Remus said. 'We should all rest and continue tomorrow.'

Zachary turned in disbelief. 'You are a guest in my city. I will not have you saying when this meeting is finished. I am the one who makes these decisions.'

Remus forced a smile and gave a slight bow. 'Please accept my deepest apologies, king. I only thought that this was what you would do. We should plan the battle while these things are fresh in our minds. What do suggest we do?'

Zachary nodded and puffed out his chest. 'We will retire until tomorrow. We will have a war council and plan our attack.'

Logan's jaw dropped. Zachary had just said the exact same thing. He glanced at Remus, who flashed a knowing smile. Logan walked to his room, wondering what the king had gotten himself into.

18

The three captains of the Legion stood in Zachary's chambers, with Logan stuck in the middle. He marvelled at how they were almost identical. The only thing separating them was their weapons. Redemption had spiked metal batons, Reckoning wore extended claws on his hands, and Retribution had twin swords.

The warlords and red wizards were scattered amongst the royal guard and council along a narrow table forty yards long. Remus and Zachary sat on opposite ends, while everyone spoke about the upcoming march on Sanctuary.

Zachary pounded the table with the hilt of his dagger. People stopped talking and he said, 'The time to march will soon be upon us. The snows will stop, and the ice will crack. That will be our call to leave this city. Two armies marching as one. We will know a better way to defeat those at Sanctuary. I thank Remus for his assistance.'

Remus smiled as he stood. 'Thank you, King Zachary. We of the Legion will do all we can to assist where we can.'

As he sat, Zachary introduced Logan, who spoke of what he knew. Once he was finished, Zachary stood. 'What if the secret tunnel does not work, and we cannot climb the high walls to attack them?'

Remus chuckled softly. 'Do not worry about your walls, King Zachary. In my world, we have giant crabs that can climb any surface and are larger than your warhorses. With a magical spell, I can bring two of these to aid us in battle. And there will be three armies to march on Sanctuary, not two.'

Zachary was confused. 'What are the three armies?'

'The kingdom army, the Legion, and the Symiaks.'

Zachary baulked. 'Symiaks? Are you mad?'

'No,' Remus replied calmly. 'I am quite sane. I have made pacts with several of the tribes, offering them a share in Oriel's treasure if they helped.'

Zachary stormed over to Remus. 'What right did you have to make a pact with those creatures? We have been enemies for generations and kill them on sight.

The royal guard stood ready with hands on sword hilts. A cold chill ran through Logan as he saw the three captains of the Legion smile.

Remus smiled. 'King Zachary, we are close to fighting in this room. Ask your men to stand down and I will speak.' Zachary waved the royal guard away. 'The Symiaks told me of the troubles with you, and I come to you with a solution. If they come to Sanctuary with us, we throw them at the wall and let them take all the arrows for us. After they die, we walk in and take what we want.'

A calculating smile spread on Zachary's face. If the Symiaks died at Sanctuary, the problem would be solved. 'How do you know they will follow your plan?'

Remus shrugged. 'Because they are greedy and stupid.'

'How many will join us?'

Remus gave a dismissive wave. 'Hundreds and hundreds. That's what they tell me.'

Zachary shook his head. 'My men will not ride with them.'

'Tell them this will rid your land of these creatures; all they need to do is march them to their deaths.'

Zachary thought for a moment before nodding. 'But the creatures must not come into the city.'

'Agreed. They will wait outside the wall until your army comes out to meet them.'

Zachary looked at Reckoning and Retribution. 'How did they come here? I thought they were in Turtha and Covedon?'

Remus smiled and spread his arms. 'You forget, King Zachary, that we come from a world of war and magic. They came here the same way Logan did and will soon return.'

Zachary smiled triumphantly. 'You could use this to bring the three armies to Sanctuary.'

Remus shook his head slowly. 'It takes a great deal of magic to move one person, and we only have so much.'

Remus did not want Zachary or anyone to know anything about their magical powers. The less they knew, the better they could be manipulated. 'Our main concern should be the dragons. Where do they come from and how many are there?'

Remus saw a reaction from Logan and glared at him.

Logan jumped. 'I almost forgot about Owain, the blind archer. He is from Shangri-la.'

'What?' Zachary said.

'What is Shangri-la?' Remus asked.

'A place with dragons.' He turned to Logan. 'Tell us more about him.'

'He is a blind bowman but can hit a target from two hundred yards. He teaches the archers, but no-one talks of his relationship with the dragons.'

Zachary nodded. 'We will deal with the dragons when we get there. We have the Symiaks to distract them. I want to leave as soon as we can.'

Zachary smiled to himself as he pictured the Symiaks running to the wall of Sanctuary being peppered with arrows and eaten by dragons, the giant beasts dropping from the sky and tearing them apart.

Then he found himself in Oriel's cavern surrounded by mounds of gold and gems, riches beyond his imagination. Little did he know that the red wizard had cast a persuasion spell, making the king see what he most desired.

Remus smiled, thinking that King Zachary was as stupid as the Symiaks. He knew with certainty the combined forces would be more than anything Sanctuary would offer as a defence.

***

The archers lined the wall with bows ready.

'Now!' Ramulas called.

Coloured bags of corn were tossed into the clearing from the trees. The bags seemed to dance in the air as they were hit before falling to the snow-covered ground. Only four arrows missed the target.

After the archers fired, they shouldered their bows and ran downstairs through the courtyard and into the castle. Within minutes, they occupied all the small balconies along the front of the castle. Each balcony held two archers with bows drawn from the first to the fifth floor.

A loud whistle cut through the air and coloured bags were thrown into the courtyard from nearby doorways. Again, arrows rained down on the bags. Ramulas walked out into the courtyard, inspecting the bags littering the ground filled with arrows.

'They are improving, Lord of Sanctuary.' Iguchi said.

He nodded. 'I know, but I want them to be faster.'

'They are good enough for the time they have trained. If we had more time, they could be better, but we do not.'

Ramulas sighed. The archers had been training for the last week in case the enemy came into town. If this was done right, the enemy would walk into a killing field of arrows.

Iguchi smiled at Ramulas. 'Man is always afraid of the unknown. We will use that on our enemy when they come. By the time they arrive, they will be very tired. The people of Sanctuary will be well rested. This is a good start for battle. Now I will take the archers for riding lessons.'

***

Iguchi stood on the middle platform in the forest and looked down at the road. Three archers stood on each platform waiting for the signal. A few minutes later, a couple of clay pots were thrown from the trees onto the road. They broke, spreading a dark liquid. The archers fired at the liquid.

Then they jumped onto their horses and rode to Sanctuary. Five sets of Angels stepped out to stop them, only to be pushed back. Iguchi had run down the road inspecting the arrows and smiled when each one had hit the mark.

If this part of the plan worked, the Fallen Angels would have their fun with the Legion soldiers. There would be much blood and screaming.

He looked back at the platforms that were partially hidden. Once the archers fired, the enemy would be mad and want to attack them. Iguchi imagined himself as the enemy as he ran up the hill through the snow and reached the platforms in thirty seconds. The enemy would take twice as long. He ran down the path where a surprise awaited the enemy.

***

The Fallen Angels had dug four holes in the road, and cloths were placed over the holes. Shigar and the druids cast spells over the cloth to harden it enough for people to walk over but collapse when a wagon or cart came along.

***

Pip followed Grace, who led a group of children to the statues of the fallen. This had become a ritual for them. Grace would lead an ever-growing number of children here every day. Today Pip counted almost fifty young ones.

Grace would touch each statue and talk about them to the children and a light would shimmer across the statue. Pip had been watching for the past few days, and curiosity had gotten the better of her.

She walked up to the group. 'What are you doing, Grace?'

Grace smiled. 'We are saying hello to the fallen.'

'You know they are just statues.'

Grace shook her head. 'Da says the way to keep people alive is to always talk about them.'

'What happens when you touch them?' Pip asked.

Grace whispered, 'I hear voices.'

'What do the voices say?'

'"We will protect you".'

Pip was confused. 'Who will protect who?'

'The fallen will protect the children,' Grace said with a smile.

19

The snows had stopped, and the sound of ice cracking could be heard as the sun rose every morning. Two days prior, Remus had sent Omega and Beta with ten soldiers to see if the Symiaks were ready, and they had returned.

Omega bowed. 'They wait for you to come and bring them down. They said that you told them you would come.'

Remus turned to Zachary, who sat on his throne. 'I will be outside the west gate with them by midday tomorrow. Have your men ready by then.'

'What of the First Legion?' Zachary asked.

'Do not worry. They will be ready.'

Remus rode his mountillo up into the mountains. Even though the snows had stopped, he held his cloak tight around his shoulders. He was accompanied by two red wizards, Omega, Beta, and one hundred Legion soldiers. The melting snows fed the small streams coming down from the mountains.

They were two hours into the mountains when he saw movement on the cliffs above them. Looking up, Remus saw Symiaks on both sides keeping pace with them. The Symiaks followed until a turn in the path led them to four larger Symiaks blocking their way.

Remus held up a hand and they stopped. The warlords and red wizards gathered on either side of him.

'Why is you coming here?' one of the creatures asked.

Looking at the creatures, Remus did not recognise the furs they wore. These ones must have come during the winter. 'We come to see Grunch,' Remus said as if talking to a child. 'We take you to get shiny gifts.'

The Symiaks huddled and spoke excitedly in their guttural language and separated after a moment. One of them stepped forward and said, 'Follow.'

The creatures turned and walked up the path, leading Remus and his group. Within half an hour, they reached the main camp at the top of the mountain. A sea of tents and dwellings stretched as far as the eye could see. Thousands of Symiaks moved through them. Remus estimated there were twice as many as when he had left before winter.

The word quickly spread of Remus' return. The creatures started hooting and stomping their feet. Grunch came out of the largest tent, held up his spiked club, and roared. The creatures fell silent. 'Bring humans here.'

The Symiaks opened, making a passage from Remus to Grunch.

Remus said, 'Omega, Beta—come with me; the red wizards stay with the Legion.'

Remus walked with his head held high, walking as if he owned the mountain. He stopped in front of Grunch. 'We are ready for you to take gifts.'

Grunch opened the flap of his tent, motioning for Remus and the warlords to enter. Once inside, they saw six chieftains sitting around a large rug. Two of them he did not recognise, and he noticed three former ones were not there. Remus took shallow breaths as he entered. The thick musky smell of the creatures was almost overpowering.

'Where are the others?' he asked.

Grunch shook his head. 'They not want gifts. Want smash humans. I send away.'

'Does everyone here want gifts?' Remus asked.

They all nodded, and Grunch added, 'We have Keah.'

Remus nodded. 'After we march to Sanctuary, I will make sure you get what you deserve. Tomorrow morning, we leave to meet Keah's army.'

They spoke in their language for a few minutes while sly smiles grew on their faces. Remus knew they were planning something. 'If you attack humans before Sanctuary, there will be no gifts.' The creatures went quiet and glanced at each other as Remus continued, 'You will have all of the gifts, but only if you listen to me.'

The Symiaks quickly spoke before Grunch looked at Remus. 'We listen, then we have gifts and Keah?'

Remus nodded. 'I promise you will get everything that you deserve. I want to leave by morning.'

Grunch nodded as the chieftains stood and left the tent, going in different directions and calling out orders. The sea of Symiaks churned as the camp was packed away.

A red wizard approached Remus as he came out of the tent. 'There are just over two thousand creatures here.'

He nodded. 'That will be enough.'

Remus looked to the west, seeing the sun setting on the horizon. His soldiers were setting up camp and he smiled. By this time the following day, the three armies would be on their way to Sanctuary. He smiled.

'Oriel, I am coming for you.'

***

The sun rose over the peaks of the surrounding mountains. The combined Symiak clans and soldiers lined up in columns ready to leave—scores of wagons and carts carrying supplies and a strange-looking catapult.

Remus walked up to Grunch. 'Remember, do not talk to the king's men about taking Keah.'

'Why?'

'Because they will attack you.'

Grunch held up his large hand, crushing an invisible object. 'We will smash them.'

Remus lowered his tone. 'No gifts and no Keah if you do.'

Grunch turned and shouted to the Symiaks for a moment before turning to Remus. 'We no talk Keah.'

The strange catapult was pushed to Grunch and he climbed into the basket.

'What are you doing up there?' Remus asked.

Grunch puffed out his chest. 'Throw us at enemy. This is good.'

Remus shook his head. 'You use rocks to throw at your enemy.'

Grunch shook his head. 'Throw Symiak, not rocks.'

Remus walked away, not knowing how to respond.

***

They saw the walls of the city as the combined army made their way to the gate. Legion and kingdom soldiers waited by scores of wagons, carts, and war machines. Remus made a quick calculation—there were almost twelve thousand marching on Sanctuary. He was confident that they had enough to crush the people guarding Oriel.

The horses, carts, and wagons stayed on the roads because the plains near the city had been inundated with water from the thawing of snow. Remus learned the hard way, with several carts being pulled out of the mud.

He felt the tension rise almost immediately between the Symiaks and kingdom soldiers. He stopped the creatures two hundred yards from the king's men. He rode to meet Zachary, whose face was a mask of shock. Behind him, his men were ready to charge.

Remus communicated with Redemption to bring one thousand of the Legion in between the creatures and soldiers. As the Legion moved, Zachary came closer to Remus with eyes as wide as saucers. 'You told me a few hundred. This is a lot more than that.'

Remus shrugged. 'I am as surprised as you are. Who knew they could not count.'

Zachary's mouth opened and closed as he looked over Remus' shoulder. Remus turned and almost fell off his mountillo. Grunch had climbed out of the basket and was walking to them.

'What are you doing?' Remus asked in disbelief.

Grunch ignored the question until he was ten feet from Remus. 'Gifts for Symiaks,' he said in a low tone to Zachary.

Remus rolled his eyes and looked to the sky. Could this get any worse?

Zachary pointed to the necklace on Grunch made from three human skulls. 'Remove that at once, or I will have your head.'

Grunch smiled, lifting his spiked club. Remus could see a fight breaking out soon outside the city gates. Everyone would lose here. He did not want any fighting until they reached Sanctuary. Remus needed the Symiaks and kingdom army to soften up Sanctuary's defences.

Grunch pointed to the skull. 'This mine. You take if strong enough.'

Zachary pulled out his sword. Remus turned his mount to face Grunch and waved to the mountains. 'If you fight here, no gifts for you. Take everything back into the mountains.'

Grunch sneered at Zachary before turning to the Symiaks and waving his club while shouting in his guttural language. The Symiaks began to hoot and stomp their feet.

Remus looked at Zachary. 'If you fight with them, you lose everything. Your men will die, and you cannot go to Sanctuary. You need to wait until Sanctuary.'

'I am the king of these lands, and no-one tells me what to do.'

'If you fight them, I will take the Legion to Oriel myself,' Remus said, watching Zachary's facial expression as he battled internal conflict.

'We will leave the creatures until Sanctuary,' he said in a strained voice.

They both turned to the gate as screams of panic came from within the city.

'What treachery is this?' Zachary asked.

Remus waved a hand toward his Legion soldiers, who remained still while the kingdom soldiers ran around. 'The giant crabs we need for battle have come from the docks. I cast a spell over winter, and they waited until now.'

Zachary baulked. He had forgotten about the crabs. How big could they be? The screams of terror came closer until the crabs walked through the gate. Kingdom soldiers backed up while drawing their swords. The Legion stepped in between the crabs and the soldiers. Two of the Legion soldiers climbed on the crabs and rode them halfway up the wall.

Remus smiled at Zachary, 'You see, the walls of Sanctuary will prove no problem for my crabs. We are now ready to go.'

***

Ramulas and Pip fought the Legion soldiers in the training room. They had separated when a faint image of Oriel appeared. 'Ramulas, I need you.'

Ramulas and Pip tucked and rolled away from the soldiers to the door, where the soldiers could not follow. They soon arrived in the throne room to find Oriel looking out the window.

'What's wrong?' Ramulas asked.

She walked over to Ramulas. 'Remus has left Keah. He wants me to know that he is coming and to feel fear. He is bringing the Legion, kingdom soldiers, and thousands of Symiaks with him.'

Ramulas fought to stay upright. He felt as if a horse had kicked him in the stomach. How were they going to survive this? 'Symiaks and humans have been enemies for generations—why have they joined the kingdom army and Legion?' He looked to the former thief for confirmation, and she nodded.

'Remus is very deceitful. Who knows what tales he has told for the three to join as one?' Oriel said.

'Where are they?' Ramulas asked.

'They have just left Keah.'

Ramulas turned to Pip. 'We must tell Iguchi to bring his Angels out to meet them.'

'Will fifty be enough against thousands?' Pip asked.

'With what he has planned, I hope so.'

***

Shigar, Iguchi, the Fallen Angels, Owain, the druids, Edwin, Rygar, and K'ayden had joined them in the throne room. 'Remus is on his way. They have just left Keah. With his Legion is the kingdom army and thousands of Symiaks—the number is close to twelve thousand.'

He observed the expressions of everyone as the news sunk in, and they collectively held their breath.

Shigar shook his head. 'Zachary would never march alongside Symiaks.'

Oriel nodded. 'It's happening, and they are coming.'

She waved her arms through the air while chanting softly. The area in front of the throne began to bend and warp. An image of the city of Keah appeared. Zachary and his army led the way, followed by the Legion, their slaves and then the Symiaks. The horses, carts, and wagons seemed to go for miles. Remus and Zachary rode side by side. The sound of distant rolling thunder came through the portal and the group moved away from the city.

'What are those creatures?' Iguchi asked, pointing at the crabs.

Oriel sighed. 'They are giant crabs. Remus will use them to climb these walls. They are very hard to kill. There are many more than last time. It will take them longer to come here.'

Rygar nodded. 'Symiaks are stupid creatures. They will look for the first opportunity to break whatever oath they took. By me thinkin', they'll cause trouble along the way.'

Iguchi faced Oriel. 'Spirit of the dragon, I will take my Angels to meet with this great army. The best defence is to elude all attacks from your enemy. Sanctuary cannot move, so we will harass them as they march.'

Oriel smiled. 'My thanks to you, Iguchi.'

Iguchi bowed and led the Fallen Angels out of the room. They would travel for days to find a place where they could attack the enemy. Iguchi had outlined what they were planning to do. It was extremely brutal and risky but also necessary for the coming battle.

Ramulas turned to Edwin. 'How long until you reach Oriel?'

The dwarf shrugged. 'The elementals and meself have been diggin' as fast as we can. We are getting closer, but not sure how much further we need to go.'

'Please return to the tunnel. We need Oriel free before the Legion arrives.'

After Edwin left, Ramulas said, 'We all know what we need to do. We need to prepare; they will be here soon.'

Everyone gave a slight bow before rushing off leaving Ramulas and Oriel alone.

'How do you feel?' she asked.

'I am excited and scared at the same time. We have trained hard and have improved so much since the last battle, but I don't know if that will be enough.'

'What worries you?'

Ramulas sighed and dropped his head. 'In the last battle, we lost twenty-eight people. I don't want to lose that many again.'

She smiled sadly. 'Do not worry; you won't.'

'Thank you. That makes me feel better,' Ramulas said as he walked out.

Oriel knew it would be a lot more, and they would be lucky to survive, but Ramulas would not be able to handle that truth.

***

Shigar sat in his chambers reading from a large leather-bound book in his lap. He was so engrossed that he failed to notice Grace had walked up beside him. He continued to study the contents when the seam of the book opened, and Shigar thought it was falling apart. Then the head of a black viper pushed its way out through the seam.

Shigar froze as the rest of the body slithered out. The black viper was one of the deadliest animals in the kingdom, and it had just slithered out of his book. Its tongue flicked out, tasting the air as it climbed his body.

'Hello, pretty snake,' Grace said, reaching over to pick it up.

'What are you doing?' Shigar said in alarm. 'The poison will kill you.'

The viper coiled around her chubby forearm. Its head rested on her hand, the tongue flicking in and out.

'He won't bite me,' she said, bringing it up to her face. 'Da taught me how to talk to animals. This snake knows I am its friend.'

The magician almost fainted when she kissed the snake on the head and then, to make matters worse, she hugged the viper.

'Grace, do you know where the viper came from?'

She rolled her eyes. 'Of course I do—it came from your book when I read the words.'

Shigar looked to a section where she pointed and noticed that she had not read the bottom line. 'Read the rest of the passage, Grace.'

Grace read the last part and he noticed the colour of the snake lighten, after a moment, it transformed into a snake of paper that still lived and breathed. Grace looked down, noticing the change in her hands, and Shigar almost laughed at her disappointment.

'You do know it's rude to read over someone's shoulder? Your father said no more magic for you. I will need to tell him of this.'

***

An hour after dawn, Miles, Benji, and Michael stopped two miles from the town of Turtha. Benji climbed down from his horse, handing the reins to Michael.

'Stay out of trouble,' Miles said.

Benji shrugged and smiled. 'Trouble always seems to find me.'

'Just look around and meet us at the lake,' Miles said.

Benji waved and jogged to the town as his two friends rode away.

***

Benji adjusted his travel cloak as he approached the gate. His armour, sword, and shield had been left with the Fallen Angels; he only had his wits to protect him. He had relied on his wits for years before coming to Sanctuary.

The guards at the gate came to attention as he came closer. Benji knew that he would be treated as a rogue while in town. They watched him closely but did not question him as he passed. He saw patrols of Legion soldiers walking the streets, but they ignored him.

He walked through the market looking at the stalls, listening to the vendors calling out their wares from the different stalls and smelling the mixture of smells from fresh vegetables and cooked foods, the animal pens and grains. He walked past the milling people to the livestock pens until he found the man he was searching for. He stood in front of the pens and waited to be recognised.

The vendor glanced at him a few times with suspicion in his eyes. Other than that, he was ignored.

Benji sighed. 'Now, Bromm, is this any way to treat an old friend?'

The vendor stopped in his tracks and looked at Benji with his mouth open. He blinked a few times before stepping closer. 'Benji, is that really you?'

'No, it's your mother coming to spank you for cheating customers.'

'It is you!' Bromm said, picking Benji up in a bear hug. The huge man was bigger than Miles and strong as an ox.

He released Benji and held him at arm's length. 'What has happened to you? You have changed.'

Benji shook his head, letting out a long slow breath. 'Man, it was a hard winter. I was with Michael and Miles. We ran into a patrol this side of Bremnon.' He stopped to rub his forehead, feigning a headache.

'Go on, tell me what happened,' Bromm said eagerly.

And the fish has taken the bait, Benji thought while hiding a smile. 'Michael and Miles were captured, and the hell hounds killed. I just got away and have been on the run since.'

'What have you been doing?'

Benji allowed his shoulders to sag. 'I have just been trying to stay alive, just living off the land as well as I could.' He showed his callused hands.

'By the gods, look at your hands. If there is anything I can do to help, just tell me.'

Benji jingled a purse. 'I need a horse. I have enough for an older one.'

'Why do you need a horse?'

'Miles has a sick mother in Covedon. I promised to look after her.'

Bromm fought back tears. 'You are a good man at heart, Benji. I have always said that about you. Show me how much coin you have, and I'll see what I can do.'

***

Benji rode the horse toward Covedon. It was worth at least twice what he had paid for it. He felt a slight pang of guilt for lying to Bromm, who was upset at his story. He had also given Benji a wheel of cheese and a leg of ham to give to Miles' mother.

The guilt was pushed to the side. This was for a greater cause—the lives of everyone in the kingdom were at stake.

20

Ramulas walked through the forest to the sacred grove. He could smell the thick aroma of the decaying foliage as the trees began to show signs of new life. He had been walking for a few minutes when he heard a buzzing in the air. He stopped and smiled, waiting for the sprite to come.

'Why are you in the forest?' she demanded.

'A great enemy is coming, and I must warn the dryads.'

Tilly pulled out her short sword. 'No-one comes into the forest uninvited.'

He smiled. 'There will be a bit too many for you to handle. That is why I must talk to the dryads.'

Without a word, she turned and flew back the way she came. He walked quickly to keep up, and before long, he was in the sacred grove to find all the dryads waiting for him.

Eady walked up to him. 'What news do you bring us?'

'The enemy army is on its way; they will be here in about a week's time.'

Eady stood proud as she looked around. 'We will be ready for them. We will attack as they enter the forest.'

Ramulas felt sick. A few hundred dryads against so many. He needed them to know what was coming. 'Twelve thousand soldiers and Symiaks are coming. Use the trees to your advantage.'

Eady smiled. 'You care for us.'

Ramulas nodded. 'Yes, I do, as well as those in Sanctuary. It will hurt me greatly if people die in this battle.'

Eady held out her arm and formed a fist. Several darts shot from her knuckles into a nearby tree, and then she turned to Ramulas. 'We have things to show the enemy that no human has seen before and survived.'

'What is it?'

She shook her head. 'If we show you, you will die screaming.'

***

Benji followed the road along the ocean and arrived in Covedon mid-afternoon and was surprised to see the First Legion standing guard on the gate. The Legion in Turtha were only in the streets. He stopped one hundred yards from the gate to weigh his options. This caught the attention of the six Legion soldiers, who rode out to meet him.

He had ridden for several hours and knew that his horse could not outrun the Legion's horses. Then he saw something that almost made him fall off his horse. The Legion's horses were different—covered in armour made from their skin.

He forced a smile as they came closer, forming a semicircle. ''What is your business in this town?' one of them asked.

'Who are you to ask my business? I answer to kingdom soldiers, not you.'

A cold smile grew on the soldier's face as he moved closer to Benji while pulling out a red-bladed dagger. Benji forced a look of terror as he leaned away. With Iguchi's training, Benji could have easily taken the knife and slit the man's throat, but he was here to gather information, so he held up his hands.

'I have come to sell my wares at the market,' he said, pointing to the saddle bags.

The soldier inspected the bags before addressing Benji. 'We are the First Legion. We were sent here by your king to watch over this town.'

Benji was confused. 'Why would the king give those orders?'

'That is none of your concern. Where have you been not to know about us?'

Benji turned and waved a hand behind him, 'I live on a farm a day's ride from here. I come into town a few times a year.'

The soldier grunted. 'You may enter, but if there is any trouble, I will show you my dagger again.'

Benji bit back a retort and nodded as the soldiers parted for him to move through.

***

Benji found himself sitting at a bar of an inn by the docks, a place frequented by sailors, thieves, and rogues. He felt as if he was at home. When he travelled with Miles and Michael, this place was like a second home to him. The windows were open, allowing the smell of the sea and the sounds of people and gulls outside to enter.

Benji saw that there was a change in people's manner and the way they held themselves. They were guarded more than usual. He also noticed as he rode through the streets that people would shy away from the groups of Legion soldiers as they patrolled the street. The people were on edge, and he saw fear in people's eyes.

Benji had traded the ham and cheese for a room and a meal at the inn. His horse was put into the stables as well. He finished his stew and waited for someone to approach him, but everyone was wary. Benji had not been there since before winter, and even old associates kept their distance.

He placed a silver coin on the bar and asked for a certain girl to be sent up to his room.

***

Benji sat on his bed, his fingers playing with the worn fabric of the blanket. He heard the soft knock on the door. 'Come in.'

A girl wearing a plain black dress walked in. Her blonde wavy hair fell past her shoulders, and her pale green eyes lit up when she saw Benji. She ran over to him as he stood and embraced Benji tightly.

'Hello, Tasha. How old are you now? You must be at least twenty summers.'

She stepped away and blushed, dropping her head and causing her hair to cover her face. 'I am eighteen summers, Benji, and you know it.'

He smiled at the girl who was like a sister to him. She had always been small and thin. He felt the need to protect her.

'Tell what has happened here since the Legion arrived.'

Her smile quickly disappeared as Tash told Benji of the Legion. 'At first, it was all nice and fancy and friendly, but after a few days, they said they were in control of the town. They have a curfew. No-one is allowed out after dark. Anyone who goes out disappears and is not seen again.'

'How many have gone?'

'Twelve of us have gone missing,' she replied, talking of the street rats. She held a blue cap in her hand. 'Marcus vanished last week, and I found this near the sewer. He always had this with him.'

'How are the other street rats?'

'No-one goes out at night anymore.'

Benji held up a hand for silence and quietly crept to the window as it opened. He crouched underneath it and motioned for Tash to continue talking. As the person came into the room, Benji pulled on the leg, and a small boy tumbled into the room.

'Robert, what are you doing here?' Tash called out in surprise.

Robert smiled at Benji as he picked himself up. 'I thought I was quiet.'

Benji laughed. 'You forgot who trained you.'

Robert looked at Tash. 'Another was taken from the docks. He tried to take his boat, but the Legion caught him.'

Benji looked outside and saw that it would be dark in a few hours. There was still much for him to learn.

'I want the two of you to stay here tonight. Buy food and drink—we have much to talk about,' Benji said, tossing a couple of silver coins in the air.

Robert's hand shot out and caught them.

***

Benji sat in the room deep in thought. He had spent the last few days talking with old associates and was not happy with what he found. The Legion had taken total control of the town.

What confused Benji was that the king allowed the Legion to control two of his towns. A knocking pattern sounded at the window—two knocks, then four, then three. The window opened and Robert climbed into the room. He looked at Benji with wide eyes and fought for breath.

'What is wrong?' Benji asked.

'Tasha said not to tell you. You must come look for yourself.'

Benji followed Robert for a few minutes until they came to a couple of abandoned houses near the south wall. They entered one of the buildings, which was known to be frequented by the street rats. They climbed the stairs to the third floor, where they came out onto the roof where Tasha waited for them. From here they could see over the wall.

What Benji saw almost caused him to fall from the roof.

Roughly ten miles away marched the biggest army he had ever seen, sending clouds of dust behind them. He turned to see the setting sun. It would be dark in a couple of hours. Iguchi had taught him that the army would have to set camp for the night.

Tasha handed Benji a cylindrical tube and he looked through the sailor's spyglass, which brought the army closer to him. He felt sick to the stomach seeing thousands of Symiaks next to the kingdom soldiers and the Legion. The three groups had separated and begun setting up camp. Benji took this as a good sign.

The trio sat on the roof watching the army set their tents and light fires until it was dusk. The sheer number was overwhelming, and Benji wondered how they could defeat them. The Symiaks alone would prove difficult to kill.

'Who are they?' Tasha asked.

Benji handed her the spyglass. 'The First Legion has come with the king's army and Symiaks to attack Sanctuary. Gather every street rat you can and leave this town."

'Why?' Tasha asked.

'The First Legion is very bad, and with this much in one place, things might be a lot worse for everyone. I have been living in Sanctuary, where we have been training to fight the Legion.'

'What do we do?' Robert asked.

'Tell as many as you can to leave and go along the coast.'

'But it's after dark. We can't be seen on the streets,' Tasha said.

'Damn it,' Benji swore. He knew she was right.

But he could not wait until morning. He had to leave that night. 'Follow me. I will bring you back to the inn.' They both nodded and he could see their uncertainty.

***

Coming out into the street, Benji saw Legion groups on patrol. He quickly observed a pattern in their movements. They stayed on the main streets and avoided alleyways.

For two agonising minutes, he led the two street rats through alleyways, narrowly avoiding the patrols until they were almost safe. They had stuck to the shadows without incident. Then Tasha ran across the street to an alleyway just as two Legion soldiers walked out of an inn.

'Hey!' one of them called, and Tasha froze like a rabbit caught in a trap.

The Legion soldiers took hold of her and dragged her into the alleyway. Tasha looked helplessly at where Benji and Robert were hiding.

'Let's have some fun with this one,' one of them said, pushing her against the wall.

She fought them as they tore at her dress, even punching one in the nose. Then a knife flashed in front of her face and Tasha froze.

Benji grabbed Robert's vest and pulled him close. 'I want you to leave here in the morning, travel south until you reach a rundown farmhouse, and wait there for me.'

Once Robert nodded, Benji raced across the street into the alleyway.

'Please let me go,' Tasha whispered.

This brought sinister laughter from both soldiers. Benji ran up and kicked the closest one in the knee, which broke with an audible snap. The soldier inhaled sharply, ready to scream. Benji grabbed a handful of hair with one hand and the soldier's chin with the other, and then twisted as he dropped to one knee. The soldier's neck broke, and he was dead before hitting the ground.

By this time the other soldier had stepped away from Tasha and held a red-bladed dagger before him.

'Hello again,' Benji said to the soldier who threatened him outside the gates.

The Legion soldier snarled, tossing the dagger from one hand to the other. 'You will suffer greatly for this.'

Benji stepped towards Tasha, who held her torn dress with her hands. 'Does he die fast or slow?'

The soldier looked dumbfounded. 'What has she got to do with my death?'

Benji smiled without emotion. 'She has everything to do with how you die.'

He rushed at the soldier, shuffling his feet, and the red dagger was thrust at him. He knocked the weapon away with his left hand and punched the soldier in the throat with the knuckles from his right, crushing his larynx.

The Legion soldier fell to his knees, holding his throat and fighting desperately for breath. Benji knelt before him holding his chin so he could look into his eyes. 'I want you to know before you die that I am one of thousands waiting for the Legion at Sanctuary. We will kill every one of you.'

The soldier's mouth opened and closed as he tried to suck in oxygen, and then his body began to convulse. Benji released him and stood to turn to Tasha, who looked at him in awe. 'Quickly, you need to come with me.'

***

When they were back in Benji's room, he handed Tasha a small purse. 'Take as much food as you can carry from downstairs. You must leave at dawn. Head north along the coast until you reach a run-down farmhouse and stay there for a few days.'

Tasha bit her bottom lip as tears welled in her eyes. 'Will I see you again?'

He leaned forward and stroked her hair. 'Do not be foolish. Of course you will.'

He left the inn knowing that things were a lot worse than they had planned for. He made his way back to the dead Legion soldiers. He had work to do.

***

Benji wore one of the Legion uniforms and he looked at the wall behind the dead soldiers where he had written a message in blood. He smiled to himself, knowing this would get the Legion's attention.

The Lord of Sanctuary is waiting for you.

The large letters stretched across the wall. There would be no mistaking who had done this. He walked toward the east gate as if he belonged, passing several groups of Legion soldiers. He soon stood outside the stables by the gate. The horses made little noise as he entered. Ramulas had taught him that they will be calm if they feel you are.

Benji chose his horse, fitted the saddle and bridle and filled the saddle bags. When he was finished, Benji cut the straps of the other saddles and then rode out of the stables.

Four Legion soldiers looked up as Benji approached the gate. He raised a hand in greeting as he came closer, and they relaxed. Benji made as if he was going to talk, then kicked the horse's flanks, riding past the startled soldiers and through the gate.

'Sanctuary!' he shouted.

Benji raced off into the night heading north-east. He wanted to ensure that the Legion could not follow.

21

An hour after dawn, the combined army approached the eastern gate of Covedon. Remus' eyes widened as he saw a thin pillar of green smoke coming from within the town. From the disturbance behind him, he knew that the Legion had seen it as well.

Remus turned to Zachary, his face an emotionless mask. 'You come with me. Your men will remain outside.'

A part of Zachary wanted to refuse, stating that he was king and the one who gave orders, but that was a very small part. The tone of Remus' voice sent chills down his spine, and for the first time as king, he knew that he had lost control.

Retribution met them at the gate. 'My lord, there was an incident last night.'

'Show me,' Remus said.

Remus and Zachary rode into the town and saw that the streets were totally deserted of people except for the Legion soldiers. As the Legion soldiers saw Remus, they gave a slight bow.

'Where are my people?' Zachary asked, looking around.

'They have been locked in their homes,' Remus replied.

Zachary turned to Remus, his cheeks flushing. 'You dare lock my people away? By what right?'

Remus sighed and spoke to Zachary as if he were a child. 'The pillar of green smoke we saw was a sign that something terrible had happened inside this town. My Legion bow their heads in mourning as we pass.

This means that one of my Legion soldiers has died, and until I find out what happened, your people will be locked away for their protection.'

Zachary shook his head. 'You have no right.'

Remus smiled. 'If your men were watching a town in a strange land and one of them died in suspicious circumstances, what would your men want to do?'

Zachary's eyes widened. 'Keep them locked up.'

***

They stood in the alleyway by the bodies of the Legion soldiers. Remus had read the message on the wall several times. He could not understand why someone from Sanctuary would come to Covedon, killing his men and then taunting the Legion. In his world, people did not like the Legion, but they only whispered this to others. The people of this land would soon fear the Legion.

He turned to Zachary. 'Did you ever have problems like this with the people of Sanctuary?'

'When thousands of people went missing across the kingdom, the Lord of Sanctuary led a small group that attacked a patrol outside of Bremnon.'

'I need to know more about who did this,' Remus said as he began to chant while tracing invisible shapes through the air. The magical symbols on his breastplate glowed. After a few seconds, the alley grew dark.

Zachary looked around in disbelief. 'What is happening?'

Remus ignored him and continued to trace patterns with his fingers through the air, and then he dropped his arms. An image appeared of the two Legion soldiers dragging a young girl into the alleyway, tearing at her dress while she cried. A man raced in after them. Zachary gasped as he broke the soldier's knee and neck.

The man spoke to the girl before punching the second soldier in the throat and speaking to him as he died. Remus quickly waved his hands and the images moved in reverse until Benji punched the soldier in the throat. Remus clicked his fingers so that Benji's image faced them.

Benji spoke. 'I want you to know before you die that I am one of thousands waiting at Sanctuary. We wait for the First Legion. We will kill you all.'

Remus clapped his hands, and the alleyway was bathed in daylight once more. Zachary blinked a few times and then saw the rage on Remus' face. A small ball of white light the size of a grape floated in the warlord's hand. He handed it to Retribution. 'I want this man to die a slow and painful death.'

The guards from the eastern gate explained how Benji had escaped wearing a Legion uniform riding a horse and ensuring he could not be followed. Remus smiled. The direction of the man was exactly where they were headed. He would soon be caught.

'What was that ball of light?' Zachary asked.

'It's like the smoke from a fire far away. No matter where this person runs to, we will find him with the ball of light.'

***

Benji found the Fallen Angels by the great lake as the sun rose and a light mist covered the water. He climbed down from his horse and Michael handed him his uniform, shield, and sword. Iguchi walked over as Benji stripped, handing Miles a length of rope. 'Tie the horse to a tree by the lake, Benji. Leave their uniform with the horse.'

'Why?' Benji asked.

Iguchi raised a finger. 'The Legion will gather around the horse and uniform. They will make camp here and search for you.'

'How do you know they will make camp here?' Miles asked.

'You ask the wrong question; you need to ask Benji where he got the horse and uniform from.'

Benji explained his last few days in Covedon and the killing of the two Legion soldiers before he left.

Iguchi nodded. 'This is good. You have angered them. They will make mistakes.'

Then Miles froze, his whole body rigid while he stared into space for a few seconds. Benji knew his friend was having another one of his visions of the future. Sometimes the visions were good, and other times they were fragmented so badly that they made no sense.

Miles gasped coming out of the trance. He looked at Benji with wide eyes. 'Benji, you angered them. You are going to die a terrible death.'

Benji grabbed Miles by the shoulders. 'How? When?'

'I don't know, but I can still hear you screaming in pain.'

The Fallen Angels looked on in disbelief as the two friends spoke. Benji wanted to ask for more information, but he knew that Miles had told him everything that he knew.

Iguchi stepped forward. 'Do not worry, my Fallen Angels. We will protect one another. As a team, we are a mighty foe to be feared by the enemy.'

While the rest of the Angels cheered, Miles could not shake the feeling that Benji would not be able to escape what was coming.

***

Two miles to the north, they passed a wagon on its side. One of the wheels had snapped.

'What is that?' Benji asked.

'That is a wagon carrying wine from Turtha,' Iguchi said with a smile. 'Scouts from the enemy will see this as a prize. They will bring it back to camp. This will help with our plans.'

'What do we do now?' Benji asked.

'We travel north-west, where we hide and rest. Tonight, we will hit them and run. It is the beginning of our harassment as they move toward Sanctuary.'

Iguchi led the Fallen Angels two miles north-west until they reached fields of waist-high grass. Half slept while the other half practised breathing exercises. Every two hours, the guard changed until midnight. Iguchi wore a grim smile. He knew this would be their first test away from home. The fate of Sanctuary rested on how they acted that night.

***

Iguchi sat as still as a rock in the middle of a sea of grass. Three miles away, the combined army of the enemy had gathered by the lake. Through the sea of bodies, he saw tents erected as dusk fell. The Fallen Angels were going to wait until the dead of night before making their move. The tools needed for that night lay at his feet.

He heard several Angels creeping behind him, and Michael said, 'Master, we are coming to look.'

'Is that my Angels stomping through the grass? I thought a herd of wild animals were crashing through the trees.'

Six Fallen Angels sat with Iguchi watching the enemy and Iguchi spoke. 'We are safe here. They have scouts to the west and the south. The wine is in the camp. We will let them know of the Angels tonight.'

***

The moon shone high in the clear sky as the fires burned low in the enemy camp. The Fallen Angels had moved into position. Iguchi was thankful mist had rolled in from the lake. It was thin and waist-high and helped conceal them.

Michael, Miles, and Benji crept towards a sentry who quietly whistled to himself. It was a Legion soldier. A twig snapped and the whistling stopped. The soldier peered to his left into the darkness.

Benji rose out of the mist behind the soldier, clamping a hand over his mouth. Miles and Michael rushed in and, within seconds, he was tied and gagged.

***

A few minutes later, the Legion soldier was tied in position, and the Fallen Angels were ready. Iguchi nodded to Benji, who took out a flint and removed the sentry's gag. Michael brought a horn to his lips and blew a long single note. Calls of alarm came from the camp.

***

A horn sounded in the middle of the night and Remus was instantly awake, coming out of his tent as the sound faded. Soldiers and Symiaks were looking around in confusion. Then a fire lit the night two hundred yards east of the camp.

The sentry's scream cut through the night as he was burned at the stake he was tied to, and at his feet was a small bonfire. Orders were called out, and both man and Symiak raced to the burning man while others were still scrambling from their tents. The Legion soldiers were ready, but the Symiaks and kingdom soldiers were slow to react.

Legion soldiers reached the man, throwing water over him, when another horn sounded from the north. Its sound hung in the air, silencing the camp. A second later, a man screamed desperately for mercy before another fire lit the night to the north of the camp.

This time it was a kingdom soldier whose legs were coated in lamp oil before being tied to the stake. This helped the flames climb his body, licking at his groin and stomach.

New orders were called out, and both Symiaks and soldiers raced to the men on the stakes. Within a minute, both fires were out and the men cut from the stakes.

Both men were alive but badly burned. Remus had them brought into his tent. His head still swam with the effect of the wine found on the wagon. All the top-ranking officers from the three armies drank from it and were equally affected. Remus cursed himself. This combined army was now without leaders.

Zachary stumbled through the flap of the tent following the injured men, and then the horn sounded once more. Rage flowed through Remus as he stormed out of the tent, knocking Zachary to the ground in the process.

Remus cast a spell to amplify his voice. 'Find them. I want search parties to the north, south, and west. Sentry patrols are to be tripled.'

The men and Symiaks who ran around without purpose or direction were now finding order, and he watched as different groups marched away from the camp.

Remus walked back into the camp as the red wizards and warlords stood over the two injured men who still screamed, casting spells of healing. It was only then that he saw how serious the injuries were. Their legs and lower bodies had been cooked and blistered; no number of spells would help.

'Remove their pain,' Remus said.

The red wizards cast more spells and both men became calm.

'Tell me what happened,' Remus said.

Both soldiers told similar stories of camouflaged men rising from the mist to take them. They were gagged and tied to stakes. After the fires were lit, they did not see where the men went.

By the time they had finished, Remus was furious. 'How dare they attack our camp.' He turned to Zachary. 'Were you attacked this far from Sanctuary?'

Zachary shook his head. 'They did not attack until we were in the forest.'

'They will not catch us unprepared again,' Remus snarled.

Remus looked down at the Legion soldier. 'You cannot recover from your burns. There can be no weakness in the Legion.'

The soldier nodded with a blank expression and folded his hands across his chest. Remus's hand shot out, and a thin beam of red light punched through his chest. He shuddered once before dying.

Zachary instantly became sober. 'What did you do?'

'I put him out of his misery,' Remus said, staring at the king. 'He would have died a long painful death. His screams would have lowered morale.'

Zachary shook his head. 'There must be some other way.'

'There is no other way. Now, what of this one?' Remus asked, turning to the kingdom soldier who shook with fear.

Zachary waved to the soldier. 'Leave him. We will take care of him.'

Remus snapped his fingers, removing the pain-numbing spell. The soldier's eyes widened before letting out screams that were louder than before. Zachary looked at Remus in shock as the warlord walked out of the tent. The screams cut through Zachary like a knife. He looked at a nearby Legion soldier holding a dagger and nodded. The Legion soldier walked over, and the screams stopped.

***

A patrol returned with a red-bladed dagger with mud on the handle. The six Legion soldiers stood to attention while one held the dagger.

Remus came forward to inspect it. 'Where did you find this?'

'A few hundred yards east of the river.'

Remus looked at Redemption. 'Take a hundred men in this direction for a few miles and then return.' Then he turned to the other captains of the Legion. 'I want defensive lines at every other section of the camp.'

Once they had left, Zachary walked up to Remus. 'What are you doing?'

'The men of Sanctuary have fooled us once, but it will not happen again. When they blew their horns and burned our men, we acted like scared animals running back and forth. This was how they wanted us to act.'

Zachary pointed to the dagger. 'But they have left a clue.'

Remus shook his head. 'How do we know that if we look to where they left the dagger, we will not be attacked from a different direction by a larger force?'

Zachary's jaw dropped at hearing this, and then he looked out into the darkness, searching for the possible army waiting in the shadows.

'Everyone, come with me,' Remus said, away from his tent.

Remus quickly spoke with the red wizards and the warlords for a moment before they broke away. 'Let's light up the sky.'

Remus shot his hand out, sending a tiny ball of light toward the stars. This was followed by the red wizards and warlords. The balls reached their height and exploded, turning night into day.

The red wizards had gathered in a circle, holding out their hands as if they held a large bowl, and then they chanted as small lights danced around them before shooting into the sky. As the balls of light exploded, they transformed into smaller ones that seemed to hang in the air before fading.

Zachary was transfixed as the balls of light exploded all around the camp, bathing the entire area in light as the kingdom soldiers and Symiaks gasped in wonder.

'They will not come here again tonight, in fear of being exposed to our light,' Remus said.

***

Half an hour later, Redemption returned with a half-eaten loaf of bread and a water skin. 'These were found a mile and a half away to the east.'

Remus looked at Zachary. 'What is to the east of this lake?'

Zachary thought for a moment before going pale and stepping back. 'The Darkwood. They are headed that way.'

'What is this Darkwood?' Remus asked.

Zachary explained that this was where the druids had come from, where they lived with monsters, and then told of his encounter with the trolls in the woods.

Remus looked around. 'We have many more men. We will follow them to this Darkwood. We will send the Symiaks to deal with any problems.'

Zachary nodded, but he was not so sure. He understood the history of the kingdom and knew that there was a lot more than just trolls in the Darkwood. He knew that Remus felt confident with the numbers, but he hadn't faced the creatures there.

They needed to sleep before morning came, but Zachary knew that after the events of that evening, sleep would be hard to come by.

<h1 style="text-align:center">22</h1>

It was midday and the combined army was within half a mile from the Darkwood. From this distance, the forest looked black, as if no sunlight pierced the trees. All morning, scouts had been returning with items left by the men of Sanctuary. The column had come to a stop while they listened to noises coming from within the dark forest. Remus waved Redemption to his side. 'Send twenty men one hundred yards from the trees and have them return.'

Orders were given, and twenty Legion soldiers mounted on their armoured horses lined up. A whistle sounded, and they raced to the mark, kicking up chunks of grass and soil from the wet ground before turning their mounts and racing back. Besides the increased noise from the Darkwood, there did not seem to be any trouble. The soldiers reported that a piece of Legion armour had been left by the tree line.

'They are hiding in the forest,' Remus said.

Zachary baulked at the notion. 'Listen to the noises coming from in there.'

'Our force is large enough to pass closely while we look,' Remus replied.

Another scout came up to them saying that the men had left a trail one hundred yards from the edge as they passed. Remus explained that they would be safe following the same path.

Remus led the force closer to the Darkwood. The kingdom soldiers were followed by the Legion and their slaves and then the Symiaks. They reached the point where the scout found the armour. The men and

Symiaks looked to their right as they passed the foreboding forest and the noises increased.

After a few minutes, a score of lanky trolls stepped out from the darkness of the trees and roared a challenge.

'Defensive lines!' Zachary called.

Kingdom soldiers formed two lines, the first row with swords and shields, the second with bows ready. Remus nodded to himself as the Legion organised their own ranks of defence. Remus looked back at the Symiaks and his mouth fell open.

Grunch yelled, waving his spiked club over his head. Like a dam breaking, the creatures surged forward towards the trolls.

'No!' Remus said as he kicked the flanks of his mount.

The Symiaks were fifty yards away from the trolls when hundreds more came pouring out of the forest, which spurred the Symiaks on. The two groups collided with a chorus of hoots, grunts, and screams. The trolls were as tall as the Symiaks but twice as strong. They had no need for weapons as they picked up Symiaks and bashed them into the ground.

What the Symiaks lacked in strength and strategy they made up in sheer numbers and rage, but Remus could see that they would soon lose this fight, and he needed them for Sanctuary. He rode down to Redemption's position. 'Help the Symiaks; we need them.'

Five companies of one hundred Legion soldiers raced toward the fray, hitting the trolls on their right flank and hacking away with abandon. A soldier cut a troll's arm and watched as it healed almost immediately.

His blood turned to ice, and he called out, 'They heal; they heal!'

He was relieved when he heard the call repeated up the line. He called a retreat, leading a section of the trolls away with them. As they passed the Symiaks, he called for them to follow, but their battle lust had taken over and they wanted to fight.

Slowly, the five companies led the trolls back toward the main host of the combined army. A group of three trolls charged forward, only to turn to stone. Then a cheer went up as more followed, turning to stone.

But the Symiaks continued to battle the trolls. Remus saw the bodies of many dead Symiaks on the ground. He knew that if he did not act, the rest would die. He cast a spell, sending a giant fireball into the midst of the trolls. The effect was instantaneous.

A group of four trolls were hit by the fireball and caught fire like dry kindling, running around in panic. Each troll they touched caught fire as well. Within seconds, the trolls were running away from the fire in all directions. Some ran into the barrier, turning to stone. The rest returned to the Darkwood.

The Symiaks were stunned as Remus rode over to them. Dead and dying Symiaks littered the ground. A quick count told him that about three hundred had been lost.

He stopped in front of a blood covered Grunch. 'What were you thinking?'

The Symiak glared at Remus. 'Why you not help us?'

Remus raised an eyebrow. 'I *did* help with the fireball. That's why the trolls ran away.'

Grunch shook his head. 'You wait until many die, then you help.'

'You led your Symiaks into battle without waiting to see if we were coming. We stayed back where it was safe. You should have waited.'

'Symiaks brave and strong,' Grunch replied, thrusting his club into the air, causing the rest to hoot and stomp their feet.

You are strong and stupid, Remus thought, but he said, 'The three armies need to work together or no gifts for you.'

'Him not help,' Grunch said, pointing behind him.

Remus turned to see Zachary coming with the royal guard, who stopped beside Remus.

Grunch leaned forward, jabbing a finger into Zachary's chest. 'Why you not help Symiaks?'

He slapped the creature's hand away. 'Do not touch me, you oaf. Only a fool would have done what you did.'

Both Zachary and Grunch glared at each other defiantly as soldiers and Symiaks readied for battle. Remus could feel the tension building between them and needed to do something before things got out of hand. 'Zachary, return to your men and take the royal guard with you.'

'You dare?' Zachary asked as Remus put himself in between him and Grunch.

The royal guard formed a semicircle behind their king. Remus saw the Symiaks readying their weapons. He would have liked to see the creatures kill Zachary and the royal guard, but that would wait until Sanctuary.

He leaned into Zachary. 'Thousands of Symiaks are about to kill you and your royal guard.'

'Then my men will slaughter them.'

Remus sighed. 'Then you will die without seeing Oriel's riches, and your daughter will be an orphan. You are this close'—Remus said, holding his thumb and forefinger half an inch apart—'to having everything that you came for. Within days, I promise you, will get what you deserve.'

Zachary nodded before leading his royal guard back to his army, and Remus walked his mount to Grunch. 'You do not want gifts, so return to your homes.'

Grunch snarled. 'Symiaks want gifts now.'

Remus slapped his own forehead. 'Then march to Sanctuary and get them. Do not attack unless I tell you to. My way is better; you will have gifts and Sanctuary after Sanctuary.'

Grunch nodded before yelling out in his guttural language and the Symiaks began to hoot and dance. Remus shook his head as he rode away. He needed to reach Oriel before everything fell apart.

***

Iguchi stood three hundred yards away from the Darkwood. He watched as the enemy moved away from the battle with the trolls. His Angels had left a trail along the border of the Darkwood before hiding in grassland nearby. They had waited through the night and morning for the enemy to arrive.

'That was a good fight,' Michael said.

Iguchi nodded. 'You are getting better. You are walking very quietly.'

'Do you think many died?'

Iguchi shook his head. 'Many died, but not enough.'

Michael and Iguchi ran back to the Fallen Angels, where they waited until night-time before tracking the combined army. A few hours after dark, they saw the distant fires.

'Bring your horns; we have work tonight,' Iguchi said.

***

Remus and Zachary agreed to triple sentries and were confident that alarms would be raised if the enemy were to attack. In addition, there were groups of soldiers and Symiaks walking around holding torches. They would not be caught by surprise again.

***

Halfway through the night, the camp was quiet, and most were sleeping. Then a horn blew to the south of the camp. People called out in alarm as the patrols ran to the sentries to see if they were tied to stakes. Men and Symiaks alike scrambled out of their tents, searching for danger.

Remus stormed out of his tent, flanked by Beta and Omega, to a sea of madness: soldiers and Symiaks running around without purpose. The three captains walked over to him.

'We need order in this camp. Send patrols out to see what they can find.'

They moved away as Zachary came up to Remus with his royal guard fighting for breath. 'What's happening?'

Remus glared at him. 'Your men are running around like frightened children. They need to find the one who blew the horn.'

Zachary nodded and moved away with the royal guard as eight red wizards walked over to Remus. 'Light up the sky.'

As the red wizards turned night into day, Remus watched the camp and men and Symiaks searched for someone who could not be found.

Reports came back that the entire area surrounding the camp had been searched and nothing was found. Zachary and Remus spoke and agreed that the camp should rest once more.

***

An hour later, the horn blew again from a different area. Again, men and Symiaks raced from their tents to find the source. This time, they were more organised. After an hour of searching, they could find no-one.

The horn sounded two more times in the early hours of the morning.

The sun rose in the east. The camp walked out of their tents with bloodshot eyes, every second person from the kingdom army yawning. Zachary and Grunch sat in Remus' tent. 'How far to the nearest town?' Remus asked.

'Turtha is twenty miles to the north.'

'We need to put a stop to this. As we march, we will send patrols miles in every direction as we travel. This will flush out the enemy.'

Remus knew that if they were harassed every night, they would be useless at Sanctuary.

***

At the time of the meeting in Remus' tent, Iguchi ran to where the Fallen Angels waited for him. A smile grew on his face knowing that his plan of burning the men and blowing the horns had worked. He knew the army would panic every time they heard the horns. No-one from the enemy camp needed to die that night—hearing the horns and worrying who was going to die was enough. They only needed to hear the horns.

The Fallen Angels lay in tall grass five miles from the enemy camp. Iguchi had sent two Angels out at a time to blow the horn and then return. He knew that once the fear of the unknown had spread through the camp, it would be hard to reverse its effects.

***

Ramulas and Oriel stood on the balcony of the throne room looking at the tunnel leading to her cavern. 'How far are they away from here?'

Oriel did not need to ask who 'they' were; she knew he was referring to the combined armies. 'They will arrive at Turtha tonight, and within two days, they will be at our gate.'

Ramulas sighed. 'The time has finally come. This is our time to be tested. If we cannot stop the Legion …'

'Then everyone in Sanctuary will die, including me,' Oriel said. 'Then Remus will move across the kingdom killing and enslaving the people.'

'I need to talk to the people, to let them know all of their training has come to this moment.'

Then two carts crashed outside the tunnel and a realisation hit Ramulas like a runaway horse. 'Two days. We need to get you out of the cavern before they arrive.'

Ramulas raced out of the throne room.

***

Ramulas walked through the tunnel with a purpose. He noticed while walking how long it was and gave polite nods to the workers as he passed. He was greeted by Edwin at the end of the tunnel.

'Hello, me lord. Yer lookin' worried.'

Ramulas sighed. 'The Legion will be here in two days. I need to know how long until Oriel is free.'

Royce and Shayne stepped away from the wall they were working on. Their transformation was complete—they were now beings of living stone with burning red eyes.

'We do not know how much more we need to dig; we just feel that we are getting very close to her,' Royce said.

Shayne smiled. 'We can feel that we are closer to her every day.'

Ramulas clenched his fists in frustration. He knew they were doing the best they could—asking them to do more would be pointless. He forced a smile. 'You have been trying your best, and I thank you for your work.'

Ramulas walked away hoping she would be free in time; he did not want to think what would happen if this was not the case.

***

Ramulas wasn't the only one who watched the digging with interest. Nathaniel moved to the side as the Lord of Sanctuary walked by in the tunnel. He was unseen in his astral form. He could feel that the earth elementals were so close to him and Oriel, it almost drove him mad.

His powers had been returning with Oriel's growing magic. When she was released, he would be free, and then he would find the ones who stole his weapons. They would be the first of many to die. Once he had his weapons, Nathaniel would see how powerful the Lord of Sanctuary really was.

***

Remus and Zachary sat inside Remus' tent outside the walls of Turtha. The daytime patrols had found no trace of the enemy. The entire camp had wrapped itself around the town's walls. The warlords and red wizards had spent the day setting magical wards around the camp. If a horn sounded, or someone entered the camp, that area would light up and hold them. The sentries were pulled back from their position. They were to be the first to attack any intruders.

'Will this work?' Zachary asked.

Remus nodded. 'Anything that disturbs the wards will be shown and caught. Anyone affected by the wards will glow in the night, easier for us to kill.'

Zachary nodded, knowing a surprise waited for anyone who dared come to the camp that night.

The sun had begun to drop over the Devil's Ridge Mountains, and fires dotted the camp. Soldier and Symiak alike knew about the wards and what needed to be done. They also knew this gave them an extra sense of security. However, the events of the last two nights kept the camp on edge.

***

Miles walked with Iguchi, Benji, and Michael a mile north of the camp. The three Angels each held a horn and had left the others to rest a few miles away. Then Michael stopped the group with a raised hand.

'What's wrong?' Benji whispered.

'There is a faint light surrounding the camp. Don't you see it?'

'Is it the fires?' Miles asked.

Michael shook his head. 'No, not the fires. The outside of the camp has blue lights. They look like walls. I do not like this.'

Iguchi grunted. 'Then we will not go. We must trust our instincts—this is how we survive.'

Benji turned to his friend. 'What do you see?'

Miles studied the camp for a minute before his eyes glazed over and he went stiff. A minute later he gasped, turned—and ran straight into Michael before falling to the ground. Benji looked down at his friend in sadness. Every time Miles had a vision, it took something from him.

Miles sat up with wide eyes. 'Don't go to the camp; it's a trap. If we go near the lights, they will kill us.'

Iguchi nodded. 'This is good. We will rest tonight and strike tomorrow.'

Benji nodded. 'I survived the Druid's labyrinth using my instincts.'

Miles looked at his friend with his mouth open. He had travelled with Benji for years with only a few words about his ordeal. Now it looked like Benji was finally about to tell his story.

Benji looked across the night-time sky with a faraway expression. 'I woke up in the middle of the maze with a sprite flying above me. I had no sword, shield, or armour. The sprite said she would help me through the maze and find items to assist me. She explained that the druids had placed me in the maze for sport—they would watch as I fought my way out of the mazes or died trying.

'After two days, I had found armour and weapons and had fought some of the foulest creatures you could imagine. Then I was captured and placed in a cell within a large dungeon. The sprite had gone, and I was alone with the monsters, who were locked up as well.'

Benji shuddered before continuing. 'Two demons as big as Lodi, full of teeth and claws, came for me the next day and threw me into a small arena with five goblins. I was given a sword and shield—they each held crude spears. I looked up to see fifty druids in seats surrounding the arena. We were told that this was a bout to the death.

'The goblins attacked straight away, but I managed to kill them and was brought back to my cell.

'Each day I was brought out to fight different creatures. When you hear the demons coming for you, you know that you are going to fight for your life again. Fear grips your heart because you do not want to die.

'After a few days of killing, that fear leaves you. I found myself pacing my cell, wanting to kill more creatures. You see death as a way of escape. As the fights to the death continued, I gained the trust of the druids, who came for me instead of the demons.

'Then, one day after killing a Symiak, I collapsed to the ground and I saw how they disposed of the bodies: there was a chute to the side, and the body was pushed into it. After a week of watching and planning, I made my escape.

'I fought against a giant spider in the arena. Its feet were covered in cloth to prevent it from climbing the walls. During the fight, I concentrated on cutting away these cloths, and soon it went over the wall and attacked the druids.

'I dived into the chute and found my way to the surface.'

Benji lost his faraway expression.

'Let us go to the other Angels and rest,' Iguchi said.

23

Ramulas sat on his throne. Pip, Oriel, Rygar, and Shigar stood before him. Owain, the druids, and K'ayden had just entered the throne room. Word had quickly spread that the Legion would arrive the following day. People had gathered in the courtyard, waiting for the Lord of Sanctuary to address them.

'As you all know,' Ramulas began, 'the enemy will be here tomorrow sometime. I want no training today. I want the people to celebrate what they have here.'

He had rehearsed what he was going to say and was happy that they agreed with him. 'Is everyone ready, and do they know what their roles are?'

Everyone nodded.

'Iguchi and his Fallen Angels are harassing the enemy as they come. This will make them tired.'

Rygar spoke. 'We might have a small problem. Only half o' the people fought in the last battle. The others will be new to this.'

'But you have been training them,' Ramulas said.

The dwarf nodded. 'Ye can teach a man to kill an' show him who he needs to kill, but to do that killin' is a different thing.'

Ramulas knew this to be true. All the training in the world would be useless if the person was unwilling to fight when the time came.

***

Ramulas walked out onto the balcony holding Jacqueline's hand. Kate and Grace followed. Pip and Oriel stood on either side of the family. A roar erupted from the people below as they came out. After a few seconds, he raised his hands for silence.

'As you all have heard, the Legion will arrive tomorrow. With them is the kingdom army, which we defeated before.'

Another cheer rose from the crowd.

He raised his hands once more. 'Thousands of Symiaks have also joined them, which makes twelve thousand marching for our home.'

The people of Sanctuary looked up in stunned silence.

'But we have learned from the mistakes that we made last time. I have watched you train, and you are better than I could have hoped. The Legion will be in for a surprise when they come to our home. I see everyone here as a member of my family and will do everything that I can to keep you safe.'

He pointed down into the sea of people. 'Are you going to allow them to come and take everything that we have fought for?' Ramulas shouted.

'No!' the crowd roared.

'What will we do when the enemy comes to our doorstep?'

'Fight!' they roared.

Ramulas felt a warm sensation explode in the pit of his stomach and allowed it to flow through him, holding his hands high. Purple flames covered his arms and arcs of energy danced between his hands.

'Let them come. We will give them a beating they will never forget,' he said as the crowd erupted into a frenzy.

Ramulas watched as his people danced around feeding off each other's energy. 'Today will be a day of celebration. Spend time with your friends and family and celebrate how far we have come. Tomorrow, we will show them the error of their ways.'

***

Iguchi stood in the darkness with Michael, Benji, and Miles. They watched the enemy camp a mile away. The Fallen Angels had stayed ahead of the enemy as they came toward Sanctuary. The camp was three miles from the edge of Sanctuary's forest and Michael pointed out the thin blue walls of light.

'This time there are not as many. I can see a few areas that we can walk through,' Michael said.

Iguchi nodded. 'Last night, we did not trouble them. They have false confidence that the walls of light protect them. Gather the other Angels; we have work to do.'

Michael led the Fallen Angels through the magical walls. They came across a lone sentry who stifled a yawn looking out into the darkness. A few patrols carrying torches walked through the tents. The rest of the camp was quiet.

The Angels spread throughout the camp, entering tents. They knew what needed to be done. Michael was the only Angel who did not participate, and Iguchi took his place. Michael waited for the Angels to finish.

Ten minutes later, they started to make their way to Michael, and everyone wore a grim expression. Their work was harsh but necessary. Michael led them from the camp and into the forest where horses were waiting for them.

A mile from the camp, Benji and Miles both pulled out their horns. Iguchi nodded to the rest of the Fallen Angels, who ran to the trees. Benji counted to one hundred before blowing his horn, followed by Miles, before they ran after their companions.

***

The horns shattered the night's silence. A ward flared in the north of the camp and sentries raced to see who was there. Remus stormed out of his tent, followed by his warlords; their faces showed no emotion.

They turned to the north. Seeing one of the wards had been activated, orders could be heard through the camp as soldier and Symiak moved north.

Then came the first scream of terror.

Remus' head snapped in the direction of the scream, and from what he could gather, a kingdom soldier had been killed in his tent. Blood still flowed from his neck, meaning it was a fresh kill. Before Remus had time to react, calls of alarm and panic spread throughout the camp as more bodies were found.

Remus began to shake as fury welled up inside. How had the enemy got past the wards into the camp?

'Silence!' Remus shouted with a spell that amplified his voice.

Every soldier and Symiak focused on him. 'Men have been killed in this camp during the night. I want all their bodies brought before me. I want to see how this was done.'

The camp exploded into a flurry of action as the search went on for those who were murdered. Zachary walked out of his tent with his royal guard.

'My men have been murdered while they slept,' the king said in anger. 'Treachery by the Symiaks. I say we attack them now.'

Remus rolled his eyes. 'And how convenient for them to blow horns to tell us of their deeds. If the Symiaks had killed your men, they would do it in silence.'

Zachary was at a loss for words as the bodies were laid before him and Remus.

***

One hundred bodies lay before Remus and Zachary—fifty kingdom soldiers and fifty Legion soldiers. But there was not one dead Symiak. Remus inspected the dead and found that each had their throat cut or was stabbed in the heart. These were not the wounds from any Symiak.

The next issue would be to find out how the enemy made it past the magical wards, killed one hundred, and left without a trace. Remus organised for every person who was in those tents to come see him, Zachary, and the three captains of the Legion.

The warlords stood behind Remus as the kingdom and Legion soldiers told their stories, all stating the same thing—they were unaware that something was wrong until they woke. This surprised Remus—for someone to enter a Legion tent, kill one of them, and leave undetected was a feat. He had underestimated the enemy.

By the time everyone had been questioned, it was three hours before dawn and the bodies still needed to be buried. From what Zachary had told Remus, it was only a day's travel until Sanctuary. He needed his men to have as much energy as possible and ordered the camp to rest.

Zachary turned to Remus. 'Is it wise to rest again? They might come back and attack again.'

Remus shook his head. 'They would have attacked already. The men need rest, or we will be fighting half asleep.'

Remus shook his head. Having Zachary and the Symiaks was like dealing with children. What he wanted was to find those responsible for causing unrest in their camp.

***

The Fallen Angels rode into Sanctuary and found Pip, Ramulas, and Rygar waiting for them. The Angels were sent to their quarters with a wave of Iguchi's hand.

'Hello to you, Lord of Sanctuary,' Iguchi said, climbing down from his horse. 'How did you know we were coming through the night?'

'The dryads told me. Come inside and we will talk.'

Iguchi looked around at the deserted streets. It would be a few hours until dawn. He hoped the people of Sanctuary would have enough rest before the battle.

Iguchi walked into the throne room. 'The three armies come today. They are tired and angry.'

'What happened?' Ramulas asked.

Iguchi outlined how the Angels had harassed the enemy from the great lake to the border of the forest and finished by saying the Angels were sent to rest.

'We all need rest. The dryads will tell when the enemy comes close,' Ramulas said.

***

As the sun rose, the kingdom and Legion soldiers buried their men in long trenches dug by the giant crabs—Legion soldiers in one and kingdom soldiers in the other. There were no ceremonies or speeches, just a few quick words before the soil covered the bodies.

Remus wanted to reach Sanctuary that day. The sooner he arrived, the sooner he would have Oriel's power. He also looked forward to the kingdom soldiers and Symiaks dying.

The camp was ready to march, and the combined armies walked through the last of the grasslands. Zachary and Remus led them into the forest.

Zachary turned to Remus. 'At the end of this road is Sanctuary. It will take us a few hours to reach it.'

With a wave of his hand, Remus sent scouts down the road as two scores of dryads watched from the trees. They wanted to attack this force, but now was not the time. They needed to tell the people of Sanctuary.

***

The sound of a bell rang through Sanctuary. People froze and looked up to the castle. Another bell sounded and everyone exploded into action. They had trained for months for this day. Each person knew what their role was and ran to their station ready for battle.

Ramulas heard the first bell in his quarters. He kissed his wife and girls before embracing them. 'I want you all to stay here.'

Grace's eyes lit up. 'Da, can I be the boss?'

'Yes,' Ramulas replied as he ran into the hallway.

The second bell sounded as he came into the throne room. Oriel stood at the window looking at the mountain. 'Welcome, Ramulas,' she said without turning.

'They are in the forest and will be here soon.'

Oriel turned to face him, and it cut Ramulas to the core seeing the fear and sadness on her face. It felt like a dagger in his stomach. 'What's wrong?'

'I wanted to be free before Remus arrived, but that will not happen. He will capture me…'

Before Oriel could finish, Ramulas raced out of the room.

***

The Lord of Sanctuary raced out into the courtyard. People filled the streets in armour and carrying weapons; others manned the supplies. Women hugged their husbands and sons before the battle, and everyone could be heard wishing loved ones good luck.

People gave him slight nods as he passed on his way to the tunnel. At the end, he found Edwin and the elementals hard at work. 'The enemy has entered the forest.'

The dwarf smiled. 'We know. We heard ye bell.'

Ramulas looked at the wall and his heart sank. They had gone a few feet deeper but had not reached Oriel. He knew they were doing all they could to reach her. 'I have faith in you. I know that you will do your best.'

As Ramulas walked away, the trio redoubled their efforts on the tunnel.

***

Coming out of the tunnel, Ramulas noticed lines of people making their way to the rear of the town. He followed them and soon found out where they were going. The people slowly filed past the statues of the fallen, asking for help in the coming battle. The magical flame above the altar had grown to twice its size.

He saw Pip with Emily watching the people as well. He was surprised that he had not seen Emily in a while and wondered what she had been doing as he walked over to them.

'Look at them,' Pip said, nodding to the people as they walked by the statues. He glanced across and instantly knew what she meant. As the people filed past the fallen, their chests swelled with pride and their eyes lit up. This was giving the people hope and faith in themselves.

Ramulas turned to Emily. 'Bad people are coming here today. I want you to stay safe.'

As he spoke, he thought it strange to tell someone as powerful as Emily to stay safe, but he could still see the child inside.

'I don't like bad people,' Emily said before walking away.

Pip sighed. 'There is a lot to be done.'

'I know. For now, stay by my side.'

'The hell hounds?'

'They are in the castle. They will protect our families. Shigar and the druids will help us with the Legion.'

Pip nodded and followed him to the wall.

***

Ten archers rode out of Sanctuary, followed by Iguchi and the Fallen Angels. Ramulas knew that these groups would be preparing surprises for the enemy as they came closer. Companies of soldiers began to form into columns on either side of the courtyard as barricades were pulled into the street, making it hard for the enemy if they entered Sanctuary.

The barriers were made of wood and stone, six feet high and ten feet long. If the Legion and kingdom soldiers made it through the maze, they would have to navigate through this while fending off attacks. Every inch of ground would be paid for in blood.

Buckets of water dotted areas near the wall, manned by boys who would run to any who needed it. Cooking fires were started, and food prepared—Rygar had said that it was better to fight on a full stomach.

A sharp intake of breath caused Ramulas to look at Pip. Her mouth hung open and her eyes were wide in shock. He followed her gaze and said, 'Oh no.'

***

Zachary and Remus had been leading the combined armies for half an hour. The scouts returned twice to say that the way ahead was clear. The forest went quiet. Birds that were singing suddenly went quiet. Legion soldiers saw movement in the trees, and then the kingdom soldiers reported the sightings as well.

Lone figures would appear from behind trees and run to another. Soldiers would give chase only to find no trace of anyone. However, when the sightings were made, it was only one or two soldiers who saw them and called out the alarm. After five minutes, the column stopped, and soldiers were ordered to search both sides of the forest.

'Did this happen the last time you came to Sanctuary?' Remus asked Zachary.

The king shook his head. 'We were attacked closer to Sanctuary. I have not seen anyone in the trees.'

'Your men and mine have seen movement. We will flush them out,' Remus said before turning and speaking softly to Redemption. A moment later, arrows were fired into the trees. They waited a minute to see if there was any reaction. When there was not, Remus gave the signal to move on.

'We have either killed or scared those in the forest,' Remus said.

****

The dryads stood inside the trees, watching as the enemy slowly made their way to Sanctuary. They now knew how long it would take for them to get there. This would help when they attacked them later.

****

Lodi walked along the top of the wall, holding a huge boulder almost as big as he was over his head. As the giant walked, he swayed from side to side, looking as if he would fall at any moment. The archers on the wall moved out of the way.

Ramulas and Pip raced up the stairs as fast as they could. Lodi had almost reached the cliff on the right-hand side when they caught up with him.

'Lodi, what are you doing with that rock?' Ramulas asked.

The giant quickly turned and almost lost his balance. The rock swayed more violently, forcing Lodi to drop it into the clearing. He looked at the fallen rock, then at Ramulas and Pip. 'I didn't do nothing with the rock,' Lodi said, eyes wide in fear. 'It was already there.'

Pip tapped Ramulas on the elbow and pointed behind the giant where there were three other rocks stacked in the corner.

'Are those your rocks, Lodi?' Ramulas asked.

The giant's mouth opened as he stepped sideways trying to hide the rocks. 'I didn't see any rocks. I didn't do nothing with them.'

Pip smiled. 'Are you going to throw the rocks at the enemy when they come?'

Lodi nodded. 'I will squash them.' Then he realised his mistake and covered his mouth with his hands, his eyes wide in terror. 'Not to tell Rygar.'

Ramulas nodded. 'It will be our secret. But no more rocks on the wall. I will let you throw the ones on the wall.'

***

Owain walked over to Ramulas and Pip as Lodi left the wall. 'I am happy the giant has left so we can prepare.'

'He is just trying to help. When the Legion arrives, let Lodi throw his rocks. They think he is dead—this will unnerve them.'

The blind archer nodded. 'I understand. '

'How are things on the wall?'

Owain waved to a pot of iron ore hanging over a fire. Forty such pots lined the wall. He explained that they had twice as many as last time and would be used in two waves—they would expect the first but not the second. Quivers full of arrows were piled near archers, and each archer had one of the exploding spears made by Rygar. The druids had taught them how to handle the arrows covered in bubbles.

Ramulas looked out into the forest, wondering how Iguchi and the Fallen Angels were.

24

Iguchi and the Fallen Angels stood by the trees on the side of the road as the sun streamed through the trees. They were almost invisible with their camouflaged uniforms and faces. Iguchi had given each of the Angels a small green seed and showed how it could be chewed and then send out a stream of green mist. This could travel five feet and surprise the enemy. They were told to use it wisely to win the battle.

Iguchi left his Fallen Angels and ran up the hill to the platform where the archers were waiting, his bright blue vest quickly vanishing in the thick foliage. Each group of archers had a lantern.

Iguchi waved to the archers. 'When you see my signal, light your arrows on the lantern and shoot at the road. You must leave after this and block the path behind you when you leave. This will cause them much grief.'

Iguchi inspected each platform, ensuring they were ready. 'You need to rest until you see the enemy pass below you, then wait for the signal.'

The archers nodded and Iguchi ran back down to his Angels.

***

Joshua and Rain stood in the middle of the empty courtyard. Both were eager for the enemy to arrive and then they would enter the maze to fight any soldiers or Symiaks they found. Joshua swung his iron ball in lazy circles by his side while Rain held his sword before him, a wall of mist cascading to the ground.

213

'We have hours before they come,' Rain said.

Joshua growled while shrugging. 'I don't care, as long as we are in the maze before them.'

Rain glanced to where Joshua nodded and saw both half-giants, each holding a large broad sword. A bet had been wagered to see which duo could kill most of the enemy.

***

Iguchi froze and cocked his head. A moment later, the sound of hooves could be heard coming down the road. Six riders slowly trotted passed the Fallen Angels. There were three kingdom soldiers and three Legion soldiers.

The scouts scanned the forest as they rode by the Fallen Angels, who could have reached out to touch the horses. However, Iguchi did not give the signal, and the scouts were allowed to live.

The Fallen Angels saw the darkened eyes from lack of sleep and could smell stale sweat from the six as they passed. Their harassment had taken a toll.

***

The scouts arrived at the edge of the clearing and looked up at the wall of Sanctuary. Sanctuary's archers had their bows trained on them. The scouts moved their horses back up the road leading into the forest.

'You are bad men,' Emily said as she stepped out of the forest.

All six soldiers were startled by the appearance of this young girl. Then one of the Legion soldiers laughed, which broke the spell. A kingdom soldier joined the laughter, waving at her. 'Run along, child.'

'Leave now, or you will die screaming,' Emily said.

They were all shocked at not only what she said but at the calm way she spoke. Then one of the Legion soldiers climbed down from his horse and walked to Emily with a cold smile.

The irises of Emily's eyes turned black, and her hair danced on end as dark energies crackled around her. The nearby trees shook violently as a cold wind came from the forest.

Oblivious to the danger, the Legion soldier came forward pulling out his red-bladed dagger. With a thought, Emily transformed the weapon. One moment the soldier was holding a dagger and the next he held a very angry red metal spider, which began to attack his hand.

He screamed as he shook his hand frantically trying to dislodge the spider, but it held on and continued to bite into his hand, causing blood to flow to the ground. The other scouts did not see what had happened until he turned. The two Legion soldiers jumped to the ground to assist him.

Emily's arms shot out and dark energies flowed from her hands into the two Legion soldiers. They screamed as their bodies danced a few inches from the ground and they were cooked from the inside. By the time their burnt bodies fell to the ground, the red spider had made its way up to the soldier's neck. Blood spurted from open wounds as he fell to his knees on the grass.

The kingdom soldiers had seen enough—they turned their horses to see the road behind blocked by a score of dryads. The three screamed in horror at the creatures before them. Creatures that seemed half-man and half-tree watched the kingdom soldiers, who attempted to find a way back to their army.

The three soldiers screamed at seeing the creatures before them. A buzzing was heard a second before Tilly burst from the trees holding her short sword. 'Get out of our home.'

The sight of a sprite—a two-foot-tall mythical creature holding a sword against three armed soldiers—would have been comical, but they were truly terrified. Each of the dryads raised their right hand towards them and made a fist. The horses collapsed under the hail of darts shot by the dryads.

The three kingdom soldiers were thrown off the horses as more dryads rushed from the trees to grab hold of them. Their eyes were wide in terror and were too scared to talk or even move. Vice-like hands held them in place while thirty dryads surrounded them, and they did not look happy.

Eady stepped forward. 'Why have you entered our home?'

One of the soldiers opened his mouth but was unable to talk. Then Eady nodded. 'We need only one to bring back the message.'

The soldier on the right was released by all but one dryad, who ran, dragging the screaming soldier halfway into a tree before releasing him. The soldier's scream was cut short when his body exploded on the side of the tree, sending blood and body parts across the forest floor. The coppery taste of blood hung in the air, quickly overriding the damp earthy fragrance of the forest.

Seeing the way their colleague died, the remaining two screamed for mercy while struggling to break free. Eady smiled without compassion. 'What mercy would you have shown those in Sanctuary?'

The second soldier was pulled screaming into another tree, trying to grab at the foliage and roots before he exploded in a shower of gore. Eady walked up to the remaining soldier. She smiled while stroking his cheek with the back of her hand. He flinched at the texture of her rough skin against his.

Her smile vanished, replaced with a look of disdain as she pulled her hand away and slapped him hard across the cheek. His eyes widened as he felt minute things crawling under his skin.

Eady smiled. 'The bugs under your skin will burrow their way into your heart. The only way to remove them is through fire. If you try to cut them out, they will poison your blood and kill you. Go tell your army to leave.

The soldier was released and ran screaming hysterically down the road.

***

Iguchi and the Fallen Angels heard the screaming as he ran towards them. When he passed, Iguchi spoke to his Angels. 'I have spoken with Oriel the spirit of the dragon. She has warned me of the Legion. Do not allow them to take you alive. They will give you a slow and painful death.

'It is a game for them to see how long they can keep you alive. We are fighting an enemy that will not stop until they have destroyed everything in this world.'

The Fallen Angels nodded, knowing this would be a life-or-death situation.

***

The kingdom soldier ran screaming around the bend of the road, falling over and kicking up a cloud of dust. Zachary and Remus stopped their horses while the royal guard formed a protective circle around them. The soldier fell to his knees in front of Lucas and begged for help as the left side of his face bled. Lucas ignored him while searching the road behind the man.

When he was confident that no-one else was coming, he looked down at the scout from his horse. 'Tell me what happened.'

The soldier absently touched his face with panic in his eyes. 'Monsters in the forest,' was all he could say before he felt the bugs burrow down to his neck. The soldier's eyes bulged. 'Get them out of me. I'm going to die. I need fire to kill them,' he screamed while clawing at his neck.

A thin stream of fire shot past Lucas to hit the soldier in his face. The captain of the royal guard looked back in shock to see Remus lower his hand. 'That could have hit me.'

Remus ignored Lucas, watching the scout holding the burnt side of his face as he calmed down. 'It did not hit you, though. We need him calm for questioning.'

The following columns came to a stop. Remus made signals to his captains before continuing. 'Now that he is calm, King Zachary and I can talk to him.'

Zachary rode forward, stopping in front of the scout. 'Where are the others?'

The scout looked up at Zachary with wide, frantic eyes. 'There was a small girl in the forest with dark magic, and so many creatures coming from the trees.'

'What did the creatures do?' Zachary asked.

'They did terrible things …' he said before losing his sanity. The scout began to laugh on his knees. His body convulsed as the laughter became maniacal.

Zachary turned as Remus pulled his horse next to his. 'Your soldier has seen more than his mind can handle. His behaviour will spread throughout the camp.'

A beam of light shot from Remus' hand and the soldier shuddered once before he collapsed.

Zachary looked at Remus. 'You killed my man.'

'No. He sleeps. He would have lowered morale. He will wake later. Put him into a wagon.'

Remus and Zachary turned to see kingdom soldiers with uncertain expressions. They had witnessed the scout's behaviour and were concerned.

Remus forced a smile and waved to them. 'The people of Sanctuary are scared. They dress as creatures of the forest to frighten us like children. My warlords and red wizards will protect you from this trickery.' Remus swept his hand around the forest. 'The people of Sanctuary know we are coming, and they fear us.'

The kingdom soldiers cheered.

***

The front column of the enemy passed below the archer's platforms; the archers silently watched as the first column of kingdom soldiers rode by, scanning the thick foliage and trees on either side of the road. The sounds of marching feet and wagons squeaking travelled up to the platforms. They recognised King Zachary with his royal guard riding with a man wearing a red robe.

They waited for Iguchi's signal while holding their bows and special arrows ready. They watched in awe as the soldiers kept marching past their position, with wagons, machines of war, supply wagons, and strange-looking horses.

They marvelled at the differences in the two armies. The kingdom soldiers walked while the Legion soldiers seemed to march as a single unit, each step taken simultaneously.

From what Iguchi had told them, the main supply wagons would be somewhere in the middle. The urge to fire their arrows was almost overwhelming, and yet they waited for Iguchi.

*****

The archers saw the flash of red cloth through the trees, then came about thirty large wagons down the road. They all nocked arrows and waited. A minute later, the wagons were passing by. Clay pots full of lamp oil were thrown from the trees onto the wagons. They broke on contact with a crash.

The archers dipped their arrowheads into their lamps to light them. They lifted their flaming arrows as calls for alarm were made by the enemy army. Legion soldiers searched the forest as the archers fired their arrows.

The arrows fell in slow, lazy arcs before hitting the wagons covered in oil.

Five wagons in the middle burst into flames with enough force that it shook the surrounding trees, and people called for the fires to be put out. The archers let their second lot of arrows fly, hitting wagons not yet alight. The enemy now saw the archer platforms, and orders were given to kill them.

A wall of flame had leapt up from the wagons, sending plumes of dark smoke curling towards the sky. The smell of the oil and material burning drifted up the hill. Men and Symiaks were forced back by the intense heat, the other wagons were pulled away, and horses cut from their traces to run from the flames.

Like red and black ants, the Legion soldiers swarmed up the hill towards the platforms, followed by kingdom soldiers and Symiaks. The enemy cut paths through the foliage. The archers climbed onto their horses and rode down the path to Sanctuary as if a horde of demons were chasing them. They steered with their knees, holding their bows and searching for the enemy.

After a minute, they arrived at the place where they would block the path. One archer stopped as the others rode on. He hacked at the rope holding the logs and rocks. As the rope broke and the logs fell with a rumbling sound, he saw several Legion soldiers coming.

He climbed onto his horse and rode with a smile on his face. The Legion soldiers had begun to climb over as he rode, but it would slow them down enough for the archers to ride home safely.

***

They rode through the gate of Sanctuary to be met by Ramulas on his warhorse. 'Did it go well?'

'It did,' one of them said. 'Man, they were fast coming up the hill.'

'Did you do much damage?' Ramulas asked.

The archers turned and pointed to a column of black smoke rising in the forest behind them. 'We helped their wagons catch fire,' one said.

Ramulas watched the smoke rise, hoping that Iguchi and the Fallen Angels were faring well.

25

Iguchi watched as the first volley of arrows sailed down to ignite the wagons. A wall of flame leapt up, sending soldiers of the Legion into a panic. They ran from the flames while calling out in alarm for people to help. He knew that his Fallen Angels would be breathing shallowly to avoid choking on the dense smoke coming from the nearby fires.

As the second volley of arrows came down, the Legion saw the archers on the platforms. Orders were called out and the soldiers stormed up the hill eagerly. All eyes were focused on the archer platforms.

Iguchi nodded and stepped forward out of the trees with his Angels. Each of the Angels silently walked behind a Legion soldier. Benji winked at Miles and Michael before casually walking to stand next to a Legion soldier.

'Nice fire,' Benji said with a smile.

The soldier jumped in shock and pulled out his sword. Benji rushed forward, thrusting his sword through the soldier's neck. He pulled the blade out and danced away from the blood as calls of attackers rang out. Iguchi and the Fallen Angels cut down another one hundred Legion soldiers.

And the element of surprise was gone.

Legion soldiers formed columns, holding shields in front of their bodies and swords over the shields. Iguchi pulled his Angels past the burning wagons, leaving only enough room for them to come through one at a time to attack between the burning wagons.

Iguchi and the Fallen Angels formed a semicircle with their backs to the trees. Several Legion soldiers rushed through the gap, only to die by the Angel's swords. Bodies began to pile in front of the Angels. Out of the corner of his eye, Iguchi saw a man in red robes floating towards them.

'We must go to the gully,' he called before running into the trees.

The Fallen Angels turned as one and followed. Forty Angels sprinted ahead while Iguchi and the remaining ten ran at a slower pace. Iguchi looked back in mock terror as he saw the pursuers charging through the trees. Birds flew from the trees with calls of alarm as the Fallen Angels ran through the forest.

'We must hurry,' he called out loudly. 'We have come the wrong way. We are surely doomed if they catch us. We will die.'

Benji and Miles took the hint and fell over each other near a grove of trees. The rest of the Angels slowed down to pick them up. This had the desired effect as the Legion soldiers howled with rage seeing their enemy so close.

Iguchi knew that the Legion soldiers wanted blood. He would give it to them deeper in the forest.

***

The red wizards and warlords were at the rear of the Legion columns when shouts of alarm and smoke rose into the sky five hundred yards ahead. Omega cast a spell and floated towards the chaos. He could hear shouts of attackers.

He looked behind him to see the red wizards running toward the fire, pulling components out of their robes to douse the flames. To the left of the smoke, Omega smiled seeing a thin shaft of red light shooting into the sky. He knew instantly that this was the person who killed Legion soldiers in Covedon.

After finding the bodies and a message written in their blood on the wall, Remus took this as an insult. He wanted an example made of this person and cast a spell that would activate when the warlords were nearby.

Omega's hands flashed before him, and he floated higher in the air towards the beam of light. He came closer, watching eleven men running through the trees that were so well camouflaged that they were almost invisible. He saw his prey trip and fall, only to be picked up again.

After a few seconds, he lost sight of them as they disappeared into thicker forest; however, he continued to follow the shaft of red light. Once the man stopped, Omega would teach him not to disrespect the Legion.

***

Iguchi and his group continued to run through the forest at the right pace—too fast and the pursuers would lose sight of them, too slow and they would be caught. So, they ran just fast enough to give the enemy the illusion that they would soon be caught.

They came into a small gully alongside a narrow stream. The Fallen Angels ran along the banks of the stream, scores of Legion soldiers close behind howling for blood. They passed through a narrow section where cliffs on both sides were covered in moss and vines. After a few minutes, they came into a small clearing with cliffs all around them.

The Fallen Angels were trapped with nowhere to go. They pulled out their swords and shields as the Legion poured into the clearing. The Fallen Angels each looked around with worried expressions, searching for a way out. The Legion soldiers slowed down, seeing the Angels were trapped.

'Oh, woe is me,' Iguchi wailed. 'We have come the wrong way, and we are doomed.'

The Legion soldiers walked slowly towards the Fallen Angels, savouring their expressions of terror.

Then Benji began to laugh.

He could not help it. It started off as a giggle and the more he tried to fight it, the worse it became. He laughed so hard that he held onto his side and fell to one knee. The Legion soldiers stopped in their tracks, unable to understand this behaviour. They were used to their victims begging for mercy.

Iguchi ignored the Legion soldiers, walking in front of Benji and shaking a finger at him. 'We are supposed to fear them, and now you have hurt their feelings. Do you have anything to say to them?'

Benji stood as his expression changed from mirth to pure rage. 'You are all going to die.'

The Legion soldiers came back to their senses and took a step forward as the cliffs on either side of them exploded in movement when the other Angels came out of their hiding places. The tide had quickly turned, and the Fallen Angels took full advantage of this.

The Legion soldiers turned their attention to the Angels coming out of the cliffs. Benji and Miles led their group into the stunned soldiers while the other group attacked. To the Legion's credit, they put up a good fight against the Fallen Angels, even injuring some of them.

But they had walked into Iguchi's trap, designed to cause maximum damage with minimal losses to his Fallen Angels. An observer would have called this a slaughter more than a battle. After a minute, the remaining Legion soldiers ran away down along the stream. The Fallen Angels were surrounded by scores of dead Legion soldiers.

Omega floated down from the trees, casting a spell on Benji, who yelled as his body floated up towards the warlord. His sword and shield became extremely hot, and he dropped them. Other Fallen Angels called out for Benji and tried to grab him, but he was just out of reach.

Omega floated just above Benji, waving his hands. Benji's body stiffened as his muscles contracted. Benji pulled the seed pod out and popped it into his mouth.

Miles pointed up to the warlord. 'He's the one that will kill Benji. I saw it in a vision.'

Iguchi pulled out a small bow in a fluid motion and shot two arrows at the warlord. They were deflected half a yard away by an invisible shield.

Benji floated up to be level with Omega. His muscles had all but seized up. 'Now I have you. Remus wants you to suffer.'

Omega laughed at Benji's attempts to move his body. Then, with great effort, Benji spat a cone of green mist, hitting the warlord in the face and chest. The Fallen Angels below cheered in the small victory.

Omega looked at Benji with absolute fury while waving his hands through the air. Balls of white light surrounded Benji. Large hooks on the end of chains shot out from the light, Benji screamed as the hooks entered his body. Within seconds, twelve hooks pulled at his body. Omega smiled down at the Fallen Angels before clicking his fingers.

Omega and Benji vanished with a pop.

'Where did they go?' Miles asked.

***

Remus, Zachary, and the royal guard rode back to the burning wagons and could see the smoke rising in the distance while hearing calls from attackers for the fires to be extinguished. Lucas kept telling kingdom soldiers to move out of the way to allow them room.

One hundred yards from the burning wagons, they saw the fires dying down, with the red wizards using their spells on the fire. With each wave of their hands, a small sheet of water would be thrown into the wagons.

Remus looked at a nearby Legion soldier. 'Tell me what happened.'

The soldier explained how pots of oil were thrown from the trees onto the wagons, then flaming arrows came down from the platforms up the hill, orders were called, and soldiers ran up the hill. That was when camouflaged soldiers came out behind them and killed one hundred before anyone knew they were there. Omega and several hundred Legion soldiers had chased them into the forest a few moments earlier, and they had not returned.

Remus was fuming. He had a feeling that these were the ones who had been tormenting them on the road for the last few nights. Remus closed his eyes and held a hand out toward the forest. After a short while a smile spread on his face.

'Omega has caught the one who left us the message in Covedon. Move the wagons to the side and salvage what we can; we need to keep moving.'

A small bundle of leaves was thrown out from the trees. Remus watched it with curiosity as it arced through the air. The bundle struck a Legion soldier on the arm and unravelled. A swarm of wasps gathered around the soldier, attacking all that were nearby. People ran away waving at the wasps.

Remus was confused and looked back to where the bundle came from. To his astonishment, scores of bundles flew out from both sides of the forest. 'Beware the wasps!' Remus called out.

Everyone looked at him as the multiple bundles hit the ground. Wasps were attacking soldiers up and down the lines. Men ran around screaming while waving their hands around.

After a few moments, a line of fire shot over their heads and dead wasps fell to the ground. Red wizards shot more flames over the soldiers until the wasps were dead or disappeared. Several soldiers had swollen faces, hands, and arms from the stings.

Remus was both shocked and angered. He had never heard of someone using insects in battle before. He saw the pain and discomfort in his Legion soldiers, but they did not complain. The same could not be said for the kingdom soldiers.

Fifty yards from Remus, a creature that appeared like a walking tree stepped out onto the road. Remus was stunned and did not know what to think.

'Dryad,' Zachary whispered.

Before Remus could ask what a dryad was, the creature picked up a screaming Legion soldier as other soldiers jumped out of the way. The dryad dragged the soldier halfway into a tree before releasing him, causing a shower of blood and gore to cover those close by.

Scores of dryads stepped out of the surrounding trees. The kingdom soldiers panicked, backing away from the creatures. The Legion soldiers formed battle squares, five men by five men, with their shields facing outwards.

Remus wondered if these were the creatures the scout rambled about before he went mad. He raised his hand, sending a bolt of energy at one of the creatures. It was hit in the side and tumbled to the ground.

The dryad's response was instantaneous and brutal—four of the dryads raised their hands towards Zachary, Remus, and the royal guard, sending a wave of their poisoned darts at the group.

Remus quickly waved his hands to erect a magical shield just in time to stop the darts from hitting them. Zachary hid behind his shield as his horse was struck and fell to the ground. Three of the royal guards had also been hit. It seemed that Remus' shield only covered him and his party.

Then Remus saw the dryads attack both kingdom and Legion soldiers. The kingdom soldiers were picked off as they ran around screaming. They were brought to the trees where they died painfully. The kingdom soldiers attempted to fight back with their swords, but the dryads moved in a way that was so fluid and graceful that they could not seem to hit them.

The dryads approached the Legion battle squares in a different manner—five dryads ran at the wall of shields before leaping into the air. The Legion soldiers could only watch as the dryads landed in their midst. The creatures struck out with their hardened fists and the battle square crumbled. Soldiers were picked up and dragged into the trees.

Omega, Alpha, and the red wizards sent streams of flame at the creatures, only hitting two, these dryads ran screaming into the trees. The dryads sent wave after wave of darts at the group of magic-users. Wards and magical shields were erected, and their sole focus was to defend themselves.

This allowed the dryads to take a red wizard from the group into a tree, where he exploded after screaming for Remus to save him. The remaining magic users teleported themselves to a space next to Remus.

Remus cursed as he saw men being dragged into the trees and darts flying, and then the Symiaks came charging from the rear. He had seen the dryads run in and out of the trees, and he knew this was part of their magic. As he called the other magic-users into a circle, Remus saw two dryads grab a Symiak and sink into the ground up to their knees.

They released the Symiak and it screamed in pain, doing everything it could to escape before it exploded, and the dryads ran for their next victim. The red wizards and warlords waved their hands in tight circles while chanting. A disk of faint green light formed in the middle of the circle.

A moment later, the disk flared and shot into the sky before it exploded. Rolling waves of energy flowed through the forest up and down the road. The dryads were thrown to the ground and pulled out of the trees. Try as they might, the dryads could not enter the trees.

Remus cast a battle-lust spell over the kingdom and Legion soldiers. 'Kill them all,' he shouted.

With howls of delight, the men and Symiaks charged the stunned creatures.

***

The Fallen Angels looked up to where Benji and the warlord had vanished. They could hear faint whispers through the trees. These soon became distorted screams of pain coming from Benji begging for help. These screams drifted away from the Angels.

Miles took the lead in following the screams downstream. Iguchi stepped in front of him, placing a hand on Miles' shoulder and sadly shaking his head.

'He is alive, and he needs us,' Miles said softly.

Iguchi shook his head as his sad smile grew. 'Benji has left us and is beyond our help. His screams will be used to lure us into a trap. Use your vision to look into the future. Tell us what will happen.'

Miles blocked out the screaming, closed his eyes, and concentrated.

Miles led the Fallen Angels in formation, running along the bank of the stream and into the forest. The screams were louder and more desperate as they ran. After a minute of running, scores of Legion soldiers jumped out from behind trees. In the initial clash, ten Angels were killed, and then more Legion soldiers joined the battle.

Miles gasped as his eyes snapped open. 'They want us to follow them into an ambush where we will all die.'

Miles fought back emotions of anger and frustration as he looked to where Benji's screams came from. Michael walked up to place a hand on Miles' shoulder. 'Benji has left us. Our deaths will not bring him back.'

Miles started to shake. 'I want the one who took Benji.'

'We must follow our plan and travel back to Sanctuary,' Iguchi said.

Miles nodded and led the Fallen Angels up the moss-covered cliff. When they were in the forest once more, Iguchi held up a hand and cocked his head. The sound of men screaming in terror came through the trees. 'The dryads are attacking the enemy so that we can make it home. Do not let this be in vain.'

They raced through the forest until they came to the clearing and found Ramulas and Pip waiting for them.

'How did you fare?' Ramulas asked.

Iguchi smiled sadly. 'Benji has left us. He now roams the kingdom in the clouds.'

'Damn,' Ramulas swore, looking behind the Fallen Angels, half expecting Benji to jump out from behind the trees. He pushed away these feelings and led the Fallen Angels into Sanctuary.

***

Soldier and Symiak alike swarmed into the forest chasing the dryads. Swords chipped away at their skin hurting, but not killing, them. It was the Symiaks with their clubs and heavy swords that did the most damage. Within the first few minutes, seven dryads were chopped to pieces in a wild frenzy.

A group of kingdom soldiers had a dryad on the ground, hacking at it with swords and laughing as it pleaded for mercy. Sap wept out of an open wound, and then an angry buzzing came through the trees.

A soldier looked up in time to see Tilly fly out with her short sword leading the way. She flew past, cutting him on the forehead and causing blood to flow into his eyes. He screamed as Tilly threw herself at another soldier.

***

A dryad ran through the trees with soldiers and Symiaks in close pursuit. A club clipped its shoulder, causing the creature to fall, sliding along the ground until it stopped at the base of an oak tree. It was quickly surrounded by its pursuers.

'Look how it cowers in fear before us,' a Legion soldier said as he placed the tip of his sword under the dryad's chin, forcing the dryad to stand.

The dryad stood and rested its back against the tree. Its body blended in so perfectly with the tree that it was almost invisible. Then its eyes widened, and the dryad smiled.

'Why do you smile?' the Legion soldier asked.

The dryad stood confidently. 'I am not afraid to die. You are the ones who need to fear death.'

The sword tip had found the softer skin under the dryad's chin. He lifted the dryad's chin as the rest of the group closed in. They were angered at the creature's defiance.

Then it happened.

The dryad reached out grabbing the Legion soldier by his wrists before pulling him halfway into the tree and releasing him. An explosion of blood and gore covered all who were nearby.

Before the soldiers and Symiaks had a chance to react, dryads emerged from the surrounding trees to drag them screaming into trees. The remaining soldiers and Symiaks lost their nerve and ran back to the road, followed by extremely angry dryads. Remus' magical spell had been countered by the magic within Sanctuary's forest.

They would wait until the enemy moved on before retrieving their dead from closer to the road. They did not want to deal with the magic-users again.

Men and Symiaks returned with news that the creatures were fighting deep in the forest. Remus talked with Zachary before giving the order to move on towards Sanctuary. As the wagons moved, Remus turned to the king. 'Tell me of the dryads.'

Zachary took a deep breath before explaining that they were just myths, and that, before that day, no-one had ever seen one before.

Remus shook his head. 'Your myths killed a lot of men today. Are there any more myths I need to know about before we reach our destination?'

'I only know of the dragons that I told you about. Will the dryads be able to attack us again?'

Remus shook his head with a smile. 'Do not worry. Our magic is more than a match for them. But what are the chances of dragons attacking us in the forest?'

Zachary searched the canopies of the trees above searching for the flying beasts. 'In our last battle, they only came when we were outside Sanctuary.'

'In your mythical tales, did the dryads kill people or throw wasp nests at them?'

Zachary could only shake his head.

***

The army was on the move again. Between the Fallen Angels and the dryad attacks, they had lost just over three hundred men, a handful of Symiaks, and hundreds were injured; however, they still had thousands to retrieve Oriel.

The red wizards were close to collapsing from exhaustion after their magical battle and needed time to recover.

***

The Fallen Angels walked into the barracks emotionally drained. The loss of Benji was sinking in. Miles was the most affected. Sitting on his friend's bed, images flashed through his mind of the adventures they

231

shared before coming to Sanctuary, and then after becoming a Fallen Angel. Benji was always the person who had a wisecrack whenever Miles felt down.

Miles laughed as bitter tears flowed down his cheeks. The laughter turned to sobs of despair that shook his body. After a few moments, he felt a hand on his shoulder. He saw Iguchi standing before him.

'You must let go of your sadness and anger. A true warrior does not have emotion during battle. This will only bring death. You can plan revenge or move on with his memory.'

'I want both. I will move on after I get my revenge.'

Iguchi shook his finger. 'You must release your anger before it kills you in battle.'

***

The dryads came out onto the road to gently pick up the ones they had lost and wounded. They were taken to the sacred grove to be healed and buried. This was a very sad time for them. There had not been a dryad death in over one hundred years.

The dead were buried at the base of an old oak tree, and the wounded bathed in the mystic pool until they healed. A great sadness fell over the dryad community. There was no anger toward the enemy, only grief for their loss. After such a tragedy, they had lost the will to fight.

26

'We are close,' Zachary said as the Devil's Ridge Mountains came into view through the trees. It would only be half an hour before they arrived at Sanctuary.

Calls of alarm caused both Remus and Zachary to turn. Two hundred yards behind them, the giant wheel of the catapult had fallen into a hole. The large machine of war groaned as it tipped. There was a resounding *crack* before it toppled to the ground and smashed into the trees, sending birds flying from the trees.

Remus, Zachary, and the royal guard made their way to the catapult to inspect it. Redemption stood by one of the holes that were dug and covered. The front wheel was still in the hole next to the fallen machine.

'What is this?' Remus asked, fighting his rising anger.

'A hole has been dug and covered in the road. There could be more,' Redemption replied.

Remus turned to the front of the column while holding up his hands and chanting. After a few seconds, three rectangular shapes glowed just under the surface of the road. He walked over to each of these sections, murmuring until the light faded.

When Remus was finished, he looked at Redemption. 'Get the Symiaks to move the catapult. We march for Sanctuary.'

***

Remus and Zachary walked out into the clearing in front of Sanctuary. They stopped by the tree line as Remus scanned the wall, seeing archers lining the top, each holding a bow. He scanned the clearing for any other threats before turning to Zachary.

'We need to finish this quickly. Once the people of Sanctuary see our combined armies, I might be able to persuade them to hand over Oriel in exchange for their lives.'

'What of Oriel's treasure and the people in Sanctuary? They must be punished.'

Remus smiled. 'Once I have Oriel, I will make sure you get what you deserve. Now, let's bring in the armies.'

Zachary signalled for Lucas and instructed him to bring the kingdom army out to the far side of the clearing. Then the Legion would follow.

'Leave some of the men in the trees; they can come out after,' Remus said.

Zachary turned to him, confused. 'Why?'

'With thousands of soldiers and Symiaks, we would fill this clearing and be taken out by the archers on the wall.'

Zachary agreed and passed the word along. This time, there would be too many men for the cowards in Sanctuary to attack them from behind again. As the columns passed, Remus kept a watchful eye on the sky. He had a surprise for any dragons if they came.

Supply wagons and two trebuchets were brought into the clearing, closely followed by the first ranks of the Legion soldiers, and still, the archers had not moved. As the machines of war came halfway across the clearing, someone from the wall whistled.

Lodi jumped from his hiding place with an earth-shaking roar, and all eyes were locked on the far right-hand side of the wall where the giant appeared.

All movement in the clearing ceased.

The appearance of the giant on the wall had shocked everyone in the combined army. Lodi bent down to pick up a man-sized rock and threw it at one of the trebuchets. The rock hit the machine of war, snapping its arm, its net full of rocks falling to the ground. The spell was broken, and soldiers ran in all directions as the giant threw a second rock.

Then the archers opened fire.

A wave of arrows came down amongst the soldiers running from the rocks. Twenty fell dead before the next wave came.

'Shields!' Lucas called out.

Both kingdom and Legion soldiers raised their shields in time to hear the arrows bouncing off. Still, five more fell, and Lodi threw another rock. This rock headed towards the supply wagons, causing the men nearby to scatter toward the trees. A third wave of arrows came down at those running from this rock as it smashed into a wagon.

***

When Lodi jumped up, Remus was in shock. Logan had said the giant had been poisoned and then burned in a warehouse, but clearly, the giant was alive and well. Then the archers shot into the clearing, killing soldiers from the kingdom and Legion ranks.

Remus was caught in a dilemma—should he protect the soldiers from the arrows or attack the wall, and if he did attack the wall, would he target the giant or the archers?

His mind was made up instantly as Remus raised his hand and shot a line of flame at the giant as it threw the third rock. A yard before reaching the giant, the flame hit an invisible barrier, sending light blue ripples above the wall.

In a mix of astonishment and anger, Remus shot his hand out again, sending flame to a different part of the wall where the archers were, but again, it hit the invisible barrier, sending out blue ripples.

'The wall has defences against magic. Archers, shoot at those on the wall,' Remus ordered.

Legion archers stepped forward and shot up at the wall. To Remus' relief, the arrows sailed over as the people ducked.

Remus turned to Zachary. 'The giant is not dead as we were told.'

Zachary turned to one of the royal guards. 'Find Logan and bring him to me now.'

A minute later, a very nervous Logan stood before Remus and Zachary. The columns of Legion soldiers still waited to come into the clearing, and behind them, the Symiaks were becoming restless.

'I did not know the giant still lived—' Logan began.

'What other surprises await us?' Remus asked in a soft tone.

Logan held out his hands while shrugging, and Remus threw a handful of red dust over him that surrounded him in a soft red glow, which showed Remus that he spoke the truth.

Remus turned to the warlords and red wizards. 'Erect a magical barrier to protect those coming into the clearing.'

They stepped out of the clearing chanting and waving their hands through the air while spreading out. A transparent wall rose from the ground fifty yards in front of them, and it covered the whole clearing.

Remus motioned with his hand and the columns came marching forward. A wave of arrows came down, striking the shield and bouncing off. The magic-users strained to hold up the barrier. Remus gave orders for the soldiers and Symiaks to move faster.

***

The soldiers and Symiaks were in columns across the clearing, and Remus called back the warlords and red wizards. Thirty seconds later, the magical wall began to collapse on itself. Large portions of it crumbled in silence until all the pieces turned to dust and floated away. The front lines of men and Symiak were one hundred and fifty yards from the wall.

A wave of arrows came down. Remus swept his hand, and they were knocked away. He walked forward a few steps while holding both hands out.

'Why do you resist?' he said in a low, hypnotic voice that carried to the archers. 'Our numbers are far greater than yours. Why do you wish to throw your lives away? Your people have attacked us from the town of Covedon and we have only defended ourselves. Stop this foolishness, open the gates, and leave Oriel to us. Once we have her, we will leave you to live your lives in peace.'

Remus watched the wall to see who would respond. The archers on the wall spoke to each other but ignored him, and then they parted to allow a warrior in purple armour and a green dragon on his breastplate. He stopped to look down at the clearing. The man's face was covered, only showing his eyes.

'They hear your words well enough,' Ramulas said. 'But you cannot blame them for not trusting you.'

'I have done nothing to warrant the mistrust of the people in Sanctuary,' Remus said in his hypnotic voice.

'Oriel has shown us your true colours. That is why everyone behind this wall will gladly die for her.'

Remus looked up at the wall with a friendly smile. 'You judge me before getting to know me and hearing my side of the story. Oriel is the one you need to fear. She has done terrible things in our world. That is why she ran away and must be brought to justice. Come down and speak with me on equal terms. You have my word that no harm will come to you.'

Ramulas nodded. 'I will come down.'

The gates opened and Remus gasped as he saw down the passageway into Sanctuary. Ramulas walked into the clearing and the gates were shut by four soldiers. Remus' mind raced as Ramulas walked toward him. All he needed to do was break through the gates, and then the combined armies would flood into Sanctuary.

Ramulas stopped six feet from Remus. His face shield melted into his armour like water running down a wall. This showed the marking left by Iguchi's sword.

As one, the Legion soldiers fell to one knee, casting their eyes to the ground.

'The Avenger,' Remus whispered in shock.

For generations, the people in the world of Lodec had spoken in whispers about the prophecy of the Avenger. It was said that he was the only one with the power to overthrow the warlords and free the people. In his mind's eye, Remus saw the prophecy.

The day will come
When the Avenger steps forth.
The warlords and wizards will tremble,
For the spirit of the dragon lies within.
Legion soldiers shall kneel before their new lord,
For he holds the power of two worlds.
His face bears hope and freedom;
Dance and rejoice the day
The Avenger will set us free.

Even though Remus did not believe in the prophecy, he still ordered the death of any male child with any markings on their face, and yet, standing before him was the man he fought with on the mountain range. He remembered the shock when he first laid eyes on this man whose features were so similar that it was almost like looking into a mirror.

However, things had changed; the last time they met, the man was unsure of himself, surprised at his ability to use magic. Now before him stood a man of confidence and full of power, and he had acquired the marking on his face.

It was the writing from the old ways, the ways that the people still clung to. The mark meant freedom and hope.

Ramulas smiled at the expression on Remus' face. Oriel had told him of the Avenger prophecy and how this would affect the Legion.

'Oriel is under the protection of the people in Sanctuary. Everyone inside is willing to die for her.'

Remus turned to see the Legion soldiers still kneeling with heads bowed. 'On your feet!' he shouted.

They rose to their feet and watched the wall. Remus turned to scowl at Ramulas, his friendly façade gone. 'Tell me, are you willing to die for Oriel?'

Ramulas' smile grew. 'Of course.'

Red energy leapt from Remus' hand and went through the image of Ramulas standing before him.

'I knew you could not be trusted. That's why I sent an astral image of myself to you.'

The image began to flicker as Remus stepped forward and put a hand through the image. His eyes widened in shock. He turned to his Legion soldiers. 'Look upon this trickery. This is just an illusion. The mark of the Avenger is another part of the illusion. This shows how much they fear us.'

Legion soldiers glared at Ramulas with open hatred.

'The show of force on the wall was impressive,' Remus called, 'as were the attacks on us as we came here, but if you do not surrender Oriel to us, you will all suffer before you die.'

Remus turned slightly and made a gesture with his hand. The Legion soldiers parted, and Logan walked proudly smiling up at those on the wall.

'Thanks to this man,' Remus said, waving to Logan, 'we know all of Sanctuary's weaknesses and secrets. I will give you one hour to bring me your terms of surrender.

Ramulas' image looked at Logan in shock 'We took you in, and this is how you repay us?'

Before Logan could answer, the image of Ramulas vanished.

***

Ramulas opened his eyes to find himself in the throne room with the druids, Shigar, and Oriel. 'That worked better than we expected.'

Oriel smiled. 'What happened?'

'He thinks we are weak thanks to Logan and is confident of entering Sanctuary soon. He attacked my astral image, thinking it was me, and offered us an hour to deliver our terms of surrender.'

'I want to deliver this to him,' Miles said, walking into the room with Iguchi close behind.

Ramulas saw that Miles was determined and would not take no for an answer. He gave Iguchi a questioning look.

'Hello to you, Lord of Sanctuary. Do not worry—Miles can do this thing.'

Ramulas looked at the magician. 'Prepare him for what needs to be done so he can return after the message.'

Shigar nodded and took Miles over to the druids to explain his plan for how the Fallen Angel could go out and return safely.

A short time later, Miles returned to Ramulas. Shigar held his sword and shield. Miles gripped a small glowing stone in his hand and knew that he would return to the throne room as soon as he released the stone.

The druids had given him a scroll, which he held lightly in his other hand; he did not want the spell within the scroll to activate early. Just before the Fallen Angel left the room, Ramulas placed a hand on his shoulder.

'Please return as soon as you deliver the message.'

For the first time since Benji had died, Miles smiled. 'You know me, my lord.'

Ramulas returned the smile 'I know I do. That is why I am a little worried. Do not try anything silly.'

Miles attempted to pull an innocent expression and failed miserably.

***

The gates opened, and Miles walked out into the clearing. His heart beat faster as he saw the enemy so close. The trees beyond the clearing seemed to be filled with the enemy as well. He concentrated on walking slowly with one foot in front of the other. Their numbers were vast— many times that of when the kingdom army had last attacked, and with Symiaks to the left and Legion soldiers to the right.

Miles walked straight towards the royal guard and men in red robes who stood by King Zachary. As he came closer, Miles saw the one who appeared like lord Ramulas wearing a red breastplate covered in strange symbols. From what Oriel had told him, Miles knew this to be Remus.

On either side of Remus stood two others in red robes. A cold chill ran down Miles' spine as he saw that the one on the left had green stains on his face and robes—this was the one who had taken Benji.

Miles stopped a few feet in front of Remus while the warlord chanted softly. A moment later, Miles' hands glowed red.

'What magic do you hold?' Remus asked him.

'In one hand I hold the terms of our surrender and, in the other, I have a way of returning safely home.' The air around Miles glowed red, showing that he told the truth.

Remus nodded. 'You speak the truth. If you had lied, you would have suffered a painful death.'

A cold smile spread across Miles' face. 'I do not fear death.'

'Were you one of those who harassed us from the town of Covedon?' Remus asked.

Miles nodded.

'You are good,' Remus said with grudging respect.

Miles shook his head. 'The Fallen Angels are the best.'

'One of your friends died in this forest,' Remus said, referring to Benji. 'That does not make you the best.'

Miles fought the angel rising inside of him, glanced at the man with the green stains on his robe, and handed the scroll to Remus.

Remus unrolled the scroll, and an expression of confusion crossed his face. Miles had to bite his tongue to stop himself from laughing. Remus looked at a blank page with four green bubbles on it.

Miles leaned forward and flicked the back of the scroll, causing the bubbles to explode, covering Remus and the warlord next to him in green sticky goo.

Both were in shock. 'That is our terms of surrender,' Miles said.

Miles released the glowing stone in his hand and jumped at the man who had killed Benji. By the time Remus cast a spell to counter the web, Miles and Omega were gone.

****

Ramulas and Shigar jumped in shock as Miles and the warlord appeared in the throne room. Omega chanted softly while moving his fingers in front of him.

'Beware!' Shigar shouted. 'He is casting a spell!'

Miles grabbed Omega's hand and twisted it sharply. The warlord gasped and Miles punched him in the throat. Omega rolled around, fighting for breath, looking like a fish out of water. Iguchi ran over and stuck two rigid fingers into the side of Omega's neck. The warlord shuddered once before collapsing.

Miles said. 'This was the one who killed Benji.'

Iguchi shook his finger at Miles. 'This one could have used magic. Now, he will sleep for an hour.'

Shigar nodded. 'Good. Drag him to the stone oak tree. I have something to stop this one from causing any trouble. I have manacles that will cancel his magic.'

Shigar left the throne room and returned a short time later with a length of chain and the manacles, securing the warlord to the tree.

Oriel gasped, and everyone looked at her. 'They are attacking,' she said.

Ramulas turned to the magician. 'Make sure he cannot do any damage, and then meet me on the wall.' He looked at Oriel. 'Do not worry; they will not come near you.'

Ramulas ran to the balcony and jumped over the edge as a warm sensation exploded within him. Oriel's magic, combined with his own, helped him float down into the courtyard. The people looked at their lord in awe. As soon as he touched the ground, Ramulas raced for the stairs and up to the top of the wall.

27

When Miles flicked the back of the scroll and broke the bubbles, Remus closed his eyes and looked away as he was covered in the sticky goo. He cast a quick spell to turn the goo into dust. He heard cheering from the archers on the wall. Remus opened his eyes to find the warrior and Omega had gone. 'What happened?'

'He grabbed Omega before they both vanished,' Zachary said.

Rage flooded through Remus as he thought of being played for the fool. 'Where is Logan?'

Zachary pointed to the west at the mountain range. 'He is near the secret entrance with a group of men waiting for the signal to enter.'

'Are your kingdom soldiers ready?'

Zachary puffed out his chest and looked at the small hut in the clearing. 'My men are as ready as your Legion soldiers. Pull the lever.'

A kingdom soldier ran out to the hut and entered. A few seconds later, a rumbling could be heard as the ground shook. A passageway of stone rose out of the ground in front of the gates. It was fifty yards long and provided the perfect cover for those attacking the gates.

Both Remus and Zachary smiled as Symiaks and soldiers rushed for the passageway with arrows coming down from the wall. The archers were shocked for a few moments and did not start firing until half had already entered.

Grunch led the way with a group of Symiaks holding a metal-tipped battering ram. Kingdom and Legion soldiers ran into the passage with their shields held above their heads, and the arrows bounced off harmlessly. Legion and kingdom archers stepped forward to provide cover, keeping those on the wall too busy to shoot.

Then the sound of the battering ram could be heard.

***

The last wave of arrows came over the wall just as Ramulas reached the top of the stairs. He found Pip, Owain, and Rygar sitting with their backs against the wall. He investigated the clearing to see the enemy archers retreat.

'Fire!' Ramulas called.

Archers along the wall jumped up and fired into those running away. A few pots of molten ore were thrown as well but landed short. He could feel the battering ram hitting the gates as the vibrations travelled through his body.

He looked down into the maze when he heard stone grinding against stone. The two sides of the maze had now merged into one. As the battering ram continued, Ramulas prayed that Shigar's magical trap would work.

***

Logan waited at the base of the cliff near the secret entrance with nine others. In the surrounding forest, there were other groups of ten waiting for their chance to enter Sanctuary. There were just over two hundred kingdom and Legion soldiers in total.

Logan had instructed each group what to do to cause the most damage in the shortest time. After his group entered, others would wait their turn and follow. Then a soldier came running through the trees.

'It's time.'

Logan reached up and pushed the stone into the cliff. As the secret door opened, torches were lit and handed to the group. Logan led them into the circular room and the door closed behind them. He walked over to the lever and pulled it.

The walls of the room fell away, and they found themselves in a long dark cavern. The light from the torches only showed the space around them. The men looked at Logan with uncertainty. He watched the light from the torches throw shadows along the floor, unsure what to do.

A cold wind swept through the cavern followed by a woeful moaning; men shivered as the wind seemed to pass through them.

'So long have I waited,' a voice whispered in Logan's ear, causing him to jump and spin around.

What he saw chilled him to the bone—a creature wearing a tattered dark robe. Most of the flesh on its face had rotted away, giving the appearance of a constant smile.

'To my side,' Logan called, drawing his sword.

They drew their swords and fanned out on either side of him.

The creature sighed as it slowly floated towards the group, who huddled together with swords out.

'I have waited so long, and now you are here,' it whispered, moving closer and reaching out with a skeletal hand.

'What do you want from us?' Logan asked with a tremor in his voice.

'I wish to make you whole.'

Logan's instincts screamed for him to run away from this thing as fast as he could, however, his muscles refused to obey his commands. The creature shot forward with unnatural speed, grabbing the Legion soldier to Logan's left. The spell broke as the soldier was dragged away screaming.

Logan turned and ran deeper into the darkness of the cavern. He heard the other close behind him, and then they heard screams of agony from the Legion soldier.

'We need to find a way out of here,' Logan said as they ran.

A kingdom soldier turned to him. 'What happened to the room with the lever?'

He shook his head, not knowing what to say. They soon found refuge in a small cave. Logan was transfixed watching the shadows dancing along the walls. Soon, men hugged themselves as plumes of steam came out of their mouths. Logan felt uneasy, knowing that something was in the cave with them.

A cold gust of wind passed Logan, almost blowing out his torch, and then the shadows on the wall took shape. Hands of shadow came from the floor and walls. Logan screamed as they entered his chest, and he fell to the floor while the others raced out.

Logan screamed louder as his bones began to break inside his body one by one. His ligaments and muscles stretched and reformed. In a few minutes, Logan was on his hands and knees sobbing uncontrollably. Then it turned into maniacal laughter.

Logan stood and observed his new body. He was taller and thinner, with spikes protruding from his arms and legs. The creature in the tattered robe floated near the entrance of the cave, and behind him was another creature like Logan.

'Show the others what it is like to be free,' the creature whispered.

Logan stepped out of the cave and leapt twenty feet toward the fleeing torchlight. His spiked companion landed next to him before they both jumped again. They repeated this three more times before landing in front of a terrified kingdom soldier.

Logan pulled the man's head to the side and bit deeply into his neck while he screamed, then he let the man drop to the floor, where he convulsed and transformed. His screams echoed throughout the chamber until the transformation was complete.

The rest of the soldiers ran for dear life, knowing what would happen if they were caught.

***

The next group waited to enter through the secret door in the cliff face. The rock on the wall disappeared and they began searching for another way to open the door. After a minute of searching, they could hear faint blood-curdling screams coming from within the mountain.

They jumped back when trickles of blood seeped out from the cliff. The two hundred soldiers gasped as they saw it as well—something had gone wrong, and they needed to inform Remus and Zachary.

***

Shigar sat on the floor in his chambers watching the clay pot in front of him. It was full of seawater, with a small piece of coral in the bottom. The surface of the water would ripple each time the battering ram would hit the gates.

He took a deep breath before putting his hand into the pot. Water spilled over the sides as he held the coral. Shigar squeezed it tightly and felt the coral puncture his skin. As his blood flowed into the water, Shigar released the spell.

***

Grunch stood near the gates as the battering ram swung back and forth, slamming into the gates of wood and iron. He was yelling at the Symiaks, telling them to hit the gates three times and then rest.

They had hit the gates two times and pulled back for a third when Grunch felt moisture on his arm. He turned to see that the gates had gone and in their place was a wall of water. He could even see fish swimming just out of reach.

A cold realisation washed over him—he needed to stop the battering ram. He turned in time to see the tip punch through the wall of water. Grunch had time to yell before being swallowed up in a torrent of seawater. The Symiaks holding the battering ram and several rows of soldiers were engulfed by the wave.

Those further down the passage heard the dull thuds as the gates were hit, and then a hole twenty feet wide opened at the entrance of the passage. Shouts of alarm were heard as two score Symiaks and soldiers fell into the hole.

Then the roar of water could be heard over the screams from within the passage. Remus and Zachary sat on their horses and watched in disbelief as soldiers and Symiaks were pushed out of the passage and into the hole with a torrent of water.

Symiaks and soldiers in the clearing ran as the water flooded out. The tangy smell of seawater was heavy in the air. Then the roaring water stopped, and the passageway began sinking back into the ground. The silence that followed was deafening.

A cry of panic from the men and Symiaks in the watery hole broke the silence. The water level dropped as the edges of the hole closed. Legion and kingdom soldiers rushed forward to pull out as many as they could. Within a minute, the hole had closed, leaving many buried alive. The archers on the wall cheered.

'What was that?' Zachary asked.

'That was a magical trap. I would like to speak with Logan to thank him for showing us the passageway,' Remus growled.

'He was with the first group to enter the secret tunnel into Sanctuary,' Zachary replied.

Remus sighed, looking at the area where the passage had been. They had lost a couple of hundred men with this trick. Sanctuary seemed to have struck an early blow. It was time for the people of Sanctuary to feel his wrath.

A group of Legion and kingdom soldiers came racing from the trees. They explained that something had gone wrong with the secret entry into Sanctuary. By the time they had finished, Remus could not believe his string of bad luck. His hand shot out at the wall in frustration, and red energy shot out at the gates.

Multi-coloured sparks flew in all directions for a few moments before Remus lowered his hand. The gates seemed unaffected by his magic; however, the colour of the gates was slightly darker, which meant a magical ward protected the gates. How many times could it withstand attacks?

Then Shigar appeared on the wall and Zachary cursed. 'You traitorous dog.'

***

After releasing the water spell in the passageway, Shigar quickly made his way from his chambers to the wall. He thought of how devastating the spell would have been for those trapped in the passage. When he collected the octopus, Shigar removed the piece of coral from deep in the ocean. This section of water was used for his trap.

He reached the top of the wall fighting for breath as Ramulas clapped him on the shoulder. 'That was a good trick.'

'Thank you, my friend. I have a few more. Tell them to leave or you will call the dragons.'

Ramulas saw the magician holding several scrolls and books under his robes and then glanced over to Remus and Zachary. 'If you do not leave us, I will call my dragons.'

Soldiers looked around and up at the sky with anxiety while Zachary turned to Remus and spoke. Before the warlord climbed down from his mount and came a few steps forward, Alpha and the red wizards came to stand by his side.

'We will stay here,' Remus called. 'We do not fear your dragons.'

Not expecting this response, Ramulas looked at Shigar in shock and shrugged. 'Give them the dragons.'

The magician dropped everything except for one leather-bound book. He flicked through the pages until he found the right spell. Shigar stepped away from the wall as he began to chant. Dark energies filled the clouds above, accompanied by the sound of rolling thunder. Men and Symiaks were transfixed by the shapes moving within the swirling clouds.

First the people on the wall, and then everyone in the clearing, gasped. Their skin was covered in goosebumps as the temperature dropped and magical energies intensified.

Zachary turned to Remus. 'What magic is this? What should we do?'

Remus shrugged. 'This is a simple spell. Let us see what transpires.'

The warlord knew that this was more than just a spell—it was different magic, and not knowing how to counter it could be very dangerous. The clouds formed into one and darkened even more and Shigar threw a stone into it.

With a clap of thunder, the cloud transformed into a black dragon. Soldiers and Symiaks began running into the forest with shouts of alarm as the dragon's head snaked down. As the creature dropped into the clearing, more people and Symiaks headed for the trees. Remus and the other magic-users stood together chanting while waving their hands through the air. They waited until the dragon was fifty yards from them before raising their arms into the air.

Red strands of energy shot into the sky forming a giant net that dropped over the dragon and wrapped around it. With a command from Remus, the net was pulled and tightened. The dragon roared once before exploding into a cloud of dark smoke.

Remus dropped his hands in shock and the net vanished. It was meant to hold and control the dragon, but then the creature was gone in a puff of smoke. Then he saw Shigar move on the wall, and it dawned on him—the dragon was nothing but an illusion.

Remus smiled coldly up at the wall. 'The dragon was an illusion, as was the Lord of Sanctuary who bore the mark of the Avenger. You wish to fight us with just illusions?'

As the soldiers and Symiaks came back out of the forest, Remus thought about what Zachary had told him about his magician joining the people of Sanctuary. For him to create the dragon on the clearing, their magical barrier must be down.

He shot a hand out, sending a stream of energy at the magician. As before, blue ripples flowed in front of Shigar. *The magical barrier must drop each time Shigar casts a spell,* Remus thought. He would test this theory.

He took three small crystals from his robe and handed them to Alpha. 'The next time he casts a spell, throw these over the wall into Sanctuary.'

Alpha took the crystals and murmured a spell that would carry them far over the wall. Remus was about to order the archers to fire when something comical caught his eye—a Symiak went flying toward the top of the wall and missed it by ten feet, disappearing over the other side.

Remus walked over to the Symiaks as another hopped into the basket of their catapult. He watched as this one landed on top of the wall. Archers on both sides shot arrow after arrow into the creature before it fell dead into the clearing.

'Where is Grunch?' Remus asked.

Slesht stepped forward. 'He die in water tunnel. I rule Symiaks. I take gifts.'

Remus recognised this creature as the one who had fought Redemption in the mountains. Then an idea came to him on how the Symiaks could help. 'I can help lots of Symiaks get onto the wall. Have twenty of them line up in front of you and tell them to wait.'

Slesht growled. 'Why is you say wait?'

Remus rolled his eyes while looking to the sky before waving to the combined army. 'If we work together, then Symiaks get gifts sooner.'

The Symiak chief nodded and sent twenty to line up in front of Remus. Then the kingdom and Legion archers fired at the wall, forcing the archers of Sanctuary to duck. Alpha shouted, causing Remus to turn. Alpha pointed to the left-hand side top of the wall, where he saw a giant snake made from stone slithering over the edge. Shigar waved his hand while chanting a spell from a scroll he held.

'Now!' Remus shouted at Alpha, who threw the three crystals over the wall to land in separate parts of Sanctuary.

'Attack the magician!' Remus called.

Arcs of red energy leapt from the red wizards' hands. Two of them hit Shigar, knocking him out of sight before the magical barrier returned and the blue ripples echoed above the wall.

Remus watched as the head of the stone snake buried itself in the ground at the base of the wall. He chanted while waving his hands through the air in tight formations. A bolt of lightning came down to strike the snake's stone skin with a crackling sound, which caused the snake to burrow quicker.

Remus soon realised that this was no illusion, and he needed to work out a way to deal with something this big and made from stone. The ground in the clearing moved and rippled as the snake came towards Remus.

28

Holding the spell book in one hand, Shigar chanted, bringing forth the giant stone snake. Oriel had told him of Sanctuary's magical barrier which would activate when the enemy entered the clearing, protecting those on the wall.

The barrier would only drop when someone on the wall used magic, or if it received too many magical attacks. Shigar knew that he was vulnerable when casting and had an invisible shield in front of him as he brought the stone snake to life. Shigar shuddered as the snake came out of his book and down into the clearing. It was at least twenty feet long and thick as he was.

Then he was hit by two arcs of energy; the first weakened his shield and the second broke through, knocking him over. He looked up in time to see the barrier block the other shots.

Ramulas ran over to the magician. 'Are you alright?'

'I am fine,' Shigar lied, looking down at the burn marks on his robe.

With help from Ramulas, Shigar stood and felt every muscle in his body ache. 'I knew there was a risk when casting, but there was no other way.'

Then the magician's jaw dropped as twenty Symiaks flew up to land on the wall. Ten landed on either side of the pair. Ramulas turned to see the archers aim their bows at the creatures, but there were too many in such a confined space. The archers were in trouble.

'Pip, Rygar, to the left,' Ramulas said as he ran to the right. A warm sensation exploded within him, and his whole body was bathed in purple flame. The closest Symiak was shot by an archer before it reached down to pick him up and throw the archer off the wall screaming into the clearing. Rage spurred Ramulas as he reached the Symiak and swung with his war hammer, knocking it into the maze.

Being close to the creatures once more brought back memories of his first encounter with them when he went into the mountains with Pip. Their musky odour was something he could never forget.

He saw Symiaks and archers fighting. The archers were at a disadvantage because they had spent their time training with bows, not swords. Their attacks on the Symiaks were clumsy, desperate swings with their swords. Ramulas yelled out a warning as he came to the next fight, giving the archer time to move out of the way before he killed this one. Four Symiaks had been killed by arrows, and the one Ramulas killed had ten arrows in its body.

The grunts and howls of the Symiaks were mixed with shouts and cries of the archers, a dozen of whom were lying injured. Ramulas saw a Symiak take a bow from an archer and snap it in half. This Symiak was covered in arrows and seemed unaffected. The archer reached back and picked up one of Rygar's exploding spears, ready to stab the creature.

'No!' Ramulas called out running towards them, but it was too late. The archer thrust the spear into the Symiak's midsection, detonating the weapon with a clap of thunder. The top half of the creature was blown off the wall—its legs took a few steps before collapsing. The archer stared at Ramulas with wide, vacant eyes. Both of his arms were missing, and he had holes through his chest and stomach.

Ramulas ran fifteen feet to the archer in time to catch him as he fell. He did not know what to say or do. Ramulas had never seen injuries like this on a person before. The archer gurgled one last breath and died in his arms. Ramulas fought back tears as he looked down at the man's blood on his armour.

He gently lay the archer on the ground before looking at Pip and Rygar fighting the last two creatures on their side of the wall and then down at the combined army in the clearing. There were so many—if twenty Symiaks did this much damage on the wall, he shuddered to think what would happen if more came up. Then Ramulas' heart skipped a beat as the two giant crabs came out of the forest toward the wall to the cheers of the Legion soldiers.

***

Remus looked back at his Legion soldiers. Their weapons would be virtually useless against this thing. He would need to rely on magic. He called for Alpha and the red wizards to gather around him as the ripples beneath the surface came closer.

Fifty yards.

The magic-users chanted while waving their hands, causing a soft glow to form in the middle of their circle.

Thirty yards.

They were forced to move back as they continued to cast the spell. Soil and grass bulged and split as the head of the snake came out of the ground bringing forth a rich earth smell into the air. A red wizard shot fireballs into its head and face, causing it to rear back as the others finished the last words of the spell.

The snake reared up ten feet in the air, shaking its head as Remus clapped his hands. The ground where the snake came out of had turned to stone, trapping it, but Remus knew it would not hold for long.

Remus and Alpha cast another spell, shooting thin jets of green mist at the snake. The mist had an instantaneous effect when it hit the snake— stone scales sizzled on the snake before they fell to the ground revealing green scales beneath. This enraged the snake, and it slammed its body to the ground repeatedly, causing those nearby to lose their footing.

Glancing up at the wall, Remus knew that Alpha and the red wizard were busy with the stone snake. He saw the twenty Symiaks lined up and cast a spell, sending them flying up to the wall. The giant snake bit at the ground trying to free itself. 'Attack the green scales!' Remus called as he cast another spell holding the snake in position for a few moments. Scores of arrows were shot at the snake, half hitting their mark.

Remus turned to the nearby Symiaks and pointed to the snake. 'Hold it down.'

As one, the Symiaks charged the snake. Three were crushed by the snake before it was covered with the creatures and fell to the ground under the weight, only its head remaining free. Redemption danced in and thrust his twin swords into a vulnerable spot beneath its eye. The snake shuddered once before dying.

'Bring the crabs,' Remus called.

The Legion soldiers cheered as the crabs came out of the forest, tearing trees from the ground. Remus looked at those on the wall with an evil smile.

***

Ramulas' eyes widened as he ran to the middle of the wall. 'Pip, I need you to send the giant-kin into the maze and send Joshua and Rain up here.'

Once Pip ran down the stairs, he turned to Shigar. 'We need some time before the crabs reach the top of the wall. Do what you can.'

The magician nodded and searched through his scrolls, and Ramulas saw the injured archers and dead Symiaks along the wall. He called for Rygar to bring the injured to Oriel and dump the Symiaks into the clearing.

Ramulas attempted to use his magic to communicate with the crabs but could not understand their language, while Shigar read from one of his scrolls, waving his hands in wide arcs as he stepped to the edge of the wall.

The red wizards sent fireballs at the magician as he cast, causing him to duck for cover. He smiled at Ramulas. 'Watch the clearing.'

Ramulas turned to look at the combined army and then saw patches on the ground begin to glow beneath their feet. Several patches flickered rapidly before the soldiers and Symiaks standing on them just vanished into thin air.

Shouts of alarm and confusion spread throughout the clearing and Redemption made the connection. 'Step away from the light.'

Every man and creature obeyed the command, and after a few seconds, the flickering lights faded until they were gone.

***

Shigar stood and pointed to the gaps in the formations of the enemy army. 'I have been working on this trick for some time—it's a teleportation spell. Those missing are somewhere between here and Turtha. It will take them a day to return to the battle.'

Shigar explained how he had placed components of the spell in the clearing days before. And had asked Iguchi to drop off another part when he took his Fallen Angels out. This component would act as an exit point.

Then they were distracted by a large explosion below them. Pip ran over to them as Remus unleashed wave after wave of energy at the gates.

'I think we made him angry,' Pip said.

'Where are the injured archers?' Ramulas asked.

'With Oriel. She is healing them.'

'Good. We need them back as soon as possible.'

***

As kingdom and Legion soldiers vanished before his eyes, Zachary turned to Remus in shock. 'What's happening?'

Remus ignored him as he tried to understand it himself. Then he heard Redemption call out the warning and knew what the spell was. He walked over to one of the patches of ground that glowed, held his hand above it, and cast a minor spell. A moment later, his eyes widened in realisation. This was a teleportation spell.

He walked to Zachary. 'Your magician Shigar teleported our men far away. How powerful was he?'

Zachary shrugged. 'I took no notice of what he did or how powerful he had become. I only knew he was a magician.'

'Well, your magician sent several hundred of our soldiers and Symiaks to a place unknown. That was no minor feat.'

'He is a traitor and no longer *my* magician,' Zachary shot back.

Remus fought his rising anger. 'Well, did you know that he was able to teleport large groups?'

Zachary shook his head and shrugged. 'A lot of his time was spent in private; I know not what he did.'

Remus felt his anger boil over and wanted so much to feed the king to his giant crabs, but he would wait until he had Oriel. He needed the kingdom soldiers and Symiaks.

'Send the crabs to the wall and have the men ready to enter Sanctuary,' Remus said to Redemption.

The captain of the Legion walked off calling orders. Columns of soldiers and Symiaks slowly made their way forward. The two giant crabs waited at the base of the wall. Each had a length of knotted rope tied to their shells.

'Attack the gates, 'Remus shouted as he sent a blast of energy at the gates.

Alpha and the red wizards joined in the magical assault. Kingdom and Legion archers fired up onto the wall to provide cover. Two columns of Legion and kingdom soldiers carried battering rams, holding shields above their heads. The archers on the wall ducked as Shigar began casting another spell.

'I have you, magician, 'Remus growled.

He had been hoping and waiting for this and cast a counterspell. Shigar threw something from the wall. It flew twenty feet before it came back toward him. Shigar was hit in the chest and disappeared in a cloud of black smoke. People nearby on the wall backed away quickly in horror. Covering their faces.

'Enjoy your own medicine, magician, 'Remus said.

***

Shigar finished casting his spell when Joshua and Rain came onto the wall. He threw the component at Remus, knowing it would be a severe blow to the enemy. Then, to his horror, it flew back at him.

The spell hit Shigar and he was lost within the black cloud. He fell to his knees choking and gasping for air with tears rolling down his cheeks. He had thrown the carcass of a dead fish. Anyone who was hit with this would carry a nauseating stench that clung to them.

People backed away from him and they covered their faces as they dry-retched. Shamed as never before, the magician ran down the stairs and to his chambers.

29

Pip pointed down at the clearing and Ramulas saw the giant crabs come to the wall digging deep trenches in the ground with their feet, followed by those holding battering rams. Then movement near the trees made his heart drop. Twenty Symiaks lined up and waited to be thrown onto the wall. If the Symiaks came up with the crabs, those on the wall were in a lot of trouble.

Owain faced the clearing, clicking his tongue to understand what was happening. 'Archers, bring the pots to the wall and throw half when they reach the wall.'

The attacks on the gates stopped as the soldiers came closer. Joshua and Rain came to Ramulas. Rain had drawn his crystal blade, which had mist cascading to his feet. His blue crystal eyes showed his eagerness for battle while Joshua swung his iron ball in lazy circles by his side while softly growling.

Ramulas nodded. 'I need you two to take care of the giant crabs. Will that be too much for you to handle?'

Joshua barked a bitter laugh. 'We have been waiting to fight.'

Pots of molten iron were thrown down onto the upturned shields. It splattered and seeped through the gaps, sending soldiers running away. But this time, the Legion and kingdom archers were ready—they stepped in, firing at the top of the wall. The archers on the wall ducked as the arrows shot over.

That was when the twenty Symiaks were thrown up to the wall. Owain, Joshua, and Ramulas were the only ones who did not duck. 'Archers, aim for the Symiaks coming for the wall.'

The archers on the wall sprung up with bows nocked with arrows. They fired at the Symiaks as they flew to the wall.

'Archers, shoot them as they come up,' Owain said.

The archers sprung up and shot at the Symiaks as they came closer. Owain clicked his tongue as he fired as well. A warm sensation exploded inside Ramulas as the Symiaks came closer. He was soon bathed in purple. He held out his hands, sending purple streams of energy at two of the creatures. They roared before exploding in midair.

A stream of ice shot past Ramulas to turn one of the Symiaks into ice. It shattered when it hit the wall. The rest of the Symiaks were dead by the time they hit the wall. An arc of red energy hit the invisible barrier in front of Ramulas, who waved at Remus with a smile. A few of the clay pots were dropped onto the crabs as they climbed the wall, but the creatures were unaffected, and archers ran to either side of the wall as the crabs climbed over the top of the wall.

Joshua gave a wet growl before charging to the one on his left.

Rain shot a blast of ice to the left before running to his right. This enraged Joshua.

***

With the archers at both ends of the wall, it was safe for the combined army to move forward. Remus and Alpha opened with one last stream of energy at the gates before allowing the battering ram to hit the gates.

Kingdom and Legion columns moved away from the main force toward the ropes left hanging by the crabs. They ran with shields held high to ward off any attacks from above. Symiaks ran forward in scattered numbers, with no pattern or formation.

Owain clicked his tongue rapidly and called out for the archers to shoot the Symiaks and those climbing the ropes.

***

With an angry roar, Joshua launched himself at his crab, swinging his iron ball as the creature turned. A giant pincer opened as Joshua came down swinging his ball, and it broke with an audible crack. The crab scuttled away with foaming bubbles coming from its mouth.

Joshua raced forward with another growl, angry that his opponent moved away. The broken pincer shot forward, hitting Joshua in the chest and sending him back a few feet. The crab came at him leading with its good pincer. Against all common sense and logic, Joshua ran forward to hit the crab in between its eyes, causing it to back away.

As it moved back, Joshua attacked the two front legs on its left and within moments, they had broken off and Joshua was covered in green blood. Then he found himself in the grip of the good pincer. The crab lifted him up and started to squeeze his body. Joshua leaned back with his iron ball to strike, and the chain was jerked out of his hand by the other pincer. Joshua fought for breath as the giant crab crushed the life out of him.

Rain's arm pumped as he ran toward his crab. It was hit with several blasts of ice, and small icicles hung from its body. It scuttled to meet Rain with both pincers snapping.

Rain skidded to a stop, sending a stream of ice and covering one of the pincers, and the crab hit the pincer against the wall a few times until the ice broke into fragments on the floor. It came forward, its pincer moving in slow, jerky movements.

Rain held the blue crystal sword before him and summoned a wall of mist to fall from the blade. He picked up the sword and waved it around his body and above his head until he was surrounded by thick fog.

He heard the crab's legs clicking against the stone as it came forward. With a thought, Rain lifted the mist and found a surprised crab five feet from him. Ice exploded from his sword and trapped all its legs to the wall. With a flick of his wrist, Rain covered the pincers as well.

He rushed in, stabbed the crab in its mouth, and unleashed the sword's power, freezing the crab from the inside. Once the crab was frozen solid, he removed the weapon.

He looked back at Joshua when Ramulas called out. He saw the giant crab lift Joshua, who had lost his iron ball. He took a slow breath before aiming his sword at the other crab and firing a blast.

***

Joshua was frustrated and pounded on the pincer with his gauntlet. Then a blast of ice hit the crab in its mouth and Joshua was dropped to the ground.

Two quick steps brought him to his chain. He picked it up with a growl and began to swing his iron ball. The giant crab busied itself with breaking the ice on its mouth. Joshua leapt through the air and smashed his iron ball into the crab's shell. The crab froze in shock, and Joshua repeatedly struck the creature's body, legs, and pincers.

After ten seconds, all that was left of the crab was a mound of smashed shell and goo. Joshua looked around for another enemy to attack, ignoring the sticky fluid from the crab that covered him. He noticed the ropes attached to its rear legs, and without a second thought, he jumped down into the clearing below.

***

As Rain and Joshua fought the crabs, the archers on the wall fired at the soldiers and Symiaks climbing the ropes. Every now and then, they would have to duck a volley of arrows from the clearing. No matter how many fell from the ropes, more still climbed.

Those on the battering ram stepped aside as Remus and Alpha shot arcs of energy at the gates. Multi-coloured sparks flew in all directions. Then Rain saw a Symiak pop his head over the top of the wall. He ran along the wall, tilting the tip of his swords at the Symiak. A blast of ice hit the Symiak in the face, and it disappeared. A Legion soldier climbed up the other rope. He saw Pip dance across and slit his throat.

Rain looked over the wall to see over twenty men and Symiaks climbing the ropes, and more waited below. He severed the closest rope with a chop from his sword, and then he saw Pip's eyes widen as she looked past him. He turned in time to see Joshua falling down the wall. Joshua grabbed soldiers and Symiaks on his way down to slow his descent.

Ramulas raced along the wall to where Joshua had jumped off with Rain close behind. Pip cut the remaining rope, letting men and Symiaks fall into the clearing.

***

Joshua hit the ground to find scores of the enemy surrounding him and even more running to his position. Joshua smiled, swinging his iron ball. He was in his element. Soldiers and Symiaks were sent flying in every direction as he let loose with his ball. They soon learned to keep their distance.

A group of Symiaks pushed through and charged Joshua. The first two were knocked aside, but the third barrelled him to the ground, sending chunks of grass and soil into the air, and the surrounding enemy pummelled him as he tried to rise.

Then the first explosion went off.

***

Ramulas watched Joshua fight the soldiers and Symiaks and was not sure how long he would last. The nearby columns of soldiers and groups of Symiaks rushed toward him. The archers on the wall fired their arrows, but it did not seem to discourage them with shields above their heads.

'Spears!' Ramulas called out as he picked one up lying nearby and threw it in the middle of a group of Legion soldiers running to Joshua.

The spear hit one of the upraised shields and exploded, sending men flying. Archers on the wall dropped their bows to pick up spears and throw them into the clearing.

The combined army broke and ran back to the trees as the archers on the wall picked up their bows and fired at them. Kingdom and Legion archers returned fire as their men returned, but the damage had already been done.

Scores of soldiers and Symiaks lay dead near the wall, and even more were wounded. Remus, Alpha, and the red wizards created a magical barrier to protect their army from the arrows.

'Stop firing!' Owain called.

The archers on the wall leaned their bows on the wall. Rygar made a few signals and they sat with their backs against the wall. The young boys ran up and down the wall offering water and food. The dwarf hoped for a break in the fighting.

***

Ramulas looked down at the bottom of the wall. Joshua looked across at the enemy camp surrounded by scores of their dead. 'Are you coming back up, or waiting for them to return?'

Joshua looked up at Ramulas in pure rage and growled a challenge.

'I'll take that as a yes,' Ramulas replied.

Hand over hand, Joshua quickly made his way back up again just in time for Rain to greet him. He shot a blast of ice at Joshua that seemed to pass right through him. Joshua growled for a few moments and then calmed down.

Rain turned to Ramulas. 'I am the only one who can help him control the gauntlet.'

Rain severed the ropes hanging from the wall and walked to the middle of the wall. They found Owain had walked down a section of the stairs clicking his tongue. Ramulas walked over to him. 'What is wrong?'

Owain shook his head. 'I heard a crack when they used the battering ram. I am afraid the magical ward has gone, and the gates are cracked, and it won't take much for them to open.'

Ramulas' heart sank. This was happening too quickly. The wards were supposed to last for days. The enemy's magic must be strong. He looked at the dwarf. 'The gates are broken. We need something to block them with.'

Rain stepped forward. 'I can block it for you.'

'How?' Ramulas asked.

Rain tipped his crystal blade into the rear of the gates and shot a stream of ice, and for a minute, everyone watched in silence as the ice grew to fill the passage behind the gates with a solid block of ice. 'It will take them a while to break through that.'

***

Pip waved from the top of the stairs and Ramulas came over to see that the enemy had moved out of arrow range. The dead and wounded still littered the clearing.

'They've had a hidin', Rygar said. 'Ye won't be getting any more trouble for a while. Ye showed 'em too much of a fight.'

A feeling of sadness washed over Ramulas as he looked down at the clearing with the dead and dying then at the archers along the wall. Several had been struck by the enemy arrows.

'Take the injured from the wall to Oriel. Everyone else can rest,' Ramulas said to Pip.

As she walked away, Ramulas turned to the dwarf. 'How do you know they will not attack soon?'

Rygar shook his head. 'They will need to remove their dead and injured from the clearing. Tell them you will offer a truce while they do this. They won't be finished until dark. This will give us time to rest.'

'They will attack us after dark.'

The dwarf nodded. 'We know that, but they don't know that we know.'

With a deep sigh, Ramulas called out to the enemy. 'Collect your injured and dead. You will not be harmed as you do so.'

A few groups came out into the clearing while glancing warily up at the wall with shields held high. When nothing happened to them after they brought back a few injured, more groups came out without worrying about being attacked.

Rygar elbowed Ramulas in the side. 'Ye need to bring men up onto the wall if yer restin' the archers, that way they won't know we're restin.'

His eyes widened at this and ordered two hundred soldiers up from the courtyard, once they were on the wall and in place, the archers closed their eyes and tried to sleep.

***

Pip raced up to Ramulas, very animated. 'The tunnel—something has happened. You need to go to the tunnel.'

'Oriel,' Ramulas said before racing down the stairs.

He navigated around the barricades, past the columns of soldiers, and into the tunnel, where he ran into Edwin. 'Me lord, Royce and Shayn have broken through, but we have a problem.'

'What?'

'Ye need to see for yerself,' Edwin said, walking deeper into the tunnel.

The dwarf struggled to keep up with Ramulas' urgent pace. Two minutes later, they came to the end of the tunnel, where it opened to a giant chasm. The earth elementals stood on the edge looking across.

One hundred yards across was a glowing golden door. The surrounding darkness made it impossible to know how deep the chasm was.

'Is that where Oriel is—behind that door?' Ramulas asked.

Royce nodded. 'We think she is behind that door.'

Shayn pointed across the chasm. 'We need to build a bridge across to the other side. Once the bridge is completed, the door will open. We can tell by the glyphs written around the door.'

'How long will this take you?'

Royce shook his head. 'We are not sure, but we should have it done by tomorrow. We will not stop until we reach the door.'

Ramulas nodded. 'Come for me when the door opens.'

Both elementals smiled as Ramulas left the tunnel.

***

Ramulas came out and realised it would be dark soon. He walked past the barricades and soldiers near the courtyard. The people were more relaxed knowing the enemy had moved away from the wall.

He smiled at the people. 'Please, try to relax. They will attack again soon. Rest while you can.'

He made his way into the castle, politely thanking the people as he passed them. Ramulas wanted one last chance to see his family before the fighting renewed.

He walked into his family quarters to see that Pip was already there. Fenris barked and wagged his tail.

'Da,' Grace said as she ran over to him.

He smiled as he scooped her up. Kate came over as well. Once both girls were in his arms, Jacqueline came over with tears in her eyes. 'The girls have been worried about you. We could hear the fighting from in here,' she said, embracing him.

With his wife and daughters holding him, all Ramulas wanted to do was stay there forever; however, his family was one of the main reasons that he was fighting—to keep them safe from the Legion and the rest of the army outside.

Ramulas was doing this for his family and all the families across the kingdom. If the Legion were victorious here, they would enslave and kill as they moved across the land.

Pip softly coughed behind him. He turned to see her arms crossed and her foot tapping on the floor. 'We can't stay here all night; we have things to do.'

Ramulas released himself from the tangle of bodies. 'Everything will be fine. I will return soon. Stay in this room and you will be safe.' Then he turned to Grace. 'Little one, I do not want you using magic while I am gone. I want you to promise.'

After a moment she nodded. 'I promise.'

He quickly kissed his family and left with Pip.

***

They walked into the throne room to find Oriel looking out of the window, and Ramulas said, 'The earth elementals have found the doorway to set you free. As soon as they build a pathway across, you will be free.'

She turned and smiled sadly at Ramulas and Pip. 'There is not much time. You need to reach me before Remus.'

'Do not worry. We will hold them outside the wall until you are free,' Ramulas said.

'I know you will, but I don't think you can make it in time.'

'Do not worry,' Ramulas said before leading Pip out of the room.

Oriel was worried. She was so close to being released, but she felt the energies of Sanctuary and knew that the ward on the gates had collapsed. The Legion would soon find their way into Sanctuary, and the people would not stand a chance against them.

She also wanted to tell them about Nathaniel and how her freedom was tied to his and that, once he was out, Nathaniel would unleash his anger on everyone.

30

Remus, Zachary, the royal guard, and the three captains of the Legion sat in the command tent. Five Symiak chieftains came in and sat before them. Zachary was surprised at the drop in temperature as the sun dropped. It was never this cold early in spring.

The kingdom and Legion soldiers could be heard singing and laughing by the campfires. The Symiaks were hooting and stomping in the distance. Remus explained the sound of this would unnerve the people in Sanctuary.

'They have given us a few surprises, and no doubt there will be a few more, but the magic in front of the gates has weakened and we will break through in the morning. When the gates are open, everyone will need to charge at once,' Remus said.

'Should we attack now while it's dark?' Zachary asked.

Remus looked at Zachary as if he were a child who asked a stupid question. 'They will be expecting an attack tonight. Let them wait and worry while we rest, but I have a plan for tonight.'

The red wizards sat in a separate tent casting spells to activate the three crystals that had been thrown over into Sanctuary. If the crystals were ready in time, Remus could use them in the attack on Sanctuary. The red wizards would need to cast spells through the night.

***

Three hours after nightfall, Ramulas and Pip stood on the wall watching the enemy in the clearing and forest with small plumes of steam coming out of their mouths with each breath. Pip's eyes glowed a fierce green as she studied the Symiaks and soldiers, both within tents and around campfires. She had been searching for the last hour for patterns in the camp.

She smiled. 'They won't be attacking any time soon. Maybe by morning. They need to do a lot of work before they are ready.'

'How do you know? Ramulas asked.

Pip shrugged. 'I have seen soldiers take turns at the campfires. They sit there in shifts of no more than an hour before going into a tent for rest.'

'Hello to you, Lord of Sanctuary. The thrower of knives is correct,' Iguchi said, appearing next to Ramulas. 'Their laughter is forced to make them appear relaxed and ready for battle.'

'What are they doing?' Pip said, grabbing Ramulas by the arm and pointing into the clearing.

Ramulas followed where she was pointing and saw two Symiaks creeping up to the wall holding a ladder. Pip picked up a bow and loaded it with an arrow that had bubbles on its tip. She leaned over and shot them as they reached the bottom of the wall. The arrow hit the ladder, and both Symiaks were covered in green sticky goo. They both tripped and fell several times running back to their camp.

As Pip and Iguchi suspected, the response from the camp was non-existent. Over the next hour, Pip watched several pairs of Symiaks run to the wall and drop ladders before returning to their camp. The ladders were less than half the height of the wall, and Ramulas knew this was just a diversion.

Then a shaft of bright white light shot from the cliff face where Logan had taken his group into the secret entrance.

***

Logan had adapted quickly to his transformation. He brought his arm up in front of his face and flexed his muscles. He grunted as spikes of bone came out of his forearm and knuckles. He had never felt so powerful in his life.

However, with this power came an almost insatiable hunger. Saliva drooled freely from his jaw full of sharp teeth. The creature in the tattered cloak floated in front of Logan and the others. 'Go out into the night and feast upon the flesh of men.'

The door to the outside world opened, allowing twilight to light the cavern. The demons raced out into the night, almost driven mad at the thought of food so close.

***

'Look over there,' Pip said, pointing to the east.

Ramulas and Iguchi peered into the darkness but were unable to see what she could. Then Pip gasped as she saw the demons emerge. 'The torches on the wall. Quickly, put them all out.'

Ramulas was about to ask why, and then he saw the expression of absolute terror on her face, so he ordered the torches to be doused.

As the wall of Sanctuary fell into darkness, the singing and laughing of the enemy camp turned into shouts of alarm and screams for mercy. Those on the wall watched the shadows of the enemy forces silhouetted by the campfires race from whatever terror Pip had seen.

***

The demons tore through the first lines of kingdom soldiers before anyone knew what had happened, and then they began to eat the soldiers alive. The audible sound of bones cracking could be heard over the screams of pain as the demons gorged on flesh.

A group of kingdom archers formed a line and began firing at the demons. The arrows bounced off the demon's hardened skin. The arrows were nothing more than an irritation to them.

A warning was called out as a group of cavalry rode at the demons with their swords drawn. The demons were happy to drop their food to pull these soldiers from their horses to feast on them. The cavalry had time to gasp as their swords bounced off the demons before they were dragged off their horses, had their armour torn open, and demons ripped at their bodies.

A bolt of lightning shot from the trees, hitting one of the demons and causing a shower of sparks from its body as it looked up from its feast with blood dripping from its mouth. It saw a nervous Alpha who could not understand how his spell had no effect on the creature.

The demon that was once Logan dropped its meal and roared; the other demons stopped their feasting to glare at the warlord. Soldiers formed a loose circle around the demons, holding swords and shields. They were uncertain as to what they had to do because their weapons seemed to have no effect on the demons.

Columns of Legion soldiers pushed their way through the kingdom soldiers towards the demons. The demon that was once Logan leapt through the air toward Alpha, and a blast of red energy knocked it aside, sending it into one of the campfires.

***

Remus and Zachary's heads turned at the calls of alarm and screams of terror. 'They are attacking us,' Zachary said.

Remus did not respond as he rushed out of the tent leading the others. He could feel the dark energies in the air. They saw the chaos at the edge of the kingdom camp. Alpha walked towards the fighting as the cavalry rode by.

The riders were pulled from their horses, and Alpha cast a spell that hit one of the creatures. With a roar, it jumped at him. Remus' hand shot forward and a blast of red energy knocked the demon aside.

He watched its path as it crashed through the campsite. Soldiers ran forth, hacking away with their swords, but the demon seemed unafffected. Spikes formed on its arms, and with sweeps of its arms, it sent screaming soldiers flying in all directions.

A Symiak came crashing through the campsite, tackling the demon. Both fell into a barrel of water, which exploded sending water everywhere. A high-pitched keening sound escaped the demon as steam rose from its body. A Legion soldier thrust his sword through the demon's back.

The demon screamed while clawing at the air in front of it. It turned suddenly, causing the Legion soldier to lose grip of his weapon. The tip of the sword could be seen coming out of the creature's chest. Other soldiers rushed in and cut it to pieces.

'Water makes them weak,' the Legion soldier called out.

Remus and Alpha cast water spells on the remaining demons and the soldiers ran forward in rage. The demons lashed out at the first few but were soon overwhelmed and cut down in an onslaught of swords.

Once Remus was certain that the danger had passed, he walked over with Zachary to inspect the bodies. What they saw was truly disturbing—through the spikes and deformed bodies, they could see the uniforms of kingdom and Legion soldiers.

'This was the group Logan took into the mountain,' Remus said.

Zachary was dumbfounded. 'How did this happen?'

'A strong dark and powerful magical power was at work here.'

'The people of Sanctuary are to blame for this,' Zachary said.

Remus doubted this but did not voice his opinion. This magic was on a different level than he had ever seen before. They needed to prepare the camp for the following day's attack and see what other surprises came their way. But first, they needed to remove the bodies of the demons. The smell of decaying flesh was almost overwhelming.

***

At dawn, the combined army stood in columns facing the wall with the Symiaks scattered amongst them. As they came forward, Pip pointed to the groups with the battering rams. 'They're ready for our arrows.'

Ramulas grunted and he watched them come. They walked four abreast with shields above their heads, and he could make out the extra padding on their bodies making their walking cumbersome.

Remus and Alpha opened their hands and directed streams of energy at the gates, sending showers of multi-coloured sparks in all directions.

'How long?' Ramulas asked Pip asked as she leaned over to see the magical ward in front of the gates begin to break.

'Very soon.'

Ramulas turned toward Sanctuary and waved both hands above his head. A moment later, he smiled. 'Joshua, Rain, and the three giant-kin have just entered the maze—they are going to be part of our welcoming committee.'

Then Ramulas saw Shigar sitting with his back to the wall. After his last spell had backfired, it had taken the magician a lot of time to wash away the smell. Shigar had one more spell left in him, and Ramulas hoped it would be a surprise for the enemy.

***

Remus and Alpha lowered their hands and the streams of energy stopped. The battering ram units shuffled forward, and the archers on the wall remained still. Not one arrow was fired.

'Now,' Ramulas said to the magician.

Shigar began reading from his book, and Ramulas could feel the magical energies build around them. A small glowing ball of light lay in Shigar's hand, and he placed the book on the ground to stand closer to the edge of the wall. He dropped the ball of light into the clearing, and everyone on the wall turned away. It hit the ground, sending a bright wave of the brightest light rolling across the clearing.

Those looking at the wall became temporarily blind as their retinas went into overload. Shields and weapons were dropped, and hands went up to faces as they screamed in pain and panic.

'Now!' Owain called.

The archers turned and began firing down at those in the clearing. Soldiers and Symiaks screamed while running around blindly. Orders to calm down were ignored as panic overrode their senses. The soldiers regained their senses as their eyesight returned, and they quickly ran to the trees and picked up shields.

Alpha and Remus shot more energy at the gates, and after a few seconds, the magical ward broke with the sound of shattering glass. The battering rams rushed the gates.

'Bubbles!' Owain called.

Archers carefully nocked their bows and fired at those closest to the wall. Shouts of alarm were called out as soldiers were bound together by the sticky goo. A quick count told Ramulas that around two hundred had died in the assault.

The Symiaks and soldiers struggled in the green web. As the red wizards stepped out of their tent, Remus and Alpha sprayed a mist over the green nets, which dissolved them.

Pip pointed to the red wizards. 'They have been working on their magic all night. They have been working on something, and now that the gate is unprotected, I do not know what will happen next.'

Ramulas saw her serious expression and scanned the archers on the wall. The enemy would break through the gates and everyone on the wall would have to run down the stairs into the courtyard and then into the castle.

'The block of ice is behind the gates,' Ramulas said.

Pip looked below her feet and her eyes glowed fiercely as she saw the block of ice through the floor she was standing on. A large crack ran through the block. 'It won't take them long to get in the gates.'

'Iguchi, I need the soldiers off the wall. Then take your Fallen Angels out with the druids,' Ramulas said.

Iguchi bowed before calling out orders while running down the stairs, closely followed by the soldiers. Ramulas walked over to the blind bowman. 'Owain, they will come through the gate soon. Have the archers fire a few arrows each before coming into the castle.'

'Five arrows!' Owain called out.

A wave of arrows came down on raised shields in the clearing as the battering ram pounded on the gates. After the third wave of arrows, the enemy archers responded, and those on the wall were forced to duck. While they were out of sight, Owain ordered that they go to the castle.

After a few moments, only Ramulas and Pip remained on the wall. Then they heard the gates break open.

Pip smiled at Ramulas. 'Time to go.'

They raced downstairs to the courtyard.

***

They arrived in the throne room to find a doorway of light, and Oriel was nowhere to be seen. She had discussed the door of light with Ramulas. It was a way to even the odds of this battle. He took one last look for Oriel before stepping towards the door and he glanced at Pip.

'Wait here for me to return.'

As the doorway began to close, Pip shrugged and jumped in after Ramulas.

***

The three magical crystals thrown into Sanctuary had grown rapidly in the last hour with help from the red wizards. All three stood like translucent arches and remained dormant. They would activate and become visible when the final spell was cast.

***

Twelve druids walked through the forest, followed by Iguchi and the Fallen Angels. They were coming up behind the combined army as they rushed the wall. The druids were the only ones making noise as they moved through the trees. When they were two hundred yards from the army, the Fallen Angels split and flanked the druids from the trees.

A few sentries from the kingdom army turned when they heard the snapping of branches and leaves and saw the druids when they were fifty yards away. Primal fear gripped their chests as the druids came closer. Every child of the kingdom had been brought up with horrible stories of druids coming to take people away in the dead of night. These soldiers were too scared to move or speak.

The druids took wands out of their robes as they came closer, making the childhood nightmares come to life. This broke the spell and the soldier screamed.

Kingdom soldiers turned, and their eyes widened at the sight of the druids. This was their undoing. The druids sent streams of bubbles of all sizes at the soldiers. The druids waved their hands, sending the bubbles to the startled soldiers.

Shouts of shock and alarm rang out as the bubbles exploded, sending sticky green webs that attached soldiers to each other and trees. Kingdom and Legion soldiers were joined by Symiaks as they ran around the webs and trees to attack the druids.

Hands dropped into pouches and threw stones into the air. These transformed into stone wasps that attacked the enemy. Men and Symiaks swatted at the wasps and tried to run as more bubbles came out of the trees to explode around them, covering everyone.

Soldiers and Symiaks ran into the webs as they tried to escape the wasps. When the numbers became too great, the druids retreated into the forest. Men and Symiaks saw this as a sign of weakness and chased them as the Fallen Angels stepped out from the trees.

The Angels hit both sides of the enemy simultaneously. Swords slashed through the enemy before they knew that they were under attack. The combination of druids and the Fallen Angels decimated the enemy's rearguard. The movements of the enemy soldiers appeared slow compared to that of the Angels. They danced around slashing and stabbing at the confused mass.

Miles led his side into the enemy's flank with controlled fury. The memory of Benji still fresh in his mind, he acted without thought as he swatted away attacks as if they were flies, then he would deliver a vicious thrust or slash before moving on.

Then Benji appeared next to him, smiling and saying one of his smart remarks about Iguchi's training. Miles blinked and Benji was gone. The pain of losing his friend deepened. Miles roared and attacked with renewed fury, and the surrounding Symiaks and soldiers soon kept their distance.

Iguchi led the attack on the other side, dancing up and down the line with rapid thrusts of his swords. Exposed arms, legs, and faces were cut, causing a moment of distraction—more than enough time for his Fallen Angels to kill the enemy.

***

A fireball flew over their heads to hit one of the webs in between the trees. The web, and three soldiers trapped within, burst into flame. The sound of the explosion and the soldiers' screams caused enough distraction.

'To the forest!' Iguchi called.

In the blink of an eye, the Fallen Angels and druids vanished.

***

The red wizard cursed himself for using a fireball as Alpha walked over to him. Then they both jumped as an image of Ramulas appeared before them. 'If you wish to end this now, step into my image, and we will see who has the greater power.'

This was an offer they could not refuse. They looked at each other once before stepping into Ramulas' image. After a bright flash, all three had vanished.

31

The red wizard found himself in the training room that Ramulas and Pip had been using. He saw that he was in a small stone room bare of any furnishings. Ramulas walked out of the shadows ten feet away.

'Where is Alpha?' the red wizard asked.

Ramulas held out his hands. 'He will come after I have defeated you.'

The red wizard sneered. 'What makes you think that you can beat me?'

Ramulas shrugged. 'I am the Avenger. The warlords and red wizards are supposed to tremble before me. That is part of the prophecy, is it not?'

The red wizard's eyes opened in shock as Ramulas recalled what Oriel had told him. The red wizards mastered the lower levels of magic and were intimidated by the warlords. Ramulas needed to strike first. A warm sensation exploded within his stomach and flowed through his body.

Purple flames danced along Ramulas' arms. His right hand shot forward, sending a stream of fire at the red wizard, who countered with a water spell. The flame hit the water, sending a hissing wall of steam to the ceiling.

With a left-right-left combination, Ramulas sent three more streams of fire at the wizard, each one countered with a water spell.

'I have defences for fire spells,' the red wizard said.

Ramulas winked. 'I know.'

Ramulas waved his arms, turning the flame on him from purple to blue, and then he brought both hands together in a thunderclap, sending a blue shockwave across the room. Ramulas had released a high-level water spell, and the red wizard was now encased in a block of ice and still wore a shocked expression with a hand held out defensively.

Ramulas walked forward holding his war hammer. Using two hands, he swung the war hammer in an overhead chop. The block of ice shattered, sending frozen pieces of the red wizard across the floor.

In a flash of light, Alpha stood before Ramulas and unleashed an energy blast that pushed Ramulas back a few feet, almost knocking him over.

Ramulas held his war hammer before him in both hands as he regained balance. His weapon had absorbed most of the blast. He stepped forward and brought the hammer down, sending a shockwave of purple energy at Alpha and knocking him back. This gave Ramulas time to take out his battle axe.

With a thought, Ramulas' body and weapons were covered in purple flame.

'Battlemage,' Alpha spat in disgust.

Ramulas shrugged as he smiled. 'One thing makes me better than you.'

'What is that?'

Ramulas crossed the handles of his weapons, and a shaft of white light shot at Alpha, who erected a barrier just in time, sending white light in all directions.

Enraged, Alpha shot both hands forward, sending streams of red energy at Ramulas. They exploded as they hit the purple flames surrounding the Lord of Sanctuary. Ramulas and Alpha unleashed spells and counterspells, sending multi-coloured sparks in all directions. Their spells were cancelling out each other. They had come to an impasse.

Ramulas decided to use his weapons. He turned his body and spun both before him. As the weapons gathered magical energy, he would send arcs at Alpha. He needed a moment's respite to unleash a spell that would win the battle, but he and the warlord were equally matched.

Two throwing knives came spinning out of the shadows, hitting Alpha's robes, but the spell surrounding the warlord deflected them and they clattered to the floor, causing Alpha to look down.

This was the distraction Ramulas needed—he rushed forward, holding up his battle axe, and Alpha cast a spell that put a magical shield above his head. Ramulas focused on his magical ability and placed a small flesh-eating worm inside Alpha's head.

Alpha's eyes popped open and froze as he felt something crawling through his brain.

Ramulas smiled at him. 'What's wrong? Something on your mind?'

Alpha's eyes darted around, and he still did not move. Ramulas swung his foot with all his might, catching the warlord in the groin and lifting him a foot into the air. As Alpha collapsed, Ramulas swung down with his battle axe. As the warlord's head rolled, Pip stepped out of the shadows.

Ramulas sighed. 'You were not supposed to be here.'

'You're welcome,' Pip said as she picked up her knives and wrinkled her nose. 'This room will smell if we don't clean it.'

Ramulas shook his head. 'That can wait. We have a battle to fight.'

They raced out of the room. Ramulas needed to reach the balcony on the sixth floor facing the courtyard. This would give them a good view of the maze and the chance to oversee his people.

***

Royce and Shayn had been working continuously building the bridge across the chasm and were ten yards from the golden door. The image of Nathaniel appeared in the doorway. The earth elementals stopped and watched as Nathaniel waved to them, encouraging them to hurry.

'What do we do about him?' Shayn asked.

Royce shrugged. 'I do not know, but we need to free Oriel.'

***

The gates had broken away and all that stopped the combined army was a thick block of ice. The Symiaks had grabbed the battering ram and were making short work of the ice. Showers of ice exploded with each hit. Kingdom and Legion soldiers pulled away the chunks to make room.

Then, with a final crack, the right-hand side of the ice block shattered and collapsed. Men and Symiaks pulled away at the ice in a frenzy to reveal a way into the maze. A group of kingdom soldiers and Symiaks were the first to rush into the maze. After a short while, they heard stone grinding against stone and shouts of alarm.

The turned to see a part of their group being cut off by the walls moving in the maze. All they could do was continue through the maze until they reached Sanctuary.

They continued to hear the walls move. Along with shouts from soldiers and Symiaks, it seemed that the combined army was being split into smaller groups as they entered the maze.

The walls were twelve feet high, and the top would shift, dropping any Symiak or soldier if they tried to climb them. Soldiers and Symiaks heard faint echoes of their steps as they walked. Then a kingdom soldier saw an intricate carving of an octopus on the wall, and he noticed the octopus' eye following him.

'Look at this,' he said, stopping to touch the engraving.

His mouth fell open as he touched the stone, and the octopus began to move along the wall. One of the tentacles reached out to caress his face before pulling away with half the soldier's face.

Warm blood flowed from his face as the soldier let out an horrific scream before he fell to the ground in shock. Another octopus leapt from the wall to land on a kingdom soldier's shoulders. It wrapped its tentacles around his neck and squeezed. He fell to the ground trying to pull it off before his neck snapped.

Nearby soldiers ran away in fear as screams could be heard throughout the maze. A Symiak stepped forward to pick up an octopus and grinned, snapping off one of the tentacles. It moved and sprayed a jet of acid into the creature's face. The Symiak fell to its knees, holding its face, as steam poured out between its fingers.

The walls within the maze came alive as scores of octopuses swam along the walls and leapt out at soldiers and Symiaks. The octopuses seemed to float as they left the walls with tentacles reaching out for their next victim. Soldiers attempted to run, but in the confines of the maze, there weren't too many places they could go.

***

Lodi and the two half-giants were running through the maze when they heard the first scream. Lodi held his club and the two half-giants held long broadswords. As they went deeper into the maze, they saw the octopuses moving along the walls. They wanted to reach the enemy before Joshua and Rain.

A wager had been placed to see which group could kill the most enemies within the maze. After a minute, Lodi roared and lifted his club. A group of Symiaks came out of an intersection before them.

With a powerful sweep of his club, Lodi hit the first creature against the wall before jabbing the end of his club into the face of the nearest Symiak. The remaining four Symiaks ran at the half-giants, thinking they were easier prey.

With the movement of seasoned fighters, the half-giants parried the clumsy strikes of the Symiaks then, with economical thrusts and strikes, the four Symiaks soon lay dead. The half-giants looked up to see Lodi pound his two Symiaks to a pulp. They were already dead, but that did not seem to matter to Lodi.

***

Joshua and Rain jogged through the maze as the first screams could be heard.

'The giant-kin,' Joshua said.

Rain shook his head. 'No. Too much terror—if it were the giants, they would be laughing.'

Joshua smiled as they went deeper into the maze. Joshua swung his iron ball and Rain held his blue crystal sword, which left a trail of mist as they walked. They came to an intersection and saw a score of soldiers and Symiaks.

Rain pushed Joshua back and shot blasts of ice at the mass. The ice stopped six feet from the enemy and formed an ice wall. It was an inch thick and high as the walls of the maze. The Symiaks began bashing on the ice with their clubs and swords.

After a few seconds, the ice wall shattered. Symiaks and soldiers were shocked to see Joshua swinging his iron ball just a few feet away. With a growl, he stepped forward and swung his ball.

A Symiak was hit in the chest and thrown back into two soldiers, the trio falling into a heap by the time Joshua moved onto his next target. Rain stood twenty feet behind, pointing his crystal sword. He stood back, allowing Joshua to have his fun. A blast of ice would hit any who tried to get behind Joshua.

***

Remus watched with a grim smile as soldiers and Symiaks entered the maze. Oriel would be his once again.

'We are ready, lord.' He turned to see a red wizard.

'Where is Alpha?'

The red wizard shrugged, and Remus said. 'Never mind. Prepare the openings.'

The red wizard returned to the others, and they began to chant while waving their hands through the air. After a few moments, three doorways of light appeared near the trees. This meant that the crystal arches within Sanctuary were open.

Remus gave the order for Symiaks and soldiers to enter the doorways. He knew that the doors would vanish after two hundred entered; however, with the whole of Sanctuary facing the wall, six hundred soldiers and Symiaks could do a lot of damage.

Symiaks and soldiers formed lines in front of the door, eager to enter Sanctuary. The three captains of the Legion also joined them as they entered.

Remus nodded, knowing that hundreds would die in Sanctuary before they knew what had happened.

***

The crystal arches in Sanctuary hummed as the first group of soldiers and Symiaks stepped out near the waterfall with the three captains of the Legion. Looking around, they saw that the streets were empty. They could hear fighting and screaming coming from the maze. Redemption saw the castle and knew that they were to enter and find the throne room. Logan had shown them maps of how to get there.

Three young boys came out of a nearby house carrying food and buckets of water fifty yards from the enemy. They froze when they saw Legion and kingdom soldiers. The three stood perfectly still, too afraid to move. Their heartbeats and heavy breathing seemed deafening to them.

A Legion soldier nocked his bow and sent an arrow flying to hit the middle boy in the chest. As the body flipped in the air, the other two boys ran towards the wall, screaming for help. Arrows flew passed them as they ran for their lives. The boy on the left jerked as an arrow punched through his neck.

Fuelled by sheer terror, the remaining boy picked up speed and screamed louder. He turned a few corners before hitting someone and falling to the ground.

He looked up to see Iguchi and the Fallen Angels.

***

The second group came out two hundred yards from the statues of the fallen. Groups of women and children were frozen in fear as they saw the enemy walk through the arch. They screamed as the Legion soldier gave chase.

The women and children ran to the statues of the fallen. Fifty in all dropped to their knees begging for mercy and for the statues to help them. The hundred Legion soldiers surrounded the crying women and children smiling as they closed in.

A Legion soldier reached down to pick up a small girl who screamed for the fallen to help her.

Then the statues of the fallen opened their eyes.

***

Iguchi and the Fallen Angels rushed to where the boy said the enemy was. Redemption, Reckoning, and Retribution saw the Angels come around the corner just as another hundred soldiers came through the arch.

'Go into the castle and find Oriel,' Redemption said to them.

The Fallen Angels saw the kingdom and Legion soldiers run to the castle, leaving the three captains behind. The Angels charged and the three captains calmly spread out drawing their weapons.

Miles saw the arch behind the three that allowed the enemy into Sanctuary, but he knew that the three before him were important to the enemy. If they were killed, it would aid Sanctuary.

Miles screamed as he led the attack on the three captains. After they were killed, the Fallen Angels would deal with those who came through the arch.

Then something strange happened.

As Miles thrust his sword at Redemption's stomach, his opponent smiled and turned away at the last possible moment, knocking Miles' sword away with a swipe of his baton. Before Miles could react, he was struck on the inside of each forearm with the batons.

Pins and needles ran up Miles' arms and he dropped his sword and shield. Redemption spun, kicking Miles in the face. To his surprise, Miles fell to the ground. All the months of exhausting training in the snow and now he was disarmed and on the ground in under two seconds.

As Miles picked up his sword and shield, he watched the other Fallen Angels fight the three captains and he was stunned. Each of the three moved like Iguchi, but they were faster, stronger, and younger.

It was at that moment that Miles knew that the Angels were in trouble.

The three captains seemed to dance amid the Fallen Angels with their spiked batons, curved claws, and twin swords batting away all Fallen Angel attacks.

To Miles' horror, he realised they were just playing with the Angels.

Then, without warning, three Fallen Angels were brutally killed. Reckoning reached out with his claws, catching an Angel's breastplate and pulling him off-balance. Redemption spun in a tight circle, catching the falling Angel on the temple with a spiked baton, and then he rushed another Angel, kicking him in the chest.

Reckoning danced to the left to grab the Fallen Angel from behind. With his claws in the Angel's face and throat, he shook his body violently, tearing out chunks of flesh, and the Angel died in a pool of his own blood.

Retribution spun to the side, cutting off an Angel's arm at the elbow, then thrust both swords through his breastplate. This Angel fell to his knees, drowning in his own blood.

***

Iguchi had allowed his Fallen Angels to go ahead, confident that they would have no problem against the three captains. To his dismay, he realised his error when he saw three of his Angels fall.

'My Angels, retreat,' Iguchi called as he ran forward.

Without hesitation, the Fallen Angels stepped away from the three. Iguchi's heart broke seeing three of his Angels dead before him. He pointed to the enemy that came out of the arch. 'Kill them, my Angels. Leave these three to me.'

With one last look at their dead companions, the Fallen Angels ran off. Iguchi walked into the middle of the three captains and looked each one in the eyes, his expression devoid of all emotion.

'You have harmed my Angels; I will bring you much sorrow,' Iguchi said as his heart bled, for he saw each of his Angels as his own sons.

The three smiled as they closed in on Iguchi.

***

The group of kingdom and Legion soldiers raced to the rear entrance of the castle. As they entered, a group of Khilli warriors led by K'ayden saw them from two hundred yards away and gave chase, their shouts echoing throughout the hallways. At the stairway, the Khilli found fifty kingdom and Legion soldiers waiting for them. The rest raced toward the throne room.

The Khilli warriors threw themselves at the kingdom and Legion soldiers in a fury never seen before. Here they were, face-to-face with those who imprisoned their families for generations, and Oriel had shown them what the Legion would do if they were victorious.

Screams of the fighting echoed up the stairs.

The sounds of the fighting travelled down the hallway into Ramulas' quarters. Kate and Grace ran to their mother and held onto her tightly. She looked down to see fear in the eyes of her daughters.

'What do we do?' Jenna asked. Jacqueline looked at Pip's sister holding her two small children, and then she saw the hell hounds. They were the only protection they had. Then she thought of something. Oriel was in the throne room—she could help protect them.

'Come with me,' she said.

She led the small group and hell hounds to the throne room, and as they entered the room, the fifty Legion and kingdom soldiers came out of the stairway and saw them.

Jacqueline and the girls slammed the door shut as the hell hounds began barking. The door shook as the soldiers hit it from the other side. They were not able to put the beam in place. Then it opened an inch before Jacqueline and the girls pushed it shut once more. Jacqueline and Jenna picked up the wooden beam to lock the door, and then with an explosion, the door flew open.

Chaos reigned.

Jacqueline and Jenna were thrown back. Kate and Grace ran back, picking up Makayla and Tao as they went, and soldiers poured into the room. The hell hounds attacked. The sounds of women and children screaming were mixed with armour being torn from the soldiers and grunts of pain.

Jacqueline grabbed Jenna by the hand and dragged her to the throne. A dozen kingdom soldiers ran out of the room, followed by the hell hounds, and the rest of the soldiers closed in on the women and children.

A kingdom soldier rushed forward swinging his sword, and Kate danced forward to meet him. She grabbed his wrist and twisted it as she turned her body flipping the soldier. She caught his sword as it fell.

Kate stood strong with her shoulders back and full of confidence. 'Leave now or die,' she whispered.

The kingdom and Legion soldiers were shocked at this.

'Kate, come here this instant,' Jacqueline called.

Kate shook her head and walked toward the enemy. At this moment, Kate knew that this was her destiny. Two Legion soldiers charged, one coming in low, the other high. Kate shook her head and spun her body, falling to her knees, and with a dazzling display, she deflected the low strike while avoiding the high thrust, stabbed the first soldier in the thigh, and quickly stood to slash the throat of the other. She tilted her head at the soldiers. 'Leave now.'

The Legion and kingdom soldiers were beyond stunned. Here was a young girl who dispatched two Legion soldiers with ease. How could this be?

Four Legion soldiers rushed in, eager to avenge their companions. Kate spun as she met them, her swords constantly moving up and down, deflecting strikes while her body twisted and turned at impossible angles. Every now and then, she would score a minor hit on a soldier's arm or leg, but she mainly focused on keeping herself in between the soldiers, so they worried about hitting one another to get to her.

Kate was gaining the upper hand when four more soldiers rushed in, one of them striking high, bringing her guard up and exposing her body, when another kicked her hard in the side, sending her sprawling across the floor.

These were Legion soldiers after all, and this insult needed to be rectified. They slowly walked over to Kate lying on the floor holding her side wanting so badly for the pain to cease so she could continue fighting. Jacqueline stepped over her daughter and picked up the sword to stand protectively in front of her.

32

Royce and Shane laid the last stone to complete the bridge. Nathaniel punched both fists into the air in triumph. The magical door pulsed as the golden glyphs fell away. Then the door exploded, sending shards flying across the chasm. Royce and Shayne were thrown from the edge and fell into the darkness.

'I am free!' Nathaniel shouted, stepping onto the bridge. He took a few steps, stretching his wings, before leaping into the air. He flew down the tunnel towards Sanctuary. His sword and gauntlet were nearby. He could feel them calling to him.

The entrance of the tunnel was guarded by one hundred soldiers facing outward. Without a second thought, Nathaniel flew out of the tunnel, sending the soldiers flying like leaves in a storm. He flew above the town and an invisible force pulled him towards the castle. He flew up to the balcony on the sixth floor where he saw a man of great power. He would be the first one Nathaniel would fight after he retrieved his weapons.

Archers on the wall of the castle looked at Nathaniel in shock. Not one of them fired any arrows. Nathaniel turned to the maze as an ice blast shot into the air. He flew to be reunited with his weapons.

***

The statue's eyes burned a fierce purple. The Legion soldier holding the girl hesitated when he saw their eyes open. With jerking movements, the

293

statues stepped down onto the ground, their swords and shields held ready.

The Legion soldier released the girl and stepped back. Smiles vanished as the Legion soldiers prepared for battle. The children ran up to the statues with tears of relief running down their cheeks. The fallen took slow stiff steps towards the Legion soldiers, each step becoming smoother than the last.

The Legion soldiers waited for the fallen to come. A fallen used his sword as he came forward. The Legion soldier blocked the slow strike and stabbed the fallen in the throat. His eyes widened as the tip of his sword snapped. The fallen smiled as it brought its sword down in a vicious arc, cleaving the soldier from shoulder to hip. The rest of the fallen attacked the soldiers.

It did not matter how fast or how many times the skilled Legion soldiers attacked the statues; they were unaffected. Each time they were hit, they would lash out at the Legion soldiers. Most times, the soldiers were able to move out of the way, and they learned not to block with their shields, as the statues' swords broke through.

After a fierce battle, only thirty-five Legion soldiers remained standing. The statues of the fallen had formed a protective semicircle around the women and children. Each time a Legion soldier attempted to pass, he was cut down. Bodies of dead Legion soldiers lay strewn near the statues. The remaining soldiers looked at each other before running to another fight.

The fallen did not give chase. They remained in a protective formation around the women and children. Their purpose was to protect the children.

***

Iguchi stood in the middle of the three captains as they slowly circled him. Then, in a fluid movement, Retribution sheathed his swords, crossed his arms, and stepped back.

Redemption and Reckoning rushed at Iguchi. Iguchi spread his feet and lowered his centre of balance with both his swords out in front of him then, without warning, he shuffled to the left and delivered a sidekick to Redemption, hitting him squarely in the chest. Then he turned to face Reckoning's claws.

A claw was thrust at his face, which he parried, and the other claw came in for Iguchi's stomach. Iguchi danced out of the way, barely missing it, and then he attacked Reckoning with a flurry of his swords, and each blow was blocked or parried by the claws.

Iguchi heard a faint shuffle behind him. He moved to the right and dived into a forward roll. A spiked baton swung through the air where his head had been. Iguchi stood in a fluid movement and waited for the duo to make their next move.

They ran at him and separated ten feet from him. Redemption and Reckoning worked in concert—one would attack Iguchi while the other would stand back and watch, and then they would swap. Iguchi continued to dance back and forth between the two, not able to strike any major blows. It was as if they were somehow communicating with each other.

Iguchi saw an opening in Reckoning's defence. He slashed at his head with his swords, forcing the claws up, and then leaned forward and thrust his sword into his exposed stomach. With lightning speed, a claw came down to entrap the sword. Without thought, Iguchi rammed the hilt of his short sword into Reckoning's ribs. The other claw came down, trapping this sword as well.

With both his swords trapped, Iguchi was left with no choice but to release them and fall to the ground just as a spiked baton hit Reckoning in between the eyes, killing him instantly. Iguchi twisted and rolled around on the ground with Redemption close behind trying to hit him with the batons.

Iguchi rose to his feet to find Redemption blocking him from his swords. He glanced to the side to see that Retribution still stood with his arms crossed. Seeing Iguchi unarmed, Redemption came forward, swinging both batons. Iguchi twisted and turned, narrowly avoiding them. Some of the strikes came so close he could feel the air as they passed.

Then Iguchi found an opening.

He ducked under a right swing and, when Redemption's arm was fully extended, Iguchi thrust two rigid fingers into his armpit, which temporarily paralysed him. Iguchi stepped to the captain's front and slapped both his hands over Redemption's ears, shattering the eardrums, and then punched him in the throat, with his knuckles crushing his larynx.

Iguchi turned from the dying man as he fought for breath and retrieved his swords.

He turned to see Retribution with his arms still folded. 'You are next.'

He walked forward and stopped ten feet from the remaining captain, who smiled as he uncrossed his arms and slowly tapped the hilts of his twin swords.

Retribution laughed. 'I know the moves you are going to make; you have already lost.'

Iguchi closed his eyes, slid his right foot forward, and held the hilt of his long sword in a reverse grip. His eyes were closed, and his left hand was out as if holding up a wall.

Retribution gasped. He had seen this very stance many years ago. It was said that only a true master could defeat any attack from that position, but Retribution had killed that master and would do the same to Iguchi.

Iguchi moved as he heard the gasp, shuffling forward quickly, pulling his sword up and across, opening the captain's stomach and ribcage. He then thrust the tip of his sword down into Retribution's collarbone and into his heart.

Both fighters fell to their knees.

Retribution had thrust his sword into Iguchi's stomach as he attacked. Iguchi fell to the side, watching his lifeblood flow from his body.

***

'Ma, I can help,' Grace said behind Jacqueline.

'No, Grace. You promised your father that you would not use magic.'

Grace lowered her head as the Legion soldier stepped forward. 'Drop the sword and you will not be harmed,' he lied.

Jacqueline shook her head and raised the sword, knowing she was her daughter's only protection. 'Leave us—'

Her sentence was cut short as the soldier thrust his sword through her breast, killing her instantly. He yanked his sword out and her dead body collapsed to the floor. The soldiers smiled as they walked to Jenna and the children.

Then Grace broke her promise.

A warm sensation exploded inside her stomach and spread throughout her body. She held out both hands, her chubby fingers opening like flower petals. Arcs of purple energy jumped from her fingers. Ten soldiers jerked as they were lifted into the air when the energy hit them. Their weapons dropped as they were slammed back to the floor.

She looked at the branches of the stone oak tree behind her. With a thought, Grace pulled off five stone acorns and sent them flying at blinding speed at the soldiers. Five soldiers screamed as their armour was punctured by the acorns.

Grace looked down at the dead body of her mother and was filled with a sense of great sadness. This was quickly replaced by feelings of anger.

She saw the dropped sword and made it float in the air before it shot at the nearest soldier, puncturing his breastplate. It came out and, as the soldier died, Grace waved her hands. The sword was bathed in purple flame. Her hands moved, controlling the flight of the weapon. It flew to a group of soldiers, slashing and thrusting, causing them to duck and run, and then the sword spun, spitting out purple fireballs that hit the soldiers.

The ten soldiers she first attacked had recovered and crept towards her with weapons drawn. Grace clicked her fingers, and they were picked up and slammed to the ground again, their weapons sent flying across the room.

***

Omega sat on the ground, chained by his ankle to the stone oak tree, watching the battle and unable to do anything. He had seen the girl's magical ability, but his manacles prevented him from helping.

Then a miracle happened.

When Grace slammed the soldiers to the ground, a crossbow skidded across the floor and stopped at his feet. He picked it up awkwardly, as he had only used magic to fight. Now he pointed the weapon at her.

He took a long slow breath before pulling the trigger. He watched the bolt travel in slow motion as it flew towards Grace. It hit her in the middle of her back. The flaming sword stopped spinning and fell to the ground with a clang. Its flame spluttered once before disappearing.

Grace looked down at the head of the bolt coming out of her chest, wondering how it got there. Kate and Jenna screamed as Grace fell to her knees with bubbles of blood coming from her mouth.

Then, with a shrill scream, K'ayden led the Khilli warriors into the throne room. K'ayden saw Jenna and the children backing away from the soldiers, Jacqueline's lifeless body on the floor, and Grace swaying on her knees with a crossbow bolt in her chest.

K'ayden rushed to Grace as the rest of the Khilli killed the soldiers, catching her as she fell. He felt a deep sorrow for Ramulas, who had been through so much protecting his family. Now his wife lay dead, and his youngest daughter would soon follow.

K'ayden knelt, holding Grace gently to his chest. He could feel the bubbles forming as she slowly drowned in her own blood. A few moments later, when the soldiers had been killed, K'ayden turned to Kate. 'Who shot your sister?'

With tears streaming down her face, she pointed to the warlord. Several Khilli warriors screamed as they ran for the stone oak tree.

'No!' K'ayden shouted. 'Leave that one for the Lord of Sanctuary.'

***

Oriel was free. She looked out of her cavern and saw a stone bridge across a chasm. She could feel that the earth elementals were very close to freeing her, so she left the throne room to return to her cavern so she could prepare for her freedom.

Oriel walked tentatively out onto the walkway. These would be her first few steps on her new world. Oriel had previously only used astral travel. She took a few steps before jumping into the air and floating to the tunnel.

Oriel drifted towards Sanctuary with her green robes floating behind. A flood of emotions ran through her mind as she experienced feelings through her human body.

Oriel felt weak from helping to erect the magical ward outside the wall and preparing for freedom. She was extremely weak and needed to find Ramulas quickly. The battle of Sanctuary had been going on for one day and night. She was assaulted by feelings of anger, sadness, despair, fear, pain, and heartache. The wave of human emotions was almost too much to bear.

She had felt Remus searching for her since the Legion arrived the previous day. Oriel came out of the tunnel and into the sunlight. The people of Sanctuary saw her and began to cheer. She smiled at them and floated towards the castle, where she could feel Ramulas' presence. As she moved, Oriel could feel her strength returning.

***

Ramulas and Pip were watching the combined army come through the maze. They had faced the stone octopuses and now faced Joshua, Rain, and the giant-kin. Pip grabbed Ramulas roughly by his arm and turned him to the left. His eyes widened as Nathaniel flew up to the balcony. Nathaniel glared at him before diving into the maze.

33

Joshua growled as he swung his iron ball at a Legion soldier's upraised shield. It broke along with the soldier's arm. He grunted and fell before three more took his place. A blast of ice struck the soldier in the middle, and Joshua threw himself at the other two.

He stood in between the two, swinging left and right repeatedly until the soldiers were a mess of meat and bone.

Then Nathaniel dropped in the middle of the duo.

Instinctively, both knew that he was the rightful owner of their weapons; however, they were not going to give them up without a fight. Joshua raced forward, swinging his iron ball and releasing it to hit Nathaniel in the shoulder. The angel grunted, turned, and held out his left hand. The gauntlet melted from Joshua's hand as he howled in protest, and it returned to Nathaniel.

Joshua picked up the ball to swing it at Nathaniel once more, hitting him in the chest and sending him back a few feet. Nathaniel grunted and smiled. 'You still have some of my power.'

Nathaniel struck Joshua with a backhand, sending him crashing into the wall ten feet away. A blast of ice hit the angel, covering his wings in a solid block of ice. Nathaniel flexed his wings and the ice shattered. He slowly turned to Rain and smiled. 'Do you really think you can hurt me with my own weapon?'

Rain shot him with another stronger blast of ice as the angel came forward. Nathaniel laughed as the blast seemed to pass right through him, and then he reached out to take his sword out of Rain's hand.

'Now let me show you what my sword can do,' he said with a cold smile.

He tilted the tip at Rain's feet and fired a blast of ice. A large claw formed of ice came out of the ground to wrap around Rain, pinning his arms to his side and crushing him.

Joshua groaned as he pulled himself up, and Nathaniel hit him with a blast of ice. Then he hit both Rain and Joshua with his gauntlet. Both fell to the ground. With his weapons returned, Nathaniel flew out of the maze searching for his next opponent.

His eyes locked on Ramulas.

***

Ramulas and Pip stood on the balcony watching Nathaniel fight Joshua and Rain. Then the angel flew out of the maze with the magical weapons. As Nathaniel hovered in place, beating his wings, Ramulas knew this was the being that Oriel told him about.

Without warning, Nathaniel flew to the balcony. Ramulas looked down into the courtyard and saw Rygar. 'The maze—'

Ramulas pushed Pip aside before being yanked off the balcony. She screamed as he and the angel flew into the air. As they rose into the air, he heard Oriel call for him from below. She was free and needed him.

He saw Rygar lead the soldiers into the maze and realised his mistake. He did not want them going into the maze—he only wanted to say that Joshua and Rain were injured in the maze.

Then he saw Oriel floating towards the castle, and he beat on Nathaniel's chest. 'Let me go. She needs me.'

'No, you must fight me,' Nathaniel replied before tossing Ramulas up high and shooting a blast of ice at him.

***

Remus' head snapped up. Oriel's magical energies hit him like a wave, and he knew that somewhere behind the wall, she was out in the open.

She was weak and vulnerable—he needed to take advantage of her in this state. He looked at the gate in frustration. Soldiers and Symiaks blocked the gates trying to get in.

In frustration, he shot an arc of red energy at the top of the wall. To his amazement, it was not stopped by the barrier. Remus closed his eyes and cast a quick spell. A moment later, his eyes opened, and he smiled. The barrier was no longer there.

Remus held both arms out and levitated over the wall. The maze and town of Sanctuary came into view, and then he saw Nathaniel fly out of the maze and fight Ramulas.

He saw Oriel slowly make her way to the castle. His heart skipped a beat. After all this time and effort, now he had her. Oriel was alone and no-one could stop him.

***

Just when Oriel needed Ramulas the most, he was fighting with Nathaniel, with streams of ice coming at him. A warm sensation exploded inside of him and spread throughout his body.

This time, something was different. Ramulas was able to access all his magical abilities. He thrust his hand out. The ice parted and went around him. Purple flame covered him as he pulled out his weapons. Nathaniel raced towards Ramulas, leading with his crystal sword as he began to fall and everything around him slowed.

Ramulas knocked Nathaniel's sword aside with his war hammer and hit him in the chest with his battle axe. The angel shrugged it off and punched Ramulas, who twisted, narrowly avoiding it. Ramulas began to fall before activating a levitation spell as he fought Nathaniel.

Then time returned to normal as a blast of ice hit Ramulas in his chest, causing him to lose concentration and fall to the top of the castle. Then Ramulas felt Oriel's fear. Remus had found her, and she was too weak to defend herself.

Ramulas allowed himself to fall as he heated the air around him. Nathaniel folded his wings and dived after him. The ice around Ramulas broke away as he crossed the shafts of his weapons, emitting arcs of purple energy. The angel flew with his wings flapping wildly.

Ramulas glanced down to see Remus attacking Oriel as the townspeople attempted to help, but energy blasts from the warlord kept them at bay. Ramulas guided his fall away from the castle.

Nathaniel grabbed Ramulas and threw him at the roof, causing tiles to fly in every direction as he slid across. He reached out for the edge to slow himself. Nathaniel slammed into Ramulas and pounded away at him; the pain was so overwhelming that Ramulas almost blacked out. Then pain exploded behind his eyes and purple arcs of energy came from Ramulas' eye to hit Nathaniel in the chest.

The angel was knocked back ten feet from the roof, screaming. Ramulas stood placing his weapons on his back and ran along the roof before jumping off and hitting Nathaniel in a bear hug, wrapping his arms around him. Purple strands of energy wrapped around his wings.

They both fell to the courtyard ten stories below. At the last moment, Ramulas twisted so that Nathaniel took the brunt of the fall. They hit the ground one hundred yards from Remus and Oriel and the people scattered.

Ramulas rolled off Nathaniel, fighting for breath, and crawled to Oriel, who was desperately trying to fight off Remus. Ramulas held out a hand, sending a solid beam of white light that knocked Remus off Oriel.

'Behind you,' Oriel said as a tremendous weight hit him from behind.

Nathaniel slid his arm under Ramulas' chin and tightened the grip to choke him. Ramulas fought back, thinking of a way to defeat the angel.

'No,' he gasped as Remus jumped back on Oriel.

Then he heard Oriel's voice in his mind. *You must let him defeat you, that is the only way to help me.*

Against his better judgement, Ramulas stopped struggling and let his body go limp. He fought the panic inside as Nathaniel continued to squeeze. Then, without warning, the angel jumped off him.

Ramulas sucked in a lungful of air as Nathaniel flew at Remus.

***

The walls in the maze had stopped moving, allowing the enemy to flow through to Sanctuary. The giant-kin stood at an intersection—Lodi at the front and the half-giants behind him. Symiaks and soldiers soon learned to avoid these three and searched for alternative routes.'

A group of the enemy was spotted running away, and the half-giants gave chase. Lodi soon found himself facing ten Legion soldiers twenty yards away. They seemed hesitant to come near him as he swung his club. Another Legion soldier had found a way behind the giant and waited out of sight.

***

Rygar ran through the maze leading a group of soldiers. They travelled blindly, heading towards the sounds of battle. Then he rounded a corner in time to see a Legion soldier thrust his sword into the back of Lodi's thigh. The giant roared and fell to one knee.

Then, as if by magic, Lodi was covered in Legion soldiers who hacked away and stabbed his son. They appeared like red and black ants swarming over a larger insect. An invisible cold hand squeezed his heart.

'Not me boy!' Rygar cried as he ran to his son.

With a primal roar filled with rage, Lodi stood and attempted to shake them off, but they continued to stab him. Then he fell forward and lay very still ten feet from the dwarf.

'Aaaaargh!' Rygar screamed as he leapt into the air. Rygar's axe hit a soldier in the middle of his face, sending a spray of blood into the air. Then, without any thought for his safety, the dwarf allowed his rage to consume him. Swinging his axe left and right, Rygar chased down every soldier who attacked his son.

The soldiers from Sanctuary arrived in time to kill the few that remained. When it was finished and Sanctuary's soldiers went deeper into the maze, Rygar stood on top of Lodi's chest and sobbed uncontrollably. A few came past and tried to comfort the dwarf, but he was inconsolable.

They left Rygar with his son and continued fighting in the maze.

***

Nathaniel landed in front of Remus and grunted as a shower of sparks hit him in the face. He pointed his crystal sword at the warlord, unleashing a blast of ice at him.

Remus had time to gasp before Nathaniel kicked him. Remus flew ten feet before hitting a wall. Nathaniel leapt after him.

***

Pain shot through Ramulas as he attempted to stand. He pushed through the pain and made his way to Oriel. He knelt next to her, cradling her head in his hands.

Oriel smiled and whispered. 'You have come just in time.'

Ramulas shook his head. 'I am sorry I could not be here any sooner. Did Remus hurt you?'

Oriel reached up to touch his face. 'That does not matter now. My time is coming to an end.'

'What do you mean?' Ramulas asked in shock.

'You need to understand something about me. From the moment of my birth, I was destined to die after a few years when I reached maturity, and that time is almost here.'

Ramulas felt as if someone had kicked him in the stomach. He did not want to believe what Oriel was saying. An invisible hand gripped his chest and a lump formed in his throat. 'So, I have done all of this for nothing?'

She took her hand away from his face, clicked her fingers and Ramulas' world turned white. 'This is my true form.'

Oriel's body was translucent blue with shades of black. Her eyes crackled with black and her hair moved as if a soft wind blew, and she wore a green tattered robe. The image vanished and Ramulas was back in Sanctuary with Oriel in his arms.

'My end is near, and I want to give my power to you,' she said with a smile.

'No; I want you to live,' Ramulas replied, choking back his emotions.

'I will live inside of you.'

'But there must be another way.'

Oriel smiled sadly and shook her head.

The invisible hand constricted his chest, and his heart felt as if it were in his throat. A sense of helplessness washed over him.

Oriel grabbed Ramulas by the face, pulled him closer, and kissed him on his forehead. He screamed as her spirit entered him.

Knowledge poured into him at unbelievable speed. Each spell Oriel had learned was now being passed onto Ramulas. He saw her whole short life in a few seconds, experienced when she was happy, sad, lonely, or content, and then her power entered him.

A thunderclap rolled across the sky as a ring of bright purple exploded from Ramulas.

'No,' Remus protested as he saw Ramulas floating and covered in purple flame.

'Yes,' Ramulas replied as he saw Remus and Nathaniel still fighting.

Arcs of energy leapt from Ramulas' outstretched hands, throwing Remus and Nathaniel into the air.

34

In the forests of Shangri-la, the family of dragons all looked to the sky at once. They had been resting in the sun when the call came. The spirit of the dragon had been born and they would answer the call. A score of green dragons beat their powerful wings, took to the air, and flew towards Sanctuary.

***

Ramulas looked down at himself and saw that he now wore long flowing purple robes of energy. The sounds of fighting continued, and he shook his head. With a thought, Ramulas floated up holding out his hands. Ramulas' robes turned to dragon's wings.

He stopped at the top of the castle and saw the fighting, wounded, dead, and dying. A deep sorrow filled his soul. *What a waste of life*, he thought.

He clapped his hands and a wave of energy washed over the town, maze, and clearing. Soldiers and Symiaks were knocked to the ground. Then every living thing looked up at Ramulas floating in the sky. The fighting was forgotten.

'This is enough,' Ramulas said in an amplified voice. 'I have Oriel's power. There will be no more fighting or killing. There is nothing here for the Legion, kingdom soldiers, or the Symiaks.'

He glared at Remus before waving his hands in front of him. Purple trails of energy weaved in front of him until they formed a living ball that constantly moved. Ramulas sent this into the middle of the maze, where it exploded into a bright light, which transformed into a portal. Then Ramulas waved his hands again and the walls within the maze moved so that all paths led to the portal.

'Those of the Legion, I have opened a portal back to your world, which you will find in the maze.' A bright light shot into the air from the portal.

'You have one hour until it closes. If you have not left by then, my people will hunt you down and kill you.'

'What right do you have to talk to my Legion?' Remus screamed.

Ramulas saw that Remus and Nathaniel had recovered and the angel was preparing to leap up to attack Ramulas. The Lord of Sanctuary snapped his fingers and a bolt of lightning lanced down from the sky to strike him down.

Remus opened his mouth to talk when a dark shadow moved across the ground, followed by several others. The green dragons had arrived.

Ramulas could hear the dragons calling to him as they circled above. He used his magical ability to communicate with them. They were calling him 'spirit of the dragon'. They had a connection with Ramulas and could feel his sadness.

'How can we take away the sadness?' one of them asked in his mind.

'Show me the dead and injured.'

Ramulas' eyes turned a deep purple as he saw through one of the dragon's eyes. As it circled Sanctuary, Ramulas was filled with more sadness seeing a close-up view of the carnage. So many of his people were injured or dead.

His heart skipped a beat when he saw Rygar lying on the body of his adopted son, and instantly he knew Lodi was dead. As a father, he could empathise with the dwarf's pain. Ramulas could not imagine what he would do if something happened to his family.

Then he saw Iguchi lying near three dead Fallen Angels and knew he would be dead in a few moments. Without a second thought, Ramulas floated down to the warrior. He saw where the wounds were in his friend's body and pulled out the sword with one hand as his other hand sent purple energy into Iguchi, healing the wounds.

A moment later, Iguchi opened his eyes and smiled weakly. 'Hello to you, Lord of Sanctuary.'

'Rest, my friend,' Ramulas said, patting him on the shoulder.

Then Ramulas' dragon vision returned, showing Nathaniel and Remus fighting once more. He leapt into the sky to land before the duo. Both hands shot out, sending streams of energy at the pair. Within seconds, both were bound and struggling on the ground.

'I have said no more fighting.'

Nathaniel was red in the face as he tried to break free.

'Ramulas,' a familiar voice called behind him.

He turned to see K'ayden on the balcony of the throne room, his face a mask of sorrow and despair. He knew instantly that something was terribly wrong. He leapt up to land next to the Khilli warrior.

K'ayden's body slumped. 'I am truly sorry, my friend. We came too late.'

Ramulas' heart beat faster as he investigated the throne room. What he saw made it feel as if someone tore his heart out of his chest. Among the dead Legion and kingdom soldiers, he saw the body of Jacqueline, and next to her was Grace with a crossbow bolt in her chest.

Grace's eyes were closed and her skin pale. Kate knelt next to her younger sister, supporting her head. She looked at Ramulas with eyes full of pain. 'Help her, Father.'

It was at that moment that Ramulas' heart broke. His wife lay dead, and Grace would soon follow. An enormous lump grew in his throat as tears streamed down his face. Then Fenris barked.

Ramulas was pulled out of his pit of sorrow and despair. It was then that he saw both hell hounds next to Grace and the Khilli warriors behind Kate. Ramulas pushed away feelings of sorrow and an expression of determination came over him. He walked with a purpose to his daughter, waving his hands through the air.

In a second, Grace was bathed in a nimbus of purple light, showing him the extent of her injuries. The bolt had pierced her spine and punctured both of her lungs. He could not remove the bolt and heal her in the way he had Iguchi. If he tried anything, she would die.

A wave of helplessness washed over him. He had just been given all of Oriel's powers, and now he had the choice of watching his daughter die slowly or removing the bolt and killing her.

He slowly shook his head before looking at Kate. 'I am so sorry. I cannot help Grace. Who did this to her?'

K'ayden pointed to Alpha, who sat chained to the stone oak tree. Ramulas walked towards him while the warlord cowered in fear. 'First, you kill Benji, then you kill my own daughter.'

Ramulas felt a small hand take hold of his own and looked down to see Emily.

'I can help her,' she said.

'How?'

Without answering, she released his hand and walked over to Grace to sit in front of her. Placing a hand on Grace's shoulder, minute strands of blue energy flowed from Emily into Grace. Ramulas watched as Grace's injuries glowed from within, and after a moment, Emily's body started to replicate these wounds. By this stage, Emily's eyes had turned black.

The injuries throbbed inside both girls with the same intensity, and then Grace's wounds began to heal as Emily pulled out the bolt. At the same time, the injuries inside Emily intensified. By the time Grace's wounds had fully healed, Emily struggled with pain. Holding the bolt in her hand, her wounds flared in a fierce light. The last of the blue energy flowed from Emily to Grace.

Then Emily collapsed dead on the floor.

Ramulas was shocked and did not know what to do. He knew that Emily had taken Grace's injuries and saved his daughter's life. He was torn between happiness for Grace being healed and the pain of losing Emily, who was like a daughter to him.

Then he noticed a subtle change in Emily. He reached out and touched her arm. The power that flowed through Emily was no more. Lying before him was the body of an ordinary girl.

'Da,' Grace said softly.

Ramulas spun around to his daughter, who softly moaned with her eyes shut as she leaned against Kate. Ramulas felt powerful magical energies build up around him. Kate's and Grace's hair stood on end. Ramulas stood and searched the room. The last time he had felt this energy was when he first met Emily, but she had died.

Grace opened her eyes and Ramulas gasped. Her eyes were completely black.

***

Shigar and the druids burst into the throne room. 'Oh my,' the magician said, looking at Ramulas and Grace.

Shigar could see that Ramulas' magic had grown and had infused with Oriel's power, which pulsed from within him. Grace's magical power had also grown, but in ways greater than her father's. The dark ancient energies surrounding her told him that she now possessed Emily's magic. It was then that he saw Emily's body.

Then he saw Jacqueline. 'Oh, my friend, I am so sorry.'

Ramulas shook his head. 'I cannot bring her back.'

People began screaming outside and Ramulas saw a green dragon fly past the balcony, followed by another. He looked at his daughters, Shigar, the druids, and then at Jacqueline. After losing so much, the last thing he wanted was to leave his family, but he had unfinished business outside.

He smiled at Grace and Kate as an idea came to him. 'Would you girls like to see a dragon?'

Kate's mouth dropped before she slowly nodded, and then the old Grace returned quickly as she became excited. Ramulas communicated with the dragons and found the smallest of them and asked it to come into the throne room. Everyone gasped as a green dragon landed on the balcony and crawled through the window.

The Khilli rushed forward with weapons ready.

Ramulas raised a hand. 'Hold! The dragon is a friend.'

The Khilli stepped back as the dragon folded its wings and slowly crawled into the room, its claws clicking on the tiles with each step. Its body was twenty feet from the snout to the barbed tail. *Protect my daughters*, Ramulas communicated to it.

As the dragon came closer to Grace and Kate, the hell hound stood in front of the girls ready to attack. Ramulas quickly communicated that the dragon was a friend and the hound calmed down. The dragon circled its body around the girls. Kate sat in disbelief while Grace patted the creature.

Ramulas turned to K'ayden and Shigar. 'Watch my daughters until I return.'

Ramulas flew out of the room. Shigar and K'ayden looked at each other. Ramulas had just called a dragon in to protect his girls—how powerful was he?

***

Ramulas flew out of the window and saw the people of Sanctuary cowering with dragons flying overhead, so he amplified his voice. 'Fear not, people. The dragons will not harm you—they are now friends of Sanctuary and all who reside here.'

Once the people relaxed, he dropped down in front of Nathaniel and Remus. 'Both of you behave. I will be back to deal with you later.'

Remus struggled against his bond as his fury showed on his face, 'You dare talk to me that way? When I am free, I will come for those close to you.'

Something inside of Ramulas snapped. It began in his chest and slowly spread through him. He clenched his fists and purple flames erupted along his arms. He leaned in until his nose was two inches from Remus. 'My wife was killed by your soldiers and my youngest daughter was mortally wounded by your warlord. I want nothing more than to burn you alive for what you have brought to my world.' A cold smile spread on Ramulas' face. 'But there are far worse things than death.'

'Like what?' Remus asked defiantly.

'This,' Ramulas said as he waved his hands in front of Remus while he chanted. The warlord's eyes widened as he felt the change. Remus screamed in terror and desperately tried to escape. Thin red strands of energy flowed from Remus into Ramulas as the warlord continued to struggle. Within a few moments, Ramulas had absorbed all of Remus' magical power.

'I will return soon,' he said before flying away.

For the first time in his life, Remus felt extremely vulnerable.

***

Ramulas flew over the maze and was happy to see lines of Legion soldiers flowing into the portal. He saw the confused faces of the kingdom soldiers and Symiaks. They did not know where they stood with the shifting of power. Ramulas stood on the top of the wall, looking down at the clearing.

'Those from the kingdom army and Symiaks—you will leave here by nightfall and return to your homes. There is nothing here for you. If you are here after dark, I will let the dragons hunt you.'

King Zachary stood next to the command tent surrounded by the royal guard and a score of Symiaks. 'You talk of treason,' he shouted.

With a thought, Ramulas floated down to land ten feet from the king. Symiaks and the royal guards moved away, not wanting the purple flames to burn them.

'I claim everything within this forest as a place for the people of Sanctuary. If you return you will be killed.'

'You, you …' Zachary sputtered, trying to find the words.

'Leave my home,' Ramulas said. His robes moved around him as if a soft wind blew around him. His robes seemed to have a life of their own. Zachary glared at him, enraged, but his anger turned to fear when he saw the confidence in Ramulas' eyes and knew he could not win.

Zachary turned to the royal guard, 'Pack everything; we leave here soon.'

A Symiak walked to Ramulas holding two large stone-bladed swords. 'Where is gifts for Symiaks? Remus said if we help, we get shiny gifts.'

Ramulas shook his head, thinking that the creatures had been fooled.

'Now Symiaks have all of Keah,' the same Symiak said as the creatures nearby nodded.

This comment brought Zachary and the royal guard rushing back. 'What did you say about my city?'

'Remus said if help him, we get Keah,' the Symiak replied.

'You betray our peace?' Zachary roared.

Symiaks and kingdom soldiers faced off, drawing weapons and ready for a fight. Tension filled the clearing.

Ramulas became frustrated and brought his hands together, sending a thunderclap across the clearing. Soldiers and Symiaks within twenty yards were thrown to the ground. The rest dropped their weapons.

The Symiaks with the stone swords stood and Ramulas jabbed a finger into the creature's chest. 'You will return to your home in the mountains. If the Symiaks attack any people along the way, I will send the dragons to eat you.'

The Symiaks looked up in fear, seeing the dragons flying.

Zachary strutted over while smiling smugly. 'If you are not careful, my soldiers will attack you before you reach the mountains, and if you fight back ...' He finished by pointing to the sky.

Ramulas was enraged that the king would act like this after what had happened to his family. 'You dare! My dragons will hunt any who starts fighting after this.' Then he turned to the Symiaks. 'You have been tricked. There is nothing here for you.'

Ramulas leapt up and flew over the wall. He had business in Sanctuary.

***

He landed in front of Nathaniel and Remus. The angel still struggled with his bonds while Remus was subdued. Ramulas waved his hand and Remus was free. The warlord stood slowly, looking at Ramulas warily.

'I have one more thing for you,' Ramulas said.

He rubbed his thumb and forefinger together and they glowed softly. Then he opened them, and a minute speck of white light shot into

Remus' left eye. The pain was immediate, and Remus clutched his eye and struggled to stand, and then his jaw dropped.

Ramulas had given Remus the memories of when they were younger: growing up together as children, working for the warlord, and the love they shared as twins. Then the wraith came, and Remus chose power over family. All of this flashed through his mind in an instant.

'Brother,' Remus whispered as what he had done dawned on him, 'I am so sorry.'

'So am I, 'Ramulas replied as he waved his hands.

Both floated up and into the maze to where the portal was, and the Legion filed in. Ramulas stood at the portal and could feel the wind being sucked into it. Legion soldiers stepped back when the pair landed.

Ramulas grabbed Remus by his breastplate and turned his brother to the portal. 'How will you survive on your world without your magic?'

Without waiting for an answer, Ramulas pushed him into the portal.

***

Ramulas stood with Iguchi near the portal. In front of them was Omega, still wearing the manacles, as the last of the Legion walked in. The warlord attempted to look as small as possible.

Ramulas moved to stand in front of Alpha and Iguchi moved to the side of the warlord. 'You killed Benji and hurt my daughter. My people have asked for your death, but I will show you mercy. Hold out your hands and I will remove your manacles.'

Omega's eyes widened in shock upon hearing the words. How foolish was the Lord of Sanctuary? As soon as the manacles were removed, he would send Ramulas into the portal. He fought back a smile as he slowly raised his hands.

Iguchi danced to the side, pulling out his long sword. In one swift movement, Iguchi brought the sword up and down. Omega felt a slight tug on his wrists and barely had time to register that both hands now lay by his feet before Iguchi spun and kicked him in the chest. As the warlord vanished into the portal, Ramulas looked into the sky.

'Return to the castle, Iguchi. I will soon follow.'

Ramulas returned to the sky, communicating with the dragons and telling them to return to Shangri-la. They were allowed to take as many of the dead from the enemy as they wanted, but the people of Sanctuary were off-limits.

The dragons dropped from the sky, took their food, and flew east. He could feel that even the small dragon who watched his girls had gone. Ramulas saw the carnage of the dead below. He focused on the dead from the combined army.

He waved his hands through the air and chanted. Each of the bodies glowed and slowly rose to him. He increased the movement of his hands and the bodies glowed. As the bodies came to his height, they formed a giant circle around him. Ramulas waved his hands in a different manner, and the bodies danced around him in stiff jerking movements.

'Through that portal, you will find my enemies. You will go through and show no mercy.'

Ramulas watched as they floated through the portal, dancing as they went. When the last of the undead passed, Ramulas clicked his fingers and the portal closed with the sound of rushing air.

Ramulas felt a shift in the magical energies and knew that Nathaniel had broken free. He leapt into the air the same time Nathaniel did, blasts of ice flew in his direction, and arcs of purple energy shot across to shatter them. Then Ramulas found himself in a thick fog, and Nathaniel's gauntlet hit him in the face.

He was knocked out of the mist, and the angel was close behind. He had said no more fighting, and Nathaniel would not listen. He needed to stop this. Ramulas held out both hands, unleashing a powerful spell. Lightning came from all directions to hit Nathaniel; he tumbled from the sky to land hard in the courtyard.

Ramulas landed as Nathaniel tried getting to his feet on unsteady legs. He saw Ramulas and pulled out his crystal sword to aim it at him. Ramulas' hand shot forward, sending streams of purple energy at Nathaniel, throwing the angel against the wall.

Ramulas walked up to him in frustration. 'Stay down. I do not want to hurt you.'

Nathaniel grunted while trying to stand, his intentions clear, and Ramulas clicked his fingers and was covered in purple flame.

Then Michael stepped in between them. 'Lord, do not do this, I beg of you.'

There was something in Michael's manner that caused him to pause. 'Why?'

Michael smiled. 'He is my brother. I have come to take him home.'

Michael removed his Fallen Angel's uniform and tunic until he stood bare-chested, and then Ramulas gasped as a pair of white wings grew out of Michael's back. Michael was bathed in white light as he turned to Nathaniel. 'It is time for you to return home, but you must leave your anger and weapons behind.'

Nathaniel stood as the anger drained from him. The blue crystal sword and gauntlet fell to the ground.

'Goodbye, Ramulas,' Michael said, gripping his shoulder.

Michael walked over to his brother and hugged him. Both angels glowed for a few moments before the light became too intense for Ramulas to look at. He turned away for a second. When he looked back, they were gone.

The calls of the wounded could be heard. Ramulas had work to do.

35

He organised for all the able-bodied people to gather the injured and bring them to the courtyard. While this was happening, Ramulas walked into the throne room to find the Khilli, the druids, Shigar, and the hell hounds had formed a circle around Jacqueline and his girls.

The hollow, empty feeling inside of his chest started to ache. He knew what needed to be done. With a sad smile and his arms open, Ramulas walked to his girls, who embraced him. After a moment with his girls, he looked up.

'I need some time with my family. We need to say goodbye.'

Without question or hesitation, everyone left. When the door was closed, Ramulas looked down at his wife. It felt as if someone was tearing out his heart with a rusty blade. As tears rolled down his face, he could not believe even in death how beautiful his wife was. Then the thought came to him—what could he say to comfort his daughters?

Ramulas stood by Jacqueline's lifeless form. The room seemed to blur around him, his heart heavy with grief. His daughters clung to him, seeking solace in his presence, but inside Ramulas, a storm of emotions raged.

How do I console them? His voice was just a whisper in his mind. *How do I find the strength to guide them through this pain when my own heart is shattered? Jacqueline my love, I wish I could speak to you again, to hear your voice, to feel your touch. I need you; the girls need you …*

His outward demeanour remained composed, but the internal battle was fierce. Ramulas pushed the sadness aside. His daughters needed him to be strong.

Ramulas took a deep breath and began talking without thinking. 'I have spoken to your mother's spirit,' he lied, as both girls looked at him with hope and awe.

Tears began to burn his eyes as he fought back the racking sobs he could feel just below the surface. He needed to be strong for his girls. 'Your mother told me that she loves you both very much and will always be with you in some way. She will look down on you and always be proud of you. You will see her at night-time. She is the brightest star in the sky. Kate is the lady of the castle and Grace is the princess.'

Both girls were very happy with what their mother had said. Then Ramulas told them of a way to honour her. Kate and Grace were both excited. The girls said their final goodbyes before running off to prepare for their mother's ceremony.

When they left, Ramulas held Jacqueline's hand. It was cold and clammy. He knew that her soul had left. He looked at her face and allowed the floodgates of grief to open. Sobs racked his body as tears rolled down his cheeks. With the grief came frustration and anger. He had all this magical power but was unable to save his wife.

Ramulas remembered to first time they met, started seeing each other, and their first kiss. Each memory was gut-wrenching, but he held them close. He wanted them to stay with him forever. His whole life had revolved around Jacqueline and his girls. Now a major part of him was missing.

Ramulas did not know what he was supposed to do without her in his life. He felt so alone.

***

There was a soft knock at the door. He turned to see Shigar enter. 'The injured are in the courtyard, my friend. The people still need you.' Ramulas looked at the magician as if he were a stranger. Then he nodded and stood, composing himself before walking to the balcony. The people gave a light cheer as he came out. The word had spread about Jacqueline, and everyone remembered her as a kind and gentle soul.

He saw over two hundred wounded in the courtyard, and there were more in the streets. They had injuries from minor cuts to broken bones and severe bleeding. With a smile, he chanted while waving his hands through the air. Red mist flowed down to the people. This continued until all the people had been fully recovered. Their bodies would still be stiff, but their wounds were healed. Ramulas smiled, thinking how Remus would feel knowing it was his magic that healed the people of Sanctuary.

Ramulas sat in the throne room with his daughters and the hell hounds. He had not gone into his quarters yet. He was unsure how he would react to seeing signs of Jacqueline. Then Jenna walked into the throne room with her children, and she was worried.

'We cannot find Pip. Have you seen her?'

The statement shocked Ramulas. The last time he saw Pip was a while ago, and so much had happened since then, but he forced a smile. 'I am sure she is fine. Pip will turn up soon.'

***

Zachary rode through the forest, feeling dejected. This was the second time he had marched on Sanctuary and had been forced to walk away in defeat. He could not understand how they lost again—he'd had the Symiaks and Legion with him.

Thinking of the smelly, stupid creatures made him shake his head. The Lord of Sanctuary had forbidden any fighting as they returned home, or they would be eaten by dragons. There was a disturbance at the rear of the column where the Symiaks followed his army. He sent his royal guard to investigate.

A moment later, a royal guard rode alongside him. This one had his face helm pulled down so only the eyes were showing. After a few moments, the royal guard spoke. 'How many people have you sent to Gullytown?'

Zachary turned in surprise—the speaker was female, but all the royal guards were males. Then a lock of purple hair fell from the helmet. Zachary was speechless as Pip removed her helmet.

'My parents died in Gullytown; tell them I said hello,' she said softly.

Zachary realised he was in trouble and opened his mouth to scream. Pip raised her left arm and fired her crossbow into his open mouth. Zachary's head snapped back as the bolt entered his brain, killing him instantly and knocking him to the ground. By the time he hit the dirt, Pip had disappeared into the forest.

***

The next morning, Kate and Grace walked through the maze with the hell hounds. The dead of Sanctuary numbered one hundred and twenty-three. Ramulas had asked for all of them to be brought to the castle to be honoured. Lodi was the only one missing.

Ramulas had tried a few times to talk to Rygar, but the dwarf would not listen. He had spent twenty-four hours with his adoptive son and would not respond to anyone. Kate and Grace stopped ten feet from Lodi with Rygar still lying on top.

'Da said to come to the castle,' Grace said.

The dwarf lifted his head, annoyed that Ramulas would send his daughters. His eyes were red from crying, his face a mask of despair. 'Leave me be. Ye cannot know the pain of losin' me own boy.'

'Legion soldiers killed Mother,' Kate whispered.

Rygar's head jerked up. 'What did ye say?'

Grace smiled sadly. 'Da said she was very brave, fighting them with a sword.'

'They killed yer mother?' Rygar asked.

Both girls nodded, and with a roar, Rygar jumped off Lodi with his axe. He could see the heartache in the girls' eyes. 'Where's the dog that killed your mother?'

'The Khilli killed them,' Kate said.

'I would have shown them the blade o' me axe,' the dwarf said as he began chopping a nearby wall in frustration at not being there for his son and Jacqueline. Then he dropped the axe and began to punch and headbutt the wall.

Kate and Grace looked at each other before they started giggling. After a moment, he stopped and looked at them. 'Do you think this is funny?'

Both girls nodded with smiles growing on their faces. This brought Rygar out of his world of pain.

'Take me to yer da.'

***

As Remus was pulled through the passageway, he noticed that the ceiling and walls still moved as if by an invisible wind. Long, dark shapes still swam just beneath the surface. The last time there, Remus had marched, but now he floated along like a leaf in a storm. Then, before he knew what was happening, Remus stumbled out into his castle.

He was caught by one of the warlords who had been unable to come to Oriel's world. He looked around to see a few hundred of the Legion soldiers, who stood to attention when they saw him.

'Where are the others?'

The warlord gestured behind him. 'They are in the barracks. Where are the three captains? And what of Oriel?'

Remus shook his head. 'We were defeated, and if the captains did not come through, they are dead. Oriel has given her power to another, and my magic has been stripped from me.'

This statement shocked the warlord as he looked at Remus. Remus had ruled for generations with magic. What would he do now? Then Alpha came through the portal, falling to the ground. Remus saw that he was dead, and both his hands were cut off. He had wondered what happened since the Fallen Angel took him.

He ordered four red wizards to take the body away so he could examine it later. The golden arch began to glow, catching everyone's attention. Remus watched the portal, wondering what could be coming through. He jumped back in shock as the first wave of undead came through. His hand shot forward and he cursed when nothing happened.

'Attackers coming through the portal!' he called.

Warlords and red wizards raced forward as Remus stepped back. Spells were thrown at the undead as they came through the portal, but still more undead soldiers and Symiaks poured through, attacking with fury.

Remus swore, wishing he had the means to help.

***

One of the dark holes in the passageway had a claw probing the edges. When the journey to Oriel was planned, great care was taken to ensure nothing could go in or out of these holes. But as Ramulas sent everyone back, it damaged this hole just enough to catch curious eyes. This hole led to a very dark world, and the creatures here would be very pleased to find a new home.

The claw disappeared as the creature returned to tell what it had found.

***

The people of Sanctuary gathered around the fallen. A thick wall of fog blocked the statues and the cliff behind. The mist curling around the silhouettes and the diffused light added an otherworldly quality to the surroundings. After the battle, rumours had spread about how the fallen had protected the children. Only after the last of the enemy left Sanctuary did they break their protective circle around the children and walk back to their platforms.

***

Ramulas stood facing the crowd with Kate and Grace by his side. He had been working with Edwin through the night to honour the dead, and now he was ready to reveal his work.

'People of Sanctuary, we have fought and won our second battle; we have suffered far too many losses, but we have saved this world from a great evil. Now, it's time to honour our fallen.' He waved his hand and the tendrils of mist lifted. The crowd gasped as one. The original fallen were on their platforms, and above them, alcoves had been cut into the cliff face where the newest fallen stood.

Each statue stood strong and proud holding a sword and shield. The magical flame from the altar was reflected in all the statues' eyes. Then people asked where Jacqueline and Lodi were. Ramulas knew this time would come. He would let the people find out later—for now, was a time for his girls and Rygar.

He took Kate and Grace by the hand and led them to the courtyard, where the dwarf waited.

***

The entire courtyard was covered in swirling mists. Ramulas and his girls stood near Rygar. 'Are you ready, dwarf?'

'Oh, git yer fog away.'

Ramulas waved his hand and the fog lifted. Rygar fell to his knees as a sob escaped his lips. A statue of Jacqueline dressed in flowing robes stood with a welcoming smile. Behind her towered Lodi, standing protectively, holding his club high with a scowl. The message was clear—this served as both a welcome and a warning.

'Da, can we touch her?' Grace asked excitedly.

'Of course.'

Kate and Grace ran forward to hug the statue of their mother. As Kate embraced her mother, memories rushed in like a tide. She remembered Jacqueline's gentle voice, her warm embrace, and the stories she told by the fireplace. Tears blurred her vision, but amidst the sorrow, a spark of determination ignited.

'Mother believed in me and said that I was the lady of the castle. Can I really live up to that? Do not worry, Mother. I will make you proud.'

As soon as Kate spoke, a chime sounded throughout Sanctuary, and Ramulas was hit with a magical wave of energy.

He looked around to if anything had changed, but everything seemed normal. He could feel that something had changed but was unsure what it was.

Pip raced into the courtyard, stopping in front of Ramulas with a smile. 'Something wonderful has happened. Come with me.'

He saw that his girls still hugged their mother and communicated for the hell hounds to stay with them. Pip led him into the castle and out to the statues. Then he saw a group of people gathered around a section of the cliff that had opened. The Fallen Angels stopped anyone from entering.

'How did this happen?' Ramulas asked.

Pip smiled. 'We heard a chime and the cliff just opened. Where does it lead?'

'We will find out,' Ramulas said, communicating with his warhorse.

The crowd parted as he came forward riding Rufus, and Ramulas looked at Iguchi. 'We will return soon. Watch over everyone until we return.'

Iguchi bowed as they rode down the passage. The path slowly twisted and turned so they were unable to see more than one hundred yards ahead. They were both tense, not knowing what lay ahead.

They turned the last corner and were shocked to see a large valley open in front of them with fields, forests, and one thing that stood out—a familiar town in the middle of the valley. They rode toward the town and Ramulas noticed the bird life in the trees. He used his ability to find out what other animals were in the valley and almost fell off the warhorse when he discovered how many there were.

'What is this place?' Pip asked.

Ramulas shook his head. 'I do not know, but it has been a very long time since people have lived in this valley.'

'What about the town?'

'We will find out soon.'

They rode for ten minutes before stopping in the courtyard of the town in front of the castle. They climbed down from the warhorse, unable to speak for a while.

'In the night sky, how many moons do we have?' Pip asked.

'There is only one moon,' Ramulas answered.

'Then I think we are a long way from home,' she said, pointing to the sky.

Ramulas looked up and was shocked to see a larger moon in the late afternoon sky with another, half of its size, next to it. Then he scanned the wildlife in the valley once more and almost fell off the warhorse,

'I am not familiar with any of the animals here. After we look around, we will return with Iguchi and Shigar to see what they think of this place.'

'Is this real?' Pip asked in awe looking at the town in front of them.

'Yes. This looks exactly like Sanctuary.'

'How do you explain that?' Pip said, pointing to the statues in front of them.

The statues were of Lodi and Jacqueline, but they were not new. It looked like they had been there for years. Ramulas looked around the town. Every building, door, and window was the same as Sanctuary. The only difference was the lack of cliffs behind the town.

As they walked through the town, they could see that no-one had lived there in years. Where had the people gone? And why was there another town like Sanctuary hidden in this valley?

At the rear of the town, Pip grabbed Ramulas roughly and turned him. 'Can you hear that?'

He cocked his head and could hear faint crying. They looked at each other and ran to the sound. They came around the corner to see the statues floating in the air in the same order as those in Sanctuary, but these were bathed in purple light with the magical flame dancing in the middle.

The crying came from a small girl kneeling in front of the altar. Ramulas and Pip walked up to her.

'What's wrong?' Pip asked.

The girl stopped crying but did not look up. 'The monsters took Mother and Father.'

'We can help you find them,' Ramulas offered.

The girl slowly turned to look at them. Ramulas and Pip jumped back in shock when they saw her.

The young girl was Emily.